'Do you think a man with my power, having what I went through as a child, will be willing to stand idly by while *my* child is shuffled between minders, aeroplanes, movie locations and court-ordered visiting rights?'

Goldie's mouth trembled for a second before she caught hold of it. 'Gael—'

He broke off mid-pace and planted himself firmly in front of her. He needed her to see the intent emblazoned in his heart and in his mind. 'Let me answer for you, Goldie. The scenario you propose will happen *over my dead body*.'

'You can't just rule things out, Gael. We need to agree to a compromise.'

'Why compromise when I have a solution?' he asked.

Her smooth forehead clenched in a frown. 'We confirmed the pregnancy less than ten minutes ago. How can you have a solution already?'

'Very easily, when the situation is this important.'

She gave a slight shake of her head, but her gaze didn't leave his. She blinked, her expression turning trepidatious. 'No. I think we need to talk about this some more.'

'I'm done talking, Goldie. The soundest solution to the situation we find ourselves is for you to marry me.'

Rival Brothers

When rivalry is thicker than blood...

Estranged brothers Alejandro and Gael Aguilar are titans of technology and each other's biggest rivals.

It will take two special women to help these sexy Spaniards put the past behind them and join forces to become more powerful than they ever dreamed!

Battle commences in
A Deal with Alejandro

And find who will be victorious in
One Night with Gael

ONE NIGHT WITH GAEL

BY
MAYA BLAKE

MILLS & BOON

First Published in Great Britain 2016
By Mills & Boon, an imprint of HarperCollins*Publishers*
1 London Bridge Street, London, SE1 9GF

© 2016 Maya Blake

ISBN: 978-0-263-92138-0

Our policy is to use papers that are natural, renewable and recyclable
products and made from wood grown in sustainable forests. The logging
and manufacturing processes conform to the legal environmental
regulations of the country of origin.

Printed and bound in Spain
by CPI, Barcelona

Maya Blake's hopes of becoming a writer were born when she picked up her first romance at thirteen. Little did she know her dream would come true! Does she still pinch herself every now and then to make sure it's not a dream? Yes, she does! Feel free to pinch her, too, via Twitter, Facebook or Goodreads! Happy reading!

Books by Maya Blake

Mills & Boon Modern Romance

Signed Over to Santino
A Diamond Deal with the Greek
A Marriage Fit for a Sinner
Married for the Prince's Convenience
Innocent in His Diamonds
His Ultimate Prize
Marriage Made of Secrets
The Sinful Art of Revenge
The Price of Success

Rival Brothers

A Deal with Alejandro

The Billionaire's Legacy

The Di Sione Secret Baby

Secret Heirs of Billionaires

Brunetti's Secret Son

The Untameable Greeks

What the Greek's Money Can't Buy
What the Greek Can't Resist
What the Greek Wants Most

The 21st Century Gentleman's Club

The Ultimate Playboy

Visit the Author Profile page
at millsandboon.co.uk for more titles.

For Romy, for your invaluable help
with all things South Africa.
Any mistakes are mine!

CHAPTER ONE

POR EL AMOR de todo lo que es santo! For the love of everything that's holy!

Gael Aguilar gritted his teeth and stopped short of invoking actual martyred saints as he listened to excuse after excuse roll off the tongue of the man he was talking to on the phone.

At the end of his very short tether, he cut across yet another effusive apology. 'Let me get this straight. You're supposed to be here, in New York, holding auditions, but instead you chose to go skiing, in *Switzerland*, and are now laid up in hospital?'

'It was just supposed to be a weekend thing for my wife's birthday, but… Look, believe me, no one's more sorry than I am, okay?'

Not okay. Gael jerked his head back against the car's headrest none-too-gently. 'What's the medical verdict?'

'Leg's broken in two places. It's going in a cast tomorrow. Provided there are no further complications I'll be back in New York on Thursday, to pick things up, but we can't miss the Othello Arts Institute slot today. It's been arranged for months.'

Ethan Ryland, his director, was almost pleading. Gael barely stopped himself from pointing out that he should have known better then than to indulge himself with a continental trip. He also barely stopped himself from uttering the pithy words that would have brought him immense satisfaction right then and there. But temporary relief wouldn't alter the facts facing him.

He couldn't fire the director. Somewhere in the small print of his multipage contract was the perfect excuse for what was happening now, Gael was sure. Had he not had bigger matters demanding his attention, he would have taken the time to seek out other small print, words that swung in his favour, and used them. Hell, he wouldn't even need to lift a finger himself. That was, after all, why his company had a whole firm of lawyers on retainer.

But he couldn't do that. For one thing, embroiling the Atlas Group, the staggeringly successful but still infant global conglomerate he'd birthed with his half-brother in litigation right now would be bad for business. Not only would his half-brother Alejandro take satisfaction in demanding his head on a platter, their Japanese partners the Ishikawa brothers would also have a thing or two to say about the matter.

The merger between their three companies was barely six months old—as was his personal relationship with Alejandro, following decades of their actively and conspicuously avoiding each other.

While the business side of their relationship had flourished after a few initial setbacks, personal interaction between him and his brother had taken a two-steps-forward-one-step-back approach. Their once-a-month business meetings had grown decidedly stilted in the past three months and, frankly, Gael was on the verge of deciding it was time to take a permanent step back and run his side of the business from his Silicon Valley base.

It didn't matter that he knew the reason why.

The past. Always the past. And not just *his*. His mother's. His father's—the father who'd been woefully lacking in being worthy of the name. Alejandro himself.

He pushed the recent confrontation with his mother aside, stepped back from the thoughts of torrid retribution he harboured towards his director, and forced himself to speak. 'What exactly do you wish me to do?' he snarled.

'Just sit in on a cast call. You know my work—that's

why you hired me. You also know what you want. It will be filmed, of course, so I'll see it when I get back. But nothing beats experiencing the raw, visceral performance in person. Tapping in to the emotions of acting is only potent on camera if it's saturating in real life.'

Gael exhaled and curbed the urge to roll his eyes at the melodrama of the director's speech. 'Send me the details. I will attend this meeting you've set up,' he snapped into the silence thickening in the back of his limo.

A breath of relief shot from the sleek phone console at Gael's elbow. 'Thanks, Gael. I owe you one.'

'You owe me more than one. You owe me a first-class Atlas Studios maiden movie, to be unveiled—hiccup-free—as part of my digital streaming relaunch in six months' time. Make no mistake: you only get this one free pass. Let me down again and you'll be out. Is that clear?'

'Crystal.'

Gael hung up before more useless platitudes reached his ears and instructed his driver to alter their destination. It looked as if he was staying in New York for one more night.

Activating the phone again, he dialled a familiar number in Chicago. As he waited for his brother to pick up Gael admitted to himself that he felt the tiniest sliver of relief to have avoided the Chicago trip for one more day. Because, contrary to the challenge he'd thrown down to Alejandro a year ago, about his brother acknowledging him as his blood, Gael himself had never been inclined to claim the Aguilar name. No matter that there wasn't any doubt as to his parentage, the name had never sat well on his shoulders.

After all, he was a bastard whose mother had tried to cloak his name in imagined respectability by naming him after the father who hadn't wanted him. Had his mother not pleaded with him, Gael would've changed his surname to

Vega years ago. But she'd beseeched him—out of the same bewildering devotion to the man she'd chosen to reproduce with, he was sure. And he'd relented. He'd withstood both the blatant and the silent mockery from strangers and gossipmongers from childhood into adulthood for as long as he could. Then, like his half-brother, he'd retreated to the other side of the world.

The news that their father was once again indulging in the extramarital affairs that had brought Gael into the world had turned his stomach. Alejandro, for his part, after a series of conversations with his parents, seemed a lot less bitter about the whole thing. Not so much Gael.

And, on top of that stomach-turning news, his last conversation with his mother hadn't ended well when he'd found out *she* was entertaining his father's advances again. Nor had the exchange he'd had with Alejandro lent any insight into why their respective biological parents were hell-bent on perpetuating chaos.

'Do I want to know what you're thinking?'

Alejandro's question, posed after one too many whiskies in his brother's office a few short weeks ago, slashed into Gael's brain.

'No.'

His brother's brooding gaze settled on him. 'Tell me anyway.'

'I'm wondering why polygamy was ever banned,' Gael had responded.

Low, bitter laughter had spilled from his half-brother. 'Trust me, I'm a one-woman man, but the same thought has crossed my mind many times about our parents.'

'You know what? I don't think they'd be happy with polygamy, even were it an option. They'd still find a way to make their lives—and ours—a living hell.'

Sour amusement had disappeared under the cloud that always accompanied thoughts of his father and mother.

He didn't like to lump them together as *his parents* because they'd never been that to him. Sure, Tomas Aguilar had attempted to make a mockery of a family with his mother when Gael was a child, but that had been more to do with his twisted game to hurt the wife who had worn his ring and borne his firstborn than with love for Gael or his mother.

His father, his mother…his past…had nothing to do with the issue that confronted him now. And he'd never been one to expend energy on fruitless ventures.

Gael arrived on the doorstep of the Othello Arts Institute late—courtesy of an accident on the Queensborough Bridge—and alighted from the back of the limo in a fouler mood than he'd been in two hours before.

Not because of the call with his director, or even the chaotic traffic. No, his teeth-grinding could be laid firmly at his brother's feet.

Alejandro had been nauseatingly understanding of Gael's excuses, even going as far as to put Elise, his fiancée, on the line, to reassure Gael that all was well and they would welcome him to Chicago any time he pleased.

Wondering whether his brother's brooding tone had been meant to reassure him, or to deliver a subtle message that Alejandro still maintained an arm's-length approach to their relationship, despite Gael himself wishing it so, was what had thrown him into a worse mood.

He pushed open the glass doors to the sharp-angled building and entered the world-renowned institution, clearly aware he was spoiling for a fight. He didn't bother taking a steadying breath because it would be of no use. Only two methods restored his control when he felt like this—losing himself in computer code or losing himself between the thighs of a woman. One had made him richer than his wildest dreams. The other never failed to restore equilibrium to his very male aggression.

The urge to pull out his phone and arrange his next assignation with his flavour of the month was only curbed by the reminder that this inconvenient detour was still business. And business *always*—without exception—came before pleasure.

He sought directions to the room he needed and entered to find two casting directors ready and waiting.

An hour later Gael's mood had taken a sharp dip further south. The auditions had gone worse than abysmally— and he'd arrived from the viewpoint of an outsider. Tense handshakes with the directors and a swift exit preceded his urge to go back on his word and fire his director immediately. If this was what he had in store then he was better off parting company with Ethan Ryland before the process advanced beyond salvaging.

Sí, someone most definitely needed to atone for his mood. He pulled the phone from his pocket.

And stopped.

The door to his left was only partially ajar, but he heard her clearly. Her voice, filled with pure, unadulterated emotion, carried even without being raised high.

Removing his hovering thumb from the call button, he pushed the door with his forefinger. When it started to creak he stopped and stepped back. Glancing up and down the quiet hallway, Gael saw another door farther away at the end of the auditorium. Quick strides granted him silent entry into the shadowed rear of the cavernous room in time to catch her impassioned speech.

'You won't leave me. I won't let you. You think you love her, but you don't. And, yes, I know you enough to tell you what is in your heart. I love you that much, Simon. Enough to forgive. Enough to take another chance on us. But for us to happen you need to stay. Please...take the chance.'

Gael realised he was holding his breath as he watched tears stream down her face. She raged for another minute, then collapsed onto the stage. Genuine sobs convulsed her petite body.

Against his will, he was riveted, the breath he'd scoffed at needing moments ago locked in his throat. He watched her struggle to her feet, saw a hiccup shake through her as the last of her emotion rippled free. She swiped at the tears with her wrists and walked to the edge of the stage, chest rising and falling, her gaze expectantly on the audition director—who stared at her for uncomfortably tense seconds without speaking.

A fizzle of irritation wove through Gael's body and his already black mood darkened further at the director's deliberate silence.

'Your performance was…commendable, Miss Beckett. I can tell you poured your heart into it.'

A tiny hopeful smile from the performer. 'Thank you. I did.' The response was firm, but husky, probably owing to her emotional expenditure.

The director regretfully shook his head. 'But sadly I need more than that. Heart is great, but what I need is *soul*.'

The actress frowned. 'I don't understand. That *was* my heart—*and* my soul.'

'In your opinion. But not in mine.'

Gael felt her acute disappointment from across the room. She gave a slight shake of her head, as if to refute the director's words. Then she gathered herself with admirable pride. 'I'm sorry you think so. But thank you for your time.'

She started across the stage towards a shabby-looking rucksack near the door.

'That's it?'

The smirking taunt from the director tightened the knot of anger in Gael's gut.

She paused. 'Excuse me?'

'According to your opening speech, you want this part more than you want your next meal. And yet you're walking away without so much as a fight?' the director sneered.

Her eyes widened. 'I thought you said… You mean I have a chance?'

'Everyone has a chance, Miss Beckett. What stands between you and the opportunities you receive, however, is how much you *want* it. Are you prepared to do whatever it takes?'

She nodded immediately. 'Yes, I am.'

The director crooked his finger. She retraced her steps to the middle of the stage. Impatiently he beckoned her further forward. She approached without hesitation.

The beginnings of distaste filled Gael's mouth as he watched naked hunger fill her face.

Somewhere in the middle of her performance she'd lost her shoes. Her bare toes breached the edge of the hardwood stage as she looked down at the director. He extracted a silver card from his pocket, traced it over the top of one foot down to her toes before laying it between her slightly parted feet.

'*This* is what it'll take, Miss Beckett. Pick it up and the part is yours.'

Gael had been on the receiving end of propositions for long enough to know what was going on. *Dios mio*, hadn't he had the row of all rows with his mother only two weeks ago over just such an issue?

He expelled his breath in a quietly seething rush as he watched her slowly sink down and retrieve what looked unmistakably like a hotel room key card.

The disappointment that lanced through him was strong enough to make him question why the scene unfolding in front of him was affecting him so deeply. Perhaps today of all days, when the past seemed to be dogging him with its bitter memories, he'd wanted to be pleasantly surprised by the elusive integrity of the human spirit. To experience a pure character to go along with the pure performance that had stopped him in his tracks, touched him in ways he was still grappling with.

More fool him.

As the director's hands moved to touch her feet Gael retreated as silently as he'd entered, his rigid gaze firmly averted from the sleazy scene unfolding on the stage.

He was looking for a fairy tale where none existed. Just as he'd once—futilely and childishly—prayed for a family that included a father who didn't wish him out of existence.

He should know better. No. He *had* known better—for a very long time.

Even before he exited the building he knew those dredged-up feelings would be crushed beneath the immovable titanium power of his ambition and success. Emotional needs and futile dreams were far behind him. What he'd done with his life since that time in Spain was what mattered.

Everything else came a very pale second.

CHAPTER TWO

So why was he back here mere hours later, pulling up in front of Othello? And at a time of night when there was guaranteed to be no one around?

Gael had resisted admitting it all day. But, despite the stomach-turning denouement, something about the woman's performance itself had stayed with him. Enough to make him pass a few precious hours re-reading the carefully selected script he'd searched through thousands for before settling on two years ago. Enough to convince him to put aside his personal feelings and revisit the actress's flawless performance.

And it *had* been flawless. With a true visionary's direction she would be able to pull off the project he had in mind for his movie launch without a hitch. Help him achieve the best possible premiere for what would be the world's largest independent streaming entity.

The project wasn't by any means the only thing sustaining the launch, but if done right the results and the benefit to the whole conglomerate would be incomparable. His partners were counting on him to get this right. *He* was counting on himself to make this vision come true.

That was why he was here, approaching the front desk with little more than a surname and a firm grip on his distaste.

The receptionist looked up, did a double take that would have amused him had his mood been anything but grim.

'Uh…may I help you, sir?' she asked eagerly.

'You have a student—a Miss Beckett. She was performing in room 307 this afternoon. I'd like to speak to her, *por favor.*'

The enthusiasm dimmed a touch. 'Do you have her first name?'

Gael frowned. 'No.'

The receptionist grimaced. 'I'm sorry, sir, I can't locate her without a first name.'

'You have a lot of students named Beckett?' he enquired.

'I can't give out that information, or even tell you if she's a student here or not. The thing is, she may not be. We hold outside auditions here from time to time. She may have come in with a director...' She stopped and cast a slightly uncomfortable glance at him, probably due to his increasing irritation with her babbling. 'Sorry, sir, but if you want to leave a card...or your contact details...I'll see what I can do?'

The smile was re-emerging, and the flick of her hair was transmitting signals he didn't want to acknowledge.

With reluctance, Gael extracted his card and handed it over. She glanced at it, her eyes going wider still as she gave a soft gasp. He watched, his cynicism growing, as realisation and an accompanying degree of avarice entered her eyes.

His former company, Toredo Inc., had been a serious player on the streaming media platform—a hit with students and young professionals long before he'd teamed up with Alejandro and the Ishikawa brothers to form Atlas. Since then, he and his partners had rarely left the media's attention.

He and Alejandro had only finished their world tour scouting to find satellite partners to enter into a joint venture with Atlas a few short months ago. During that time they'd conducted numerous media interviews, which meant his face had been plastered all over the news for weeks on end. Anyone with a decent search engine knew what the Aguilar brothers looked like, and how much they were worth—and, if their search had been thorough enough, their relationship status.

From her expression, the receptionist was no exception. He watched her cast an amusingly exaggerated look round the deserted reception area before clicking on the keyboard in front of her.

'I think you're looking for Goldie Beckett?' she stage-whispered.

The name brought to mind corkscrew golden curls and honey-toned skin. Surprisingly fitting. *'Sí,'* he confirmed. The chances of the name being wrong were minimal. If it was, he could always resume the search.

The receptionist nodded. 'I really shouldn't be doing this…but she was practising in the music room until five minutes ago. You just missed her.'

Gael stifled a curse. 'Did you see which way she went?'

'No, but I know she lives in Jersey, so she may be headed for the subway?'

'Thank you,' he bit out.

'Uh…you're welcome…'

She looked as if she wanted to continue the conversation. But Gael turned away, cutting short the familiar look that preceded a gentle but firm demand for something. A phone number. A favour for a friend. A *personal* favour. At any other time he would have been inclined to grant the mousy receptionist another minute of his time, even reward her for her help. He'd long accepted how things worked between him and the opposite sex. He gave when the mood took him. They took *all* the time—until he called a halt to their schemes and often naked greed.

But not tonight.

Not when an alien urgency rubbed under his skin, demanding he find the elusive Miss Goldie Beckett.

He rushed out into the street, already condemning the futility of his actions. This was New York City. Finding a single person in a throng of people on the sidewalk, even after nine at night, was insane. And yet his feet moved inexorably in the direction of the subway station. Behind him his chauffeur kept pace in the limo. Probably he was wondering what had possessed his employer, Gael mused.

He knew her name. All he had to do was pass it to his security people and let them find her. He'd witnessed her naked ambition for himself. All he needed to do to entice her was offer his name and the once-in-a-lifetime project he had in mind and she would come running. There was absolutely no need for him to pound the pavement.

He'd slowed his footsteps, thinking how idiotic he looked when he heard a scuffle in the alleyway.

Gael almost walked past. Unsavoury characters lurking in dark places were commonplace in cities such as this.

A husky cry and the flash of golden curls caught the corner of his eye. He stopped in his tracks, wondering if he was conjuring her up in his irritated desperation.

The alley was poorly lit, but not deep. His eyes narrowed as he tried to peer through the wisps of smoke pouring out of a nearby restaurant vent.

'No, damn you, let go!'

The distinctive voice coupled with the decisive sound of clothing being ripped firmly altered his course, hurrying him towards the night-shrouded scene.

'Lady, I won't say it again. Give me the bag.' A low, menacing voice sounded through the gloom.

A bold, mocking laugh. 'At least you have the good manners to call me *lady* as you attempt to steal my property.'

'It'll be more than an attempt in a second if you don't let go of the damn bag!'

The warning was followed by more sounds of a tussle. Then a muted scream, the distinctive thud of a body landing heavily and a hiss of pain.

Gael arrived at the scene in time to see a dark shadow loom at him, then rush past. The blocking move he threw out missed by a whisker, and the assailant was already rushing out of the alley. He had a split second to debate whether to go after the mugger or aid the victim. Gael chose the latter.

The vision before him scrambled upright from the grimy concrete. 'God, no! Stop him! He's got my purse!'

This time he caught the bundle that attempted to launch past him. Arms flailed in his hold. A firm, sinewy body twisted in his arms as he held her tight.

'Dammit, let me go. He's got my belongings.'

'Calm yourself. You won't catch him. He's long gone by now,' he replied, attempting to keep hold of the wriggling creature.

'Only because you're letting him get away. For God's sake, let me go.' She stopped suddenly. 'Hell, you're his accomplice, aren't you?' she accused.

Gael reeled back in amused shock. '*Perdón?* You think I'm a *thief*?'

'I don't know what the heck you are. All I know is you're stopping me from going after that piece of scum who's just stolen my purse. What am I supposed to think?'

She pulled at his hold. Gael thought it was probably wise to let her go, but his hands wouldn't co-operate.

'You're supposed to thank a person who has just come to your aid,' he suggested.

Eyes of an indeterminate colour widened in disbelief. 'He got my stuff *before* you arrived. You let him get away—and you think I should be *grateful*?' she spat with quiet fury.

She had fire—he granted her that. But it was the shaking in her voice that drew his attention.

Gael gripped her arms in a firmer hold, careful not to spook her further. Although he was still mildly amused she thought him a thief, her agitation meant she might take flight if he let her go. 'I'm not a thief, Miss Beckett. I assure you.'

She froze. And in the darkness he was beginning to become acclimatised to her gaze searched his with growing suspicion.

'How do you know my name?' she demanded, her voice husky with a different kind of emotion.

Fear.

That didn't sit well with him. He let her go and stepped back, although he made sure to keep himself between her and the exit. Now he had her before him he wasn't in the mood to go searching for her again should she bolt.

'You have nothing to fear from me.'

She laughed mockingly, but her trepidation didn't abate. 'Says the man who's keeping from leaving. Don't think I didn't notice the body-block. I'm warning you—I know Krav Maga.'

Again a tendril of amusement twitched at a corner of his lips. 'So do I, *pequeña*. Perhaps we can spar some other time, when we're both in the mood.'

'I don't spar just for the fun of it. I fight to defend myself. Now, either tell me why you're here wasting my time, and how you know my name, or get out of my way.'

'Your assailant is long gone. If you wish to report the incident I'm willing to lend you my phone.'

'No, thanks. If you want to do something useful will yourself into getting out of my way instead, why don't you?'

Gael shook his head. 'Not until we've talked.'

'I don't know who you are or what you could possibly have to talk to me about that involves us standing in a dark, smelly alley.'

She started to skirt him. He let her go until she faced the exit and her perceived freedom.

'I'm here because you're of interest to me.'

'I highly doubt that.' She took a few steps backwards. Stumbled. Her breath caught as she righted herself. 'I don't know what your problem is, but I assure you I'm not worth stalking, if that's your thing. And the sum total of my worth—which was eighty dollars—is now headed for the other side of the city, thanks to you. Anything else you want won't be given willingly.'

She retreated a couple more steps, until she stood beneath the single lit bulb gracing the mouth of the alley.

Gael inhaled sharply. He'd thought her performance captivating across the wide expanse of an auditorium. At the time he hadn't paid much attention to the woman herself. But he was looking now. And up close Goldie Beckett was…something else. Her dark honey-toned skin, even under the poor lighting, was vibrant and silky-smooth, her high cheekbones, velvety pouting lips and determined chin, a perfect enough combination to make his breath snag somewhere in his chest.

He wasn't by any means new to the art of appreciating beautiful women. His electronic contact lists were filled with more than his fair share of phone numbers from past and possible future conquests. But there was something uniquely enthralling about Goldie Beckett's face that riveted his attention.

Perhaps it was her eyes. Gael wasn't sure whether they were blue, or the violet he suspected, but the big, alluring pools, even though they currently glared at him, were nevertheless absorbing enough to keep him staring.

As for her body… She couldn't be more than five foot five, but even her lack of height—he preferred his women taller—didn't detract from her attraction. Nor did it diminish the curvy frame currently wrapped in a black sweater and denim skirt in any way.

A *torn* black sweater, which gaped wide enough at the

shoulder to reveal the strap of a lilac-coloured bra and the top of one voluptuous breast.

A thick silence ensued, during which she noticed where his gaze had landed. He admonished himself to get control in the few seconds before her hand snapped up to cover herself.

Her glare intensified even as her other hand crept around her neck and patted in a puzzled search. 'Oh, great!' she muttered eventually.

'Something wrong?' Gael asked, forcing his gaze from the hand covering her breast.

'Don't you mean something *else* wrong?' she snapped. 'Yes, something else *is* wrong. That…that lowlife didn't just take my purse, he took my scarf too.'

Again there was a thin tremble in her voice that struck him the wrong way.

She was probably no longer apprehensive of his presence, but she'd been attacked and robbed. A closer scrutiny of her showed another rip in her tights and muddy scuff marks on her skirt and boots.

'Are you hurt?'

Her mouth pursed and her eyes darkened. She regarded him, debating whether to furnish him with an answer. Slowly her free hand opened to reveal a bloodied deep welt across her palm.

A quiet fury rolled to life in his belly.

He balled his fist in his pocket to stop himself from reaching out to examine the wound more closely. He was absolutely sure she wouldn't welcome the move. 'My car is parked over there.' He indicated with a jerk of chin. 'If you come with me I'll get you cleaned up. Before we talk.'

Her laughter mocked again, deeper this time. 'I'm from New Jersey, Mr…whatever your name is, not Narnia. I don't step through cupboards or into limos, however flash they look, out of naive curiosity.'

Gael gritted his teeth, reached into his pocket and brought out his business card. 'My name is Gael Aguilar. I'm working on a project I think you might be interested in. I saw your…performance this afternoon and came back to look for you. The receptionist mentioned you'd just left. I came in this direction in the hope of finding you. Need I go on?'

She eyed him warily. 'You hesitated before you said *"performance"*. Why?'

Gael was a little surprised that she hadn't immediately jumped at the mention of his name, and that she wasn't preening at the thought of being pursued as he'd pursued her. Most women would find that a compliment. But what shocked him more was that she'd cut through everything he'd said and singled out the slight trip in his voice triggered by what he'd witnessed after her audition that afternoon.

It wasn't a flaw he wanted to dwell on. This wasn't personal. It was business.

The reminder, and the fact that he'd been in this alley too long, tautened his voice. 'It's not productive to dwell on the cadence of my speech, Miss Beckett. You have my word that I mean you no harm.' His gaze dropped to her hand. 'My advice, though, would be to see to that wound before it gets infected. I can help. Then we can talk. I don't want anything more from you.'

A slight frown marred her forehead before she looked over his shoulder at the limo. His driver stood to attention next to the back door and inclined his head at her. Her frown cleared.

Pressing home the advantage the sight his burly bodyguard and driver provided, Gael continued. 'Unless I'm mistaken, you now have no means of reaching your destination tonight or contacting anyone for help?'

'I'm far from as helpless are you're making me sound,

Mr Aguilar,' she muttered, although her voice lacked conviction.

He remained silent, gave her time to arrive at the conclusion he needed. After a minute she held out her hand.

He handed her his card and she stared down at it. If she recognised the information there she gave no indication. She looked from him to the car, then at the card, and back to him.

'You have a first aid kit in your car?' she enquired, quietly but firmly.

He probably did, but he shrugged. 'Possibly. I've never had occasion to use one. But my hotel is fifteen minutes away. We can get you cleaned up more efficiently there.'

She immediately shook her head. 'No, sorry—that won't work for me. That Narnia thing again, you know…?'

Gael stopped himself from growling his frustration. Never had he had to work this hard to get traction with a member of the opposite sex. Had he been in a better mood he would have been vastly amused. He shoved both hands into his pockets and thought fast.

'I was supposed to attend a dinner party tonight, with thirty other guests, on the Upper East Side. I pulled out because of the prospect of a business meeting with you. We will go there. Is that enough reassurance for you?'

She stared back at him, her injured fist slowly curling. Gael knew the abrasion would be causing her discomfort by now.

'Maybe…but how do I know the party is real and not some made-up fantasy?'

He compressed his lips before reaching for his phone. A few clicks and Pietro Vitale's face filled his screen.

'Gael, your presence has been missed. I've tried not to be insulted by a few of my female guests complaining that the party isn't the same without you,' his friend complained.

Gael's gaze shifted from the screen to Goldie. Her mouth was set in a firm, mildly disapproving line. He angled the screen towards her and addressed Pietro. 'I can remedy that, provided I can bring a guest?'

'Of course, *amico*. More is merrier, *si*? Also, the sooner, the better. *Arrivederci!*'

The Italian signed off.

'Will that suffice or do I need to request a police escort as well?' he drawled.

Goldie slowly shrugged. 'This is fine.'

Gael exhaled, a curious tension leaving his body as he nodded. 'Then come.'

Her eyes widened a fraction at his curt command, but she fell into step beside him. She summoned a tiny smile for his driver as he opened the back door for her. When she stooped to enter Gael forced his gaze from lingering on her rounded backside and shapely legs.

He entered after her and settled back in his seat. When she slid as far away from him as possible he experienced that mild irritation again. Considering what he'd witnessed in the auditorium this afternoon, her stand-offish behaviour was getting old.

'We've established that I'm not about to force myself on you, Miss Beckett, so perhaps you could drop the terrified lamb routine?'

'I'm not a lamb,' she snapped. 'And this isn't a routine.'

'Are you saying you're *always* this suspicious of everyone?'

'I'm suspicious of men who come out of nowhere and accost me in dark alleys—and, yes, men who are possibly wolves dressed in lambs' clothing.'

'And yet here you are,' he said.

Her expressive eyes snapped at him. 'What exactly are you saying?'

Gael stared at her as the car slid into traffic. 'I mean

your options aren't looking very good right now. So perhaps a little gratitude wouldn't go amiss. I might decide you're not worth the effort and leave you to your fate. Is that what you want?' he asked, watching her closely.

'I've just been attacked. I'm within my rights to be wary,' she replied.

'Yes, but I think you trust your instincts too—which is why you're here, *no*?'

'You think you know me?' she enquired, narrow-eyed.

'I think my assessment is right. Instinct first, then after that you let other…urges guide you.'

'What's that supposed to mean? What urges?'

His mouth twisted. 'You tell me.'

'I have no idea what you're talking about. And if this is the way our supposed business meeting is heading perhaps I'm better off cutting my losses right now.'

Gael sighed. 'While you decide on that will you allow me to put your seat belt on for you? I wouldn't want you to suffer another injury en route to what you imagine is your gruesome end.'

Her eyes narrowed. 'You're mocking me?'

He reached for the seat belt. 'I'm trying to find a way to have a conversation without getting disagreed with at every turn.'

She inhaled long and hard, her gaze going from the buckle in his hand to his face. When he cocked an eyebrow she nodded and pressed herself back against the seat. Moving closer, Gael wondered whether his offer had been a good idea. Underneath the distinctive smell of her intimate acquaintance with alley concrete he caught the scent of apples and honeysuckle. And at close quarters he saw her pulse racing at her throat, her skin flushing when he drew the belt between her breasts.

The stirring in his groin wasn't surprising—he was a red-blooded male, after all—but he cursed its presence all the same, especially when he cradled her hip for a precious few seconds before the lock slid home and his blood heated up to discomfort levels.

When he finished the task and sat back it wasn't without a modicum of relief.

He was almost glad when she cleared her throat. 'So, what do you want to talk to me about?'

He brought his mind firmly back to task. To business. 'I have a proposition for you. If you're agreeable we'll get you cleaned up first, then we'll talk, *si*?'

CHAPTER THREE

GOLDIE TRIED TO FOCUS as the sleek, luxurious car rolled down Columbus Avenue and turned on to Central Park West. She didn't think she'd hit her head when that horrid brute had wrestled her purse away from her. And yet a hazy sensation, as if she'd fallen down a rabbit hole, swirled all around her, making her wonder if her faculties were intact. Making her wonder if she'd heard him right.

What had this unfathomably riveting stranger said? A *proposition*.

She wanted to snort under her breath. Nothing good could come out of a proposition from a man like *that*. A man with the face of a fallen angel, hell-bent on practising his sorcery on unsuspecting women. A man with a voice so hypnotic she wondered if he'd practised that precise cadence and for how long before he'd attained that perfect sizzling-you-to-your-toes note that accompanied each faintly accented word.

He was the kind of man who was everything her mother had always yearned for and never achieved. The exact type of man Goldie had sworn off after witnessing time and again the way they used their God-given attributes mercilessly.

Goldie didn't hate *all* men. But she drew a particular line at playboys with enigmatic eyes and captivating faces that defied adequate description and bodies to match. Throw in the type of wealth and raw power this man next to her exuded and her warning bells clanged loud enough to be heard on the Long Island Sound.

So what was she doing in his car?

Goldie frowned, then answered her own question. Circumstances had forced her into it. But that didn't mean she wasn't still in control. Of her mental faculties *and* of her body. That zing she'd felt when he'd secured her seat belt had been a temporary aberration. The whole last hour had been a surreal sequence of events she intended to put behind her as soon as possible.

She glanced at him from the corner of her eye. When she was certain his phone had absorbed his attention, she turned and stared at his profile.

Seriously, he was like a Roman statue she'd once seen at the Museum of Natural History when she'd visited with her mother. Their trip had occurred on one of the rare times when her mother had been sober and coherent enough to make the visit. They'd stared at the statue for what had felt like an eternity, absorbing its unspeakable beauty. Her mother had sighed wistfully before her eyes had filled with tears.

Goldie had known what those tears were about. What they were *always* about. Wishes unfulfilled. A past thrown away because she'd made the wrong choices. The biggest one of which had been letting Goldie's father get away. A lump had risen to Goldie's throat as she'd watched her mother stare hard at the statue, wishing it was flesh and blood.

It had been a fruitless wish, of course.

Except Gael Aguilar was a living, breathing version of that statue.

A version who turned his head and stared straight at her in the next moment, blasting her with long-lashed light hazel eyes. Goldie attempted to look away, but for some stupid reason she couldn't drag her gaze from him.

'This proposition of yours...what's it got to do with your occupation?'

The scrape in her palm was filthy and stinging badly. Enough that it made unclenching her hand difficult. She dropped her other hand from her ripped sweater long enough to pull the business card from her pocket. It read *'CEO, Atlas Group'*. She'd made it her business to research every TV and movie production company in New York, Hollywood and Canada, just so she wouldn't miss any opportunities that might whisper past the hallowed halls of Othello. She'd never heard of Gael Aguilar's company.

'It's a new arm of my company.'

'So you were trolling the halls looking for guinea pigs?' she asked.

For some reason that amused him. Both sides of his sensual mouth lifted. Even that small action lightened his face in a way that made her breath catch. Made her wonder what it would be like to be the recipient of a full, genuine smile.

'We really need to get off the subject of animal references. I'm a man. You're a woman. Let's refer to ourselves as such, *si*?' he drawled with a raised brow.

Something in his gaze made her self-conscious. She cursed silently when heat rushed up to redden her face. Because of her chosen career she'd needed to train herself not to blush at the drop of a hat, and yet she was doing just that, simply at the droll, slightly mocking look in his eyes.

'My question still stands,' she sniped, to cover her uneasiness.

'And it will be answered in the fullness of time. I need your undivided attention for that discussion.'

'What makes you think you don't have that now?'

'You mean in between trying to hang on to your modesty and the swelling of your hand?' he enquired, his tone almost gentle.

For some reason that made something tighten in her midriff. Before she could form a disagreeable response he was leaning forward. He snagged a bottle of water from the well-stocked bar at his side of the car. Snapping the plastic top free, he wet a handful of tissues and turned to her.

'May I?' he requested, again in that gentle voice she didn't want to associate with him. Men like him weren't gentle. Men like him were predators, only intent on taking, taking, *taking* and leaving behind callously discarded husks.

Goldie wanted to refuse on principle, in solidarity with her poor mother and with the bitterness that sometimes spilled into her just from being close to it. She didn't doubt that her mother's bitterness had stained her in some way, made her wary of certain types of men. Men like the casting director from today's audition, for instance.

She silently shook her head, veering away from the subject even while admitting she was old enough to know some of the blame for her mother's current circumstances came from Gloria Beckett herself. It took two to tango, after all.

Tango.

Okay, she wasn't going to allow an image of her tangoing with this man to cloud her already dizzying thoughts. Determinedly she clenched her gut against any more fanciful thoughts and held out her right hand.

Gael Aguilar cupped her hand in his. Goldie forced herself to ignore the alarming tingling where they touched and watch clinically as he cleaned her wound as best as the meagre supplies allowed. He worked quickly and efficiently, his manner gentle but firm. When he was finished, he disposed of the tissues and eyed her with a steady look.

'Better?'

She tested the flexibility in her hand and gave a short nod. 'Yes, thank you.'

'You see, we're not above civility after all, Miss Beckett.'

Despite the amusement in his voice there was a thin veil of something else in there...something she couldn't pinpoint. Or perhaps she wasn't willing to pinpoint it?

She'd puzzled over this man for far longer than common sense dictated was wise. 'Are we there yet?' she asked instead, then cringed at the juvenile question.

His amusement increased.

Certain he was about to make another joke at her expense she hurried to add, 'I don't have all night.' She glanced at her watch, her heart lurching when she realised the time. 'In fact, I don't think I can do this thing tonight after all. I need to be somewhere else.'

Her mother needed only the smallest excuse to regress into depression and fall off the wagon. Goldie had assured her she'd be home by ten. Any later and her mother would fret. Fretting would inevitably lead to her seeking solace at the bottom of a bottle. Goldie could only pray that her mother had fallen asleep watching TV tonight.

'You need to be somewhere else? And you didn't think to mention that before you got into my car?' His amusement had vanished. Light hazel eyes narrowed incisively on her. 'Is this some sort of game?'

'Excuse me?'

'Are you wasting my time, Miss Beckett?'

Irritation rushed up her spine. 'With respect, *you* insisted on this meeting. Granted, I'm curious to find out just what this *proposition* is, but I hadn't realised how late it was—'

'And suddenly you need to be somewhere else? You have someone waiting for you, perhaps? Boyfriend?' His gaze dropped to the hand curled into her lap. *'Husband?'*

The word held a sneer that stiffened her back, and again she caught that look in his eyes. As if he held her far below his normal regard.

Puzzlement and that growing irritation made her frown. 'That really isn't your business, is it, Mr Aguilar? Are you in the habit of interrogating your potential business colleagues like this? It *is* business you intend to discuss with me, isn't it? If not, then I suggest you let me out right now—because I wouldn't want to waste more of your time!'

His jaw flexed for a second before his expression turned neutral. Eyes that had been mocking and mildly amused became opaque. 'It *is* a business proposition. If you need to be elsewhere, then so be it. But will you be able to live with yourself if you don't find out whether this is an opportunity you want to miss or not?'

There was a taunt in those words. There was also a look in his eyes as if he wasn't sure whether he wanted her to say yes or no.

'Does that line usually work for you?'

A sculpted eyebrow went up. 'What line?'

'The "do things my way or you'll kick yourself for ever" scam?'

He gave a half-sigh, half an irritated huff. 'I grow tired of this vacillating. You have one minute to say yes or no. Starting right now.'

He had the temerity to stare pointedly at his watch.

Dear God, she really *had* fallen down a rabbit hole! She thought she'd hit bottom with the sleazy proposition from that casting director this afternoon. It still made her skin crawl. But had she merely fallen into another dimension? One where the person making a proposition wasn't even certain whether he wanted his offer accepted or not, but went ahead and dared her to consider it anyway?

About to shake her head to clear it, she saw his eyes sharpen.

'Make up your mind, Miss Beckett. We're here.'

Goldie looked out of her window. Sure enough, they'd pulled up in front of one of those flashy-looking high-rises that dotted the Manhattan skyline. This one came complete with liveried doorman, shiny awning, and a uniformed concierge behind an imposing reception desk.

She redirected her attention to the man whose posture held more than a whiff of impatience and arrogance. 'Twenty minutes. That's all I have.'

His mouth thinned. 'We shall see.'

About to ask him what he meant, she found her words choked off when he opened his door and alighted, then turned to hold out his hand.

She didn't want to touch him. Not after the way it had felt the last time. And because she didn't want to let go of the tear in her top that showed half her boob. She shifted along the seat, and was debating how to exit with as much dignity as she could muster when he reached in and scooped her out as if she weighed nothing.

'What are you— Put me down!' she spluttered, outrage filling her as he marched her through the double doors being held open by the doorman and into a waiting lift.

He set her down and immediately the doors slid shut. The whole thing had happened in less than two minutes, and yet Goldie felt as if she'd just experienced the headiest, longest rollercoaster ride of her life. Impressions of heat, masculine scent, tensile strength, strong capable arms and…absurdly…above all, safety, buffeted her as she stared at him in astonishment from her side of the lift space.

Once he'd pressed the button for the penthouse he stepped back with a cool look. 'You said twenty minutes. I wasn't about to have the time eaten away while you decided which leg to use to exit the car.'

'My God, you're insane!' Or maybe *she* was. She hadn't been given the chance to dissect things properly yet.

His jaw flexed and his hands were rammed into his pockets. 'Far from it, *querida*. Someone has to remain rational in what is fast turning into a farce. Tell me—do you always make a huge production out of every small decision?'

'You don't know me well enough to label me a drama queen, Mr Aguilar.'

Suddenly the air in the lift thickened. The glance he levelled at her held the heavy weight of judgement. 'I've seen enough to reach a conclusion, I think.'

'What's that supposed to mean?' she countered.

One hand emerged from his pocket long enough to wave her away. 'We will not waste time discussing inconsequential subjects.'

'Do you go out of your way to ride roughshod over *everyone* you meet, or am I the lucky recipient of your special attention?'

He shrugged, sent her a sardonic whisper of a smile and exited the lift, once again leaving Goldie looking at him askance.

She followed him out, then drew to a halt when the double doors before them were flung open to reveal a stocky Italian with twinkling brown eyes, shoulder-length hair and a wide grin.

'Gael! *Amico!* You're here. Now my night is complete.' His gaze swung to Goldie, looked her over, and his grin dimmed a touch. 'Okay, this is…interesting. My friend, do you care to tell me why your plus one is in this state? I trust you implicitly, of course, and I'm sure in a fight you'd come out the winner, but I'm not averse to attempting to kick your butt if you had something to do with the lady's um…state…'

'"The lady" is standing right in front of you,' Goldie offered with a saccharine smile. 'And trust me, she's quite capable of answering for and defending herself.'

The man's concerned look dissolved, to be replaced by the wide smile again. 'Of course. Tell me your tale, sweet one, and allow me to vanquish those that need vanquishing.'

Goldie felt a reluctant smile tug at her lips. 'I'm fine. Really. And it wasn't…your friend's fault.'

'So he was your rescuer?' the Italian asked hopefully.

'I wouldn't stretch it that far.' She looked at the man in question to see mockery and a tight little smile playing at his lips.

'*Sí*, Pietro, we're still trying to work out the finer details of our…association. But perhaps if you would be so kind as to point out the bathroom Goldie can clean up?'

Pietro nodded. 'Of course, of course. Come with me.'

He led them through the double doors and immediately turned into a bright hallway. Goldie got an impression of grey and gold decor, loud but not intrusive music, and lots of laughter coming from the living room before Gael Aguilar's presence beside her grabbed her focus. He really was imposing. And taller than she'd thought in the alley. As for those broad shoulders—

'Here you are.' Pietro turned a door handle and nudged it open to reveal a large bedroom. 'The bathroom is through there. You should have everything you need. If not, please let me know.'

Goldie found another small smile. 'Thank you.'

'*Prego.*' Pietro returned her smile, then with a nod at Gael walked away.

Gael remained, his eyes on her. Her senses began to jump and dip in that alarming way again.

'I'm fine to take it from here,' she said, when he made no move to leave.

He made an impatient sound. 'I think we've established that I'm not going to attack you, Miss Beckett. Accepting my help won't dislodge your feminine independence. Besides, trying to see to your wound with your non-dominant hand is going to eat into my twenty minutes. Unless you want to restart the clock?'

Goldie pressed her lips together, wanting to be annoyed with him for the way he made her feel a touch ridiculous. But, short of telling him she tended to refuse help from men like him on principle alone, thus probably seeming even more ridiculous despite her beliefs, she couldn't think of how to counter his assertion.

'Okay, thanks.' The words came out far too easily. Her brain knew it and her accelerating heartbeat acknowledged it as he stepped into the room and shrugged off his jacket.

His navy shirt clung to thick, sleek muscle as he flung the jacket away and moved towards the bathroom. She followed slowly, trying to hold at bay the sensation of orbiting close to a ravenous vortex.

She arrived in the spacious bathroom to find him setting out first aid materials on the double-width vanity unit. When he had finished he started to fold back his shirtsleeves.

Goldie tried to look away from strong, brawny forearms feathered with dark wispy hair as they were revealed. But the urge was hard to resist.

Her breath caught lightly as he glanced behind him and cocked his head at her.

'Come to the sink. We'll wash your wound properly before I apply some antiseptic.'

She joined him at the sink, taking care not to stand too close when his presence registered so insistently next to her. Gael Aguilar was dominating. His body seemed to vibrate with a force field that mercilessly drew every living thing into its orbit.

He turned on the taps, tested the temperature, then held out his hand. Recalling the tingling when he'd touched her in the car, Goldie wanted to refuse. But this silly dance had gone on long enough. She needed to get this over with and go back to her life. Her mother.

Thoughts of Gloria spurred her on.

She gave him her hand and once again he cupped it in his. And once again the tingling started. Only this time the sensation was twice as intense. Whether it was to do with the bright lights of the bathroom, which cast their skin to skin contact in a vivid tableau, or with the fact that he was much closer to her than he'd been in the car, she wasn't sure. All she knew was that touching Gael, having his thumbs move across her palm as he rinsed the angry gash, was like nothing else she'd ever felt.

When her breath felt strangled the sound was audible in a silence marred only by their mingled breathing. Like in the car, his movements were gentle. But the fire he created with his fingers was not. Growing alarmingly short of breath, Goldie wanted to snatch her hand from his. But then he made a sound. And she looked up. Their eyes met in the mirror. She forgot to breathe all together.

Gael's eyes had grown darker, stoked with a dark fire that made her belly clench tight. Recognising the feeling as her first ever genuine sexual attraction, Goldie gasped. His gaze dropped to her parted mouth. Stayed riveted until the almost visceral stare made her lips twitch with a need that bordered on alien.

Beneath the running tap his hands continued to caress hers. But neither of them moved their gazes except to drift them over each other's faces, returning over and over again to their mouths.

She wanted to kiss him. Be kissed by him. Now.

Her lips parted.

Gael made a sound beneath his breath. A guttural, primitive sound. And he broke his gaze from hers.

Released from the power of that rabid scrutiny, Goldie gulped greedily on the air flowing back into her lungs. Along with even more alarm at what had just happened. The thoughts she'd entertained, the want coursing through her…

Dear God… What's wrong with me?

After that sordid, grossly insulting proposition the casting director had flung her way this afternoon, sex should be the last thing on her mind. It should be buried even deeper than normal, beneath the tight, rigid focus of her ambition and her need to make something of herself. Her need not to end up like her mother—a slave to her sexual needs and emotional wellbeing, dependent on others for her happiness.

And yet here she was, letting this man touch her, trail his long fingers over her skin as if he were caressing a lover. And she...she *liked* it.

She withdrew her hand abruptly, almost knocking it against the side of the sink in her haste to dislodge the electricity his touch created.

'I... Thanks. Can we get on with it now, please?' she said, avoiding another look into those burnished gold eyes.

He muttered something beneath his breath in Spanish. But he snagged a hand towel and wrapped it around her hand before he drew her to the vanity unit.

'Sit down.'

The order was firm enough to put her back up, but she wasn't in the mood to argue any longer so she sat down where he indicated and held out her now slightly less throbbing hand.

The antiseptic stung, made her wince.

'Are you okay?' he enquired, in a deep, low voice.

Goldie wanted to look up, felt almost compelled to look into those eyes again, but she forced her gaze to remain on the clinical movements of his medical attention.

'Yes, thank you.'

He completed the cleansing, then applied a light bandage over her palm. Her hand felt a million times better by the time he was finished.

'Now for your head.'

'What?'

He held up another cotton bud. It was then that Goldie registered the slight throb at her temples. Something like relief poured through her. Then she silently grimaced at being *glad* of the minor head injury. The small gash which Gael was now cleaning didn't really explain her temporary lapse of control or the low hum through her veins. But she clung to it as the cause just the same.

Once he was done he stepped back. His gaze dropped to the hand she still had on the wide tear in her sweater. A hand growing numb from holding the torn garment in place.

'What are we going to do about this?' he enquired.

She bit her lip, recognising that she couldn't very well go out into the party with a rip in her sweater. The ripped tights she could take care of by removing and disposing of them. But the tattered sweater would stand out—and not in a good way.

'I…I couldn't impose on you to find me a sewing kit, could I?' she ventured.

His eyes widened a touch, dark gold lightening to its natural hazel colour as mockery returned. 'I sincerely doubt Pietro would have something so domestic lying about. But I will do my best.'

He balled the hand towel he'd used and threw it into the laundry bin before he left the bathroom.

His departure infused the room with a lot more oxygen and a lot more clarity.

Goldie jumped off the vanity unit and stared at herself in the mirror. Besides the notable evidence of her tussle with the mugger, she didn't look as horrid as she felt. But she had lost her phone, the little money she had and, more importantly, all the details of the casting directors and agents she'd planned to contact in the hope of landing a job.

Her last paying job had been an infomercial three weeks ago, which had paid enough to sustain her and her mother's bills for another month. Her mother's part-time job as a waitress paid very little. Things were getting more than a little tight.

She'd gone into today's audition with more hope than expectation. When it had gone well she'd allowed herself to hope even harder. Until her hopes been dashed by the slimy words rolling off the director's tongue.

'My hotel room. Nine p.m. Perform well between the sheets and I'll make your dreams come true.'

Goldie had barely managed to stop herself from being sick before she ran out of the auditorium and into the bathroom. Locking herself in a stall, she'd been ashamed of the tears she'd allowed to fall. But she was proud that she had picked herself up and returned to the music room to practise her singing. She wouldn't give up because of one casting director who gave his profession a bad name. She couldn't afford to.

Taking a deep breath, she tugged off her boots and cleaned them with tissues, then finished tidying herself up as best she could. Spotting a dressing gown hanging behind the door, she quickly took off her clothes, disposed of the ripped tights and shrugged on the gown. She was securing the belt around her waist when Gael knocked.

Self-consciousness assailed her, even though the gown draped her from shoulder to ankle. Sucking in a deep breath, she opened the door.

What Gael Aguilar held out to her was most definitely not a sewing kit. 'My assumption was correct, it seems. This will have to do instead. Courtesy of Pietro's absent niece.'

Goldie eyed the scrap of material in his hand. The black cloth had probably started life in a designer's imagination as what a dress looked like. But even without examining it too closely she could tell it would be too small. On some level she knew Gael was probably trying to help. But the man's presence aggravated her on such a raw, subliminal level that she shook her head firmly in refusal. 'No, I don't think this will work.'

His mouth firmed. 'Go against your wish to fight me on every front, Miss Beckett, and just try it on. You might be surprised. Unless you wish to join the party in that dressing gown?'

Since that was out of the question, she bit back a grimace and took the dress. Eyeing the garment, she fingered the label, her breath catching slightly when she caught sight of the exclusive designer name. 'Okay, I'll wear it.'

She'd expected her acquiescence to draw another mocking response from him. Instead a hard look settled in his eyes.

'I'm glad you find *something* agreeable. Try not to keep me waiting too long, *sì*?' he drawled.

Goldie shut the door without responding. She suspected dealing with a man like Gael Aguilar would be trying enough at the best of times. Add the circumstances of their meeting, and the fierce awareness that showed no signs of abating whenever they were in close proximity… She admitted that her spinning senses weren't up to dealing further with the torrent of emotions he elicited.

Returning the gown to its hook, she stepped into the dress and tugged the inch-wide straps onto her shoulders. One look in the mirror drew a gasp. The material was luxuriously elastic enough to accommodate her curves but still give her room to breathe. Reluctantly fingering the hem that ended at mid-thigh, she admitted it looked spectacular, and it felt like heaven next to her skin. But the back…

Goldie eyed the exposure of her skin from nape to waist and swallowed deeply. No way could she carry off wearing her bra with this dress. Heat rushed into her cheeks as she took a deep breath and unclipped her bra. Stuffing it into the vanity unit drawer, she grabbed her boots and tugged them on. Their familiarity brought a touch of balance and, after combing her hands through her hair again, she turned and opened the door.

He was standing at the far side of the bedroom, his surprisingly brooding gaze focused out of the French windows onto the New York night skyline.

Goldie walked in and drew to a halt in the middle of the room, her gaze once again homing in with almost helpless intent on the man who leaned with such loose-limbed indolence against the wall.

His head turned and his gaze hooked on hers before his scrutiny dropped. His sharp inhalation echoed through the room as he took her in, the hands in his pockets visibly bunching as he straightened abruptly.

And stared.

Sexual awareness, now recognised as the potent substance it was, was unstoppable as it lanced her. Intensified just from the look in his eyes.

Beneath the expensive silk and elastic blend heat suffused her, rushing through her body in a maddening dash she had no hope of stopping. But she tried. Heaven help her, she had to. Or she'd lose her mind.

Slicking her tongue desperately over her lower lip, she cleared her throat. 'I'm ready to hear your proposition now, Mr Aguilar.'

CHAPTER FOUR

THE HEATED LOOK didn't abate in his eyes. But her words, like so many others tonight, seemed to trigger a response within him.

A negative one this time.

After a few charged seconds his expression grew shuttered, and his aura when he approached her vibrated with repressed emotions she couldn't place her finger on.

'Gael,' he clipped out as he passed her and headed for the door.

'Excuse me?'

'My name is Gael. I prefer it to Mr Aguilar. Use it.'

'That sounds curiously like an order,' she replied.

He stopped abruptly, turned to face her. A deep sustaining breath lifted his chest before he speared her with his incisive gaze. 'We've both had a trying day, Goldie. Can we attempt to make it slightly *less* trying before we part ways?'

She was sure it was the use of her name, spoken so smoothly, so sizzlingly, that drew the fight from her, made her lift one shoulder in a feeble shrug. 'Sure, I can try.'

'Gracias,' he intoned. Then added, 'Thank you.'

'Um…no problem.'

A tinge of amusement lit his eyes before he shook his head. '"No problem" aren't words I associate with you.' He abruptly held up one hand. 'Not that I want to test the theory right now. Come, we shall get a drink and find a place to hold our discussion, yes?'

At her nod he resumed his exit, slowing his long stride to accommodate hers.

They entered a large, rectangular living room, decorated with a severely modern and minimalist hand. The centrepiece of the room was the futuristic-looking light fixture that seemed to take up almost a quarter of the ceiling space. Beneath this gleaming white and silver masterpiece Pietro's guests laughed and mingled. The man himself was the centre of attention, surrounded by a coolly elegant circle of females.

His grin widened when he spotted them approaching, and he beckoned them with open arms.

'Ah, there you are. Confirmation of our adventures in the Andes is needed, my friend. Sadly, I don't think these fine ladies here believe a word I'm saying!' he said to Gael.

Gael's gaze drifted over the ladies in question, who sparkled and preened even harder under his attention. Although he smiled, Goldie noticed the mirth didn't touch his eyes. Not that the action didn't have the desired devastating effect. Almost without exception every woman in the group strained towards him, their gazes rabidly checking him out.

'That particular pleasure will have to wait, my friend. I have more important things to attend to right now.' He turned to the waiter who had appeared next to him and snagged two glasses of champagne.

Goldie dragged her attention from the nearest fawning woman to shake her head as he offered her one of the glasses. 'No, thank you. I don't drink.'

She caught more than one woman sniggering.

Pietro frowned, his features almost comical with alarm. 'You don't drink? You're not underage, are you?'

'No, I'm old enough to drink, but I choose not to,' she repeated.

Her mother's dependency on alcohol to get her through tough times and the depressing consequences when that crutch failed to work had taught Goldie at a very early age never to go near the stuff.

His eyes turning speculative, Gael returned both drinks to the tray and steered her outside towards a bar set up on the terrace. After taking her order for an apple spritzer and getting mineral water for himself, he led her to a quiet part of the hardwood floored space. Between two tree-sized ferns a white sofa had been set up beneath a heated lamp, which threw a lovely warm glow over the area.

'Why don't you drink alcohol?' he asked abruptly once they were seated.

'Do I have to have a specific reason?' she prevaricated.

He shrugged. 'Most people tend not to do it for two reasons—a natural aversion or an active life choice stemming from experience. I want to know which applies to you.'

Her fingers tightened around her chilled glass. 'Why?'

'Because one reason doesn't require further explanation, but the other might warrant further discussion if we're to work together.'

'So you're saying if I happen to be a recovering alcoholic it may ruin my chances at this imaginary job I'm yet to hear about?'

'I'm saying situations and flaws can be dealt with if they're known up front. I don't want to be blindsided by issues further down the line.'

'Mr Aguilar—'

His jaw tightened—a tiny movement, but she saw it nevertheless.

'Gael,' he intoned.

'Gael.' She stopped, unwillingly savouring the name on her tongue. Wanting to say it again. She cleared her throat and forced out a laugh. 'We seem to be getting way ahead of ourselves. Can we start this whole thing over? Please?' She held out her hand. 'I'm Goldie Beckett, graduate of Othello with honours in Acting and Musical Art. Currently unemployed and, yes, looking for a job.'

Gael stared at her hand. That mockery was swirling through his eyes once more.

After a beat, he took her bandaged hand in a firm but gentle hold. 'Gael Aguilar. My accolades are too numerous to name, but suffice it to say I'm in a position to make your dreams come true.'

Ice drenched her. She snatched her hand from his as words from earlier in the day, albeit without the sleazy overtones, fell into her lap.

His expression turned brooding. 'Something wrong?'

'Yes. You presume to know what my dreams are when you don't know me from a stranger in the street.'

'You just stated that you are unemployed. My response only pertains to an attempt to reverse that. Unless you wish to remain in a state of unemployment?'

She swallowed the bile of distaste the reminder of the day's earlier events had elicited and attempted to remain calm. 'I'm sorry. You mentioned before that you'd seen some of my audition this afternoon. I didn't notice you there, I must admit. Did you…did you see all of it?' She fervently prayed that he hadn't witnessed the sleazy exchange with the casting director immediately following the audition.

'I saw enough to make up my mind. Enough to make me return to find you.'

She lifted her glass and took a sip of her drink, her mind frantically ticking over. If he'd seen enough of her performance to make him hunt her down, then did she dare think he'd only seen the acting part, not the unsavoury denouement?

'You have a part you want me to play?' she queried, making sure to bleed her voice of hope.

It was that vulnerable hope that the casting director had exploited this afternoon, to make that demand of her. She planned not to let this man even close to the feverish hope burning in her heart.

'I have a part I *potentially* want you to play,' he amended. 'Subject to a few stipulations. And the usual auditions, of course.'

'Stipulations?'

He nodded, the light bouncing off his jet-black wavy hair. 'Very rigorous stipulations.'

'Such as?'

'We will discuss them later. Right now the broader questions concern your availability and your commitment to a long-term film project.'

Her heart skipped a beat, despite her promise to herself not to let hope take over. 'What's the role and how long are we talking about?'

'Female lead in a psychosexual thriller. Three to four months, travelling all over the world.'

Excitement fizzed through her blood. 'I'll need to read the script.'

'You'll be given a full synopsis to familiarise yourself with the story. But first you need to tell me whether you're free.'

About to say yes, she stopped when her mind veered to her mother. Despite the fierce ambition burning in her heart, the thought of leaving her mother on her own for four months made her heart lurch. But at the same time she knew this was what her mother wanted for her.

Goldie just hoped that pride in her daughter would make Gloria stick to the straight and narrow.

She returned her attention to Gael's face and experienced a slight chill at his expression. 'I'm sure I can work something out.'

One side of his mouth ticked with a hard twitch. 'Time to put your cards on the table, Goldie. Are you married?' he asked in a clipped voice.

She frowned. 'What? No.'

'Do you have a lover or a partner who will be displeased at your long absence from home?'

'I…no.'

His eyes narrowed. 'That hesitation doesn't fill me with confidence. I prefer *not* to start any association with lies.'

Affront stiffened her jaw. 'I'm not lying. The person I'm concerned about is my mother. I still live at home. With her. And she's…'

'She's what?'

She swallowed. 'Fragile.'

'In what way?'

'In ways I prefer not to divulge until something—if any-thing—comes out of this discussion. But I'll make sure, if it comes to it, that my home life doesn't interfere with my job.'

Silence ticked by as he stared at her. 'You're ambitious,' he drawled, with a touch of censure that grated over her skin.

'You say that like it's a bad thing. Did you not get where you are today by pursuing *your* ambition?'

He nodded. '*Sì*, but I've come to learn there are vari-ous types of ambition.'

She opened her mouth to answer, but a church clock nearby chimed, reminding her of the lateness of the hour. Whatever Gael's views on her ambitions were, they'd have to wait to be discussed some other time.

She placed her glass on a nearby table and stood up. He rose up before her, effectively blocking her from leaving.

'Where are you going? We haven't finished talking.'

She dragged her gaze from his broad shoulders and imposing body to meet his gaze. 'I can prolong our meet-ing, but first I'll need to call my mother. I was just going to ask Pietro if I could use his phone.'

His mouth compressed for a second, then he reached

into his pocket and brought out a sleek, ultra-modern-looking phone. One she hadn't yet seen on the market. Not that she paid much attention to such trendy luxuries.

'Use mine.'

He placed the phone in her hand. She swiped her hand across the screen. Nothing happened. He cupped her hand and performed something magical with his fingers. The phone buzzed to life.

'How may I help you, Gael?' a sultry voice queried.

Goldie's eyes widened as he sent her a sly smile. 'Guest call coming up,' he said into the phone. Then he held it up to her.

'Speak the number into it and you'll be connected. When you're done with your call come and find me.'

He left her alone on the terrace and headed back inside as she recited the number of her next-door neighbour. The time on the phone read just gone ten p.m. If by some miracle her mother was asleep, the last thing Goldie wanted to do was wake her.

Mrs Robinson, on the other hand, rarely slept, and was always glued to her TV screen, watching her favourite shows. Sure enough, the old woman answered her phone on the third ring.

'Mrs Robinson, it's Goldie. Do you mind checking in on my mother for me, please? I don't want to wake her if she's asleep, but I don't want her to worry—'

'Of course I will, dear. I took her a slice of peach cobbler earlier, and she said she'd be heading to bed early. I'll go and peek in on her now. If she's up I'll stay with her until you get home. If she's asleep I'll call and let you know.'

Goldie bit her lip. 'Um…you won't be able to reach me, Mrs Robinson. I lost my phone earlier tonight. My phone *and* my purse.'

'Oh, no—are you okay?'

The old woman's concern touched her heart.

'I'm fine, thanks. I'm so sorry, but do you mind checking on her now, while I'm on the phone, please?'

'Of course. Hold on.'

Goldie breathed a sigh of relief as she heard the sprightly woman head for the door. Goldie had given her a key to their apartment years ago, when Mrs Robinson had offered to keep an eye on Gloria whenever Goldie was away. The arrangement had helped Goldie maintain peace of mind when she was at college, then later when she was out at auditions and at work.

She heard Mrs Robinson let herself in. After a minute she heard the soft snick of a door shutting.

'She's sleeping, dear. Don't worry about her. I'll keep watch. Now, what about you? Will you be okay to get home?'

Goldie hadn't quite worked it out, but she wasn't about to add to the kind old woman's burden. She looked towards the living room, where the party guests milled around, some spilling out onto the terrace to enjoy the view. Gael Aguilar wasn't one of them. When she found herself searching harder for him, she abruptly averted her gaze.

Crossing her fingers, she told a little white lie. 'I'm with a friend at the moment. I'll be fine.'

'All right. I'll see you later, honey.'

Goldie pulled the phone from her ear, not sure how to hang up. When the phone went dark she assumed it had shut itself off. She looked up to find one of the women who'd been in Pietro's circle smiling at her from the bar.

Only her smile held a whole lot of speculation. The green-eyed kind.

'So, *you're* with Gael, are you?' The slight slur, figurative and literal, was hard to miss.

Goldie forced herself not to bristle. 'No, not really.'

The blonde took her answer as an invitation to stroll

closer. Expensive perfume and the faint traces of alcoholic over-indulgence reached Goldie's nostrils.

'No? If you're not together then why hasn't he been inside with us?' she demanded.

Goldie glanced towards the living room and shrugged. 'He's in there now, if you want to go talk to him.'

The blonde laughed—a brittle sound that spoke of more than just a passing interest in Gael Aguilar. 'This may be a time of equality and all that, but a woman still likes to be chased by a man.'

'Right. Okay.'

Wanting an end to the conversation, Goldie searched for her glass, only to find it had disappeared—probably taken by one of the super-attentive waiters dotted around the place. Sure enough, one of them saw her drinkless state and darted towards her with an eager smile and a tray full of drinks.

Goldie started to shake her head. 'No, thanks. I don't—'

'She doesn't drink,' the blonde stage-whispered to the waiter. When he started to turn away she stopped him with a hand on his arm. 'Wait, this is fruit punch, isn't it?' She indicated a pink drink with a gaily coloured umbrella and a straw sticking out of it.

The waiter nodded. 'Yes, ma'am.'

The blonde snagged the glass and held it out to Goldie. 'Here you go. Problem solved.'

Goldie took the drink, having no intention of drinking it. Her smile grew stiffer as the blonde examined her critically from head to toe.

'Interesting boots.'

Again, the observation came with a smile that was meant to take some of the sting out of her words.

'Interesting...dress,' Goldie replied.

Her unwanted companion laughed. 'You have a spine. I'm Heidi, by the way. And if you weren't here with the man who broke my heart last year—the man who now looks at me like we've never even met before, never mind *dated*—I'd almost like you.'

Something tiny but sharp lodged itself in Goldie's side. 'You and Gael were an item?' she asked, even though she told herself she didn't care about the answer.

Heidi's nose wrinkled, but Goldie saw the dart of pain in her eyes.

'An *item*? How quaint. We were *lovers*. I shared his bed for six glorious weeks. Then I hit my inevitable use-by date and was bade, *Hasta la vista, baby.*'

'Inevitable?'

Her laugh held more of the pain that was slowly emerging from the bottom of her champagne glass. 'As regular as clockwork. No one, to date, has exceeded Gael Aguilar's famous month-and-a-half dating limit. So don't get your hopes up.'

Goldie frowned at the umbrella and the straw. 'You've got things completely wrong. I only met him tonight.'

Heidi's eyebrows went up. 'And he already looks at you like *that*?'

'Like what?' she asked, growing a little hot under the blonde's scrutiny.

'Are you *serious*?'

Uncomfortable with where the conversation was going, she lifted the drink to her mouth and took a long sip.

When Heidi continued to stare at her as if she was dim, Goldie shrugged with more than a hint of irritation. 'I really don't know what you're talking about. And I don't think you have anything to worry over…you know…if you want to…um…rekindle things?'

This time the laughter was pure white-hot bitterness. 'Second rule of dating Gael Aguilar. There is no second chance. Once he's done with you, you're finished for good.'

She took another drink, then hiccupped. Then grimaced as if she was in actual pain.

Goldie wanted to tell her to stop. That she really didn't need to know any more unsavoury details about the man who'd come to her aid—the man who seemed taken enough by a fraction of the ten-minute performance he'd seen today to pursue her.

But Heidi was on a roll.

Goldie sipped at her drink and racked her brain for a convenient excuse even while she kept one eye on the living room doorway. Now she was sure her mother was safely asleep there was no need for her to rush back home, but she still needed to come up with a way to get home that wouldn't mean tapping into the emergency money she kept in her closet at home. She'd already used too much of it earlier this month, when her mother had been too depressed to go to work.

With each minute that passed Goldie saw her choices dwindling. It was too late to make her way back to Othello to ask to stay with one of her friends there. Just as with each passing minute she was learning way too much about Gael Aguilar. His preference in women—sleek, tall blondes. How many homes he owned—eight at Heidi's last count. His love of fast cars—immeasurable. His favourite food—authentic Spanish-made *paella*. His bedroom skills—

Um...no!

'I think I'm going to head back in now,' Goldie interrupted, before she could be made privy to gossip she didn't want to hear. 'Will you be all right?'

Heidi waved her empty glass at her. 'Of course! Go get my... I mean *your* man. Enjoy your six weeks!'

The statement ended with another hiccup that sounded uncomfortably close to tears.

Her heart went out to the woman. She started to reach out, wondering why her arm felt so heavy. 'Heidi—'

'Is everything okay here?' Gael's deep voice enquired.

They were both startled, and both swayed on their feet as they turned to face the source of their conversation. Gael reached out for her arm and Goldie gasped with surprise at the dizziness that assailed her.

But even in her confounding state she saw how he completely ignored Heidi.

'I...yes. I'm fine—'

'I thought you said you didn't drink?' came the sharp, cold query.

Goldie frowned. Or at least she attempted to. Her face suddenly felt funny. 'I don't. This is fruit punch.'

He calmly took his phone from her, then her glass, eyeing her with deep censure. 'It is fruit punch. Laced with rum and vodka.'

'Wh-*what*?' She turned her head with growing difficulty, met Heidi's unrepentant gaze. 'But you said it was...'

Too late, she realised what had happened.

Gael turned to his ex. 'Are *you* responsible for this, Heidi?' he gritted, his voice filled with black ice.

'Oh, so you *do* remember my name,' Heidi retorted waspishly.

'*Santo cielo!* Word of advice: playing stupid games like this with me is guaranteed to put you even lower in my regard. Grow up!'

Tears welled in her eyes. 'Damn it, Gael. Do you *have* to be so cruel?'

'Only when you pull stunts like this. I suggest you find a quiet place and get yourself together. Goldie—we're leaving.'

Goldie, beyond stunned at how easily and gullibly she'd fallen into such a dangerous situation, could only nod. She couldn't even summon pity or anger for the other woman as Gael led her past the avidly gossiping guests, a protesting Pietro, and back into the lift.

The buzzing in her ears and the thumping of her heart prevented her from speaking as she walked, plastered to Gael's side, to the limo. He helped her in, secured her seat belt as her mind reeled.

'Oh, God, I can't believe I was so… That she just…' She started to shake her head, then stopped abruptly when her vision swam.

'Believe it. Some people tend to regress into childish behaviour when they feel slighted. Heidi has perfected the art.'

She wanted to ask then what he'd seen in the woman to make him date her, but the question was redundant. The blonde was a goddess. And, according to her, just the type of woman Gael favoured.

The car started to move, turned a corner. Goldie slapped a hand to her mouth as her stomach roiled. When he passed her a white paper bag she grasped it gratefully.

When the car had steadied, she risked a glance at his wavering figure. 'I'm sure you think me…naive and gullible.'

She wasn't sure whether he'd shrugged or not, but his voice held a distinct bite. 'For someone who claims not to drink, I'm surprised you didn't recognise the peculiar taste straight away.'

'I wasn't…I didn't…I've never tasted vodka before. Or rum.' She grimaced. 'Does this mean I've lost my chance with you? I mean with the audition?' she ventured, feeling her tongue slurring her speech.

God, how many times had she heard her mother sound like this? And how many times had Goldie's spirits dropped with disappointment and pity?

Hard hazel eyes sliced into her. 'Just as you claimed earlier, I too have to be elsewhere tomorrow. And since I can't have a conversation with you now, in this state, I'll have to see when my schedule opens up again.'

Her fingers curled around the lowered paper bag. 'Just give it to me straight, Gael. Tell me whether I've blown it or not so we can say our goodbyes.'

'What difference will it make?'

She licked her lips, desperation beginning to claw through her. 'If I haven't blown it completely I'd like the opportunity to fix it. I...I need this job. I need *a* job!'

His nostrils flared slightly. 'And how would you propose to go about *fixing* it?'

She shook her head, then groaned. 'I don't know. Maybe you can tell me what I can do...how I can—?'

His pithy curse dried up her words.

Goldie knew then that she was digging herself deeper into the hole she'd unwittingly found herself in. It was too late. She'd messed up a shining opportunity. Through ignorance and gullibility.

She snorted, her insides shredding with disappointment and chagrin. How *could* she have fallen into the same trap she'd condemned her mother for for so many years?

'What's your address?'

'My...address?'

'My driver will deliver you home,' he stated, his voice neither gentle nor harsh.

It was almost as if he'd become indifferent to her.

Goldie fought to dismiss the slight pang that thought brought and focused on a much more troubling problem.

'I can't go home,' she muttered, the words filling her with even more distress.

'Excuse me?' His voice was filled with chilly cynicism.

She grimaced, her hand shaking as she lifted it to her numb cheek. 'I can't go home in this state.'

Gael's gaze sharpened on her face. 'Why not?'

Shame dredged deep inside her. 'I… My mother is a recovering alcoholic. I can't… She can't see me like this.'

He regarded her for several charged seconds before his jaw clenched. *'Dios mio.'*

'I know how this looks, okay?' she pre-empted, before he could voice the condemnation bristling over his frame. 'But I can't do this to her! After everything she's been through, I can't—'

'Calm yourself, Goldie. I was merely going to say I'm not blameless in all this. I should've suspected Heidi would try something like this. I shouldn't have left you on your own for so long.'

She heaved in a breath and fought the clogging in her throat. 'I… Thanks.' She clenched her unhurt hand, ashamed at how low she felt. 'I know you probably think I'm pathetic right now, but I'm responsible for my mother. If she sees me like this it'll destroy her. In many ways I've been the adult for a long time. Every choice I make…she's my number one priority.'

His mouth tightened. 'Even when the choices you make aren't sound?'

She shrugged. 'I'm not perfect. I make mistakes like everyone else. That doesn't mean I should rub her nose in it. She has enough to deal with.'

'I see.'

'Do you?'

'Let's not enter another debate, hmm…?'

Her eyes widened when he shoved his door open. She stared around her, not sure when the car had stopped.

'Where are we?' she asked.

'My hotel. Since you don't want to go home, you can stay here tonight,' he said.

A different emotion, separate from the ones she was already battling, fizzed through her. 'I'm not sure—'

'I'm staying in the presidential suite. Besides the master suite there are two more bedrooms. With locks. You're invited to use either one of them. If you don't feel safe enough with that, tell my driver where you'd like to go and he will deliver you to whatever destination you require,' he stated in implacable tones.

The same instinct that had told her she could trust him enough to get into his limo after the mugging told her she could trust his offer. But suddenly Goldie wasn't sure she could trust *herself*.

She'd let herself down spectacularly once tonight. Did she dare trust that she wouldn't make another mistake on this surreal night?

But what alternative did she have that didn't involve wandering the streets in an intoxicated state, with a bulls-eye on her back for every creep out there?

She swallowed hard and accepted that this was the best possible, safest choice on the table.

'I accept your offer. Thank you.'

Twenty minutes later Goldie was in the most comfortable bed she'd ever slept in, the double doors to the princess suite locked after a solicitous Gael had brought her a glass of water and turned down the bed.

Now, stripped to her underwear, Goldie sighed and drifted off to sleep among the dreamiest of pillows.

CHAPTER FIVE

SHE WASN'T SURE what made her jerk awake. Perhaps it was the muted sounds of the city, when she was used to her quieter neighbourhood just outside Trenton, New Jersey. Whatever it was, once her racing heart slowed she became aware of another raging need. Thirst.

The glass Gael had left her with was empty, although she didn't recall drinking the water. She grimaced at the hazy, alcohol-distorted memories and got out of bed. She hated it that she hadn't made it home, but after what had happened Goldie knew this option was best. Her mother wouldn't have been just disappointed, she would also have blamed herself. Didn't studies show that alcoholism was sometimes hereditary? And Gloria blaming herself would only bring about one result—depression.

For the past few months her mother had been doing well. Goldie couldn't stomach being the cause of any form of regression in her mother's wellbeing.

Rising from the bed, she looked down at her scantily clad body. The thought of putting on that clingy dress again just to go and fetch a glass of water brought another grimace. Going to the adjoining bathroom, she shrugged into a dressing gown bearing a distinctive exclusive designer's monogrammed label, belted it, and left the suite with the empty glass.

Her bare feet moved silently over marbled floors as she walked along the ornately decorated hallway and into the vast living room. Styled in white, gold and royal blue, the presidential suite was the last word in elegance, right down to the hand-scrolled stationery and the monogrammed cushions that graced the brocade sofas and antique claw-footed chairs. Also dotted around the room were gilt and mother-of-pearl framed mirrors, and expensive paintings reflected perfection and elegance at each turn.

On the far side of the living room, set back from a second grouping of blue and gold-striped settees, a black baby grand piano gleamed under the lamps left on to illuminate the space. Next to it was a tiny kitchenette, housing a fridge and a collection of expensive drinks.

It was there that Goldie went to fetch bottled water. And there she remained frozen after, having taken a large gulp, she heard the heated sound of Gael's voice as he paced the private terrace outside.

She didn't want to eavesdrop, and really she didn't understand a word of the bullet-fast Spanish he spoke into the phone, but that didn't matter. She saw his pacing grow hurried as the conversation gained intensity. His fingers spiked through his hair and Goldie's breath caught as he swore beneath his breath.

She eyed the semi-dark living room.

Leaving the small alcove would reveal her presence. But staying where she was, witnessing what appeared to be an argument—although she wasn't absolutely certain— would be a worse violation of his privacy.

Taking a deep breath, she slid her glass onto the counter and stepped out of the alcove. Just in time to hear him snarl before he ended the conversation.

Like a magnet, her gaze swung to him.

He stood frozen between the French doors, the phone tight in his grip, his eyes locked on her.

'I don't speak Spanish, so I didn't understand any of what you were saying,' she blurted.

One corner of his mouth twisted, although tightly packed anger still seethed from his tall, imposing frame. Moving forward into the room, he shut the door behind him and tossed his phone onto the counter without taking his eyes off her.

'You don't need linguistic understanding to know what's going on.'

'I guess not,' Goldie replied, her skin jumping at the sparks still lurking in his eyes. She stared at him until the breath locked in her lungs. Then she dragged her gaze away. 'Um…goodnight.'

'Are you feeling better?' he asked, and his voice contained a bite. She couldn't determine whether it was aimed at her or was residual from his phone call.

She stopped her retreat. Nodded. 'Yes, thanks.'

'Then stay. Join me for a nightcap. Yours will be water, of course.'

For some reason she felt a little bit better that a trace of mockery was back in his voice. Retracing her steps to the counter, she picked up her half-empty glass and waited for him to pour an expensive-looking cognac before she joined him on the sofa.

She noted that he still wore his shirt and trousers from earlier, although a few more buttons had been undone on his shirt, giving her a glimpse of a firm, bronze contoured chest and a strong throat.

Averting her gaze from the arresting sight, she stared around, painstakingly counting the pieces of furniture in the room as a distraction tactic.

Fifteen.

Her eyes swung back to him.

Gael was watching her. He didn't seem inclined to speak, appeared just content to sip his drink, preferring to keep his thoughts internal. Goldie licked her lips, knowing this wasn't the time to pursue the business conversation they'd begun before her inadvertent trip into Liquor Land. When his stare got too much, she glanced around again, her gaze landing on a small ornate clock on top of an antique console table.

Two o'clock in the morning. 'So, do you conduct *all* your business meetings in the early hours of the morning?'

His gaze shifted from her to the contents of his glass. 'That wasn't business. It was family,' he said, confirming her earlier suspicion.

'Family?' she intoned faintly.

'*Si.*' That crack of a smile was at his lips again. 'You're not the only one with maternal challenges.'

'You were arguing with your *mother*?'

His mouth twisted. 'You could say that.'

'Why?'

'Because there's a problem. Isn't that why people argue?' he snapped.

She frowned. 'Well, yes, but…'

'I don't wish to talk about that, Goldie.' His voice was a low, raw command.

Knowing how *she* felt about the subject of her own mother, she nodded. 'Okay. What *do* you wish to talk about?'

'You. Why acting?' he asked, his voice cold and abrupt.

'Because I'm good at it,' she stated without arrogance.

His breath huffed in a short laugh. '*Si,* that you are.'

He raised his glass in a toast that felt wrong. And not in the mocking way she was getting used to.

She stared at him, but couldn't read his expression. 'Gael—'

'How many auditions have you given like the one you performed today?' He cut across her.

'This was my second. The first was for a workshop in the East Village a month ago.'

'And the script? What play is it from?' he pressed.

She hesitated, unsure where he was coming from. Unwilling to have her work mocked. 'It's my own work. I wrote it last year.'

'Tell me about it.'

Goldie shrugged. 'It's a story about…resilience, dependency, trust. About two people who care for each other but can't be together because of perceived insurmountable obstacles.'

He took a sip. Swallowed. His eyes locked on her. 'What obstacles?'

She toyed with the ends of the gown's belt. 'Alcoholism. Infidelity…' she murmured.

'And the piece you performed today? Which of those two things did it deal with?'

'Both. Her alcoholism. His infidelity. He wants to give up. She wants to stay and fight.'

He stiffened, his eyes slowly narrowing. 'It sounds like they're toxic together. Don't you think they're better off apart? As far from each other as they can get?'

'Maybe they are—maybe they're not. But surely it's better to find a way through the conflict than to give up at the first hurdle? Stick it out for a while for the sake of the love that might be buried beneath all that? Surely they owe it to themselves to root through the toxicity and find it? Maybe that's what will heal them?'

She forced her voice past the lump threatening to rise in her throat.

'What if their so-called love is toxic too? And how long is "a while"? How much is enough when everyone around you has to bear the brunt of the toxicity?' he demanded.

His voice had grown ragged, raw with a frustration and anger that she knew instinctively stemmed from that phone call.

'I don't have the answers. But I know I'd never give up something that important that easily,' she said.

He stared at her, his gaze probing deep. Deeper.

'Do it,' he said, in a low, rumbling voice just a shade above a whisper.

Her breath caught. Strangled her. 'Do...what?'

'The piece. Perform it for me.'

Shock sent her rigid for a second. *'Now?'*

'We're both awake. We're here. You asked me in the car what you could do. *This* is what you can do. Show me what I want to see.'

It was clear that Gael was still affected by whatever had happened during that phone call. Talking to his mother had disturbed him badly. Enough to make Goldie consider saying no...consider questioning his objectivity.

Because this no longer felt like business. This had become something else. Something emotional. Something hot and heavy and dangerous. Perhaps even deeply personal.

But, on the flipside, it was just what she needed. She needed her audience to be emotionally invested, not clinically detached. Even if he didn't believe what she was selling, he would feel strongly about it somehow. And wasn't that a good thing?

Reaching out, she offered him the glass in her hand. His gaze went from it to her face and back again before he took it. Set it to one side.

The moment his gaze returned to her face she spoke the first lines.

'You won't leave me. I won't let you.'

'Maybe it's the best thing for me to leave.'

His raw, unexpected response made her heart race faster.

'You think you love her, but you don't.'

'Perhaps I'm not capable of loving anyone. Not even myself.'

The words were spoken with a quiet, strong conviction that made her eyes widen. Made her certain she was glimpsing something Gael Aguilar might not want her to had circumstances been different. Had he not been caught up in whatever emotions held him prisoner right now.

'I don't believe that. Besides, I know you enough to tell you what is in your heart. I love you that much, Simon. Enough to forgive. Enough to take another chance on us. But for us to happen you need to stay. Please...take the chance.'

'Even if staying is perpetuating the cycle? Destroying us and everyone else who comes into our orbit?' he rasped, his eyes fixed firmly on her.

Tears prickled her own eyes.

Slowly she reached out and laid a hand on his. *'We'll find a way, but we'll only find a way if we're together. Don't leave. Please...take the chance on us. I love you. Fight with me. Fight for us.'*

The powerful exposing words, spoken from a place in her own personal pain—the pain of suffering a broken family—rumbled through the room, moved through her as she blinked and raised her gaze to Gael.

The look on his face made her breath catch. It was a mixture of pain, regret and frustration. There was also hunger. A visceral need for connection that lanced her from the short distance between them.

'*Dios mio*, you're good. So very good...' he muttered, his tone gravel-gruff.

Between one second and the next the hand beneath hers moved, turned and captured hers. He drained his glass and tossed it aside. Then he used their meshed hold to drag her close.

Goldie ended up in his lap, the air knocked from her. Before she could take a needed breath Gael's mouth was on hers. Hot and sizzling and cognac-laced.

He brought every emotion bubbling beneath the surface of his skin to the kiss.

Goldie had been kissed before, either through her work or through casual acquaintance dates that had never gone anywhere. No past experience came close to what she was feeling now as Gael's lips devoured hers, slipped past her stunned senses to breach them deeper. Her hands curled into his shirt, fisted, held on tight as his tongue licked her lower lip, her upper lip, then charged inside, his intense savouring of her drawing fire through her veins, drenching her from head to toe in white-hot sensation. Need slammed hard into her, making her moan and strain closer to his tensile strength, to the heat of sleek muscles moving beneath the cotton shirt.

She slid her hands higher, closer to the exposed skin of his chest, his throat. At her first touch they both groaned. Gael dragged her closer still, his hand moving to her hips and positioning her more firmly in his lap until the bottom of her robe fell open, her legs moved to either side of him. When she was situated to his liking he speared one hand through her hair, using his hold to angle her head, fusing their mouths closer together.

The kiss was like nothing and everything she'd ever dreamed of. Goldie felt as if she was flying and drowning at the same time. Her lungs screamed with the need for oxygen. She wanted to deny their request, to just keep experiencing the incredible sensation of kissing Gael Aguilar.

Only the pressure of his hand in her hair finally broke her free. But it was only so he could set her back a scant few inches, stare up at her with a face masked in raw, edgy lust.

'I want you, Goldie. I want to have you. Right here, right now,' he rasped, low and deep, his eyes dark with ravaging hunger and fierce intent.

Beneath her, his hips flexed, his powerful erection nestling deeper between her thighs, ramming home to her the strength of his desire.

Need pounded with relentless force through her. A need she knew she should fight. But for the life of her she couldn't summon the willpower. All the same, she tried.

'Gael—'

He closed the gap between them, forcing her answer back down her throat as he kissed her again, showed her with his mouth how feeble any protest she wanted to attempt would be. Groaning, she slid her hands up his strong neck, noting the raging pulse beneath her touch, glorying in it for a second before her fingers spiked into his hair.

His guttural groan was one of encouragement. Of ferocious need. They stayed like that for endless minutes, her on top of him, kissing him as if her life depended on it.

All too soon, he forced her head back again.

'Don't deny me, Goldie. Don't deny us both,' he rasped.

His accent was more pronounced, his voice curling around the words, burning them into her skin the way his eyes burned for her.

At twenty-four, Goldie knew she was an anomaly in the virgin stakes, and would probably draw mockery from Gael if he knew the depth of her innocence. But it was an innocence she was proud of—an innocence she'd fought to retain simply because she knew what throwing it away on the wrong person would make her feel further down the line. She'd watched her mother throw her body and her emotions away on the wrong men for far longer than she wanted to dwell on.

She'd already made a mistake that might have had disastrous consequences tonight. Was she risking making another?

She sucked in a deep breath—which emerged in a rush when Gael leaned up and slowly licked her lower lip. Her whole body shook with the headiness of that bold claiming. The fingers she had locked in his hair tightened, encouraged him as he kissed the corner of her mouth, her cheek, her jaw, her earlobe.

'Let me have you, Goldie *mia. Por favor*,' he whispered

in her ear. 'Let's turn this unfortunate night into a better one. A memorable one. I can make it so good for you.'

She groaned beneath the weight of his torrid, tempting words even as she fought to rationalise what was happening. Could she do it? Could she give herself to him for just one memorable night?

The answer burned hot and urgent beneath her skin. But Goldie ignored it for a moment, pulled her dwindling faculties together for long enough to separate what was happening here from the history she knew and had fought hard to prevent repeating.

Where her mother had fallen down had been when she'd imagined herself in love with the men who had ultimately used and betrayed her. Nothing so fanciful was happening here tonight. Gael wanted her body. She wanted his. Their needs were mutual. The only emotion present here was the hunger that demanded to be answered.

'Say yes, *mi dulce*.' He kissed her cheek one more time, then drew back to spear her with flaming eyes. 'Say *yes*.'

The word, eating her alive, burst free. 'Yes.'

His harsh exhalation preceded his forceful rise from the sofa. The moment he was upright he urged her legs around his waist. Then, with one hand banded around her, the other fisted in her hair, he made his way unerringly down the hall and into the master suite.

The room, like the rest of the penthouse, was luxury personified. Tasteful and expensive antique furniture mixed with contemporary designs to produce a breathtaking setting fit for a king.

Or for an impossibly sexy, arrogant, ravenous Spaniard, whose sole attention was fixed on her with a feverish intensity that made every single one of her senses jump in mingled excitement and trepidation.

Burnished eyes trapped her in place as he set her down and started to undo the remaining buttons of his shirt. With each further expanse of golden skin revealed her mouth and fingers tingled with the need to touch, to taste.

'Take off your robe, Goldie,' he commanded gruffly as he shrugged off his shirt and tossed it aside.

Her fingers twitched, but for the life of her she couldn't move. Because he was perfect. Not a spare ounce of flesh resided on the upper half of his body. She'd been so right to compare him to that Roman statue. His musculature was streamlined, a true work of art that filled her with awe. And with a great, demanding need.

Between her thighs her flesh pulsed with an unfamiliar urgency. An urgency so great she wondered how she was still standing.

'Goldie.' His voice was a furnace-hot warning. 'Are you deliberately keeping me waiting?'

Her head moved in a slow shake and her hand reached for the belt. 'No. I just…wanted to look at you.'

His breath was expelled harshly, almost as if she'd surprised him. Colour slashed high on his cheekbones and he closed the gap between them, speared his fingers into her hair. He angled her face up but didn't kiss her, merely traced that hot gaze over her face.

'You can look at me all you want later. Right now I want you naked and beneath me. So the robe, *bellezza* Goldie. *Take it off.*'

With quick, jerky movements she pulled the belt loose and shrugged the robe off her shoulders, leaving only her cotton panties on.

His gaze stayed on hers for a long, absorbing moment before he slowly stepped back. His exhalation was half a groan, half an expression of wonder. The fingers of one hand traced her pulse, her collarbone, then moved down to the delicate space between her breasts. Then he moved behind her, fingers still on her skin, tracing over her shoulders to the top of her spine.

A shudder rushed over her—the beginning of many that rolled in a never-ending reaction to Gael's touch on her body. His fingers drifted down her spine, then back up again, eliciting a deep moan she was helpless to stop. In the next instant his nails were dragged lightly down her body and he groaned at her deep shudder. She swayed beneath the onslaught of fierce desire. It triggered a frenzied response and suddenly he was back in front of her, his fiery gaze moving down her body, savouring her anew.

'*Santo cielo*, you're exquisite,' he murmured huskily.

Catching her around the waist, his movements a touch uncoordinated, he tossed her onto the bed and tugged at his belt.

Goldie brushed her hair out of her eyes, the better to see him, and then almost wished she'd averted her gaze when his body was revealed in all its manly, almost intimidating glory. She swallowed hard when she took in the fullness of his manhood.

Heavens.

A trace of that arrogant smile touched his lips as he moved towards her. 'Your beautiful eyes stare a little too hard, *guapa*. Do you wish to unman me before we even begin?'

She blushed, hot and fierce, drawing a low laugh from him. She dragged her gaze up with monumental effort. 'You're laughing, which tells me you don't think my unmanning you is a possibility.'

His laughter drifted away, replaced by deep, stark hunger. He stalked to the bed, prowled to loom over her. One finger traced over her nose to her mouth, testing the suppleness of her lower lip before he demanded entry. When she took his digit into her mouth, he groaned.

'With a woman as intoxicating as you, everything is possible.'

His kiss this time was ten times more carnal, devastatingly brutal in its hunger. Luckily Goldie was equally ravenous for this new, dizzying sensation that threatened to drown her. But she hung on, clung to Gael's broad shoulders as he took her on a frighteningly exciting journey.

Even after he broke away and started to trail his mouth down her body she was still lost in that intoxicating kiss. It was only when he reached her breasts, tweaked and sucked on the stiff, needy peaks, then dropped lower to kiss the sensitive skin below her navel, teasing her panty line with his teeth and lips, that she fell into a different but equally exhilarating dimension of pleasure.

Her panties were tugged off in quick, expert movements. Then he was parting her legs, kissing his way up her inner thighs.

Goldie didn't even attempt to halt what was coming. She wanted it all. Was greedy enough to raise herself onto her elbows, stare in wonder as he drew inexorably closer to the bundle of need between her thighs.

His gaze locked on hers in that final second before he tasted her, his nostrils flaring one last time as he drew in her essence. He muttered something hard and pithy under his breath. Then he swiped his tongue boldly across her flesh.

Her hips jerked as sensation pounded her in a merciless wave. She collapsed back against the pillows, her breath emerging in shameless pants as pleasure surged through her. When Gael found the bundle of nerves that screamed for attention she cried out, her eyes squeezing shut to savour the sensations she knew instinctively would blow her away. The pressure between her thighs increased, and his tongue flicked urgently against her flesh as he groaned through his own pleasure.

Between one breath and the next she was flung into nirvana, her mind and body no longer her own as pure bliss buffeted her. Her moan fused into one long, earthy sound, and her convulsions were endlessly thrilling.

The moment her pulse began to slow she felt him move, heard him reach across her body. She opened her eyes to see him tearing open a condom, rolling it over his impressive girth.

Goldie debated then whether to tell him that she was a virgin, that he was about to be her first. But she knew then that two things might happen.

Firstly, he might not believe her. She hadn't forgotten the occasional glimpses of censure he'd sent her way a few times since they'd met. Men like Gael had cynicism bred into their DNA. She couldn't explain any other reason for those looks.

Secondly, he might believe her and think she had an agenda in all this—a motive for giving herself to him. It couldn't be further from the truth. Theirs was to be a coupling bred solely of attraction and need. Nothing more.

So she bit her lip and forced herself to meet his gaze. Whatever he saw in her face satisfied him enough to make him lower his body to hers, to free her lip from her teeth and take her mouth in a possessive, incandescent kiss.

After an age, he lifted his head.

'Touch me, Goldie. Hold on to me when I take you. I want you to know who it is that possesses you tonight.'

The raw demand robbed her of her already short breath. 'Gael—'

'*Sí*, say my name like that. Just like that…' he commanded gruffly as he positioned himself between her legs. One hand gripped her thigh, and the other fisted in her hair. The easy strength with which he held himself poised above her was testament to his powerfully honed physique, which was a beautiful sight to behold.

His fierce arousal spoke of a different power altogether—one that made her heart palpitate with trepidation even as her senses flared in anticipation.

Remembering his instruction to hold on to him, she slid her arms around his waist, caressing the corded muscles in his lower back.

Hazel eyes darkened as they met hers. His head dropped and his mouth fused with hers as he penetrated her with one sure, focused thrust.

Her muted scream rose and died between their kiss. But not the pain. God, not the pain. That held her rigid for a few endless seconds.

Above her, Gael's eyes flared, probed. He raised his head and stared at her. 'Goldie…?'

She wasn't sure whether it was a question or an observation. She registered her lost innocence and held on to him, unable to form words as the pain lingered, then faded to leave behind new, breath-catching sensations.

'Gael…' she murmured.

He shook his head, perhaps answering his own question. Perhaps caught in the burgeoning rapture of their union. He moved. He groaned. His head went back as he withdrew and thrust again.

'*Dios mio*, you feel sensational,' he muttered roughly.

'Gael…'

He withdrew and thrust again, his mouth dropping to hers for a searing, groan-laced kiss. 'Yes, Goldie. My name on your lips. Don't stop. I want to hear it.'

And she wanted to say it, she realised. So she did.

He set the pace—slow at first, then faster, building a conflagration within and between them that soon raged out of control. With it came a feverish need to touch, to kiss, to taste, to bite. Her nails raked and dug in as he took her higher. His fingers fisted in her hair, and he devoured her mouth as pleasure overtook them.

When the bough broke her cries mingled with his unfettered roar. Guttural words in Spanish poured from his lips as his climax pulled him under. Then Gael half collapsed on top of her, catching himself at the last moment to roll them over.

Hearts racing, they gulped air into their starving lungs, their hands unable to stop moving over each other's sweat-coated flesh.

But eventually their heartbeats calmed. Hands stilled. Breath was restored.

Gael pulled himself free, unable to find adequate words to sum up what had happened in the last hour. He left the bed and entered the bathroom without looking at the woman whose body he'd just shamelessly gorged himself on. He wasn't usually so lacking in after-sex small talk, but for the life of him he couldn't seem to locate his tongue.

Entering the bathroom, he shut the door behind him, then leaned weakly against it. His body still thrummed with what he could only describe as the most sensational sex he'd ever had in his life. But already tendrils of regret burrowed beneath his skin.

This shouldn't have happened. Not like this. Not when the phone call with his mother and her blatant confirmation that she was once again embroiled in an affair with Tomas Aguilar had set him on the finest, most dangerous edge.

Because the mere mention of his father's name had triggered more memories. Memories that had left him deeply puzzled as to why his mother—who should know better—was once again taking this degrading path.

For Tomas Aguilar, Katerina Vega had been a salacious means to a calculated end the first time round. Tomas had admitted as much when Gael had confronted him on his twenty-first birthday. Just as he'd admitted what Gael had always been too afraid to learn—that he'd been an unfortunate consequence of that game of emotional roulette.

Personally, his illegitimacy had long ceased to distress

him—simply because he didn't give it much cerebral capacity. It was a buried burr, cemented over with time and distance, and he'd learned to live with it. The taunts from his childhood were in the past, as was the village where he and his mother had been relentlessly stigmatised as outsiders and homewreckers. Even his inability to sustain a relationship past a month or two had worked out for him in the long run by diverting his focus to empire-building.

And yet all these years later he'd yet to succeed in getting that last damning statement out of his head.

'Tú estás un error...'

'You are a mistake.'

Gael knew it was partly that voiced statement that made him feel relief each time he left Alejandro's presence. His half-brother was a lot of things, but Gael knew he was not a mistake to the parents who'd created him. And while Alejandro had preceded Gael in leaving Spain, for reasons similar to his own, witnessing him taking steps to confront his past...and succeeding...left Gael still feeling an annihilating bitterness every time he thought of Tomas Aguilar.

So he'd chosen not to think of his father at all.

But now, with his mother's actions—which he was growing more convinced were of her own volition this time—he couldn't think of anything *but*!

He'd let his emotions get the better of him tonight. Perhaps even taken advantage of Goldie because of it.

Cursing, he moved from the door to the sink. About to remove the condom, he looked down. Froze. And cursed some more.

No. It couldn't be. She was in her twenties. She couldn't be a virgin. And yet the evidence of blood, the confirmation of his suspicion when he'd taken her, was glaring and unmistakable.

Dios mio.

Shock morphed into a different sensation. Had this been a trap? A way to secure a surer payday?

Disposing of the condom, he washed himself and stalked back into the bedroom, ready to confront her.

Except Goldie was curled on her side, fast asleep.

For ten minutes he paced the room, unaccustomed indecision plaguing him. Then, once he knew there was only one way to play this, he turned and headed for his dressing room.

CHAPTER SIX

THE WORST POSSIBLE CHOICE in a sea of bad choices.

She'd gone to sleep dreading those words were true but they were the first to slam across her mind the moment Goldie woke up. Because even before she opened her eyes she knew things wouldn't look better in the bright light of day.

Not after Gael had hurried away after making love to her as if hell's demons snapped at his heels.

Not after being left alone with nothing but her thoughts to occupy her.

The beginnings of doubt and disappointment at what she'd done crowded her every thought process.

The bottom line was that she'd found a neat argument to give herself permission to sleep with Gael. But in the cold light of day those arguments rang disturbingly hollow. She'd indulged herself simply because she'd been too weak to resist the temptation of the most compelling man she'd ever met.

Sure, she could forgive herself for it—eventually—but in succumbing to momentary madness had she given up more than her virginity? Had she also burned bridges in the career she'd fought tooth and nail to succeed in forging for herself? She didn't need the internet to confirm to her that Gael Aguilar had power and clout. Nor was she naive enough to think she could escape unscathed from her one mistake should he be indiscreet enough to whisper about what had happened between them.

She only had one choice. She had to talk to him—make it clear that they were to treat what had happened between them last night as the transient indulgence it was and nothing else. She wasn't above begging for his discretion if it came to that. She had too much to lose.

Turning over, she opened her eyes.

To see an empty space next to her.

She wasn't surprised to find him gone. After all he'd left her wide awake, seconds after they'd made love, and locked himself into the bathroom. Had she not been completely shattered, she would have dragged herself off to the other bedroom to avoid what must have been an even more humiliating sight for Gael when he'd emerged from the bathroom.

Had he even slept in the same bed with her? Or had he availed himself of one of the unoccupied bedrooms so he wouldn't have to look at her or deal with her? Had she been so disappointing that she hadn't merited six minutes, never mind his customary six weeks? Not that she'd intended to have that long a time with him!

Her face heated as humiliation mounted. She didn't want to acknowledge the dull pain in her chest, but Goldie was a believer in facing problems head-on. Yes, she'd given her virginity to a man who hadn't even acknowledged it. A part of her was glad of that. But another small part mourned her lost innocence because, while the experience had been phenomenal, she couldn't think about it without thinking about what had come after. Without thinking about why her chest felt tight with unsettling emotions she was too anxious to examine.

Dragging herself upright, she looked around her. The dressing gown was draped over a chair, her underwear laid on top of it. More heat surged into her face at the thought of Gael touching her things. Pushing the disturbing thought away, she rose, then gasped as her body's discomfort registered. The enormity of what she'd done grew as she gathered the clothes and made her way back to her room.

If she'd still kept the diary she'd used to as a teenager,

the events of the last twenty-four hours would have been emblazoned in red ink across her trusted leather-bound notebook. But, alas, they were to be confined in a secret vault in her mind, only to be examined on the rarest of occasions at some remote point in the future, when humiliation didn't burn this bright or this painfully.

She was debating in her mind exactly when that occasion would be when she entered the other bedroom suite.

The note propped up against her pillow was hard to miss, with the hotel's distinctive burgundy and cream stationery standing out against the white sheets, and the bold black scrawl across the paper.

Trepidation eating at her, she walked across the room and plucked up the folded paper.

Goldie,
I've decided to go a different way with the discussed
role. The driver will be waiting when you're ready
to take you wherever you need to go. Take as much
time as you need.
The contents of the envelope are a token of my
gratitude for your time.
G

Even before her numb fingers had located and opened the envelope, which had been propped up behind the note, sheets of icy rage were bucketing down on her.

Yesterday Goldie had thought that casting director asking her to go to his hotel suite for sex if she wanted the role she'd auditioned for was bad enough. Now she knew the depths of true humiliation.

She wasn't even sure why she took out the sheaf of dollar bills and counted them. Perhaps she wanted to know just how much her degradation was worth to Gael Aguilar. It certainly wasn't because she intended to use a single cent of it.

Ten thousand dollars.

Hot, humiliating tears filled her eyes. When they dripped down her cheeks she angrily swiped them away. Was this how her mother had felt each time she was used and discarded?

Goldie wasn't proud that she'd inadvertently walked in her mother's shoes. But she hadn't done it through choice. She didn't deserve this!

Her anger wiping away the last of her humiliation, she dressed in last night's clothes, uncaring of how she'd look walking across the famous hotel's lobby. Her rage would insulate her just fine.

She stopped in the bathroom long enough to wash her face and tidy her hair before she exited the suite, the note and the envelope full of cash clutched tight in her fist.

A butler of indeterminate age emerged as she entered the lavish living room. 'Good morning, miss. Would you like some breakfast?' he asked in cultured tones.

Putting on her best acting skills, she smiled and shook her head. 'No, thank you. Is it possible to summon the driver?'

'Of course, miss. Would you like me to tell him the destination or would you prefer to relay it yourself?'

'I'll take care of it. Thank you.'

The butler nodded and crossed over to a nearby phone. After a short conversation he returned. 'He's pulling up now, miss. If you'd allow me to escort you…?'

He led her out to the private marble-floored foyer and into the lift that solely served the presidential suite. Stepping in with her, he swiped a gold access card and pressed the button for the ground floor. Goldie was thankful for his discretion as they exited onto a side street that led to Fifth Avenue, but she couldn't stop herself from wondering how many times this butler-driver scene had been staged to facilitate Gael's predilection for one-night stands.

The very thought filled her with even more distaste and anger, darkening her mood as she emerged into the sunlight.

The limo was parked only steps from the revolving doors, its driver standing attentively at the back door. He tipped his hat when he saw her, his face politely neutral.

Goldie hated herself for the lie she was about to tell, but she would never be able to live with herself if she let this go unchallenged. She couldn't bear the thought that Gael Aguilar would reside in his lofty kingdom, content that he'd bought and paid for her and was therefore free of wrongdoing. So she waited until the butler had retreated before she faced the driver and waved the scribbled note.

'Gael left me a message that you were to take me wherever I wanted to go?'

'Yes, miss,' the driver responded.

'Well, I'd like to go home, but now the silly man wants me to have breakfast with him before I do. And after my unfortunate mugging last night I don't have a phone to call and tell him I can't. Can you take me to where he is, please?' she pleaded.

The driver started to frown.

Goldie hurriedly continued. 'It'd serve him right for me to just let you take me home, but I don't want to get into another fight with Gael. Not for another twenty-four hours, at least! So help a girl out—please?' She put on her best smile.

After the briefest hesitation, he nodded. 'Of course, miss. He's not too far away.'

'Thank you.' Goldie expelled a secret sigh of relief as he opened the back door and helped her in. The moment the door shut she unclenched her fists and closed her eyes as a deep shudder of unexpended adrenaline rushed through her.

The limo started to move and she was thrown back to last night. She should have walked away, found the nearest police station and taken her chances with the men in blue rather than the man in a black suit.

Pursing her lips, she squashed down might-have-beens and caught the driver's eye in the rearview mirror. 'Is he... is he in a meeting?'

Now she was doing this, the thought of an audience made her cringe—but not enough to alter her decision.

'Yes, miss. The production meeting should be done in half an hour.'

She fought back slight trepidation, nodded and murmured her thanks. Trying to calm her nerves was no use. Her heart was thrumming loud enough to block out the busy sounds of New York traffic as they traversed Midtown.

When the driver pulled up in front of a sheer glass office tower Goldie almost lost her nerve. The bundle of cash clutched in her fist—the representation of the grossest insult she'd ever suffered—spurred her on.

She exited the car and nodded her thanks.

The driver said, 'He's on the tenth floor, I believe. I've called the receptionist. She'll let you in. And, miss...?'

Goldie paused. 'Yes?'

'He probably deserves what's coming to him, but go easy on him.'

Her eyes widened. The tall, heavyset man, who might easily double as a bodyguard, doffed his cap with a discreet smile before getting back into the car. Bemused, she walked into the building, wondering why the driver was giving her access to confront his boss if he'd seen through her ruse.

Maybe he felt Gael deserved it? On account of having done it before?

Her bewilderment increased as the lift rushed to the tenth floor. But by the time she exited and was shown to the conference room her anger was firmly in place. She shoved open the double doors and entered.

Gael sat at the head of a large table, flanked by executives on either side. She didn't bother to stop and count how many people were in the room, but she knew all eyes had turned to train on her.

He saw her, froze mid-speech, his eyes widening, wary and watchful. On a screen to the side of him a vaguely familiar man also stopped talking and glanced her way.

'Goldie—'

'This is how you operate, is it?' She waved the envelope at him from the opposite end of the oval table. Her voice shook with anger, but she didn't care. 'What's the twenty-first-century version of *wham-bam, thank you, ma'am*? And, seriously, after *that* mind-blowing night I would've thought I'd warrant at least fifty thousand! Are you sure you don't want to revise the sum? After all, sleeping with a big, bad boss like you would gain me upwards of few *hundred* thousand if I should take it to the press, hmm?' she sliced at him.

He surged to his feet, planting his hands on top of the table as his cold eyes glared dire warning at her. 'Goldie, this isn't the time—'

'Or the place? I beg to differ. I think this is *exactly* the time to show you what I can do. Isn't that what you asked for last night? For me to show you what I can do? And weren't your exact words something along the lines of, "*You're good. So very good*"? So what changed your mind between last night and this morning? I think I deserve to know that at the very least, don't you?'

His jaw clenched for one heart-stopping second. 'If you know what's good for you—'

She laughed—a bitter, spiky sound that didn't feel one little bit natural. 'What's *good* for me? I think we both know I made one gross misjudgement after another when I chose to trust a single word you said. I may be an actress, Gael, but you were very good at pretending too. Maybe you should try your hand at acting. But I need two small favours from you, if you'd be so kind?'

His jaw clenched. *'Sí?'* he said through gritted teeth.

'First of all, the next time you come across me being mugged, do me a favour and keep walking. I'm absolutely sure I don't need your brand of chivalry. And secondly...'

Darkened hazel eyes glared at her across the gleaming table. 'Yes?'

She ripped open the envelope, pinched the dollar bills between her fingers and flung the whole lot across the table. 'Take your sleazy money and shove it where the sun doesn't shine!'

Beneath the flying bills, stunned silence gripped the whole room. Gael's eyes blazed with incandescent rage.

Knowing she'd struck her mark, Goldie dramatically brushed her hands clean, then began to walk backwards, her eyes still connected with his, a triumphant smile curving her mouth. She'd clawed back some of her dignity. She might have cratered her career in the process, but that was a problem to be tackled another day. Her immediate problem for now was to find a way to get home. It looked as if she'd have to plough deeper into her meagre savings for a taxi ride after all—

The sound of applause froze her thoughts and her feet. Her mouth dropped open as more hands joined in with the clapping. On the screen, the man she now recognised as a famous director pumped his fist, his face split into a wide grin as he pointed an accusing finger at Gael.

'Gael, you sly, brilliant man! You spend twenty minutes laying into me for the delay to the production when all along you had *this* up your sleeve?' The man barked out another laugh, before turning his gaze to Goldie. 'You—Goldie Whoever-you-are—just made my day! I can already see the headlines…not that I court them of course. The media will lap you right up. Nothing captures the movie-going public's imagination more than a newbie blowing their socks off. I don't think it's too premature to say welcome to the team—'

'Ethan, shut up for a moment,' Gael bit out, his gaze still locked on her.

He hadn't so much as moved a muscle since she'd flung his money in his face. And with each moment that passed she feared the look in his eyes would erupt into actual flames.

She'd made her point. She needed to get out of here. *Fast.* Despite the crazy talk spewing from the mouth of the award-winning director. Another step back brought her to the double doors.

'Come on. You trusted me with this project, Gael. Gave me carte blanche to find the best actress for the lead character. I know my broken leg hasn't helped matters, but—' he tipped his head towards Goldie, another smile splitting his face '—with this gem you've discovered we can start production almost immediately.'

Goldie frowned. 'I… What…? I don't know what you're talking—'

'Gentlemen, ladies—excuse me for a few minutes, *por favor*?' Gael interrupted once more.

He was rounding the table in quick, purposeful strides, his eyes cutting into her, silencing any further speech she could muster. Galvanised by the look in his eyes, she turned sharply, slammed her hands against the door in her rush to escape. When it opened she rushed through with fast, skin-saving strides towards the lift.

She'd poked the dragon in his den. Woken it. No need to stick around and watch the resulting inferno.

She reached the lift doors just as hands closed over her arms. Turned her firmly around.

Burnished eyes blazed down at her. 'You think you can create a spectacle like that and get away scot-free?' he seethed.

'It was nothing short of what you deserved,' she launched back, her hands going to the hands holding her prisoner in a bid to prise them off her. 'Let me go.'

He dragged her close and fired under his breath, 'Not until you're made to understand the consequences of what you did back there.'

'Whatever they are, they were worth it,' she returned defiantly.

A dark cloud descended on his face. 'Are you sure?'

'Yes, I'm one hundred per cent sure! Let me go, Gael.'

Behind her the lift door pinged open.

'Take a minute, Goldie. Think about what you're doing. Any hint that what you have just done *wasn't* an audacious audition could spell the end of your career. Are you prepared to take the risk?'

'To make my point that I'm not a whore you leave money on the bed for when you're done? *Absolutely*.'

His nostrils flared and a look passed through his eyes. Regret, maybe? Or surprise? She gritted her teeth.

'I don't think of you like that.'

'Oh, good—I'm so glad we've got that established. What about your note? You've "*decided to go a different route*"? The only difference between you actively pursuing me last night and leaving me that poor excuse of a *Dear Jane* note this morning is the fact that we slept together. So pardon me if my powers of deduction are right on point!'

His jaw visibly tightened. 'Calm down, Goldie.'

'No—and stop saying my name like that.'

'Like what?'

'Like I'm a recalcitrant child you're trying to manage. I'm done talking to you. I want nothing to do with you. Let me go and I'll try to forget we ever met.'

'*Santo cielo.* You should stop pursuing a career in acting and form an international debate team. You'd absolutely excel at it.'

Without waiting for an answer to his damning of her character, he dropped his hand from her arm to her wrist and dragged her towards another set of doors.

Shoving them open, he led her into an empty conference room, making sure to block her exit.

She didn't want to look at him—didn't want to be close enough to him to breathe in his unique scent, to watch the beauty of his square-jawed face and be reminded of how she'd explored his body last night, how he'd moved so powerfully inside her. So she stalked as far away from him as possible and stared out of the window at the Midtown traffic.

'Ignoring me isn't going to make this conversation conclude any faster,' he delivered.

She placed her hands on the window ledge to steady herself. She wanted to drop her forehead to the window too, but that would be one weak gesture too far. 'I told you, I have nothing further to say to you. Nor do I imagine you have anything to say to me. Your little note and the deplorable cash buy-off said it all for you. But I'm prepared to grant you two minutes. Say what you dragged me in here to say, then I'm leaving. And don't even *think* about trying to stop me.'

She sensed him prowling behind her for a full minute before he spoke. 'The money wasn't supposed to be taken the way you took it.'

What her laughter lacked in humour it more than made up for in scorn. 'Right. And I was born yesterday.'

'*Dios...*'

She heard his deep inhalation.

'I'm good at reading people, Goldie. Reading between the lines. Deny it all you want, but you're in a fix. Otherwise you wouldn't have fought for dear life to hang on to that tattered bag last night. And you wouldn't have chosen not to call a cab to take you home if you'd been able to afford it. Unemployment means different things to different people. I suspect in your case it means near destitution.'

Shame dredged her, sending prickles of tears to her eyes. She blinked it away rapidly. 'Bravo for that incisive dissection of my life.'

He sighed. 'Hate me all you want for pointing out the obvious. But you also mentioned that you needed a job quickly. The money was my gesture of assistance—'

Pride and anger made her whirl around. He was standing a few feet behind her. Tall and imposing and altogether too much for her roiling senses. 'I'm not a charity case!'

'No, you're not. And I didn't think you were.'

He paced a few steps before shoving his hands in his pockets. She was beginning to notice it was his self-calming gesture.

She supposed he needed calming after her calling him out and making a spectacle of him at his meeting.

'Are we done?'

He shook his head in a decisive movement. 'No, we're not done. You'll accept my apologies if I didn't make it clear that the money had nothing to do with what happened between us last night. It was a gesture of generosity, not payment for services rendered.'

A large dose of the hurt that lingered in her chest abated, but she wasn't about to show her relief. 'Fine, apology accepted, but you can keep your money.'

She started to walk past him. One hand shot out of his pocket and slid over her hip. Goldie jerked out of the way, in no way wanting to be reminded of what it felt like to be in his arms.

'Please don't touch me.'

His jaw tightened but his hand balled and dropped back to his side. 'As you wish. But before you walk out the door and demolish the chance you've created for yourself, stop and think for a moment.'

'What do you mean, the chance I've created?'

One sardonic eyebrow went up. 'Are you really so blind that you can't see the bigger picture?' He stabbed a thumb in the direction of the adjacent conference room. 'In your burning need to make a point you've turned an unfortunate event into an opportunity. Are you going to cut off your nose to spite your face by walking away now?' He was almost taunting her.

She folded her arms. 'Whatever was going on in there is none of my business. If they've mistaken me for the actress you wanted to cast then you can explain their error to them. I'm leaving.'

He laughed. 'After going to all this effort to create a buzz for yourself?'

'Careful, there, or that apology you uttered a few minutes ago will seem like something out of a past lifetime and I'll resume detesting you.'

He shrugged. 'I state things as I see them. You came here to make a point. You've made it. Don't let the effort you've put in go to waste.'

'Are you seriously trying to tell me to capitalise on you treating me like a prostitute?'

A look crossed his face. 'Don't make this emotional, Goldie.'

'Wow. I'm sorry if I'm not as cut-throat as you.' She shook her head. 'Why are you even pursuing this? Your note was quite clear. You woke up this morning and decided you didn't want me after all.' She thought it best to ignore the telling gleam that reflected briefly in his eyes. 'So what's changed?'

The jaw already clenched tight hardened. Silence ticked by until she was sure he wouldn't answer.

Leave, her hammering heart urged. *Before things get any weirder.*

'Are you going to answer me, Gael?' she blurted.

Eyes raked her from head to toe before meeting hers full-on. 'You were a virgin. And you didn't think to tell me.'

Goldie swallowed. Fought the heat and trembling that had begun in her lower limbs. Suddenly she wished she'd stayed by the window, not been standing on her own two legs for this unexpected turn in the conversation. Thankfully, her legs held her up. And her chin rose when she commanded.

'I don't remember any instance during the night when we were obliged to exchange sexual histories. Perhaps you thought we'd be there all night while you recounted yours?'

The barb struck home, made his nostrils flare in pure Latin temper before he reined it in. 'Are you saying being divested of your innocence meant nothing to you?'

The harsh, condemning tone was back. But she wasn't about to stand for it any longer.

'What I choose to do with my virginity is my business. Tell me the experience was ruined for you because of it and I'll apologise.'

His eyes gleamed with pure carnal memory before he blinked, but that look singed her very skin.

'It wasn't ruined. Far from it,' he returned gutturally.

That blush she was fighting won the round. Heat surged into her face and she averted her gaze for a second. 'So what was the problem?'

'The problem is *why me*? Why now? Innocence at your age is rare. I can't help but draw certain conclusions.'

She stared at him, her brain firing wildly at her. It took a heartbeat or three for her to realise where he was coming from. Horror made her hand fly to her mouth. 'You think I hung on to my virgin status just in case a guy like you came along so I could hawk it for a huge payday?' Shock made her voice squeak.

He had the grace to look momentarily confused before his inscrutable expression returned. 'That scenario isn't a foreign concept and I'm sure you're aware of that.'

'I'm aware of no such thing! I'm not sure what circles you move in… Wait—scratch that. After my run-in with your conscience-free ex I can hazard a guess as to the depths your ilk are prepared to sink to for your sick pleasures. But think about this for a second. *If* I were that avaricious, don't you think I'd have negotiated my price *before* I slept with you?' she demanded.

He levelled a hard gaze at her, in no way swayed by her argument. 'That sort of innocence isn't always easy to prove before the event.'

Her mouth dropped open for several heartbeats before she managed to shake her head. 'My God, why…? How did you get like this?' she whispered, sheets of ice dredging her stomach at his blatant accusation.

His face closed completely and his every feature was devoid of emotion. 'I'm a bastard, *literally*—and, I'm told, figuratively. I've learned to accept that nothing that feels that good comes without a price.'

Goldie held her breath, unwilling to admit in any way that the newest emotion which had risen to join the riot of feelings inside her was sympathy for him. He was the bad guy here. He was the one causing her pain.

'Please take it from me that what I gave last night had no strings attached whatsoever. And then please let me go.'

Again a touch of confusion clouded his forehead. 'I don't think you understand why I brought you in here. Regardless of what I thought last night—and I'm prepared to concede that I may have got the wrong end of the stick with you—your performance in there has guaranteed you the part.'

There was zero pleasure in hearing that. She shook her head again. 'Why?'

'Because, believe it or not, that scene you just enacted is uncannily similar to one from the script. You weren't acting, but they thought you were. And you've won them over—especially my director.'

'Right. And you?'

He cast her an inscrutable look before he shrugged. 'What I think is no longer relevant. The only question now is, do you want the part or not?'

CHAPTER SEVEN

GOLDIE EYED HERSELF in the mirror as the make-up artist applied the final touches to her make-up. Her character, Elena Milton, was the same age as her, so there wasn't much to be done in the way of make-up for the early scenes—especially since the scene they were about to shoot was one that required her to be makeup-less.

The director, Ethan Ryland, was waiting for the sun to begin setting on the plains of the KwaZulu-Natal game park, where the next scene of *Soul's Triumph* was being shot.

In her hand she clutched the script, which she always kept close by even though she knew her part by heart and could recite every other part in the script too.

When the make-up artist pronounced her ready, Goldie jumped off the stool and headed outside. While most of the cast and crew chose to stay in the cool confines of their air-conditioned trailers and chalet when they weren't shooting, she preferred to absorb the stunning beauty of South Africa's south-eastern province every chance she got.

Probably because she still couldn't believe she was there.

The experience so far had been surreal, and Goldie couldn't believe they were already halfway to being done with the movie. She had certainly learned a lot in the last five weeks. And to think she'd never imagined she would be here at all...

After Gael had thrown his gauntlet at her feet that morning, just over a month ago, she'd spent a torn, frantic twenty-four hours weighing the pros and cons of accepting the less than wholesome opportunity he had dangled once again within reach.

At her mother's urging to do as much research as possible, she'd succumbed and looked up the man she'd given her virginity to on the internet. She'd come away stunned, albeit with a half-hearted understanding of why Gael Aguilar reacted with suspicion to everyone around him. The trait wasn't admirable by any stretch, and nor was it forgivable when it pertained to her. But it was clear that the sheer prestige and power he wielded along with his half-brother, Alejandro Aguilar, through their company, was enough to draw an army of sycophants and other unsavoury characters.

Even those who sacrificed their virginities in the hope of a pot of gold...

Whatever.

Had she believed in that sort of thing, Goldie would have toyed with the notion that destiny was hell-bent on giving her this role. Even after Ethan's repeated assurances that he was going to stop auditioning because he believed he'd found his actress she hadn't been convinced.

She didn't doubt for a second that Gael's involvement in the project was what had made her initially reticent about taking the part. Gael might have accepted that he'd got her motives wrong, but the hurt hadn't quite gone away. Probably because neither had the cynicism she glimpsed in his eyes whenever he looked at her.

It had only been after her second meeting with Ethan and his team—minus Gael—two days later that Goldie had started to entertain the idea that the opportunity *was* one she could grasp and launch a career out of.

Before that, though, there'd been her mother to contend with.

Gloria Beckett had been beyond ecstatic that her daughter had landed the plum role in a big production movie.

But even as they'd celebrated with a trip to her mother's favourite restaurant, at Gloria's insistence, she'd worried about being absent from home for the long weeks shooting the movie would take.

She'd eventually divulged her worry to Ethan, only to find out Gael had lined up a list of sober companions for her to interview for her mother. Her mother had resisted at first, but once Goldie had made it a condition of her acceptance or rejection of the role Gloria had relented and let her hire Patience, the middle-aged companion.

In the week before she'd flown to Vancouver, where the other half of the film had been shot, Goldie had been able to rest easy when she'd seen how well Patience and Gloria got along.

Now, as she watched a family of elephants foraging, from the porch of the timber chalet which housed their on-location skeleton crew, she allowed herself a peaceful sigh and a small smile.

Ethan and the crew were a dream to work with. And as for the story...

She glanced down at the script of *Soul's Triumph*. The story of Elena Milton and Alfonso Veron was unbelievably powerful, at times disturbingly heartbreaking, but utterly sublime. A tale of triumph against adversity, it charted the lives of two unlikely souls each tied to a different destiny from the moment they met. But while common sense and inevitable heartache dictated they take different paths, they were continually drawn, for better or worse, back to each other, in an often shocking and volatile relationship that spanned decades and brought untold hardship to their families.

Today's shoot was the first meeting between Elena and Alfonso. Goldie had already met her Spanish lead, an actor in his mid-twenties who spoke very little English. Although he delivered his lines perfectly, conversation off-camera was minimal—a fact for which Goldie was secretly glad.

Even now, weeks later, she was still grappling with the tumultuous twelve hours she'd spent with Gael and wasn't in the mood to deal with much else, even friendly banter between co-actors. The crew for the most part also left her alone. Sure, they'd invited her along on their free day excursions, and she'd partaken of a few, and for dinner and drinks, of which she'd accepted none. She didn't think she would be able to accept a social invitation from anyone for a while after the Heidi debacle.

'Goldie, we're heading out in five minutes. You ready?'

She nodded and smiled, gave a thumbs-up to Ethan as he joined her on the porch. He returned the gesture with the tip of the crutch he still had to use, then turned to supervise the crew loading equipment into a Jeep in the car park.

Ten minutes later they set off, and Goldie found herself smiling again as the stunning landscape unfolded before her.

Ethan caught her smile. 'Is this your first time in Africa?' he asked.

'No, but it's my first to this part of Africa, and my first time when I know I'll keep a vivid recollection of it,' she answered.

He frowned. 'You've lost me.'

She laughed, although the sound was tinged with a deep-rooted sadness. 'I'm half-Ghanaian, but my last visit to my father's homeland was when I was a child. I don't remember much of it, and I haven't had a chance to visit since then, for various reasons.'

'Oh, right...' There was a note of sympathy in Ethan's voice but he didn't probe further, for which she was grateful.

They arrived at the location of the shoot and were greeted by the animal handler who would be keeping an eye on the cheetah needed for this scene. None of the animals in the private game reserve were tame, but one or two had been hand-reared due to injury. One in particular, a gorgeous, graceful cheetah named Asha, had won a part in the movie.

Goldie kept a respectful distance from the animal as she was readied. When she got her cue she made sure her running shoes were laced properly and waited for Ethan's signal.

Being chased by a semi-tame cheetah was in equal parts terrifying and exhilarating. Doing it three times, until Ethan was happy and before the sun dipped into the horizon, was a touch nerve-racking. But she managed it, and delivered her lines alongside the actor playing Alfonso, then smiled widely when she got a fist-pump of approval from Ethan.

'Scene Three is officially in the bag. Although I would *never* recommend getting chased by a wild animal in the savannah as a way to meet the love of your life for the first time.'

Amid the laughter and high fives for a job well done, Goldie looked up. And saw Gael lounging against the hood of the four-wheel drive furthest away from the cluster of crew vehicles.

Gael watched her eyes widen as she spotted him. Shock was swiftly replaced by deep wariness as she stared at him. The wide smile on her face from a moment ago faded to nothing.

He ignored the tiny spurt of regret that look elicited and shoved his hands into his pockets. It was only a matter of time before the rest of the cast and crew noted his presence. Gael had wanted a quiet moment before he was interrupted. He'd had his quiet moment, but he'd used it to question why he was here at all.

Sure, Alejandro and the Ishikawa brothers—his partners—had questioned him extensively on how the project was going, and he had promised them an update. But he could easily have video-conferenced with Ethan for a full report, as he'd done in the weeks since the project had got underway. He hadn't needed to fly for almost a day to inspect proceedings for himself.

But, hell, he was here now. And he didn't want to examine why, for the first time since he'd reached adulthood, he'd gone for a long stretch without taking a woman to his bed. He didn't want to examine why the only woman who seemed to stir his senses was the woman he'd shared a stunningly memorable night with. One who wanted nothing to do with him. One he knew deep in his gut he needed to stay away from.

And yet here he was…

He watched Goldie glance around her, as if she was debating whether to acknowledge or ignore his presence. Gael smiled to himself. *He'd* give himself a wide berth too if he could—especially after the few weeks he'd had.

It had started with his visit to Chicago three weeks ago, and Alejandro asking him to be his best man. It had gone downhill from there.

Every aspect of the Atlas Group's business was running like a well-oiled machine. And yet he couldn't focus—couldn't get past the thought that the past seemed to be on a collision course with his future: namely in the form of the father he'd put out of his life and his mind a very long time ago.

When, at the end of a fraught business meeting, Alejandro had suggested Gael return to his home base in Silicon Valley to get his head straight he'd wholeheartedly agreed, jumped on his plane—and headed to South Africa instead.

And now the woman who'd taken up more of his

thoughts than he was even marginally happy with was trying to pretend he didn't exist.

The crew were beginning to pack up. Ethan spotted him and waved, but Gael's cool nod as he approached Goldie thankfully kept the other man away.

He reached her. Stared down at her. Her nostrils quivered slightly as she stared boldly up at him. The African sun had lent her skin an even more vibrant tone, which made her stunning violet eyes more vivid and alluring. Recalling how silky her skin was, how warm and enthralling it had felt to touch her, he was glad his hands were deep in his pockets. His senses were poised on the edge as it was. He didn't want to add touching where it wasn't wanted to his list of things to deal with. But not touching didn't mean he couldn't look his fill.

His gaze raked the khaki-coloured dress she wore with a tightly cinched belt that emphasised her small waist, then her bare legs and the ankle boots adorning her feet. She looked capable and utilitarian—as her part demanded. But with the shoot over she'd let her hair loose, and dark gold corkscrew curls bounced over her shoulders. Again the memory of having his fist locked in those waves tore through him, powerful and fierce. He clenched his gut against the sensation.

'It's good to see you, Goldie.'

'*Is* it?' She stopped, pursed her lips and shook her head. 'No. Sorry—I promised myself the next time I saw you I'd make an extra effort to be civil, so here goes.' She took a deep breath. 'Thank you for sorting out the sober companion for my mother. You didn't have to, but I really appreciate you doing that…so, thanks.'

He allowed the smile that tugged at his lips—the smile that had been nearly non-existent these last few weeks— to filter through. 'You're welcome. I wanted to give you peace of mind. I trust everything's going well in that department?'

She nodded, her eyes rising from where they had settled on his chest to meet his. She even deigned to offer a tiny smile. 'Yes, they're getting on like a house on fire, or so I'm told.'

'I'm glad to hear it.' He didn't want to begrudge her the peace of mind that was sorely lacking in his own life.

Her eyes searched his. Gael wasn't sure what she found, but her face lost a little of its tightness. He exhaled, realised he was breathing a little easier, and then turned when he sensed they were no longer alone.

Ethan approached on his crutches. 'The crew are about to head out, and the cast and I are heading for the airstrip. Goldie, do you want to join us? Or...?' he paused, his eyebrows lifted.

Gael shook his head. 'There's no need. I have my plane here. We can all fly back to Durban on my jet.' He nodded to Ethan's plaster cast. 'I'm sure you'll be much more comfortable on my plane than on the turboprop.'

Ethan laughed. 'Now, there's an offer I'm not about to refuse. We'll meet you at the plane?'

Gael nodded. Waited until his director hobbled off before he turned to find Goldie regarding him with a steady look.

'Without inciting an argument, can I ask why you're here?' she asked.

He shrugged. 'My partners wanted an update. So did I. And Durban is great at this time of year, I'm told.'

'So you're here on a working vacation?' she probed.

The inkling that he wasn't wanted deepened a pang he didn't want to acknowledge. About to tell her he hadn't taken a vacation in a decade and wasn't about to take one now, Gael paused. 'Why not? I've been told I'm "grumpy and insufferable" lately. So maybe a timeout is just what I need.'

That minuscule smile reappeared. 'Did whoever dared to make that observation get away with their lives?' she teased, and fell into step beside him as he headed for the last remaining vehicle left in the deserted dirt car park of the game reserve.

'Sadly I had to rule out homicide. Doing away with my future sister-in-law before she becomes my brother's wife—or even at any time after that—will *not* end well for me. My only choice was to remove my grumpiness from her presence.'

Her smile widened, turned into a laugh.

Something twitched in Gael's chest at the sound—a feeling of wanting to join in, to revel in her warm amusement at his own expense.

Her cute nose wrinkled when he stopped beside the truck and stared at him. 'So you're here to foist your grumpiness on us instead?'

He opened the door and saw her into the passenger seat. Shutting the door, he leaned an elbow on the open window. 'I'm in the land of cheetahs, fireflies and stunning sunsets, amongst a thousand other pleasures. I'm certain I'll find a useful outlet for my mood,' he murmured.

The sparkle in her eyes didn't dim, but her amusement altered as a different sensation arced between them. Gael recognised it. Waited for her to recognise it too. He didn't exactly plan on doing anything about it—she'd made her feelings abundantly clear that day in his conference room—but the moment felt too visceral to dismiss. So he stood there, with her breathtaking face and body mere inches away, and watched her eyes darken as sexual awareness zapped the air between them.

Abruptly, she averted her gaze from his. 'Can we go, please?'

'Of course,' he murmured.

Despite his intimation otherwise, he *was* here solely on business. Although in hindsight he accepted that he might have handled their morning-after differently, he stood by his decision to keep his hands off Goldie Beckett.

For one thing, she was now effectively his employee— and mixing business with pleasure never boded well in the long run. His brother and Elise might have proved the exception to the rule, but statistics weren't in favour of such occurrences ending well.

For another, he hadn't forgotten what he'd witnessed in that auditorium at Othello. Her virginity might have proved that she hadn't gone through with the director's proposal, but Gael had seen her allow the director's touch. Had seen her take the keycard, watched her consider the proposal. As much as he wanted to explain that away, he couldn't.

Especially as since then Goldie had as much as admitted that her career was her top priority. That she would do anything to further it. Who knows what would have happened had Gael not come along? Hell, her immediate reaction to being drunk for the first time in her life had been to enquire whether her actions had affected the opportunity he'd been offering her.

On some level Gael admired her dedication, and it was undeniable that she had the talent to back the ambition. But the thought of her doing *whatever it took* left a bitter taste in his mouth, reminding him too much of the issues he was dealing with when it came to his mother. Rightly or wrongly, he couldn't think of one without thinking of the other. They both struck a little too close to home and, despite her attempting to explain herself to the contrary, he hadn't been able to erase Goldie's last performance with that director in the auditorium from his mind.

As a tool for enabling him to keep his hands off her it

was effective, he mused as he slid behind the wheel and turned on the ignition.

The ride to the private airstrip where his plane was parked was conducted in silence, and took less than ten minutes.

On the plane, he let Goldie wander off to take a seat next to Ethan. As much as it struck an unpleasant chord within Gael, he ignored the feeling and struck up a conversation with the actor playing Alfonso, who was glad to connect with a fellow Spaniard, even though Gael only half paid attention to their discourse.

His gaze was drawn inexorably to the woman chatting in low tones to Ethan. Her occasional husky laugh bounced across the space between them and sizzled along Gael's nerve-endings.

He was almost relieved when the plane landed in Durban forty minutes later. This time an appointed driver chauffeured them to Umhlanga and the Oyster Box Hotel, where the cast and crew were staying. After agreeing to have a proper meeting with Ethan the next morning, he trailed after the departing Goldie. She was standing in front of the private lift that served his suite when he joined her.

Her eyes landed on him and widened. 'You're staying in the presidential suite too?'

'According to the bookings manager it's the only suite with a spare bedroom not already taken up by the cast and crew. I hope you don't mind sharing?'

A frown clenched her forehead for a few seconds, before a resolute look slid across her face. 'Of course not. She mentioned that the other room might be used by other people. I just didn't think…'

'That I would be your first room-mate?' he finished.

She eyed him a touch warily as he stepped into the lift beside her. 'Yes. But it's not a problem. The bedrooms are on different floors, so hopefully I won't disturb you too much.'

Her smile was less natural than it had been on their ride back from the game reserve. Gael experienced another bite of regret.

'I will let you know if I'm planning any wild parties.'

This conversation was ridiculous. He wanted her at ease, but he was aware that he himself wasn't at ease. So he let silence rule for the remainder of the short lift journey and their walk to the entrance into the suite.

'Have dinner with me,' he invited.

The offer had been delivered without much forethought when she'd started to beat a hasty retreat towards the stairs that led to the suite upstairs.

She paused. Her sumptuous lips parted. 'I don't think…'

'In the interest of fresh starts and civil leaf-turning, I also wish to make an attempt. You haven't eaten yet, have you?'

Gael wasn't bothered by the knowledge that he was pushing. He was known for remaining civil with the women he'd had liaisons with—Heidi being the only exception—so why not Goldie?

Slowly, she shook her head. 'No, I haven't.'

He nodded, a welling of satisfaction moving through him. 'Do you want to eat out or in?'

'I had planned on taking a shower, then ordering in…'

He crossed to the dining room and returned with a lavish menu, which he held out to her. 'Decide what you want and I'll have it delivered here for us by the time you're done with your shower.'

He saw a look of refusal cross her face before whatever resolution she was striving to achieve forced a nod from her.

'Okay.' She took the menu and scanned it quickly. 'I'll

have the lobster bisque to start, the chicken *involtini* and the lemon cheesecake, please.'

He took the menu from her with a wry smile. 'Nothing local for you? I can recommend something if you prefer?'

She grimaced. 'I tried a selection of dishes a couple of nights ago. They were heavenly, but sadly they didn't agree with me.' She rubbed a hand across her midriff. 'Turns out my constitution isn't as adventurous as my spirit.'

Gael frowned, his gaze following her hand. 'Are you okay?'

'Yes, I'm fine now,' she replied. 'But I think I'll stick to food that I know for now. I'll see you in half an hour?'

He nodded, watched her shapely legs stride up the stairs and then resolutely turned away. They were being civil, sharing a suite like reasonable room-mates—not two people who'd shared a sizzling, passionate few hours in bed a few short weeks ago.

So he *wouldn't* imagine her undressing, stepping into the shower, rubbing shower gel all over her incredibly responsive body...

A low curse flamed from his lips. The libido that hadn't so much as twitched around any other woman he'd come into contact with since he'd slept with Goldie was now threatening to rage out of control.

He crossed to the phone and relayed their dinner order. Then he went into his own room and showered.

She was back downstairs when he emerged, wearing a flowing *boubou* gown in a distinct African print, with her hair brushed loose and wavy. The bold oranges and reds complemented her dark colouring, making her look even more striking.

His gaze travelled from her exquisite face and down her body. When she caught his eyes on her bare feet, she grimaced and wrinkled her toes.

'I hope you don't mind? My feet have been in hot and

sweaty boots all day. I can't bear the thought of confining them again.'

For some absurd reason he couldn't pull his attention from her peach-painted toenails, nor stop himself from stepping closer to breathe in the unique scent he was sure didn't come out of a tube of luxury product. Goldie's scent was one he hadn't been able to get out of his mind.

'Of course not,' he replied, his voice curiously gruff.

Her smile dragged his eyes up. Gael found himself absorbing it, wanting to bask in it. To perpetuate it long into the night.

Dios, what was wrong with him?

'Would you like a drink?' he asked abruptly.

Her smile dimmed.

Do better. He needed to do better. As much as he enjoyed sparring with an argumentative Goldie, he admitted he liked this 'new leaf' version better. She still had the fire he was drawn to, but in this place and time he could almost forget that there was a facet of her character he quietly despised. It was a naked ambition she was willing to do just about anything to achieve, and he knew he wouldn't be able to abide it into the future.

The future? What future?

He had no plans of reinitiating or prolonging anything. He'd built an empire.

He'd dated beautiful women.

And he'd vowed never to marry any of them because, inevitably, each and every one of them showed their true gold-digging and opportunistic characters eventually.

On top of that he had known from an early age that he would never produce a child who might feel a trace of the sting of rejection he'd suffered.

Nothing would change that particular vow. Not even Alejandro's engagement and the subtle hints about revisiting old ground that he kept tossing Gael's way. That, most of all, was a grenade he intended to keep tossing back into his brother's lap.

'An apple spritzer?' he tried again, careful to keep his voice even.

Her nod was a touch wary. 'Yes, thank you.'

Although there was a drinks console nearby, Gael crossed the room to the well-stocked bar, to give himself—and her—time to adjust, regroup.

He heard her pad over to the large rectangular windows that opened onto the wide patio and the stunning view of the Indian Ocean beyond. After fixing her drink he poured a glass of burgundy for himself and joined her outside, where the table had been laid by the private butler.

They sipped their drinks and watched the rolling waves hit the shore on the beach down below for a few minutes before their food arrived.

Halfway through their first course she raised her gaze from her plate. 'How long are you planning to stay?' she asked in an even voice, but he detected the thin nerves behind it.

'Until I can no longer avoid my duties as my brother's best man.'

Her eyes widened. 'Your brother's getting married that soon?'

'In ten days,' he answered, aware that the tension he'd hoped to dispel was still very much present.

'Why is it that he's getting married but you're the one who has the jitters?' she asked, and her acuity was a touch disturbing.

'I wish him well, of course, but the inescapable truth is that a lifelong commitment like marriage more often than not fails eventually.'

She frowned. 'You think your brother's marriage is going to fail?'

He shrugged. 'We don't come from admirable stock

when it comes to the sanctity of marriage. He's…brave to want to give it a try, nevertheless.'

Troubled violet eyes connected with his. 'I… What you said back in New York about being—'

'A bastard?' His jaw clenched. He thought about evading the suddenly abrading question, thought about how they'd ended up here in the first place. 'I'm the product of an affair my mother had with Alejandro's *still married* father.'

Her mouth dropped open. 'Oh.'

He took a large sip of wine. '*Sí.* Oh.'

She shook her head. 'I didn't mean *oh* like that. I mean, I'm the last person who should be shocked…' She stopped and frowned. 'If Alejandro's asked you to be his best man, then your relationship with him must be good—so your past circumstances can't matter that much to him?'

Gael recalled their last fraught meeting. Recognised that this time all the tension had been his alone. Although Alejandro had resisted at first, lately he'd been much more open—most likely thanks to the influence of his fiancée, who was open-hearted and open-armed about embracing new family, seeing as her own family situation was lacking.

'The relationship isn't without its challenges, but it's… progressive.'

'So it's progressive now, but you think that relationship will fail too?' she pressed.

He frowned. 'There are always adverse factors at play.'

'And you intend to take those adverse factors lying down, just like you do with your businesses?' she asked lightly as she cut into a piece of chicken.

'I have never failed at a business venture,' he quipped.

'So why are you prepared to write off a sound relationship and watch it fail without putting in as much effort as you would into a business venture?' she parried.

His smile felt as cynical as his soul. 'Because business is conducted and thrives without the single detrimental component that damns us all.'

'And what's that?'

'Useless emotion.'

Her fork stilled and her eyes widened. 'You think emotions are useless?'

'They're more harmful than useless. They cloud judgement and ruin lives.'

Gael knew he'd been unable to hold back the bitterness ravaging him when her face clouded with something close to sympathy

Goldie shook her head. 'How do you…? I don't understand.'

He gritted his teeth, tried to stem the words that seemed determined to spill. And failed. 'You recall your little story about infidelity and alcoholism?'

'Of course,' she said.

'The former has been the story of my life—what my building blocks are based on. I left Seville over ten years ago and thought I was free of it. Turns out I'm not.'

'Your mother?' she queried cautiously.

A vice tightened around his chest. 'And Alejandro's married father. Version two point zero.'

Anxiety darted across her face at his tone. Her fingers toyed with her water glass before she asked, 'Does Alejandro know? Does his mother know?'

He laughed harshly. 'Alejandro knows. He seems to have found a way to accept it, but I haven't been so fortunate. As for his mother—yes, she knows. Most likely she enjoys the chaos associated with it. They all seem to thrive on it, in fact.'

Enlightenment whispered over her face. 'That's what you were talking about that night? What you meant when you referred to—?'

'Toxic relationships? *Sí,* Goldie *mia.* When it comes to those types of relationships I am vastly knowledgeable.'

Her expressive eyes shadowed. 'I'm so sorry.'

Gael frowned, wondering why those two words sank deep inside him, attempted to soothe a place he'd believed was too mauled by past pain to be still alive. The sensation was so alien it robbed him of breath and speech.

Thankfully the butler arrived with their dessert course. Gael refused the sweet platter in favour of an espresso, hoping the caffeine would clear his head and put a stay on his runaway tongue.

Goldie's cheesecake was set before her with a flourish that drew a small smile from her. He nodded his thanks when his drink was handed to him.

About to gulp down the hot beverage, he looked up, frowning, as Goldie turned green.

She bolted from the table before he could utter a single word. Gael rushed after her—only to hear the bathroom door slam shut before the sound of violent retching sounded from within.

His gut tightened in alarm. 'Goldie?'

More retching, followed by a low, miserable moan. He knocked on the door, turned the handle. It was locked.

'Open the door, Goldie.'

A grunt filled with discomfort, then a cough. 'Um... no, I'm fine. I'll be out in a second.'

He gritted his teeth. 'You're not fine. You're vomiting.'

He absently wondered why that observation filled him with alarm, why the helplessness assailing him grew with each futile second.

A half-laugh sounded. 'Yeah, I think I'm aware of that little fact—' Speech ended and retching restarted.

He resisted the urge to ball his fist and pound the door open. '*Dios,* why did you lock the damned door?'

No answer. More vomiting.

He had to satisfy himself with waiting for her to finish emptying the contents of her stomach before she answered.

'Because I didn't want you to see me.'

'Modesty is the last thing you should be concerned about if you're sick. Can you open the door—*por favor*?' He tried his most reasonable voice.

'No. I…I'm feeling better. I'll be out in a minute.'

Argumentative Goldie was back. Short of breaking down the door, Gael could only grit his teeth and resign himself to pacing the hallway until he heard the sound of the lavatory flushing and a running tap.

When she didn't emerge for another five minutes his anxiety swelled higher. 'Damn it. Open the door!'

'Sir? Can I help with anything?' The solicitous butler had appeared behind him.

Gael curbed the urge to demand the spare keys to the bathroom, accepting that perhaps he was overreacting. Goldie had mentioned having a stomach upset after some food two days ago. He could still hear movement and the occasional splash of water, so she hadn't passed out—or worse.

'No, we're fine. If I need anything I'll call.'

He waited until the butler had left, then returned to the bathroom door. 'You have two minutes to come out, *guapa*. Then I'm coming in.'

'Okay, fine.'

He hesitated for a second, then returned to the patio. He poured a glass of water and downed it, then poured one for her in case she needed it.

He knew less than a minute had passed, so he forced himself to the balustrade to stare unseeingly at the view. He *was* overreacting. Goldie being sick might disrupt the movie's shoot, but it wasn't something they couldn't overcome.

But if it was more than a stomach bug…if she was falling ill with something else…

When his practised deep breathing barely calmed his flailing control, he cursed under his breath.

'Gael?'

He whirled away from the view, his relief at seeing her standing there more welcome than he knew it should be. Her hair looked tumbled and a touch wild, as if she'd run her hand through it several times without a single care about the way she looked—which put her firmly in a unique category far from most of the women he'd dated.

Framed in the light spilling from the living room, she was a gorgeous sight, despite the paleness of her face. A sight he wanted to see more of. Much more, he realised. And accepted. Perhaps he'd been too hasty to consign them to being just temporary room-mates. The chemistry between them was beyond electric. It was unique enough to warrant further investigation. Exploration of the best, carnal kind.

Prising himself off the low wall, he walked towards her. Saw the mixture of horror and acute trepidation in her eyes. And froze.

'Goldie! What's wrong? Do I need to call a doctor?' he demanded, his voice turning harsh with barely curbed concern.

'No, I don't think so.'

'You don't *think* so?'

'I…I think I know…' She stopped and swallowed, then a charged little tremble shook her frame. 'Gael, I think I'm pregnant.'

CHAPTER EIGHT

THE LIFE-CHANGING WORDS uttered out loud locked something deep into place inside her. Goldie had no explanation for it, but she knew she wouldn't need a pregnancy testing kit or a blood test to confirm the truth burning in her heart.

She was pregnant.

From her single night in Gael Aguilar's bed she'd fallen pregnant.

And he…he looked as if he'd been hit by a giant wrecking ball.

She turned around, stumbled back into the living room, sank down onto the sofa. Despite the juggernaut of emotions tumbling through her she heard him approach, take up residence in front of her. A glance upwards showed him with crossed arms, the skin around his mouth pinched tight as eyes turned dark and turbulent pierced her.

'You're pregnant.'

The words were devoid of emotion. But they demanded confirmation.

'You don't just *think*? You're sure?' he grated out in an icily controlled voice.

She licked dry lips, went over the dates she'd spent the last ten minutes in the bathroom desperately calculating. When they fell a good fourteen days short—*again*—she nodded.

'I'm late. I'm never late. I just thought… God, I don't know *what* I thought. I know it sounds naive, but I thought having sex and…and getting ready for this job may have disturbed my cycle.' She met his gaze, saw the frigid disbelief there and closed her eyes. 'Trust me, I know how that sounds. But with everything that's happened these past few weeks…' She stopped and stared at him. 'Are you going to stand there glaring at me all night?' Her voice shook, and, oh, how she hated herself for it.

'What else is there to say? Except maybe congratulations?'

Her stomach threatened to roll again. She placed a soothing hand over it. 'I don't know about that. I haven't taken it in yet.'

'*Haven't* you?'

His voice was a stiletto, cutting through the noise in her head.

She glanced up, and her heart dropped to her feet at the look on his face. 'What are you implying, Gael? What exactly do you mean by *congratulations*? On the pregnancy or on something else?'

'You need clarification?'

'Yes!' She surged to her feet, swayed, and sat down again. 'Please don't tell me you think I did this *deliberately*?'

Light, cold eyes stared unflinchingly back at her. 'Perhaps not the failure of the condom, but I'm afraid the "naive" argument doesn't fly. You're an intelligent woman, Goldie. I don't believe you ignored your hitherto *regular* cycle at all. You knew you were pregnant but chose not to say anything.'

'Why would I *do* that? Why would I be so—?'

'Calculating? I can think of a few reasons.'

Horror clenched her heart in a vice. 'Enlighten me, then, please.' Her hands began to tremble with the force of her chagrin and the shock that was rocking through her. She curled them into her lap and fought the prickle of tears that burned her eyes.

'You're already on the fast track to stardom—thanks to a few well-placed circumstances. But this pregnancy guarantees you the fastest possible route to achieve your aims.'

'My *aims*?' she whispered.

'You want to be a successful actress, do you not?'

She shook her head in confusion. 'Yes, of course I do—the same way you strive to be successful at what *you* do. I love what I do and I'm good at it. But I've also worked hard for it. There's nothing wrong with that and I won't apologise for it.'

'Of course not. Just as there's nothing wrong with the few hundred thousand starlets who want the same thing you do. Except you saw an opportunity for a fast track and you took it.'

'An opportunity *you* told me I'd be a fool to refuse, if I remember... Oh, you're still talking about the pregnancy? You think—' She stopped, too horrified to put what she suspected he meant into words immediately.

He raised a mocking eyebrow, dared her to continue.

'You think that just because you own a production company I deliberately kept this a secret, so I'd be set career-wise and security-wise for life?'

'*Sì.* Exactly.'

She shook her head again, unable to fathom how he could read her so wrong. How could he be so twisted about her motives? Or complete lack thereof. Had his past circumstances really done such a damaging number on him that he truly believed that?

'Gael, let me make one thing clear. I didn't want to lose the opportunity you presented me with, once you yourself talked me into it. But, please believe me, I would never put my career before the welfare of an innocent child,' she stated, her heart dredged with a hurt whose depths she couldn't quite touch.

'Sadly I have no proof of that besides the words falling from your mouth. *Will* have no proof of that until the child is born,' he rasped icily.

'How…? What did I do to make you think this of me? We barely know each other—'

'I know enough.'

'To condemn me like this?' she rasped, feeling her voice, like everything inside her, threatening to go numb at the flaying condemnation she saw in his eyes.

'On the way back from that dinner party in New York did you not plead with me? Tell me that you'd do *anything* to get the part?'

'Anything within reason. Like an audition. Or a screen test. Even an initial interview to see if my credentials were what you needed. Something *within* my profession. Not… not *this*!'

His eyes followed the hand she slid low over her stomach, then his gaze rose to hers, icier, more soul-shredding than before.

'*This?* The baby is a mere *thing* to you?'

'Oh, please—why are you trying so hard to twist my every word?' she cried, blinking back the further tears that threatened. 'I didn't trick you, or keep this baby a secret from you. I've only just worked it out myself. I'm not out to get my hands on your billions, or use the baby as leverage for my career. I haven't even been able to absorb the news and you're already labelling me a heartless gold-digger who would trade her unborn child for fame and fortune!'

'You wouldn't be the first,' he drawled, the same way he had that day in New York.'

Pain, raw and bracing, ripped through her. 'You know what? Go to hell, Gael. And stay there!'

This time when she stood her feet felt more inclined to support her.

He took one step forward.

She countered by taking several away from him.

He halted. 'Where do you think you're going?' he demanded, his voice quiet but grating.

'Anywhere I don't have to continue this ludicrous, de-meaning conversation with you. I'm not one of the women you've dated in the past who came with a portfolio of agendas. Hell, we're not even dating. So leave me alone.'

'Goldie—'

'No! If you have something else to say to me that *doesn't* involve you shredding my character, talk to me in the morning. Otherwise I'll thank you to stay away from me.'

He laughed. 'Stay away from you? When you're carrying my child? Believe me when I say that will not happen in a million years. We *will* talk in the morning, Goldie, whether you wish to hear what I have to say or not.'

'Don't count on it.'

'Goldie—'

'Goodnight. I'd say sleep well, but I hope you spend the rest of the night thinking about your unfounded accusations and stewing over them.'

Her words, his warning—*everything* rang in her ears long after she'd brushed her teeth and slipped between the covers.

The shocking reality that history had well and truly repeated itself for another Beckett was so visceral it brought tears to her eyes. Goldie herself was the product of a one-night stand, conceived when her mother had been part of a charity's volunteer group in Ghana and had fallen for the charms of a local businessman. But, unlike the men who'd followed, her father had tried to make it work, even moving continents to be with her mother.

Sadly, her mother had been unwilling to settle for being a wife and mother in a picket-fenced house. Gloria had believed there were bigger and better things out there for her. Her reluctance to give their relationship a chance had eventually driven her father back to his homeland, leaving her mother to fall prey to dreams that had never been fulfilled and a lifetime of being taken advantage of by unscrupulous men.

Goldie had always known in her heart that the lessons she'd learnt via her mother's experience wouldn't lead her down the same path. But one night's wrong decision *had* led her here. Only this time she was the one being called unscrupulous. Avaricious.

She hated the tears that welled up in her eyes. Hated Gael in that moment for making her feel lower than she already felt. Because what had they created together other than a child who would hate her, and possibly its father too, for bringing it into a world where there was no chance of its parents ever being together?

Goldie knew how lonely and frightening things could get. Already she feared for her child. In light of Gael's revelations about how he felt about his family, how could she not?

Her hand slid over her stomach as weariness and inevitability washed over her in equal measures. She didn't have all the answers for how she was going to deal with what was happening to her. Far from it. But Goldie knew without a doubt that she would fight to her very last breath to make sure her child didn't suffer an ounce of preventable pain or rejection. Just as she knew that if that involved battling with Gael Aguilar she would bring the same fervour to the task.

With that resolution burning bright in her chest, she closed her eyes and willed healing sleep.

Her sleep was relatively peaceful. But twice she got up in the night to throw up. Twice she heard Gael prowling through the suite. Clearly her curse had worked, but she couldn't take any joy in that. She shut her mind to it, concentrated only on making it to the bathroom and back to bed both times.

It was almost as if now her mind had caught up with

what was happening in her body her baby was determined to make its presence felt one way or another.

She fell asleep just before dawn, her hand on her stomach, her mind whirling with a million thoughts.

Less than an hour later she was up. Determined to stick to some sort of routine, she donned the aqua-coloured bikini she'd used since coming to Durban, and threw a light matching sarong over it. Slipping her feet into gaily coloured sandals, she settled a wide-brimmed hat on her head and drew back the sliding doors to step out onto the private patio fronting her bedroom. Steps led down to the beach and the dramatic shoreline.

Pausing to breathe in the fresh air, she let her gaze drift past the iconic red and white Umhlanga lighthouse to the gleaming waters of the Indian Ocean. Seagulls flew overhead in the early-morning sun, and Goldie blanked her mind as she struck out for the quarter-mile walk along the shoreline.

Pregnant. She was *pregnant*.

She would buy a pregnancy test to confirm it as soon as she could, but even without the visual proof with each pulse of the word in her brain her breath caught. She reached the end of her walk and stopped to face the ocean, her mind spinning.

How would a child fit into her world? Where would they live? *How* would they live? How would her mother feel about being a grandmother?

How did Gael feel about being a father?

That question stood out above all the myriad hurtling through her head. It was also a question whose answer she knew she'd discover soon.

Swallowing, she raised her face to the warming sun's rays for a minute, before shedding the sarong, hat and sandals and walking into the sea.

Swimming was blissful, as usual, but already she worried about what such active exercise would do to her baby, and gave up halfway through her normal lengthy swim. Collecting her things, she strolled back towards the side of the hotel. The first thing she needed to do, once she'd had a talk with Gael, was to dig up as much information as she could on how to keep healthy during pregnancy.

Once again she was assailed with a frightening but growing thrill over her impending future.

No matter what. She'd fight to her last breath.

Discarding her things on a lounger next to the private pool that served the presidential suite, she turned on the outside shower to wash off the salt water. She was washing sand from between her toes when she heard the hurried slap of bare feet.

'Where the hell have you been?' Gael demanded forcefully. 'I was about to send out a damned search party.'

She turned, her gaze momentarily obscured by the water running down her face. Sluicing it away, she tilted her head back from the spray. He was livid, the chest beneath his white polo shirt rising and falling as if he'd run a marathon.

'I went for a walk on the beach, followed by a swim,' she said, fighting to keep her voice on an even keel. She needed to keep calm. For her baby's sake.

'Without bothering to tell me?'

'I went for a swim yesterday too. In fact I've walked and swum every day since I got here. I do it before breakfast and before we go on location. Should I have reported to you then too?'

Fury blazed across his face as he stepped closer. 'Don't be flippant, Goldie. You know what I mean.'

'Do I? A few things have changed, granted, but are you seriously expecting me to turn my life upside down because—?'

His hand slashing through the air chopped off her words.

'*Everything* has changed, Goldie. Accept that now, before we exchange further words.'

About to contradict him, she stopped. Because he was right. *So* right.

For one thing, once their child was born this man who stood brimming with fury and power before her would be connected with her for ever. And if he chose to take an interest—and judging by the look on his face he already was—he would have a say in her child's welfare.

The thought sent a shiver through her. Weirdly, it wasn't a shiver of terror. More a dread of the unknown. Because suddenly another factor loomed large in her brain. This child wasn't hers and hers alone. It also belonged to Gael Aguilar.

The thought was unsettling enough to make her words tumble out. 'Gael…I… It was just a walk. A swim.'

'And what if something had happened to you?' he rasped.

'The beach is safe. Nothing would have happened.'

He gritted his teeth for a few tense seconds, before his gaze flicked to the torrent of water cascading down her body. 'Are you done?'

She nodded and turned off the shower. 'Yes.'

Glancing round, he spotted a pile of towels and grabbed the largest one. Goldie reached up to smooth back her wet hair, then froze when she caught his eyes on her.

Slowly, Gael advanced, his hot scrutiny rushing down her body and returning on a slower trajectory. 'How could you not have known you were pregnant?' he scythed in a heated voice barely above a guttural whisper.

Her breath knotted in her lungs. 'Excuse me?'

Light hazel eyes reached her breasts, lingered for a long

moment. 'Your body is already changing. How do you expect me to believe you didn't know?'

'There was so much going on. I...I wasn't paying attention. Gael, I didn't know—I swear.'

His mouth tightened, but he handed over the towel without acknowledging her words. 'Come inside when you're done here. We need to have that talk.'

She watched him walk away, his strong, shorts-clad legs taking him from her view in seconds. She took her time to dab the excess moisture from her body, even though it didn't buy her any more time to formulate her thoughts.

Simple reason was, she had no idea what was coming with regard to Gael.

When she walked into the living room he was pacing, the phone pressed to his ear. He stopped, his gaze fixated on her as he spoke. 'Work it out, Ethan, and let me know.'

The hairs on her nape prickled as she watched him hang up and toss the phone onto the dining table. 'What was that about?'

He gave a tight, mirthless smile. 'Setting out contingencies.'

'What does that mean?'

He prowled to where she stood. Scrutinised her face and body one more time. 'First things first, *guapa*. How do you feel?'

The question was solicitous, caring. The emotions bristling from his body and eyes told a different story.

She sidestepped. 'Why are you asking?'

'You were up during the night. I have a doctor on standby—'

'I don't need a doctor. I feel fine.'

A tic manifested at his temple. 'You found out you're pregnant last night. Don't you want to know immediately how best to take care of yourself?'

She frowned, knowing she'd walked into that. 'I… Of course.'

He nodded, and strolled back to the table. Grabbing a white paper bag, he handed it to her. 'Before the doctor comes let's make absolutely sure of your state, shall we?'

Still frowning, she took the bag, looked inside. 'A pregnancy test…' She wasn't sure why the band tightened around her chest. She'd planned on getting one anyway. But Gael doing so seemed…*hurtful*.

'We need to be equipped with as much information as possible going forward, do we not?'

The explanation dissolved a little of her hurt, but not all of it she noted as she nodded and headed for the bathroom.

Gael was standing at the wide rectangular windows staring out at the view when she emerged from the bathroom. He turned immediately when she walked into the room, his narrowed eyes piercing hers before dropping to the two sticks clutched in her fist. Quick strides forward brought him unapologetically into her personal space.

'Well?' he breathed, his eyes gleaming with a feverish look.

Goldie swallowed. 'Yes.' She handed him both sticks.

He stared down at the tests, his gaze riveted on the writing displayed on the tiny screen.

Pregnant. 3+ Weeks

After an age, he tossed both tests onto the console table behind her. Closing the gap between them, he speared his fingers into her hair, angled her head up so she couldn't look away from him.

'You're carrying my child.'

The primal claim in those four words was unmistakable. Her breath shook as she nodded.

The palms cupping her cheeks firmed, as if he was focusing her attention ready for his next words. He pulled her close until their faces were inches from each other's.

'Do you accept that this fundamentally changes your life, Goldie?'

The depth of his belief in the words almost shook her enough to frighten her. But she'd worked too hard for the life she'd chiselled out for herself to cower beneath anyone's will.

'No, I don't. I'm sorry, Gael, but it doesn't.'

CHAPTER NINE

IT DOESN'T.

For a few seconds Gael was sure he'd misheard. Then he remembered exactly who he was dealing with. A woman with an iron will almost as strong as his own.

The woman carrying his child.

Surprisingly, his senses had stopped reeling somewhere in the middle of the night—between Goldie's first and second vomiting sessions. The test he'd procured first thing, when he'd thought she was still sleeping had merely been the instrument to slide that last one per cent of doubt from red to green.

The one and only time a woman had tried to trick him into fatherhood before, her quest had been tentative and ultimately bungled. Heidi had hinted at pregnancy towards the end of their time together—most likely to test the waters and her chances in the marital stakes. Gael's firm shutdown had resulted in a firm retraction of her fictional state.

Not so with Goldie. Her conviction had been firm, which in turn had cemented his.

She was carrying his child.

He was going to be a father.

But she didn't think it was a life-changing situation for her. What did *that* mean?

'Perdón?' Realising he'd lapsed into his mother tongue, he shook his head. 'What do you mean, *it doesn't*?'

She licked her lower lip, triggering a wave of heat through his groin. Nothing that had happened in the last twelve hours had changed the red-hot chemistry between them. If anything, the changes in her body had lent her skin a deeper glow, made her even more voluptuous and unbelievably stunning and heightened the awareness between them. A fact his body was reacting to in the most primal way.

'I mean *some* things will change, of course. I'm not debating that. But I'm not changing who I am because of my baby.'

His fingers wanted to tighten, to draw a more satisfactory answer straight from her mind. He cautioned himself to relax, breathe deep. '*Some* things? Tell me what you think those things are. Then tell me what you think *won't* change.'

Her mouth firmed for a second. 'I haven't laid it all out in a spreadsheet, if that's what you mean—'

'But clearly you've given it some thought, Goldie. So let's have it. Bullet-point the big things for me.'

She exhaled. 'Well, the first thing is to make sure the baby is healthy.'

'*Sí*—agreed,' he said.

'Then, once he or she is born, we'll have to discuss your visitation rights and how to work around our career schedules.'

His gut tightened, disbelief flashing through his system. 'Visitation rights? *Schedules?*'

She nodded.

He dropped his hands and fought the terrible rush of dark fury and the memories of being discarded when it suited his mother that surged high. 'And where will you be living while these rights are being discussed?'

She frowned, as if his question was absurd. 'In New Jersey, with my mother—hopefully in a place that better suits us.'

'Of course. So I'm to remain in California, where I'm based, only seeing my child when a court order stipulates, hmm? Presumably you intend to pursue your career?'

'I...yes.'

'So our child will be left in the care of minders, or your mother and her sober companion, perhaps, while you're off on location around the world? Or do you intend to drag him or her with you?'

Her violet eyes grew wide, probably at his seemingly calm tone. 'Gael, I told you I don't have all the answers yet—'

'That is exactly right. You do *not*. But I do. Before I tell you, though, I have a little tale to tell you. Are you ready to hear it?'

She blinked, then raised an eyebrow. 'Do I have a choice? Aren't you going to tell me anyway, whether I want to hear it or not?'

Gael took another step back—because right in that moment he wasn't sure whether he yearned to kiss her sensual lips in an attempt to force down the memories surging, or condemn her for making those volatile emotions rise to the fore in the first place.

She shifted in reaction to the invisible fireworks sparking round the room, drawing his attention to her body, barely covered by the wispy sarong.

He whirled, slashing his fingers through his hair, and tried to seek a little clarity from the wide expanse of the ocean beyond the window. When it remained elusive, he took a deep breath and turned around again. Facing this thing head-on was the only viable option.

'I've told you a little bit about my past...my parentage, *si*?'

'Yes...' she responded warily, her gaze tracking him as he began to pace.

'What you *don't* know is that every few years when I was growing up my father would leave his wife for a few weeks and convince my mother to go away with him. Every time it was supposed to be *the* time—the moment when he left Alejandro's mother and made a life with my mother, the woman he supposedly truly loved. At those times I was parcelled off to the local orphanage or left with casual acquaintances who were paid to mind me.'

She inhaled sharply. 'Gael—'

He held up his hand. 'I'm not telling you this to gain sympathy. This is a fact of my childhood. It's behind me now, but it's not forgotten. I have accepted that I didn't even have a broken home to call my own—that my day-to-day existence was at the whim of a father who confirmed explicitly that I was an unwanted mistake when I dared to confront him.'

She gasped, her hand flying to mouth as if to cover the sound, the pain.

'I have had no interest in becoming a father simply because it's not a role I ever foresaw for myself.'

'But—'

'But now I am faced with the prospect of bringing my child into the world, things are not as clear-cut. However, there is one thing I intend to ensure will *never* happen where this child is concerned.'

She stared, unblinking, the pulse in her throat hammering wildly. 'Wh-what is that?'

'Comparing the circumstances I've just described to you with what you proposed a short while ago, do you think a man in my position, and with my power, having gone through what I went through as child, will be willing to stand idly by while my child is shuffled between minders, planes, movie locations and court-ordered visitation rights?' he gritted out.

Her mouth trembled for a second before she caught hold of herself. 'Gael, please be reasonable—'

He broke off mid-pace and planted himself firmly in front of her. He needed her to see the intent emblazoned in his heart and mind.

'Let me answer for you, Goldie. The scenario you propose will happen *over my dead body*.'

The words sank in.

Her mouth dropped open in disbelief. 'So we're not even going to discuss it?'

'We just have.'

'No, we didn't. You're just trying to lay down the law.'

'I have told you what I intend *not* to happen with my child. We can now go on to discuss what *will*.'

'*Our* child.'

'What?'

'*Our* child. Equal parenting. Equal responsibility.'

'Yes—agreed. And that most definitely does *not* involve split homes on either side of the continent.'

'You can't just rule things out, Gael. We need to agree a compromise.'

'Why compromise when I have the solution?' he asked.

Her smooth forehead clenched in a frown. 'We confirmed the pregnancy less than ten minutes ago. How can you have a solution already?'

'Very easily when what's at stake is this important.'

She gave a slight shake of her head, but her gaze didn't leave his. She blinked, her expression turning wary with trepidation. 'I think we need to talk about this some more.'

'I'm finished with talking, Goldie. The soundest solution to the situation we find ourselves in is for you to marry me.'

Even though her senses had screamed at her that whatever Gael was about to propose would most likely push all her alarm buttons, the words still hit Goldie square in the chest with shocking and relentless force.

She swayed on her feet.

Gael cursed, caught her by the elbow and tugged her to the sofa. 'Sit down, Goldie.'

'I'm fine.'

'I didn't say you weren't. I would still like you to sit. You were up half the night, throwing up, and you've been standing for far too long.'

She rolled her eyes, earning herself a dark frown. 'Women have been giving birth for thousands of years without turning into wilting flowers for the duration of their pregnancy, Gael.'

'*Sí,* but none of them have had the privilege of carrying my child,' he bit out.

Her mouth quirked in a parody of a smile, which vanished a second later. 'Do you have *any* idea how pompous that sounds?'

'You ask the question as if I care. You're still standing, Goldie.'

She plunked herself on a seat. Then rubbed her temple as his words attacked her once more. 'You just… You just asked me…'

'To marry me, yes,' he confirmed, his voice brimming with unequivocal power and certainty.

'But…why?'

'Because my child won't be living in New Jersey. It will be living with me.'

Cold dredged through her. 'And the only way I will have access to our baby is to marry you? Is that what you're threatening me with?'

He didn't answer immediately. Silence ticked by as he paced in front of her. Then he stopped and propped his hands on his lean hips.

'Tell me a little bit about your background, Goldie.'

Her gaze flicked up to meet his. 'Why?'

'Because I want to understand why you're fighting this, when all signs indicate that you would think this a perfect solution if other factors weren't an issue. So make me understand why our child can't be with *us*, full-time, wherever that may be.'

'I don't have to *make* you understand. Just because you suddenly think marriage is a perfect solution, when only last night you were dead against it for your own brother, it doesn't mean I agree.'

'I don't think it's a perfect solution. I think it's the most viable one.'

She batted the answer away. 'I would really like not to talk about our child as if it's a commodity you're brokering.'

His head went back as if she'd struck him. 'Trust me, *pequeña*, a commodity is the last label I'd hang on our child.'

The words were soft but deadly. Too late, she remembered what his parents had done to him as a child. Gael might deny it, but that period in his life had left scars. Deep scars that still dictated his motives.

'Sorry,' she muttered. 'I didn't mean to… It's just that you speak CEO all the time.'

He lifted one eyebrow. '*All* the time?'

A fiery blush flashed into her cheeks at the blatant reference to their night together. Recollection surged into her mind, making her breath shorten. Unable to drag her gaze from his, she watched, fascinated, as his eyes turned dark and stormy. Despite the brightness of the room she suddenly felt as if they were cocooned in a dark, decadent piece of heaven.

Which was absolutely the last thing she needed to be thinking about now.

He seemed to arrive at the same conclusion. He blinked and gritted his jaw. 'I'm all ears, Goldie. You grew up in a broken home, correct?'

She winced. 'Eventually, yes.'

'And your father? Is he in the picture?'

'Long-distance.'

He pursed his lips. 'Given the choice, is that what you *wanted* to happen when you were growing up?'

She closed her eyes. Swallowed. 'Okay, you've made your point, but I still think we can make an alternative arrangement—'

'No.'

She glared at him. 'Let's explore another option. Couples live together full-time without marrying. Why do we need to be married?'

'You don't think our child's conception from a one-night affair is more than enough for it to have to deal with? You want to add to the long line of illegitimacy in his history? When you can prevent it? What have you got against marriage?'

'I... Nothing. But that doesn't mean I want to be knee-jerked into it.'

'The welfare of our child should be nothing like a knee-jerk response. It should be *everything* to you.'

Her mouth dried at the enormity of what he was saying. While she'd been lost in dreamless sleep, it was clear Gael had spent hours thinking about the situation they found themselves in. He had a brilliant mind, but she didn't think he'd put together this presentation on the fly.

Still, what he was suggesting was so...*absolute.*

'Speak up, Goldie. What's the problem?'

She laughed, unable to believe he was expecting an immediate answer from her on so monumental a subject. '*If* I decide to do this, I want a few stipulations of my own.'

His brow clamped in a frown. Then he gave a tight nod. 'Let's hear it.'

'You...you can't want to be saddled with me for the rest of our lives, nor I with you, so can we agree to a more temporary solution?'

He froze. 'You want to enter marriage with a clause that ends it on a particular date?'

'Please don't make it sound so clinical. Until ten minutes ago you were a man who didn't date the same woman for longer than six weeks! Now you expect me to believe you're willing to give up the rest of your life?'

'For the right reason—why not?'

The right reason. The baby. Not them.

'I think you're missing the point, Gael. You automatically assume that putting a ring on my finger will make this baby's life stable. I'm not denying it will, but don't you think he or she will be happier with parents who are content?'

'Are you saying marrying me sentences you to a life of discontent?'

'Don't put words in my mouth. I just want us to take a step back, think about this—'

'Five years.'

'I… What?'

'You want a fixed term? We'll give it a try for five years. After that we'll reassess the marriage. Whatever the outcome then, one thing will remain non-negotiable. We'll live in the same city and do everything to provide a smooth home-life for our child. So—five years. Do you think you can give up your independence for that long?' he bit out.

'Gael—'

'And in that time, provided you make our child's happiness your number one priority, you will receive ten million dollars per year and five guaranteed box office smash movie roles courtesy of Atlas. You say your career is important to you? This way you can rest assured it will not be unduly interrupted.'

Shock held Goldie rigid for so long she wondered whether she was in danger of turning into a fossil. When she managed to speak again, her voice shook with effort. 'And…and if I don't agree to what you're suggesting?'

Goldie was almost afraid to ask, because the purpose she'd sensed in him when he'd confronted her outside seemed to have magnified a thousandfold. She didn't need to be a genius to work out that Gael had just given her the 'either' scenario. There was a very big 'or' coming her way.

'If you don't agree, then I'll take steps to remove our child from you—completely—the moment he or she is born. I'm sorry, *amante*, this is too important for me to beat round the bush. So those are your only options. What's it going to be, Goldie? Yes or no?'

Two days.

She'd argued for time to think about Gael's proposal. He'd grudgingly given her the remainder of their time in South Africa.

So she had two days to come up with a different solution, one that *didn't* involve marrying a man she barely knew, or fighting him in court for custody of their child. And so far, a day later and with twenty-four hours' worth of filming a beach scene between Elena and Alfonso completed, she'd drawn a blank.

To fight Gael she needed far deeper pockets than she currently had. This was her first movie role, and the pay was more than she'd dreamed of, but it was nowhere near enough to take care of her child while fighting for its rights in a court of law—especially against a powerful man like Gael Aguilar. And part of her contract with Atlas involved exclusive work that might extend for almost half a year after filming, which meant that even if she wanted to be pounding the pavements on job-hunts while being heavily pregnant she couldn't.

Which brought her to the option Gael preferred. Marriage.

Her heart caught every time she thought of that, but after a few times Goldie admitted that the idea wasn't as stomach-clenching as it had first seemed.

Both their backgrounds had proved conclusively that coming from a broken home could damage a child. For the longest time Goldie had felt bitterness and anger towards her mother for not being strong enough, for pushing her father away and breaking up their family. And, although she loved and supported her mother now, she couldn't help but feel bruised inside from the times when she'd lived in constant fear that her mother would never be strong enough to make the right decisions about the men she'd let emotionally abuse her.

In her darkest moments, Goldie had wondered whether she was potentially equally fallible. It was one of the reasons why she'd hung on to her virginity for so long. She'd been afraid to find out the depths of her strengths and weaknesses.

She didn't plan on being alone for the rest of her life. And did she not owe it to her child to try and give it the best possible start in life? Even if it meant marriage, temporarily, to its father?

She didn't know everything there was to know about Gael, but he'd laid the cards that were important to him on the table. The most commendable of which involved making their child's wellbeing his number one priority. Despite the flipside being his threat to fight her for custody of their child, her rational and emotional sides felt satisfied that he was committed to his unborn child.

Enough to decide to turn his private life upside down for it within hours of finding out about its existence.

That quiet but powerful truth made her turn her head now to look at the man in question, who sat next to her as the helicopter flying them to Table Mountain soared over the breathtaking landscape.

The crew had left Umhlanga early this morning. Because of tourism restrictions, they had only a small window to shoot a scene on the mountain—which, ironically, was the scene in which Elena was proposed to by Alfonso. A scene which ended with her saying yes, and then spending the rest of her fictional life fighting to save her marriage.

Dread whispered over her skin. As if he sensed her inner battle, Gael turned narrowed hazel eyes on her. He watched her silently for a few seconds before he reached across the bench seat to take her hand.

The action was unexpected, throwing her thoughts and emotions further into conflict. Provided she kept their child as their main focus, *could* they make a go of a five-year emotionless marriage? Because she wasn't about to delude herself into thinking there were any emotions involved here. Gael was acting purely on a primal instinct to protect what was his. Much as he would in a business venture.

Whereas she…

Goldie stopped her chaotic thoughts as the helicopter landed. She honestly didn't know *what* she felt. All she knew was the pledge she'd made to protect her child.

So, although she didn't attempt to remove her hand from Gael's once they alighted and were seen into the cable car that would take them to the top of the mountain, she turned her thoughts to work and the scene in front of her.

The view from the top was unlike anything Goldie had ever seen. Enough to rob her of breath for a full minute. Enough to make her feel like a small cog in the great, unrelenting circle of life. Enough to lend her the gravity she needed to utter her lines in a way that saw the scene completed in one continuous take and Ethan give yet another pleased fist-pump the moment he yelled, *'Cut!'* But while the crew celebrated she moved off to a quiet corner of the section of the plateau, her thoughts turning inward as she drank in the spectacular view of Cape Town and the ocean beyond.

She sensed Gael before his body heat arrived behind her. Strong arms bared to the African sun came around either side of her to rest on the railing.

'Do you really need another day to think about this, *cara*? You know deep inside what needs to be done, Goldie,' he rasped in her ear.

'Do I?'

'*Sí*, you do. Don't drag this out unnecessarily.'

'I don't want to. But…*marriage*…'

He moved closer, his body caging her in tighter. She angled her head, looked up at him. Eagle-sharp eyes stared down at her, their focus unwavering.

'Don't overthink it or confuse the issue. We're not fictional characters. We can have a marriage without the melodramatic chaos.'

She gave a tiny anxiety-filled laugh. 'How can you be so certain?'

'Because we don't believe in the fairy tale. We're going into this with our eyes wide open. There is only one purpose here. We're doing this for the sake of our child. For the chance to give it the stability we were both denied. Say yes, Goldie. You stand to gain far more than you stand to lose.'

His voice was hard, almost merciless.

She swallowed hard. Slid her hands over her flat stomach, her thoughts churning.

Gael's hand sliding over hers, warming her hands, cradling their child, alarmed her almost as much as it settled her. He was claiming. But he was also protecting.

She would deal with the former if it threatened her at any point. The latter, she couldn't fault.

Taking a deep breath, affirming her pledge, she gave her answer. 'Yes.'

CHAPTER TEN

THEY LANDED IN SPAIN three days later. Once she'd given her answer things had moved at lightning speed. Papers had been drawn up, witnessed and signed, granting her unimaginable wealth and the type of acting roles that should have made her ecstatic but instead had left a faintly bitter taste in her mouth.

Somewhere along the line Gael had managed to weave her into agreeing to attend his brother's wedding. If she recalled correctly, his answer when she'd expressed reservations at attending had been a tightly voiced, 'You're about to become my wife. Who else am I supposed to go with?'

The suggestion that perhaps he might go alone had been met with a frown and a firm refusal.

'You will have to meet my family, as dysfunctional as they are, at some point. Best to get it over and done with. Besides, for once I would like to enjoy an event without Kenzo Ishikawa getting on my case about my marital status.'

'Kenzo Ishikawa…one of your business partners?'

He'd snorted, his jaw going tight before he'd replied. 'He seems to take pleasure in pointing out that I'm less of a man because I'm unattached. Our first attempt at a merger fell apart partly because of it.'

'And this is your chance to rub your attachment in his face?' Goldie hadn't been sure whether to be offended or amused. She'd chosen to be neither.

But Gael had sent her a tight smile. 'Exactly so. There is also the added bonus of beating Andro in the nuptials stakes, even if only by a few days,' he'd added with surprising relish, before absenting himself from her presence.

Now, Goldie rose from the lounger and padded to the edge of the Olympic-sized pool.

Before that wedding happened there was the small matter of *her* wedding. Special licences had been arranged. Ethan had agreed to shoot a few of the scenes that didn't involve her, then give the whole cast and crew a four-day break before they resumed filming again at the end of next week. And Gael was having her mother and Patience flown over tomorrow, for the wedding that would take place here on his estate just outside Barcelona.

The place was quintessential Spanish architecture at its best. A rambling two-storey villa, the property sat in the middle of acres of rich green valley dotted with orange and lemon trees. The villa itself, originally a Catalan manor house, modernised and extended, was made of stone, with grand arches and a vast courtyard decorated with trellises and carefully groomed vines. The house was stunning and yet homely—a place she wouldn't have immediately associated with Gael Aguilar, the ruthless and ambitious CEO who wrote computer code as a hobby.

But then a few things were beginning to surprise her about Gael—not least being this marriage he was hell-bent on in order to protect his unborn child.

In the last twenty-four hours private doctors had visited her, taken blood samples and delivered enough pre-natal advice and vitamins to stun a horse. It was too early for an ultrasound scan, but Gael had readily agreed to a suggestion to listen to the baby's heartbeat on a foetal Doppler. The loud sound echoing through the guest bedroom where she slept had brought a look of almost shocking determination to his face.

It was that determination that strengthened her belief that she was doing the right thing too.

So when Gael's housekeeper walked out a few minutes later, to announce the arrival of the stylists and the gown designer contracted to ready her for her wedding, she took a deep breath, turned around and headed for her destiny.

Goldie climbed the small hill towards the tiny chapel that sat half a mile from the villa. A tiny part of her was glad for her mother's fussing around her, because it took her mind off what was waiting for her beneath the ancient steeple. She also knew it was her mother's way of accepting what was happening.

Despite Goldie's reassurances that she was doing the right thing, her mother had voiced her worry from the moment she'd landed. Eventually she'd accepted Goldie's assurances, but it hadn't taken away the veil of concern in her mother's eyes.

Goldie's worry as to whether that concern might trigger a deeper reaction in her mother had been allayed by Patience, and the companion's brief but buoying report of her mother's progress had settled Goldie's own anxiety.

So she let her mother fuss now, because it meant *she* didn't have to do any fussing. She hadn't seen Gael in the past twenty-four hours—a surprising turn-up since she hadn't expected him to observe tradition. In his absence, questions had loomed—one in particular taking up most of her thoughts.

It was the question of sex—horrifyingly triggered by her mother's observation of the vast amounts of bedrooms in Gael's villa and how she was looking forward to seeing it filled with grandchildren.

Of course that had also brought on the question of how much of their agreement they would be sharing with others.

All those questions beat hard like butterflies' wings in her belly as she reached the doorway of the chapel. Technically, her mother was to walk her down the aisle, but Gloria wanted to walk a step behind, her hoarse insistence that this was Goldie's day, not to be spoiled by a mother who'd let her down, having brought tears to her eyes.

There'd been no time to utter words of comfort, or to take in her mother's new, more hopeful outlook on life, but something had settled in Goldie's heart upon seeing her mother again. For now, though, she needed to head up the aisle and join her life with Gael Aguilar's.

The man in question turned his tall, imperious frame and speared her with a fierce, possessive look as she walked slowly up the aisle.

He was impeccably dressed in a dark navy suit and snow-white shirt, his hair tamed and gleaming beneath the dozens of candles glowing from the cast-iron holders that hung from the ceiling, and his magnificence seriously threatened her breathing.

As his gaze raked her body she derived quiet satisfaction from the fact that she'd chosen a dress she loved, which gave her a much needed boost of confidence. The short-sleeved, cream silk lace gown that framed her figure to end in a short train behind her prohibited long strides. She'd forgone a veil in favour of a tiny tiara that held her pinned up hair in place. She wore only light make-up, and simple pearl earrings belonging to her mother adorned her ears to complete the subtly elegant ensemble.

Halfway to the altar, with her eyesight better adjusted from the almost blinding sunlight to the candlelit interior, she caught a better glimpse of Gael's face. And her breath caught.

Beneath the possessiveness, that hard look she'd never been able to fathom lurked in his eyes. A feeling of having been tried and found guilty for a crime she had no inkling of committing assailed her, causing her to stumble slightly.

She stopped to right her footing. Gael's nostrils flared as he took in her hesitation. Goldie started to shake her head, but he was already striding down the aisle.

Catching her hand firmly in his, he escorted her up to the altar. Murmurs went up in the small wedding party comprising her mother, Patience, Teresa—his house-keeper—and her husband, and the driver/bodyguard who gave her a small smile as she passed him.

They had barely stopped before the priest when Gael nodded at the tall, thin man to proceed.

The bilingual ceremony passed in a blurred rush from one moment to the next.

Her mother stepped forward to relieve Goldie of the small bouquet clutched in her fist. Then Goldie was listening to Gael's deep, firm tones as he said his vows. Her eyes widened when his driver stepped forward with two rings laid out on a small velvet pillow. Gael's was a simple broad gold band, hers a platinum double circle with yellow diamond studs holding the two rings together.

Her fingers shook as she held his ring poised over his knuckle and repeated her own vows. A furtive glance at Gael showed his complete attention on her as she uttered the binding words. When she had finished an unfathomable look crossed his face.

In that moment Goldie was certain she'd crossed a threshold she would never be able to step back from.

Gael had experienced a well of satisfaction as he slid the wedding band onto her finger and repeated the words that had made Goldie Beckett his wife. He'd secured his child's future. Ensured it would never suffer the stings of illegitimacy and rejection he'd suffered. Would never be made to feel like an obstacle or an unwanted possession, either through emotional neglect or in the face of its mother's ambition.

He forced aside the rush of bitterness that stormed him. So far he'd been able to keep his feelings under control—had been able to contain the knowledge that Goldie's *yes* had come after his offer of compensation and a promise of a flourishing career.

He wanted to keep his emotions out of it—much as he kept his emotions out of his business transactions. And yet the boulder that had lodged itself in his chest since her acceptance of his deal wouldn't shift.

It shouldn't matter. Ultimately, he'd done what needed to be done for the sake of his child.

And yet it did matter.

He knew it mattered when he was invited to kiss his bride and sealed his mouth to hers and felt her brief hesitancy before her response kicked in.

It mattered when her gaze wouldn't meet his as they acknowledged the applause and smiles of their small group of guests once the ceremony was officially over.

He had married her to secure his child's wellbeing.

So why did his own suddenly feel precarious?

'Gael?'

He shut off his thoughts and glanced at his bride. They'd returned home from the chapel to an alfresco lunch set up on a banquet-like bench beneath two orange trees in his garden. He'd invited the rest of his staff to join them, and had endured the endless toasts with an ever-stiffening smile.

'Yes?' he responded.

'Are you okay?'

His mouth twisted. 'Of course. What could possibly be wrong on a day like this?'

She frowned. 'Please don't patronise me. Have I done something wrong?'

His jaw gritted. 'Goldie—'

'You've barely said two words to me since we left the church. In fact we've barely had a conversation since we arrived here. I know we're only doing this for the baby—'

'I would prefer it if you *don't* share our private agreement with the world.'

'That's just it. Why are we pretending to everyone that this is some sort of…love-match?' she demanded in a hushed tone.

'For the same reason we are entering into the marriage. To protect our child.'

'But…'

'Enough, Goldie. If you want to discuss this further we will—but not right now, *si*?'

Another member of staff—the head of Gael's vast stables—rose just then, to make a speech, effectively stopping her from speaking. Then there followed more speeches, mostly in Spanish, which meant she was left in the dark as to what was being said. But raucous laughter gave her a general hint.

She ate selectively, having eventually worked out which foods triggered her nausea and which would mostly likely stay down.

At one point, she caught her mother's speculative gaze swinging from her to Gael and back again. Although Goldie smiled, she wasn't sure it had been convincing enough.

She waited until Gael was occupied with entertaining a couple she'd been told were vintners from two estates away before excusing herself and returning to the villa. Accompanied by a smiling Teresa, who had insisted it was tradition that she help her dress for her wedding night, and her mother, who continued to cast curious glances at her, Goldie was forced to keep the starchy smile pinned on her face.

The moment Teresa departed, her mother faced her.

'You're pregnant, aren't you?' Gloria declared, her gaze running searchingly over her daughter's negligee-and-dressing-gown-clad body.

Her damning blush was all the confirmation her mother needed.

'Oh, Goldie...' The words were softly spoken, partly in regret, partly in tearful acceptance.

'I was going to tell you when the time was right.'

Her mother nodded, but her eyes remained troubled. 'Is that why you married him so quickly?'

It's why I married him at all. But she knew she couldn't say that. 'It's the right thing to do, Mom.'

'For you or the baby?'

For some reason that softly voiced question tightened a vice around her heart. She watched her mother's eyes fill with tears again as she sank down onto the bed. 'This is my fault. I'm so sorry, Goldie.'

She shook her head. 'No, it's not. Stop crying, please.'

Her mother's smile was sad and a touch weary. 'You can stop trying to be the adult, here, sweetheart. I know I haven't been the best role model for you. If I'd tried to make a better life for you, instead of selfishly wanting things I couldn't have, you wouldn't have rushed into this—'

'I made the decision with my eyes wide open, Mom. I...I don't regret it.'

She firmed her voice against the tiny white lie. The truth was that things had seemed so clear-cut on top of Table Mountain when Gael had whispered in her ear that this was the only viable option. But as she'd made her vows in that ancient chapel there'd been a terrible moment when she'd tried to imagine saying another set of vows, at another time and place, to someone else. The stunning realisation had come that she couldn't imagine such a time, couldn't picture another man. That she wanted this time and place to be the only occasion when she said those words.

Goldie still hadn't been able to wrap her mind around that.

'Are you sure, sweetheart? Because—'

'I'm sure, Mom.' She placed her hands over her mother's and held her gaze, repeating the words to herself in the hope that they would begin to ring true.

Her mother nodded and rose. Thinking she was about to head for the door, Goldie's breath caught when her mother wrapped her in a firm embrace, laying her cheek on top of Goldie's head.

'I should've done better. I should've been a better mother, fought harder to make us happy. I'm sorry, Goldie. I hope you forgive me some day.'

Tears filled her eyes, choking her response. 'Mom...'

'Shh, it's okay, honey. You'll do much better than me—I know you will. But if you ever need me please give me the chance to be there for you, okay?'

Unable to speak, Goldie nodded, then sat in silence as her mother left. She was still perched on the bed when a knock came on the door to the adjoining master suite.

The door opened to reveal Gael, minus his jacket and tie. He prowled into the room, power and glory falling from his impressive frame. 'Should I take it as a personal affront that my bride deserts me before the wedding banquet is over?' he drawled.

Her insides tightened. 'We're alone now, Gael. You can drop the pretence.'

He kept coming, not stopping until he reached the bottom of the bed, where he leaned his long-legged frame against the post, crossed his ankles. 'Where is the pretence, *amante*? You *are* my bride, and I *did* feel deserted.'

'So what is this? A yearning to have my fawning act reprised behind closed doors?'

His eyes narrowed as he stiffened. 'Act?'

'You don't wish anyone else to know this marriage is a sham, but do *we* have to pretend that there's more to this union than there really is?'

'Correct me if I'm wrong, but isn't this our wedding night?' he demanded bluntly.

Alarm and more than a touch of breathlessness stabbed her. 'In theory, I guess...'

His harsh laugh made her wince. 'No, Goldie, not in theory. In *fact*.'

Her stomach flipped. 'What are you implying?'

His mouth twisted. 'You were a virgin the last time we were together, but surely you don't need me to draw you a picture of what happens on the night following a wedding?'

She flushed, but boldly met his gaze. 'Of course not. Except I'm certain that picture doesn't apply to us.'

He slowly straightened, his chest rising and falling in measured breathing as he closed the gap between them. Goldie willed herself to stay still and not bolt the way her senses were screaming at her to.

'Explain to me how you arrived at this interesting conclusion?' he invited, his tone deceptively casual.

The dark gleam in his eyes said he was very much interested in her answer. And that it had better be to his liking. Or else.

She licked suddenly dry lips and searched for clarifying words. 'We're doing this for the baby, aren't we? And sex...sex will just cloud the issue. Blur the lines.'

He gave a hard, short laugh. 'So let me get this straight. You're perfectly content to condemn yourself to a nun-like existence for the next five years, and presumably you expect me to willingly subject myself to the same sex-less fate?' he asked, his voice reflecting how ludicrous the idea was.

Goldie opened her mouth, shut it, then shook her head, confusion and exasperation filling her. 'This is why I wanted more time before we jumped into marriage. These are things we should've discussed beforehand—'

'So we could waste hours or days arguing it to death before you saw reason and gave in?'

Hurt and anger firmed her mouth. 'I'm not a shrew, Gael. I'd thank you not to make me out as one.'

'Very well. Tell me in simple terms that your assumption is ridiculous and we can progress with our wedding night.'

'There isn't going to *be* a wedding night! We have a deal. Sex isn't part of it.'

His nostrils flared and his eyes blazed with quiet fury. 'Only because I didn't think I needed to spell out so obvious and fundamental a point.'

'I'm sorry it's such an important thing for you. It's not to me.'

He rocked back on his heels, his features freezing like ice. 'I see. You get what *you* want out of the deal and to hell with the rest—is that it?'

'What are you talking about? I said yes because we both wanted—'

His hand slashed through the air. 'Save it, *cara*. We both know that fifty million dollars and a guaranteed five box office hit movies had a big hand in you eventually saying yes.'

Raw ice doused her. *'What did you say?'*

'Your hearing is perfect, Goldie,' he drawled. 'And I'm finished with talking.'

Her mouth was still gaping open when he took the last step and untied the belt of her dressing gown. The silk slid off her shoulders without much effort, leaving her in an emerald-green negligee.

Before Goldie could protest, one firm hand slid over her nape. He pushed her back onto the bed and prowled over her to plant his knees on either side of her hips. In the next instant his mouth plunged, hot and heavy and demanding, over hers, his tongue stabbing between her lips to take and ravage hers.

Her shock dissipated under the flames of his arrogant,

unstinting caress. Despite a large part of her brain reeling under the accusation he'd flung at her, she couldn't help but moan when one hand boldly cupped her engorged, sensitive breast. Her breasts seemed to have grown a size bigger almost overnight, their tips super-sensitive as pregnancy hormones ran riot through her. Gael was clearly appreciative of her new size, and his moans grew more guttural as impatient fingers brushed aside the straps and yanked the top part of the negligee down her arms.

He broke the kiss to stare down at her full breasts. Eyes firing a burnished gold, he took the globes in his palms and toyed mercilessly with the nerve-engorged peaks.

Her head went back as she arched under the exquisite assault. Goldie knew she shouldn't be enjoying herself this much, that what he'd said to her needed to be addressed immediately, but the sensations zinging through her body, arrowing demandingly between her thighs, were too thrilling to stop.

She cried out as his mouth closed over one stiff nipple. Several expert flicks had her hips twitching, her breath shooting out in shameless pants as liquid heat ploughed through her. Back and forth he alternated his attention between the stiff peaks. Sent her right to the edge of bliss.

And then it *did* stop.

The loss of sensation was so acute she whimpered. The sound shamed her even as she launched her fingers up to stay him, and eyes she didn't remember shutting flew open.

'Gael…?'

'*This* is why I didn't think I needed to point things out to you. The chemistry between us is as natural and vital as breathing. But if you need to be told, then hear this. Unspoken or not, sex *is* part of the deal. You may have a ring on your finger, but—trust me—this isn't a point I'm prepared to concede. So argue with yourself all you want to as long as you come back with a yes. Because tomorrow night the only bed you'll be sleeping in is mine.'

He stepped off the bed with the grace of a jungle cat and stood for a moment, staring down at her.

Words stumbled through her dazed senses—begging, pleading words that had no shame under the heavy weight of her thwarted need. With super-human effort Goldie bit them back. He'd dealt her the gravest of insults, attacked her integrity. Even if she risked expiring from the gut-clenching desire clamouring through her she wouldn't give in. Not when she knew his true feelings towards her.

Raising her chin, she firmed her mouth and returned his stare in silence.

Gael's mouth twisted with mocking bitterness. Leaning down, he traced a forefinger from her clavicle to her cleavage. 'That's how it is to be, hmm? Well…good luck, *cara*,' he murmured in a soft, deadly voice.

Then, turning on his heel, he walked away from her.

CHAPTER ELEVEN

FOR THE NEXT four days they remained locked in silent, seething battle. But they made almost comical efforts to be civil to one another in front of her mother, Patience and the staff. And Gael was an exceptional host on the occasions when they took her mother to a private gallery viewing in Barcelona and then to an open park showing of *Tosca*, both of which her mother lapped up with almost childlike joy.

But the moment they were alone his charming smile and drawling banter evaporated. He barely glanced at her as he busied himself with his newspaper or whatever meal he was consuming. The moment he deemed it acceptable he left the room, either to pound relentless laps in the swimming pool or to lock himself in his study.

Goldie had no such escape. On long walks over the estate her mother was growing to love, she endured probing questions and concerned looks. The only upside of the effort it took to maintain a happy face was that she fell into bed exhausted at the end of the day, with her sleep only disturbed at the crack of dawn by relentless morning sickness.

The day before Gael's brother's wedding—the last day of her mother's visit—she entered the dining room to find Gael pouring hot water into a fine bone china teacup. Adding two slices of lemon and a cube of sugar, he stirred it briefly before setting it down in front of her, along with a small plate of dry crackers.

'Drink this. Teresa swears by it for morning sickness,' he said gruffly.

Her surprised glance swung to his, but he was walking away to get himself an espresso. Expecting him to leave the room, since there was no one to entertain, she gulped at a hot mouthful when he sat down at the head of the table.

'Am I to assume that we're talking to each other now?' she asked, after a few minutes had passed and she'd drunk half the sweetened hot water. She was aware that her tone was a touch waspish, but she'd been unable to stem the hurt of the past few days.

'Talking has never been a problem for me. Arguing without purpose, on the other hand, bores me.'

Her breath shuddered out. 'So you either want to hear only what suits you or silence?'

He tossed back his espresso and set the cup down with a heavy hand. 'No, Goldie, the only subject I'm not prepared to argue about or compromise on is the subject of sex. And since that subject appears to be a ticking time bomb between us, I suggest you tread carefully.'

The cup trembled in her hand so she set it down. 'I know your mind isn't one-track like that—'

His harsh laugh fractured her words. 'Do you? I'm a red-blooded male, Goldie. One with a healthy sexual appetite and stringent views on fidelity. You're the woman who's taken my name and my ring but is refusing to share my bed. Since I don't intend to break my vows, I'm left with a huge, potentially insurmountable problem. So do you *really* think I'm overreacting?' he grated at her.

Her blush was fierce and all-encompassing. But then so was the ache that wouldn't budge from her heart. 'Do *you* expect *me* to have sex with you when you've accused me of marrying you just so I'll get my hands on your money?'

'Come off it, Goldie. Sex was off the table even before you signed on the dotted line. You just decided to keep it to yourself. You were biding your time before you dropped your little bombshell.'

'No, I wasn't—because I wasn't even thinking about it then. You left me in bed the first time we made love without a word. I woke up to a note that was tantamount to you telling me you'd made a mistake. And you think the natural progression from that, when we agreed to marry for the sake of our baby, automatically includes sex?'

A faint dull red tinged his cheekbones, but his expression remained rigid. 'I wasn't expecting you to be a virgin so, *sí*, I was a little…thrown. But I did return to you. Only you were asleep. I took the unselfish way of not waking you and chose to sleep in the spare bedroom. But my question still stands. You knew my views on fidelity before you married me, so what did you *think* was going to happen?'

'I expected we would talk about it. We never got the chance to discuss it so neither of us knew where we stood.'

'What about now? Where *do* we stand?' he countered.

She shook her head. 'Right now we stand with me wondering why on earth you'd want to sleep with a shameless gold-digger who would barter her child for fifty million dollars!'

He shrugged, his eyes feverishly raking her face. 'The money means nothing to me, *guapa*,' he drawled softly. 'Having your body beneath mine again in bed would be worth more than twice that to me.'

'I do *not* want to sleep with you for money!'

'Too late—you have already signed the documents, remember?'

Her hands shook so hard she clenched them in her lap before he saw. 'Why are you so determined to think the worst of me, Gael?'

'I'm merely going by the evidence before me.'

'*What* evidence? My deplorable timing because I said yes right after you threw in your supposed sweetener?'

'You signed the document,' he sliced at her again.

'Yes, I signed it. So what? Was it some sort of test that I failed? Is there no room for the benefit of the doubt in your world?'

'That is up to you, Goldie.'

'How?'

His gaze moved past her face, down her throat, to the two-button opening of her white sleeveless sundress. 'Find a way.'

He left the dining room shortly after that.

On shaky feet she got up and went to the sideboard to replenish her cup with hot water. Her mother and Patience entered as she was heading back to her seat. Greetings were exchanged. And then she went back to avoiding her mother's probing stares.

After eating a piece of toast and half a banana without incident, she begged off when her mother invited her to the local market to shop for the souvenirs Gloria wanted to take back to the US. Feeling bad, she promised a mother-daughter lunch before her mother and Patience were taken to the airport for their evening flight.

Escaping to her room, Goldie paced, her mind darting over her conversation with Gael. How could something so seemingly straightforward have become such a jumbled mess?

Was she naive not to have considered that Gael would want a wife in *every* sense of the word after he'd gone out of his way to avoid her after the first time they'd made love? He claimed he'd returned after disappearing into the bathroom for longer than was normal. But his note the next morning had left very little doubt as to his feelings.

And he'd tried to fob her off with money then too!

She paused mid-stride. It was clear that money was the issue. Gael Aguilar was used to dealing with gold-diggers and scheming women. By signing the prenuptial agreement as it stood, she'd all but drawn a bullseye on her back.

Crossing to the bed, she grabbed her purse and searched for the document. There were pages and pages of it, all wrapped up in legalese. But she eventually found the clause she was looking for. Her heart leapt as she read and re-read it. Grabbing her phone, she did a quick search for local attorneys—those who practised in English as well as Spanish.

After making an appointment, she jumped off the bed and went in search of her mother. She breathed in relief when she caught her and Patience as they headed out.

'Is it too late to join you?'

Her mother turned around and smiled. 'Of course not!'

Asking Teresa to let Gael know she'd gone out with her mother, she joined them in the SUV.

The Friday market in Villa de Gracia was bustling, with exquisite trinkets and to-die-for souvenirs at every turn. It was easy for Goldie to leave her mother happily browsing and keep her appointment with the attorney. It took a good few minutes to explain to the ageing lawyer just what she wanted, and he seemed genuinely puzzled by her request. But eventually he called in his son, who agreed to draw up the requisite documents.

Twenty-five minutes later Goldie emerged from the attorney's office with a smile on her face.

'Find a way,' Gael had dared her.

She just had.

Gael was waiting on the front steps of the villa when they returned. The three women glanced at his face as the driver braked the SUV to a stop and the easy laughter in the vehicle died.

'Well, looks like someone's headed for the doghouse,' Patience quipped under her breath. 'Goldie, honey, what did you *do* to the poor man?' the plump companion, originally from New Orleans, stage-whispered.

Goldie snorted. 'Sometimes I just need to breathe the wrong way.'

Muffled laughter ensued, quickly cut off as Gael strode to the car and opened the door.

'Everything okay, son?' her mother asked sweetly.

Gael jerked out a nod. '*Sí*, everything's fine, Gloria,' he responded, without taking his eyes off Goldie. 'Can I talk to you, *cara*?'

She could tell he was trying to keep his tone even, but the flames raging through his eyes and the white lines bracketing his mouth told a different story.

She pasted a smile on her face. 'Sure.'

He took her hand and led her into the house. Once inside, he crossed the large rotunda-shaped foyer and took the right set of sweeping wood and iron stairs that led to the second level.

'Gael—'

He stopped suddenly in the middle of the staircase and stared down at her. One hand reached out and brushed her lower lip. His fingers were shaking.

'You've been itching for an argument, *guapa*. And I'm about to give you the mother of them all. Just hang tight,' he snarled, low and deadly.

He resumed climbing, his steps quickening as they crested the stairs. It was all she could do to keep up with him as he moved to the west wing and entered his bedroom.

Goldie had only caught glimpses of Gael's suite, which was connected to hers. She'd seen it when he'd come into her room on the night of their wedding.

Seeing it in all its glory for the first time, she stopped in the middle of the room. A rich, pale wood theme was everywhere, blended from ceiling to bed to floor, interspersed with a dark marble Goldie wanted to run her fingers over just to see if it was as warm and luxurious as it looked.

Of course all that passed through her mind in a split second before the man…her husband…shut the door with a decidedly repressed click and planted himself in front of her.

For several heartbeats he just stared at her. 'You went into town with your mother?'

Goldie blinked. 'Uh…yes?'

He breathed in, long and deep. 'You went into town with your mother, and then *went to see a divorce attorney*?' he seethed with white-hot fury.

Oh, hell. Her heart lurched. 'What? No—!'

'You were seen, Goldie! The attorney's office confirmed it. So did my driver.'

He started to whirl away, one hand spiking viciously through his hair. He stopped both actions halfway through and launched himself back in front of her. He looked paler than before, a vein jumping frantically at his temple as he glared at her.

'Is this your answer when things don't go your way? Is this your way of trying to get my attention, to bend me to your will?'

She shook her head. 'You've got it wrong. Just let me ex—'

He pointed a finger at her. 'I *won't* grant you a divorce. We agreed to five years. You're going to give me those five years, and not a day less. You *do* understand that, don't you, Goldie? You *do* get that anything less and I'll make sure you're locked in a court battle you'll have no hope of emerging from for another five years after that.'

She exhaled, exasperation eating her alive. 'Well, no, I *don't* get that. *If* I want a divorce you'll have to give me one when the five years are up. That's the agreement. But—'

'But nothing! *Santa Maria*, we've been married less than a week and one argument sends you running to a— Wait… *If*?'

She tried to resist rolling her eyes. She failed. 'I'm going to explain myself to you now, Gael. Are you ready to listen?'

His brow was thunderous. 'I'm not a child, Goldie. Tell me what I need to know.'

She bit her tongue against a curt answer. 'I've told you I don't want your money.'

His nostrils flared but he remained silent.

'So I went to see an attorney to give it away.'

His eyes widened. 'What?'

'The agreement says that on each wedding anniversary I get the sum you promised wired to my account. I got the attorney to divide that money five ways—two-fifths will go to charities here in Barcelona and two-fifths to charities in the States. The fifth portion will go to a local performing arts community near where I live in Trenton.' She reached into her purse, withdrew the document and held it out to him. 'Here—see for yourself.'

Mild shock blanketing his face, he took the document from her, read it with lightning speed.

Then he frowned at her. 'You're giving away all the money?'

'All of it.'

'And did you happen to discuss divorce with this attorney while you were getting this done?' he demanded, his eyes still a touch wild.

'No, Gael. I didn't. The D-word didn't once pass my lips. You said to find a way. I found a way.'

He exhaled, his breath decidedly shaky as he bunched up the document and flung it over his shoulder. 'Why the hell didn't you say that?'

'You were on a roll. I tried to stop you, but you seemed intent on flattening me.'

He paced in a tight circle without once taking his eyes off her. '*Dios mio*. Why do I let you drive me so crazy?' he seethed quietly.

She shrugged. 'You drive *yourself* crazy. You don't need my help.'

He gave a deep, vicious growl before he lunged for her. Fingers spiked into her hair, angled her head, a nanosecond before his mouth smashed down on hers. He kissed her hungrily, deeply, then ripped his mouth from hers a minute later.

'You found a way?' he whispered roughly.

'I found a way.'

He leaned his forehead against hers, his eyes boring into her own. 'Does that mean you want to be with me, Goldie?' he demanded, his voice hoarse with need. 'Truly be mine?'

'Yes,' she replied simply.

Because her need for him *was* that simple. She'd been a fool to imagine that she could erase it out of the equation—that she would be content to sleep next door to him for five long years. Even if it were true that Gael would tire of her after six short weeks, she was still going to take that time with him.

The kiss he delivered after her answer in the affirmative was bliss-inducing. Her purse fell off her shoulder and was forgotten. The hem of her sundress was gripped in a tight hold, pulled over her head and dropped to the floor, leaving her in the white bikini set she'd planned to wear for lounging by the poolside that morning.

Gael caressed his way down her jaw, her throat and shoulders. Cupping those, he turned her around and groaned, low and deep.

'*Amante*, you're so beautiful.'

The throaty words drew a delicious shiver from her, making her tremble in his arms. His fingers catching the long ties of her bikini top, he pulled them free and turned her around. Eyes turned burnished gold devoured her seconds before his hands resumed their caress. A deeper tremble seized her as he cupped her breasts and squeezed. Her hand rose to grip his waist.

She needed to hold on to him. It was a desire and a necessity. Her gaze rose to meet his and her breath caught at the ferocious hunger in his eyes. Unable to resist, she stood on tiptoe and pressed her mouth to his. His hands left her breasts to gather her close. He groaned when her chest pressed into his. Clever fingers made short work of the bottom half of the bikini. Then, naked, she was once again caught in his arms.

After an age of glorious kissing, Gael picked her up and carried her to his king-sized bed. Quick and efficient movements relieved him of his clothes and then he prowled onto the bed, sleek and magnificent next to her.

From cheek to neck, cleavage to midriff, every inch of her skin was covered in open-mouthed kisses, while over and over his fingers drifted over her abdomen where their baby nestled.

Suddenly he snapped his head up, eyes narrowed. 'Did you take your prenatal vitamins this morning?' he asked.

Goldie curbed the need to smile. 'Yes.'

A brisk nod. 'Did you have a good breakfast?'

'Yes.'

He completed another circling caress over her belly. 'Are you hungry now? The pregnancy book says you should eat little and often. Can I get you anything?'

She suppressed a groan of frustration, sliding her hands over his shoulders, glorying in the muscles that bunched at her touch. 'I'm fine, Gael. I don't need anything. No— actually, scratch that. I need *you*. Only you.'

His grin was full and unfettered, snagging a tight string around her heart. Bending his head, he placed a deep, reverent kiss on her belly before he began to kiss his way lower.

Goldie tried and failed to stop the hot blushes that rolled over her at the expert attention he delivered between her legs. Much too soon she was crying out and soaring high.

Still buzzing, she moaned as he rose over her, kissed her lips and caught her hands together above her head.

'Open your legs for me, *querida*,' he commanded throatily.

She obeyed wholeheartedly.

'Now, look at me. Show me your beautiful eyes.'

Her breath still unsteady from the aftershocks of her climax, she lifted her gaze. He caught it easily, his eyes pinning her as effectively as his body pinned hers.

One hand holding hers captive, he used the other to guide himself into her. They both groaned as pleasure surged, pure and dizzying. Without the restriction of a condom the pleasure was more intense—a fact Gaël gutturally attested to a minute after the sensational thought flew across her brain.

'I want it like this from now on. Always. I can never go back.'

'Yes...' she readily agreed, already on a set course to flame-hot bliss.

He increased his tempo, need dictating the pace as he thrust deeper inside her. On another thick groan he lowered his head and fused her mouth with his. Tongues melding, breath mingling, they celebrated their coming together with unfettered passion, then collapsed into each other's arms as ecstasy flung them into nirvana.

Once their breaths quietened he speared his fingers through her hair and angled her face to his.

'This time when I go to the bathroom be assured that I will return,' he mock growled.

Goldie laughed, her heart lifting with a sensation she didn't want to name just yet. 'Okay.'

He left her for a minute, returned with a warmed towel. After seeing to her, he returned it to the bathroom. Her breath caught all over again as she watched his gladiator-like body move towards her. She might not be in this position for the whole of the five years they'd committed to one another but, boy, she intended to enjoy every minute of the time she did have.

'Dare I ask what's going on in that brain of yours?' he drawled.

She grimaced. 'I'm thinking we need to get up soon, before Mom comes knocking. It's almost time for them to head to the airport.'

'Right. Nothing like the thought of my mother-in-law catching me defiling her daughter to kill my buzz.'

She laughed. He joined in.

She felt another life-defining twinge of her heart.

By the time they got up to get dressed, ten minutes later, Goldie was beginning to fear the changes her emotions were going through…

CHAPTER TWELVE

GAEL ADJUSTED THE SLEEVES of his morning suit and resisted the urge to glance at his watch for the third time in
as many minutes.

'Goldie, we're going to be late.'

They were expected at Alejandro's villa at noon—an
hour before the ceremony started.

'I...I'm almost there.'

He frowned. He didn't understand her need to keep a
separate bedroom now she was sharing his bed. Granted,
it had only been one night, but her half-hearted agreement
when he'd suggested this morning that she move her things
into his suite had irritated him.

Now, with the added tension of the impending ceremony and the inevitable face-to-face with his father, his
nape felt tight. Hell, his whole body was on a knife-edge.

He whirled from the window.

And was confronted with a vision.

Dios mio, she was breathtaking! With the time she'd
spent in the sun, her *café-au-lait* skin was almost as dark
as his own, making her violet eyes stunning luminous
pools. But the flush of pregnancy had added a glow that
made it impossible for him to take his eyes off her. With
her carefully styled but already a little wild corkscrew
curls, and her body draped in a shoulder-baring, floor-
length dress, she looked as divine as an angel. She wore
the pearl earrings she'd worn on their wedding day, but
her throat was bare. She was radiant enough—didn't need
further adornment.

Gael wasn't sure why the memory had chosen that moment to return, but his insides snagged hard as he recalled

how he'd felt when he'd received the call from his driver about her visit to the attorney's office. The hour he'd paced until her return had felt like the blackest of his life.

Which puzzled and disturbed the hell out of him.

Telling himself it was just because she carried his child rang a little hollow. Now that he'd accepted he was to be a father, it was a position he was looking forward to. If nothing else, he wanted to conquer the demons that howled at him that the seed he came from was poisoned. He didn't believe that any more. He would be better. Their child would be cared for and cherished.

What he'd felt yesterday had been something different altogether. He'd been afraid of losing *Goldie*, not the child she carried. And if that wasn't unnerving enough, the sharp swing of his mood in the opposite direction when she'd revealed the reason for her visit had been so acute he'd been almost dizzy with it.

That latter feeling had continued to cascade through him all through the night and to this moment. For the first time in his life Gael didn't know whether he wanted to face the problem head-on, as usual, or back away from it.

'Um…say something? *Anything?*'

He chose to back away. 'It's way past time to go.'

She grimaced. 'Right. Fine.'

He smiled. 'And you look magnificent, *querida*.'

When she reached him she punched him lightly in the arm. He responded by catching her offending hand and trailing his lips across the back of it. And as he was rewarded with a smile as luminescent as her eyes Gael felt himself swing towards that unknown high. Felt himself lose the solid ground beneath his feet.

Shaking his head, he took a deep breath and escorted her outside.

They just needed to get today over and done with. Then

he could make the time to examine these *feelings* that had taken hold of him.

The limo ride to Alejandro's adjoining estate took fifteen minutes, and he welcomed the time to answer Goldie's subtle questions about his relationship with his brother. As he answered her he realised it was another first. He didn't find talking about Alejandro as difficult as he once had, and the half-brother he'd once believed he would never willingly accept had become more of a family symbol in his mind than his own mother.

His jaw tightened as he thought of his mother and her threatened visit. Gael hadn't gone out of his way to keep Goldie's pregnancy a secret—he'd told Alejandro and Elise—but he knew his mother kept tabs on him through his household staff. So he hadn't been surprised when she'd called yesterday and dropped subtle hints until he'd divulged the news.

Her immediate announcement that she intended to visit had rubbed him the wrong way. But, no matter how disappointed and bitter he felt over her behaviour, he'd never rejected any overtures from her.

'Gael, if you clench your jaw any harder it'll snap,' Goldie said gently from beside him. 'Same goes for my hand.'

He exhaled sharply, released the tight grip he'd unconsciously placed on her hand and kissed it better. '*Lo siento.* I should warn you—my father will most likely be at the wedding.'

She nodded, her sexy curls bounced. 'And…?'

'And I haven't seen him for over ten years.' He shrugged. 'I can't say how things will go.'

'Okay.' She frowned. 'Your mother won't be there, will she?'

He gave a bitter laugh and shook his head. 'No, but she's coming to the villa tomorrow.'

Her eyes widened. 'Does she know about the baby?'

'Yes, but not about us being married.'

'Do the rest of your family know?'

'I told Andro and Elise last week. As much as I relish being a pain in Alejandro's backside, I didn't want our news to take over their day.'

Her smile warmed him, made him feel less edgy. It felt like the most natural thing in the world to slide his hand around her shoulders and pull her close. Her face turned up to his immediately, and he lost himself in the sensation of kissing her.

His driver's throat-clearing announced their arrival and Gael pulled back reluctantly.

'You owe me another dozen of those when we get home.'

She rolled her eyes, but her smile widened as she slid her hand into his and let him help her out.

Alejandro's villa was almost a carbon copy of his, bar a few minor details—like the absence of a climbing vine in the courtyard and the presence of an art studio built for Elise. His soon-to-be sister-in-law had become an overnight Manga-writing sensation when she'd sold her thirty-story collection for a fortune last year. Now retired from her previous work as a PR consultant, she was pursuing a flourishing full-time Manga-creating career.

Alejandro was descending the stairs when they entered. Gael locked eyes with his half-brother and noted that the acrimony he'd spent years nursing was almost non-existent. In their own stilted way they'd managed to forge a bond—one Gael suddenly hoped would grow stronger.

He eyed his older brother's state of semi-undress with a mocking smirk. 'Are you sure you're getting married in an hour? You look like you've just escaped a drunken sailor's bachelor party.'

Alejandro's mouth quirked in a half-smile. 'This is the

result when I'm not allowed to see my fiancée for almost twenty-four hours. Whoever came up with that idiotic tradition deserves to hang.'

His dark hazel eyes shifted to Goldie. Lingered.

Although Gael knew the depth of feeling between his half-brother and his almost-wife, something very much like jealousy shifted inside him. 'Goldie, this is Alejandro, my bear of a brother. Andro—meet Goldie.'

'Pleased to meet you. And congratulations on both accounts,' Andro drawled.

Goldie smiled and held out her hand. Alejandro's eyes widened infinitesimally before he took her hand and brushed his lips over the back of it.

Gael bristled.

Andro sent him a *payback's a bitch* wink.

He laughed, knowing he deserved the payback for flirting with Elise the first time they'd met.

'Okay. Well played,' he replied.

Goldie looked from him to Andro. 'Am I missing something?'

Gael shook his head. 'Nothing worth mentioning.'

Alejandro laughed under his breath, then his expression sobered. When he glanced at a nearby clock Gael was sure he growled under his breath.

'Do you need my help with anything, or shall we leave you to your growling and staff-frightening?' he mocked.

'If I wasn't absolutely certain Elise would have my hide, I'd sink a double shot of bourbon right about now.' He cast another look at the clock.

Gael laughed. 'Good luck with that. I'll see you at the altar.'

Alejandro nodded, started to walk away and then stopped. '*Mi hermano*, I should warn you—our father is here. He arrived early. You can avoid him if you want, but if you're headed for the salon he'll be in there.'

His eyes narrowed and Gael saw the same ruthlessness that coursed through his veins reflected in his brother's eyes.

'For Elise's sake I would prefer it if you kept your re-union brawl-free—*entiendes*?'

Everything inside Gael tightened, but he managed a nod before his brother walked away. Gael remained where he stood, his senses once more on the finest of edges.

'We don't have to go in there if you don't want to.'

He started, having momentarily forgotten his wife's presence. Resolutely, he shook his head. 'This meeting has been inevitable and it's long overdue. Besides, I have a couple of things to get off my chest,' he said.

He saw the trepidation in her face, wished he could soothe it. But the strides carrying him into the salon demanded all his attention.

Gael's eyes zeroed in on him immediately—saw the moment his father sensed his presence. He stood next to his wife, Alejandro's mother, who was seated with a coffee in her hand.

Tomas Aguilar's gaze sharpened, then widened with a mixture of shock and shame before his expression was neutralised. Gael wished that evidence of shame soothed the part of him he'd for a long time denied was still hurting. Perhaps a few months ago—before Tomas had struck up his illicit affair with his mother once more—it *would* have gone some way to soothe the rejection.

But not now.

He strolled forward until he reached the two of them.

Evita Aguilar glanced up at him, her face reflecting neither acceptance nor rejection. For a moment he felt sorry for her, having tied her destiny to a man with such low scruples. But she averted her gaze and her opinion ceased to matter.

His eyes reconnected with Tomas Aguilar's and again

he saw that momentary flash of shame, this time accompanied by regret.

'It's good to see you…son,' his father said in his native tongue.

Shock held Gael rigid, then he replied tersely, 'English, please. My wife doesn't speak Spanish.'

Both Tomas and Evita started.

'Your *wife*?' His father recovered first, his gaze swinging to Goldie.

'*Sí,*' Gael responded.

After observing her for a few charged seconds, he inclined his head. 'I'm Tomas, and this is my wife, Evita.'

Goldie's smile was a little guarded, but sincere. 'Hello, I'm Goldie.'

Gael's smile felt tight. 'Now that we have the pleasantries over and done with, enjoy the rest of your day.'

His father opened his mouth as if he wanted to say something. Then he glanced down at his wife and shut it again.

More bitterness dredged through Gael. Tightening his hold on Goldie, he led her away.

'I thought you were going to talk to him?'

'So did I, but I find that even that isn't worth doing any more.'

They walked through the salon's French doors and out onto a wide terrace. Beyond the large white columns rolled a sea of green grass, and in the centre was displayed the wedding arch where the ceremony was to be held. Fifty white-linen-draped chairs were divided on either side of the arch for the guests, the first of whom were appearing in limos and luxury cars at the bottom of the long driveway.

'Are you sure?'

Gael was certain the answer was yes until he opened his mouth. 'Maybe not.'

'He looked like he wanted to say something. So maybe let *him* do the talking?'

He glanced down at her with a slight frown. 'Only a short while ago he loomed large over my life, dictated my choices without me realising it.' He shrugged. 'But not so much any more.'

Gael suspected the feeling had something to do with the woman in front of him. Yet another thing to be examined later.

'All the same, you have a chance to get rid of the toxin once and for all. Do you want to look back and wonder if it would've been better to reconnect, to find some answers for yourself?'

Gael remembered hinting at something similar to Alejandro last year. At the time he'd blithely dropped a suggestion that his brother reconnect with the parents he'd walked away from. He knew Alejandro's visit to Seville hadn't been easy. Just as the contemplation of today hadn't been easy for Gael.

Slowly, he nodded. 'Maybe. Now, enough about this. You owe me a dozen kisses. Make good on one of them now, please.'

He was seconds from losing his mind from a kiss alone when footsteps pulled them apart.

Alejandro, followed by his parents, had stepped out onto the terrace, followed by the first of the guests. Waiters were serving mimosas and champagne to keep the guests refreshed until the organ struck up.

When it did, Gael led Goldie to the front row and stepped beside his brother.

The ceremony went without a hitch. Elise smiled widely when Gael welcomed her into the family. Then he watched as his new sister-in-law and his wife fell into instant friendship.

All through the ceremony he'd caught his father's eyes

on him. And after countless trips to the dance floor with Goldie—because he didn't want to miss any opportunity to hold her in his arms—she pushed him towards Tomas.

'It's time, Gael. Come and find me when you're done.'

He caught her before she could walk away. 'No, you come and find *me* in ten minutes. I'm guessing that's about how long I'll be able to stand it before things head south.'

She nodded. 'Okay—deal.'

He watched her sway off the dance floor and immediately be accosted by Elise.

His father was looking his way when he turned.

Gael snagged a whisky from a passing waiter before stepping out of the giant marquee onto the green grass. Above him the night sky twinkled with a thousand stars. But he was too on edge to appreciate the view.

Tomas joined him a minute later.

Gael turned his head and met eyes the same colour as his own. 'I hated you for a very long time.'

He didn't see any reason to mince his words. A second later he realised that he'd spoken in the past tense and spoken in English, because he wasn't ready to have another thing in common with the man whose blood ran through his veins.

A wave of pain and regret passed over Tomas's face. 'I know. And I deserved all of it. For what I did to you, and to your brother, you have every right to hate me.'

'But you're still doing it, aren't you? With my mother?' he accused, and a deep cloying emotion he recognised as pain roughened his voice.

Tomas shook his head. 'No, I'm not.'

Gael snorted. 'I spoke to my mother two weeks ago. She was going to see you.'

'Yes, I met with her to end it.'

Gael stared hard at his father, wondering whether to believe him or not.

'I should never have started things with your mother again. It was selfish. But after Andro came to see me last year I thought you and I might reconnect too…I couldn't summon the courage to reach out directly to you. So I called Katerina.'

Gael cursed under his breath.

Tomas shrugged. 'I think you know that I'm far from perfect. I would go so far as to call myself unworthy of being a father to both my sons. But you and Alejandro have grown into exceptional men, and I remain selfish enough to want to be a part of your lives. I would be honoured to be in your life at some point beyond today, but if you don't think that's a possibility let me tell you now that I'm proud of you.'

Something tugged in his chest. Gael fought to resist it.

'You're *proud*? You told me I was a *mistake*—that I should never have been born! Because of you I don't trust anyone… I don't know how to *love* anyone. I'm a bastard who shouldn't exist.'

Tomas paled, his eyes anguished as he stared at Gael. 'But your relationship with your brother is thriving, and you have a beautiful wife who clearly worsh—'

His laughter cut off his father's words. 'A wife I'm incapable of loving because I don't know how. A wife I've paid for. Because on the night I found out you were still sniffing around my mother I was so angry that I slaked my anger and lust on an innocent woman. After that she fell pregnant with my child, and now I'm tied to her for life—'

The ragged gasp behind him tore through to his very soul.

Even before he turned around Gael knew the landscape of his life had changed irrevocably.

Because six feet behind him Goldie stood, ghost-pale and pain-ravaged, her eyes lost pools as she shook her head slowly.

'*Dios mio*… Goldie.' He started towards her.

Her hands flew out. 'No. Stay away from me!'

He couldn't fathom ever doing that. So he took another step. She stumbled back, her heel catching on the grass.

It was Tomas who went to her aid. Tomas who helped her to her feet with a gentle touch that turned Gael's stomach.

Get your hands off her! he wanted to scream. But the words wouldn't come. His life was too busy flashing before his eyes.

But he had to act. He couldn't lose her.

Unable to believe what was happening, he tried again. 'Please, *querida. Por favor*, let me ex—'

'I swear, if you take one more step towards me I'll scream the place down. And I'll leave you to explain to your brother what went down here.'

They stood frozen, the three of them, in a twisted tableau.

After a handful of seconds Tomas turned to him. 'Let her go, Gael,' his father said to him in Spanish. 'Emotions are too high right now. You can try and repair things later.'

Every instinct screamed against his taking his father's advice. But Goldie's raised chin and her aggressive stance spelled a no-go zone he would find impossible to breach. Still, his chest felt on fire with the idea of letting her go.

'*Amante*, please…' he tried again.

'I'm leaving, Gael, and I don't want you to come with me.'

He glanced at his father. Saw a tiny nod from Tomas.

His ragged sigh felt like a gasp of death. 'I'll tell the driver to take you home. I'll be there in an hour, maybe two. Will…will that be enough time?'

Dios, please let her say yes. He couldn't stand to be away longer than that.

Her mouth twisted. 'More than enough.'

With those two words his wife turned on her spiky heels and walked away.

And with each step she took Gael's senses screamed at him that he was making the biggest mistake of his life.

CHAPTER THIRTEEN

GOLDIE HAD NO RECOLLECTION of what she'd packed or how long it had taken for the driver to deliver her to the airport. But somehow she'd managed to talk to a ticket agent and buy a ticket home.

She still had a couple of days before the last leg of filming commenced for *Soul's Triumph*, for which she thanked God. Because the way she felt right now—the way her heart screamed as if it was being ripped out with each breath she took—she didn't think she could utter one line, never mind a few hundred.

She needed the comfort of home, of her mother, even though she would need to turn around and come right back to Spain in two days to join the cast and crew. Even though Gael would most likely still be here.

She just couldn't bear to be here right now. Because somewhere between his threats and his mockery and his smiles and his exceptional lovemaking she'd fallen in love with the man whose child she carried.

Goldie was too weary to pinpoint when exactly it had happened. It had happened. And even before she'd dared to hope that her fragile feelings might be returned he'd dashed hope in the most devastating way possible.

She only had herself to blame. Everything that had happened from the moment Gael had stepped into that alley six weeks ago had been her fault.

He'd made her no promises, save for telling her that he desired her and wanted the child she carried, and she'd foolishly chosen to let her heart loose in the frantic hope for love.

Squeezing her eyes shut and turning her head away

from the curious passenger next to her, she pressed her fist to her mouth as tears fell.

Maybe the newness of her love meant she could salvage her heart?

Dream on, her shattered heart mocked.

She'd fallen hook, line and sinker.

There was no going back.

Gael tried to outstare his mother-in-law as she bodily barred her front door.

'Sorry, son. She doesn't want to see you.'

There was nothing remotely remorseful in her tone. In fact her body bristled with enough quiet fury for him to realise where Goldie got her strength from.

'Gloria, I just want to talk to her for five minutes.' He used his most reasonable negotiating tone, despite wanting to roar and plead and beg.

Gloria Beckett folded her arms. 'She flew six thousand miles to get away from you. Hoping that a five-minute conversation will fix things is a touch foolish, don't you think?' she challenged.

Suitably chastised, he nodded. 'I'm willing to do whatever it takes, however long it takes. Can you please tell her that?'

He received a shrug in return, and the light violet eyes narrowed on him as he fought the urge to pace. A few times he opened his mouth to speak. Every time, Gloria's chin went up higher, daring him to utter more damning words.

Gael bit his tongue against cursing and tried to see past the woman's shoulder into the house that harboured the woman he loved—the woman he couldn't bear to be apart from for one more second. Gloria's subtle shifting told him he was pushing it.

He shoved his fingers through his hair and tried one more time. 'Is everything okay with her?'

Gloria tossed her blonde head. 'Are you asking about my daughter or about the baby?'

'I'm asking about my *wife*. About *our child*.'

'You should have thought about them before you messed up.'

Spikes of anguish ripped wounds through his heart. 'You're right. I messed up. Badly. But I want…I *need* the chance to fix it. *Por favor?*' he added gruffly when she remained intransigent.

Her stare bored into him for depressingly long seconds before she sighed. 'I'll tell her what you said, son. But don't hold your breath. My daughter is made of strong stuff. She may be bent a little out of shape right now, but she's not broken. If she learns to stand again without you, then you'll have missed your chance.'

His heart dropped to his feet as she stepped back and slammed the door in his face.

He raised his hand to knock again, then froze when he heard the ragged sobs coming from within.

He'd spent the last twenty-four hours in hell. But the woman crying inside the house—the woman his heart yearned for more than it wanted to beat—was hurting. And it was his fault. His being here was hurting her even more.

And yet Gael couldn't leave. Staggering away from the door, he stumbled down the front step and sank onto it. Time ticked by, marched on. He couldn't move.

A light rain began to fall. He watched the droplets form on his arms and drip down his fingers. His numbness kept him insulated. Gael looked up when his driver stepped from the limo and started walking towards him with a blanket. He shook his head once, fiercely, sending the man backtracking. He didn't deserve to feel warm. Besides, compared to the chill in his heart the rain was nothing.

Midnight slowly ticked by. He knew because a clock chimed inside the house.

When he heard a noise behind him he wondered if someone's house pet had chosen to join him in misery.

'Are you trying to make some sort of point by freezing to death on my doorstep?'

Gael stood and jerked round. One lunge up the steps and he was standing in front of her.

'Goldie...*mi amor*...please give me a chance to explain.' He wanted to touch her but he didn't dare—didn't want to risk her bolting back inside.

'I think what I heard was clear enough. You bought me and you don't think you can love me.'

He shook his head, spreading a few raindrops.

She wiped a drop from her cheek, her movements jerky.

'No...I mean, yes, that's what I said. But I didn't mean it. Not like that.'

He stopped and inhaled. How could words fail him, today of all days, when his life depended on it?

'What I meant was, I knew you were leaning towards a yes to my proposal even before I offered you the money and the movie roles. I tagged them on because I wanted to be able to tell myself you'd chosen to marry me because of money.'

Her brows clamped in a frown. 'Why?' she asked, bewildered.

'Hearing that you weren't wanted, that you're a mistake, even once, isn't something you can brush under the carpet and forget easily. Alejandro and I are true brothers now, but there was a time when I thought he was the same as our father in his contempt of me. Having two out of your three closest blood relations reject you as a child is...painful. I convinced myself I was okay with it, but it wasn't until lately—until *you*—that I realised I'd let it cloud a lot of my life's decisions.'

He stopped and took a deep breath.

'I have a confession to make.'

Her eyes grew more wary. 'Yes?'

'I was at Othello on another audition hunt when I heard you performing. I was stunned by you. But then I heard that casting director proposition you.'

She gasped. 'That's why you were so nasty to me when we met? Why you would look at me sometimes with that judgemental look in your eyes?'

He sighed and nodded. 'I saw him touch you, thought you were agreeable to what he'd proposed, but I know now I must have misheard.'

'I didn't understand what he was asking me at first. When I did, I told him to go to hell.'

'I guessed as much. But much later. I'm sorry, Goldie.'

Her lips pursed. 'You were saying about your past clouding your judgement…?'

He nodded. 'When you wouldn't share my bed I thought it was because I wasn't good enough for you, so I lashed out at you. I'm sorry, *mi amor*. I didn't buy you. I threw money at you so I could make myself feel better, tell myself that yearning for you the way I did was okay because I had controlled your entry into my life. It was wrong, Goldie, and I'd give anything to turn back time and unsay what I said about you to my father.'

He watched, cursed as tears slowly filled her eyes.

'*Dios mio*, please don't cry.'

'I won't lie to you, Gael. You hurt me.'

Pain sliced his insides. 'I'll fix it, Goldie. I swear with everything I am I'll spend the rest of my life undoing this hurt.'

Her mouth trembled. 'How?' she croaked.

'Let me love you. Let me earn the right to worship you. You and our child. I'll do whatever you want.'

She licked her lips. 'What if what I want…what I *need*… is you?'

A tremble seized him that had nothing to do with the

chilled wet shirt clinging to his back. 'Then take me. I'm yours.'

'Not until I know…until I'm sure how you feel.'

'How I…? *I love you.* I adore you.'

Her breath caught. 'Please say that again, Gael.'

He closed his eyes, dared to take her hands, bring them to his lips in a reverent kiss. 'I love you, Goldie Aguilar. It may be a new love, but I promise you it's strong, it's yours, and it *will* stand the test of time.'

She freed her hands to cup his face. 'Oh, Gael. I love you too.'

His eyes sprang open. 'You *love* me?'

'Yes. And my love is just as new as yours. I love you, and I'm willing to take a chance on us nurturing each other's love, if you want.'

'*Sí!* I most definitely want.'

She smiled. His heart threatened to burst out of his chest.

She threw her arms around him and stood on tiptoe. 'Kiss me, Gael.'

It was his turn to smile. '*Dios*, you don't need to ask twice. If I remember correctly, you owe me ten kisses.'

'And I would've delivered if you hadn't thrown a spanner in the works.'

His face sobered. '*Lo siento, mi amor.* Forgive me.'

'All is forgiven.'

She fell into his arms again. When they finally parted their eyes were misted with tears.

'Take me home, Gael. Please.'

He nodded solemnly. 'It would be my honour, *mi mujer.*' He swung her up in his arms and started off the porch. About to step off, he paused. 'What about your mother?'

'She knows where my heart is…that I belong where you are.'

His head dropped until their foreheads touched. 'Goldie, I promise I will never make you regret that.'

She settled one hand over his heart, the other over her stomach, where their baby grew.

'And we promise to love and cherish you. For ever.'

EPILOGUE

BY UNANIMOUS AGREEMENT, voted on by their entire family, they held the wedding of their hearts two weeks after their daughter was born. Melina Aguilar lay nestled lovingly in her parents' arms as they renewed their vows in front of a much bigger, much happier congregation at the cathedral in Barcelona. Beneath centuries of history and stained-glass windows, they repeated the vows they'd uttered in that small chapel on Gael's estate.

Alejandro acted as his best man, and took delight in ribbing his brother mercilessly. And they stepped out into the late December evening to the sound of church bells and Christmas carols being sung in Spanish and English.

At the kerb, a vintage car stood waiting, beyond which a police cordon had been set up to keep back the screaming fans who shouted Goldie's name.

Soul's Triumph had been released to huge box office success three months before, and Goldie had become an overnight sensation. She'd been inundated with roles, but had elected to make only one movie a year, to free her to spend the rest of her time being a wife and mother—the two roles she cherished above all else.

She stopped long enough to wave to her fans before she got into the car, which was festooned not just with wedding decorations but also with holly and dozens of sprigs of mistletoe, some of which were also strung along the inside roof. Not that the couple needed any excuse to kiss on the long ride back to the villa once their daughter had fallen into a dreamy nap.

Goldie wrinkled her nose when Gael released her after another long, heady kiss, and indicated the mistletoe. 'Sorry about this. I tried to discourage my mother from doing it.'

Gael laughed. 'So did I with *my* mother—but I think we knew the moment those two got together that we didn't stand a chance.' He flicked a finger at the mistletoe. 'Although I'm not sure whether to be concerned that they believe I need a reason to kiss my wife, or to thank them for supplying me with so many opportunities to do so.'

He pulled her close once more and thoroughly explored her mouth.

They'd chosen to keep their reception small, for family and close friends only. And they arrived back at the house and alighted to join Alejandro and a very pregnant Elise. She was just over seven months, due on Valentine's Day—a fact which was a source of endless mocking ammunition for Gael against his brother.

The brothers had grown closer in the months following their respective marriages, and Goldie counted Elise not just as a sister-in-law but as a friend.

Goldie smiled at her now, as Elise joined her in the hallway and held out her arms for Melina.

Elise waited until the men were headed for the salon before she leaned in close. 'I think Gael has another role up his sleeve for you.' She winked.

Goldie laughed. 'Oh, really?'

Elise nodded. 'I heard him talking. He was asking Alejandro when it would be best to start trying for baby number two.'

Goldie rolled her eyes. 'And do I need two guesses as to what Andro's response was?'

Elise grinned. 'He said, "Immediately, of course."'

Both women laughed, causing their husbands to turn back and stare.

'What's going on?' Gael asked, making his way back to slide both arms around her.

Goldie smiled and kissed him. 'Nothing you need to worry about. Just yet.'

Both Alejandro and Gael groaned. Elise grinned unrepentantly and joined her husband. Goldie watched him tenderly touch Melina's cheek before he caressed his wife's rounded belly.

Gael's arms tightened around her, snagging her attention. She looked up into her husband's eyes. 'I love you. Thank you for marrying me again.'

'I'd marry you every day if I could.'

They kissed until their respective mothers walked past, clearing their throats loudly.

Gael and his mother had found their way back to each other after the end of her short affair with Tomas Aguilar. There was still a little tension all round, but hearts and souls were slowly healing.

Grinning now, Gael and Goldie joined the rest of their family and their closest friends in the large salon for traditional Spanish Christmas tapas and drinks.

As toasts were given and presents exchanged, Goldie saw a look pass between Gael and Alejandro—powerful and visceral and filled with the affection they'd been denied as children but had found in abundance as husbands and brothers.

* * * * *

Don't miss the first part of Maya Blake's
RIVAL BROTHERS *duet*
A DEAL WITH ALEJANDRO
Available now!

If you enjoyed this story, check out these
other great reads from Maya Blake
THE DI SIONE SECRET BABY
SIGNED OVER TO SANTINO
A DIAMOND DEAL WITH THE GREEK
BRUNETTI'S SECRET SON
Available now!

'Are you sure we should be doing this?'

There was a slight easing of the tension around his mouth. 'We're not robbing a bank, Violet.'

'I know, but—'

'If you'd rather not then I can always find someone—'

'No,' Violet said, not even wanting to think about the 'someone else' he would take. 'I'll go. It'll be fun— I haven't been out to dinner for ages.'

He smiled a lopsided smile that made the back of Violet's knees feel weak.

'There's one other thing…'

You want it to be a real date? You want us to see each other as in see each other? You've secretly been in love with me for years and years and years?

Violet forced herself to keep her expression blank while her thoughts pushed against the door of her reasoning like people trying to get in to a closing down sale.

'We'll have to act like a normal dating couple,' he said. 'Hold hands…show affection…and so on.'

And so on? What else did he mean?

Violet nodded as if her head was supported by an elastic band instead of neck muscles. 'Fine. Of course. Good idea. Fab. Brilliant idea. We have to look authentic. Wouldn't want anyone to get the wrong idea… I mean… Well, you know what I mean.'

Cam leaned down and brushed her cheek with his lips, the slight graze of his rough skin making something in her stomach turn over.

'I'll pick you up at seven.'

Melanie Milburne read her first Mills & Boon at age seventeen, in between studying for her final exams. After completing a Master's Degree in Education she decided to write a novel in between settling down to do a PhD. She became so hooked on writing romance the PhD was shelved and her career as a romance writer was born. Melanie is an ambassador for the Australian Childhood Foundation, is a keen dog-lover and trainer and enjoys long walks in the Tasmanian bush.

Books by Melanie Milburne

Mills & Boon Modern Romance

His Mistress for a Week
At No Man's Command
His Final Bargain
Uncovering the Silveri Secret

The Ravensdale Scandals

The Most Scandalous Ravensdale
Ravensdale's Defiant Captive
Awakening the Ravensdale Heiress
Engaged to Her Ravensdale Enemy

The Chatsfield

Chatsfield's Ultimate Acquisition

The Playboys of Argentina

The Valquez Bride
The Valquez Seduction

Those Scandalous Caffarellis

Never Say No to a Caffarelli
Never Underestimate a Caffarelli
Never Gamble with a Caffarelli

Visit the Author Profile page at
millsandboon.co.uk for more titles.

UNWRAPPING HIS CONVENIENT FIANCÉE

BY
MELANIE MILBURNE

First Published in Great Britain 2016
By Mills & Boon, an imprint of HarperCollins*Publishers*
1 London Bridge Street, London, SE1 9GF

© 2016 Melanie Milburne

ISBN: 978-0-263-92138-0

Printed and bound in Spain
by CPI, Barcelona

UNWRAPPING
HIS CONVENIENT
FIANCÉE

To my dear friend Jo Shearing.
You are such a gorgeous person
and I value our friendship so much.
This one is for you. xxxx

CHAPTER ONE

IT WAS THE invitation Violet had been dreading for months. Ten years in a row she had gone to the office Christmas party *sans* partner. *Ten years!* Every year she told herself next year would be different, and yet here she was staring at the red and silver invitation with her stomach in a sinkhole of despair *again*. It was bad enough fielding the *What, no date?* looks and comments from her female colleagues. But it was the thought of being in a crowded room that was the real torture. With all those jostling bodies pressing up so close she wouldn't be able to breathe.

Male bodies.

Bodies that were much bigger and stronger and more powerful than hers—especially when they were drunk…

Violet blinked away the memory. She hardly ever thought about *that* party these days. Well, only now and again. She had come to a fragile sort of peace over it. The self-blame had eased even if the lingering shame had not.

But she was nearly thirty and it was time to move on. More than time. Which meant going to the Christmas party to prove to herself she was back in control of her life.

However, there was the agony of deciding what to wear. Her accountancy firm's Christmas party was considered one of the premier events in the financial sector's calendar. It wasn't just a drinks and nibbles affair. It was an annual gala with champagne flowing like a fountain and Michelin star quality food and dancing to a live band. Every year there was a theme and everyone was expected to be part of the action to demonstrate their commitment to office harmony. This year's theme was *A Star-Struck Christmas*. Which would mean Violet would have to find something Hollywoodish to wear. She wasn't good at glamour. She didn't like drawing attention to herself. She wasn't good at partying full stop.

Violet slipped the invitation between the pages of her book and sighed. Even the London lunchtime café crowd was rubbing in her singleton status. Everyone was a couple. She was the only person sitting on her own. Even a couple pushing ninety were at the table in the window *and* they were holding hands. That would be her parents in thirty years. Still with the magic buzzing between them as it had from the first moment they'd met. Just like her three siblings with their perfect partners. Building their lives together, having children and doing all the things she dreamed of doing.

Violet had watched each of her siblings fall in love. Fast-living Fraser first, racy Rose next and then laid-back Lily. Been to each of their weddings. Been a bridesmaid three times. *Three times. Groan.* She was always in the audience watching romance develop and blossom, but she longed to be on the stage.

Why couldn't she find someone perfect for her?

Was there something wrong with her? Guys occasionally asked her out but it never went past a date or two. Her natural shyness didn't make for scintillating conversation and she had no idea how to flirt... Well, she did if she had a few drinks but that was a mistake she was *not* going to repeat. The problem was that men were so impatient these days, or maybe they always had been that way. But she was not going to sleep with someone just because it was expected of her...or because she was too drunk to say no. She wanted to feel attracted to a man and to feel his attraction to her. To feel frissons of red-hot desire scoot all over her flesh at his touch. To melt when his gaze met hers. To shiver with delight when he pressed his lips to hers.

Not that too many male lips had been pressed to hers lately. She couldn't remember the last time she had been really kissed by a man. Pecks on the cheek from her father and brother or grandfather didn't count.

Violet was rubbish at the dating game. Rubbish. Rubbish. Rubbish. She was going to end up an old and wrinkled spinster living with a hundred and fifty-two cats. With a chest of drawers full of exquisitely embroidered baby clothes for the babies she had longed for since she was a little girl.

'Is this seat taken?'

Violet glanced up at the familiar deep baritone voice, a faint shiver coursing down her spine when her gaze connected with her older brother's best friend from university.

'Cam?' Her voice came out like the sound of a squeaky toy, an annoying habit she hadn't been able to correct since first meeting Cameron McKinnon. She had been eighteen when her brother brought Cam home for the summer—or at least the Scottish version of it—to their family's estate, Drummond Brae, in the Highlands. 'What are you doing here? How are you? Fraser told me you've been living in Greece designing a yacht for someone super-rich. How's it all going? When did you get back?'

Shut up! Funny, but she was never lost for words around Cam. She talked *too* much. She couldn't seem to help it nor could she explain it. He wasn't intimidating or threatening in any way. He was polite, if a little aloof, but he had been a part of her family for long enough for her to get over herself.

But clearly she *hadn't* got over herself.

Cam pulled out the chair opposite and sat down, his knees gently bumping against Violet's underneath the table. The touch was like an electric current moving through her body, heating her in places that had no business being heated. Not by her brother's best friend. Cam was out of her league. Way out.

'I was in the area for a meeting. It finished early and I remembered you mentioning this café once so thought I'd check it out,' he said. 'I've only been back a couple of days. My father is getting remarried just before Christmas.'

Violet's eyes widened to the size of the saucer under her skinny latte. 'Again? How many times is that now? Three? Four?'

His mouth twisted. 'Five. And there's another baby on the way, which brings the total of halfsiblings to six, plus the seven step-siblings, so eleven all together.'

Violet thought her three nephews, two nieces and the baby in the making were a handful—she couldn't imagine eleven. 'How on earth do you keep track of all of their birthdays?'

His half smile looked a little weary around the edges. 'I've set up automatic transfers via online banking. Takes the guesswork out.'

'Maybe I should do that.' Violet stirred her coffee for something to do with her hands. Being in Cam's company—not that it happened much these days—always made her feel like a gauche schoolgirl in front of a college professor. He was an unusual counterpoint to her older brother who was a laugh a minute, life of the party type. Cam was more serious in nature with a tendency to frown rather than smile.

Her gaze drifted towards his mouth—another habit she couldn't quite control when she was around him. His lips were fairly evenly sculpted, although the lower one had a slightly more sensual fullness to it that made her think of long, blood-heating, pulse-racing kisses.

Not that Violet had ever kissed him. Men like Cameron McKinnon didn't kiss girls like her. She was too girl-next-door. He dated women who looked as if they had just stepped out of a photo shoot. Glamorous, sophisticated types who could hold their own in any company without breaking out in hives in case someone spoke to them.

Cam's gaze briefly went to her bare left hand where she was cradling her coffee before coming back to hers in a keenly focused look that made something deep in her belly unfurl like a flower opening its petals to the sun.

'So, how are things with you, Violet?'

'Erm…okay.' At least she wasn't breaking out into hives, but the blush she could feel crawling over her cheeks was almost as bad. Was he thinking—like the rest of her family—*Three times a bridesmaid, never a bride*?

'Only okay?' His look had a serious note to it, a combination of concern and concentration, as if she were the only person he wanted to talk to right then. It was one of the things Violet liked about him—one of the many things. He wasn't so full of himself that he couldn't spare the time to listen. She often wondered if he'd been around to talk to after that wretched party, during her first and only year at university, her life might not have turned out the way it had.

Violet stretched her mouth into her standard everything-is-cool-with-me smile. 'I'm fine. Just busy with work and Christmas shopping and stuff. Like you, I have a lot of people to buy for now with all my nephews and nieces. Did you know Lily and Cooper are expecting? Mum and Dad are planning the usual big Christmas at Drummond Brae. Has Mum invited you? She said she was going to. The doctors think it will be Grandad's last Christmas so we're all making an effort to be there for him.'

Cam's mouth took on a rueful slant. 'My father's decided to upstage Christmas with his wedding on Christmas Eve.'

'Where's it being held?'

'Here in London.'

'Maybe you could fly up afterwards,' Violet said. 'Or have you got other commitments?' Other commitments such as a girlfriend. Surely he would have one. Men like Cam wouldn't go long between lovers. He was too handsome, too rich, too intelligent, too sexy. Too everything. Cam had never broadcast his relationships with women the way her brother Fraser had before he'd fallen madly in love with Zoe. Cam was intensely private about his private life. So private it made Violet wonder if he had a secret lover stashed away somewhere, someone he kept out of the glaring spotlight that his work as an internationally acclaimed naval architect attracted.

'I'll see,' he said. 'Mum will expect a visit, especially now that her third husband Hugh's left her.'

Violet frowned. 'Oh, no. I'm sorry to hear that. Is she terribly upset?'

Cam gave her a speaking look. 'Not particularly. He drank. A lot.'

'Oh…'

Cam's family history was nothing short of a saga. Not that he'd ever said much about it to her, but Fraser had filled in the gaps. His parents went through a bitter divorce when he was six and promptly remarried and set up new families, collecting other biological children and stepchildren along the way. Cam was jostled between the various households until he was sent to boarding school when he was eight. Violet could picture him as a little boy—studious, quietly observing on the sidelines, not making a fuss and avoiding one where it was made. He was still like that. When he came to visit her family for weddings, christenings or other gatherings he was always on the fringe, standing back with a drink in his hand he rarely touched, quietly measuring the scene with his navy-blue gaze.

The waitress came over to take Cam's order with a smile that went beyond *I'm your server, can I help you?* to *Do you want my number?*

Violet tried to ignore the little dart of jealousy that spiked her in the gut. It was none of her business who he flirted with. Why should she care if he picked up a date from her favourite café? Even if she had been coming here for years and no one had asked for *her* number.

Cam looked across the table at her. 'Would you like another coffee?'

Violet put her hand over the top of her latte glass. 'No, I'm good.'

'Just a long black, thanks,' Cam said to the waitress with a brief but polite smile.

Violet waited until the girl had left before she spoke. 'Cra—ack.'

His brow furrowed. 'Pardon?'

She gave him a teasing smile. 'Didn't you hear that girl's heart breaking?'

He looked puzzled for a moment, and then faintly annoyed. 'She's not my type.'

'Describe your type.' *Why had she asked that?*

The bridge between Cam's ink-black eyebrows was still pleated in three tight vertical lines. 'I've been too busy for any type just lately.' His phone, which was sitting on the table, beeped with a message and he glanced at it before turning off the screen, his lips pressing so firmly his mouth turned bone-white.

'What's wrong?'

He forcibly relaxed his features. 'Nothing.'

The phone beeped again and his mouth flattened once more. He clicked the mute button and slipped the phone into his jacket pocket as the waitress set his coffee down on the table between them. 'So, how's work?'

Violet glanced at the invitation peeping out of the pages of her book. Was it her imagination or was it flashing like a beacon? She surreptitiously pushed it back out of sight. 'Fine…'

Cam followed the line of her gaze. 'What's that?'

'Nothing… Just an invitation.'

'To?'

Violet was sure her cheeks were as the red as the baubles on the invitation. 'The office Christmas party.'

'You going?'

She couldn't meet his gaze and looked at the sugar bowl instead. Who knew there were so many different artificial sweeteners these days? Amazing. 'I kind of have to… It's expected in the interests of office harmony.'

'You don't sound too keen.'

Violet lifted one of her shoulders in a shrug. 'Yeah, well, I'm not really a party girl.' Not any more. Her first and only attempt at partying had ended in a blurry haze of regret and self-recrimination. An event she was still, all these years on, trying to put behind her with varying degrees of success.

But secret shame cast a long shadow.

'It's a pretty big affair, isn't it?' Cam said. 'No expense spared and so on, I take it?'

Violet rolled her eyes. 'Ironic when you consider it's a firm of bean counters.'

'Pretty successful bean counters,' Cam said. 'Well done you for nailing a job there.'

Violet didn't like to admit how far from her dream job it actually was. After quitting her university studies, a clerical job in a large accounting firm had seemed a good place to blend into the background. But what had suited her at nineteen was feeling less satisfying as she approached thirty. She couldn't shake off the nagging feeling she should be doing more with her life. Extending herself. Reaching her potential instead of placing limitations on herself. But since that party… Well, everything had been put on pause. It was like her life had jammed and she couldn't move forward.

The vibration of Cam's phone drew Violet's gaze to his top pocket. Not just to his top pocket but his chest in general. He was built like an endurance athlete, tall and lean with muscles where a man needed them to be and where a woman most liked to see them. And she was no exception. His skin was tanned and his dark brown hair had some surface highlights where the strong sunlight of Greece had caught and lightened it. He had cleanly shaven skin, but there was enough dark stubble to suggest he hadn't been holding the door for everyone else when the testosterone was dished out.

'Aren't you going to answer that?' Violet asked.

'It'll keep.'

'Work or family?'

'Neither.'

Violet's eyebrows lifted along with her intrigue. 'A woman?'

He took out the phone and held his finger on the off switch with a determined set to his features. 'Yeah. One that won't take no for an answer.'

'How long have you been dating her?'

'I haven't been dating her.' Cam's expression was grim. 'She's a client's wife. A valuable client.'

'Oh… Tricky.'

'Very. To the tune of about forty million pounds tricky.'

Forty million? Violet came from a wealthy background but even she had trouble getting her head around a figure like that. Cam designed yachts for the super-wealthy. He'd won a heap of awards for his designs and become extremely wealthy in the process. Some of the yachts he designed were massive, complete with marble en suite bathrooms with hot tubs, and dining and sitting rooms that were plush and palatial. One yacht even had its own library and lap swimming pool. But, even so, it amazed her how much a rich person would pay for a yacht they only used now and again. 'Seriously? You're being paid forty million to design a yacht?'

'No, that's the cost of the yacht once it's complete,' he said. 'But I get paid a pretty decent amount to design it.'

How much was *pretty decent*? Violet longed to ask but decided against it out of politeness. 'So...what will you do? Keep ignoring this woman's calls and messages?'

He let out a short, gusty breath. 'I'll have to get the message across one way or the other. I'm not the sort of guy who gets mixed up with married women.' His mouth twisted again. 'That would be my father.'

'Maybe if she sees you've got someone else it will drive home the message.' Violet picked up her almost empty latte and looked at him over the rim of the glass. '*Is* there someone else?' *Arrgh! Why did you ask that?*

Cam's gaze met hers and that warm sensation bloomed deep and low in her belly again. His dark blue eyes were fringed with thick ink-black lashes she would have killed for. There was something about his intelligent eyes that always made her feel he saw more than he let on. 'No,' he said. 'You?'

Violet coughed out a self-effacing laugh. 'Don't *you*

start. I get enough of that from my family, not to mention my friends and flatmates.'

Cam gave her a wry smile. 'I don't know what's wrong with the young men of London. You should've been snapped up long ago.'

A pin drop silence fell between them.

Violet looked at her coffee glass as if it were the most fascinating thing she had ever seen. The way her cheeks were going, the café's chef would be coming out to cook the toast on her face to save on electricity. How had she got into this conversation? Awkward. Awkward. Awkward. How long was the canyon of silence going to last? Should she say something?

But what?

Her mind was blank.

She was hopeless at small talk. It was another reason she was terrible at parties. The idle conversation gene had skipped her. Her sisters and brother were the ones who could talk their way out of or into any situation. She was the wallflower of the family. All those years of being overshadowed by verbose older siblings and super articulate parents had made her conversationally challenged. She was used to standing back and letting others do the talking. Even her tendency to gabble like a fool around Cam had suddenly deserted her.

'When's your office party?'

Violet blinked and refocused her gaze on Cam's. 'Erm…tomorrow.'

'Would you like me to come with you?'

Violet had trouble keeping her jaw off the table and

her heart from skipping right out of her chest and landing in his lap. *Best not think about his lap.* 'But why
would you want to do that?'

He gave a casual shrug of one broad shoulder. 'I'm
free tomorrow night. Thought it might help you mingle
if you had a wingman, so to speak.'

Violet gave him a measured look. 'Is this a pity
date?'

'It's not a date, period.' Something about his adamant tone rankled. 'Just a friend helping out a friend.'

Violet had enough friends. It was a date she wanted.
A proper date. Not with a man on a mercy mission. Did
he think she was completely useless? A romance tragic
who couldn't find a prince to take her to the ball? She
didn't even *want* to go to the ball, thank you very much.
The ball wasn't that special. All those people drinking
and eating too much and dancing till the wee hours to
music so loud you couldn't hear yourself shout, let alone
think. 'Thanks for the offer but I'll be fine.'

Violet pushed her coffee glass to one side and
picked up her book. But, before she could leave the
table, Cam's hand came down on her forearm. 'I didn't
mean to upset you.'

'I'm not upset.' Violet knew her crisp tone belied her
statement. Of course she was upset. Who wouldn't be?
He was rescuing her. What could be more insulting than
a man asking you out because he felt sorry for you? Had
Fraser said something to him? Had one of her sisters?
Her parents? Her grandfather? Why couldn't everyone
mind their own business? All she got these days was

pressure. *Why aren't you dating anyone? You're too fussy. You're almost thirty.* It never ended.

The warmth of Cam's broad hand seeped through the layers of her winter clothing, awakening her flesh like a heat pack on a frostbitten limb. 'Hey.'

Violet hadn't pouted since she was about five but she pouted now. She could find a date. Sure she could. She could sign up to one of any number of dating websites or apps and have a hundred dates. If she put her mind to it she could be engaged by Christmas. Well, maybe that was pushing it a bit. 'I'm perfectly able to find my own date, okay?'

He gave her arm the tiniest squeeze before releasing it. 'Of course.' He sat back in his chair, his forehead creased in a slight frown. 'I'm sorry. It was a bad idea. Seriously bad.'

Why was it? And why *seriously* bad? Violet cradled her book close to her chest where her heart was beating a little too fast. Not fast enough to call for a defibrillator but not far off. His touch had done something to her, like he had turned a setting on in her body she hadn't known she'd had. Her senses were sitting up and alert instead of slumped and listless. Had he ever touched her before? She tried to think… Sometimes in the past he would kiss her on the cheek, a chaste brotherly sort of kiss. But lately…since Easter, in fact…there had been no physical contact from him. None at all. It was as if he had deliberately kept his distance. That last holiday weekend at home, she remembered him coming into one of the sitting rooms at Drummond Brae and going straight back out again with a muttered apology when he'd found her curled up on one of the sofas with her embroidery. Why had he done that? What was wrong with her that he couldn't bear to be left alone with her?

Violet picked up her scarf and wound it around her neck. 'I have to get back to work. I hope your father's wedding goes well.'

'It should do, he's had enough practice.' He drained his coffee and stood, snatching his jacket from the back of the chair and slinging it over his shoulder. 'I'll walk you back to your office. I'm heading that way.'

Violet knew the tussle over who paid for the coffee was inevitable so when he offered she let him take care of it for once. 'Thanks,' she said once he'd settled the bill.

'No problem.'

He put a gentle hand in the small of her back to guide her out of the way of a young mother coming in with a pram and a squirming, red-faced toddler. The sizzling heat of his touch moved along the entire length of Violet's spine, making her aware of her femininity as if he had stroked her intimately.

Get a grip already.

This was the problem with being desperate and dateless. The slightest brush of a male hand turned her into a wanton fool. Stirring up needs that she hadn't even registered as needs until now.

But it wasn't just any male hand.

It was Cam's hand…connected to a body that made her think of smoking-hot sex. Not that she knew what smoking-hot sex actually felt like. The only sex she'd had was a surrealist blur with an occasional flashback of two or three male faces looming over her, talking about her, not to her. Definitely not the sort of romantic scene she had envisaged when she'd hit puberty. It was another thing she'd miserably failed at doing. Each of her siblings had successfully navigated their way through the dating minefield, all of them now partnered with their soul mate. *Was* she too fussy? Had that night at that party permanently damaged her self-esteem and sexual confidence? Why should it when she could barely remember it in any detail?

She had been surrounded by love and acceptance all her life. There should be no reason for her to feel inadequate or not quite up to the mark. But somehow love—even a vague liking for someone of the opposite sex—had so far escaped her.

Violet walked out to the footpath with Cam, where the rain had started to fall in icy droplets. She popped open her umbrella but Cam had to bend almost double to gain any benefit from it. He took the handle from her and held the umbrella over both of their heads. Her fingers tingled where his brushed hers, the sensation travelling all through her body as if running along an electric network.

Trying to keep dry, as well as out of the way of the bustling Christmas shopping crowd, put Violet so close to the tall frame of his body she could smell the clean sharp fragrance of his aftershave, the woodsy base notes reminding her of a cool, shaded pine forest.

To anyone looking in from the outside they would look like a romantically involved couple, huddled under the same umbrella, Cam's stride considerably slowing to match hers.

They came to the large Victorian building where the accounting firm Violet worked as an accounts clerk was situated. But just as she was about to turn and say her goodbyes to Cam, one of the women who worked with her came click-clacking down the steps. Lorna ran her gaze over Cam's tall figure standing next to Violet. 'Well, well, well. Things finally looking up for you, are they, Violet?'

Violet ground her teeth so hard she could have moonlighted as a nutcracker. Lorna wasn't her favourite workmate, far from it. She had a tendency to gossip to stir up trouble. Violet knew for a fact their boss only kept Lorna on because she was brilliant at her job—and because she was having a full-on affair with him. 'Off to lunch?' she asked, refusing to respond to Lorna's taunt.

Lorna gave an orthodontist's website smile and aimed her lash-fluttering gaze at Cam. 'Will we be seeing you at the office Christmas party?'

Cam's arm snaked around Violet's waist, a protective band of steel that made every nerve in her body jump up and down and squeal with delight. 'We'll be there.'

We will? Violet waited until Lorna had gone before looking up at Cam's unreadable expression. 'Why on earth did you say that? I told you I didn't want a—'

He stepped out from under the umbrella and placed

the handle back in her hand. Violet had to extend her arm upwards to its fullest range to keep the umbrella high enough to maintain eye contact. 'I'll strike a deal with you,' he said. 'I'll come to your Christmas party if you'll come to a dinner with my client tonight.'

Violet screwed up her face. 'The one with the persistent wife?'

'I've been thinking about what you said back at the café. What better way to send her the message I'm not interested than to show her I'm seeing someone?'

'But we're not...' she disguised a little gulp '...seeing each other.'

'No, but no one else needs to know that.'

You don't have to be so darned emphatic about it. Violet chewed at one side of her mouth. 'How are we going to keep this...quiet?'

'You mean from your family?'

'You know what my mother's like.' Violet gave a little eye roll. 'One whiff of us going on a date together, and she'll be posting wedding invitations quicker than you can say *I do.*'

There was another yawning silence.

I do?

Are you nuts? You said the words 'I do' to the man who views weddings like people view the plague!

Something shifted in Cam's expression—a blink of his eyes, a flicker of a muscle in his lean cheek, a stretching of his mouth into a smile that didn't involve his eyes. 'We'll cross that bridge if we come to it.'

If we come to it? There was no *if* about it. That bridge

was going to blow up in their faces like a Stage Five firecracker on Guy Fawkes Night. Violet knew her family too well. They were constantly on the lookout for any signs of her dating. MI5 could learn a thing or two from her mother and sisters. How was she going to explain a night out with Cam McKinnon? 'Are you sure we should be doing this?'

There was a slight easing of the tension around his mouth. 'We're not robbing a bank, Violet.'

'I know, but—'

'If you'd rather not, then I can always find someone—'

'No,' Violet said, not even wanting to think about the 'someone' he would take. 'I'll go. It'll be fun—I haven't been out to dinner for ages.'

He smiled a lopsided smile that made the back of Violet's knees feel like someone was tickling them with a feather. 'There's one other thing...'

You want it to be a real date? You want us to see each other as in 'see each other'? You've secretly been in love with me for years and years and years? Violet kept her face blank while the thoughts pushed against the door of her reasoning like people trying to get into a closing down sale.

'We'll have to act like a normal dating couple,' he said. 'Hold hands and...stuff.'

And stuff?

What other stuff?

Violet nodded like her head was supported by an elastic band instead of neck muscles. 'Fine. Of course.

Good idea. Fab. Brilliant idea. We have to look authentic. Wouldn't want anyone to get the wrong idea… I mean, well, you know what I mean.'

Cam leaned down and brushed her cheek with his lips, the slight graze of his rougher skin making something in her stomach turn over. 'I'll pick you up at seven.'

Violet took a step backwards to enter the building but stumbled over the first step and would have fallen if it wasn't for Cam's hand shooting out to steady her. 'You okay?' he asked with a concerned frown.

Violet looked at his stubble-surrounded mouth that just moments ago had been against the smooth skin of her cheek. Had he felt that same sensation ricochet through his body? Had he wondered in that infinitesimal moment what it would feel like to press his lips to hers? Not in a brotherly kiss, but a proper man-wants-woman kiss? She sent the point of her tongue over the surface of her lips, her breath hitching when he tracked every millimetre of the movement. *Keep it light.* 'For a moment there I thought you were going to kiss me,' Violet said with a little laugh.

The navy-blue of his gaze turned three shades darker before glancing at her mouth and back again. But then his hand dropped from her arm as if her skin had scorched him. 'Let's not go there.'

But I want *to go there. I want to. I want to. I want to.* Violet kept her smile in place even though it felt like it was stitched to her mouth. 'Yes, that would be taking things too far. I mean, not that I don't find you attractive or anything, but us kissing? Not such a great idea.'

There was the sound of heels click-clacking behind her and Violet turned to see Lorna coming back. 'Silly me. I forgot my phone,' Lorna said and with a sly smile at Cam added, 'Aren't you going to kiss her and let her get back to work?'

Violet sneaked a glance at Cam but instead of looking annoyed at Lorna's comment he smiled an easy smile and reached for Violet's hand and drew her against his side. 'I was just getting to that,' he said.

Violet assumed he would wait till Lorna had gone back into the building before releasing her but Lorna didn't go back into the building. She stood three steps up from them with that annoying smirk on her mouth as if daring Cam to follow through. Cam turned his back to Lorna and slipped a hand under Violet's hair, cupping the nape of her neck, making every nerve beneath her skin pirouette.

'You don't have to do this…' Violet whispered.

Cam brought his mouth down to within a whisker of hers. 'Yes, I do.'

And then he did.

CHAPTER TWO

CAM PRESSED HIS lips to Violet's mouth and a bomb went off in his head, scattering his common sense like flying shrapnel. *What are you doing?* But he didn't want to listen to his conscience. He had wanted to kiss her from the moment he'd walked into that café earlier and now her annoying workmate had given him the perfect excuse to do so. Violet's mouth tasted like a combination of milk and honey, her lips soft and pliable beneath his. He drew her ballerina-like body even closer, his body responding with a fierce rush of blood to his groin. Her small breasts were pressed against his chest, her slim hips against his, her hands gripping the front of his jacket as if she couldn't stand upright without his support. Hell, he was having trouble keeping upright himself, apart from one part of his anatomy.

It's time to stop. You should stop. You need to stop. The chanting of his brain was attempting to drown out the frantic panting of his body. *Yes. Yes. Yes.* Clearly it had been too long between drinks. His self-control was usually spot on. But he didn't want the kiss to end.

He felt as though he might *die* if it did. Lust pounded through his body, rampaging, roaring lust that made every cell in his system shudder with need. Intense need. Need that made him think of sweating, straining bodies and tangled sheets and blissful, euphoric release.

She gave a little mewling sound when he shifted position, her mouth flowering open to the hungry glide of his tongue. He explored her sweet interior, his pulse rate going off the scale when her tongue came into play with his. Her tongue was hesitant at first, but then she made another whimpering sound and grew more and more confident, flirting with his tongue, darting away and coming back for the sensual heat of his strokes. He put his hands on her hips, holding her to the throbbing ache of his body.

She felt so damn good, like she was made for his exact proportions. Had he ever felt so aroused so quickly? It was like he was a hormone-driven teenager all over again. He seriously had to get his work/life balance sorted out. How long had it been since he'd slept with a woman? Too long if his trigger was being tripped by just a kiss.

A car tooting on its way past was the only thing that got through to him. Cam put Violet from him, holding her by the hands so as to help her keep her balanced. He did a quick glance over his shoulder but Violet's workmate had disappeared. Not surprising given he'd lost track of time during that kiss.

Violet blinked as if trying to reorient herself. Her

small pink tongue did a quick circuit of her lips and his groin groaned and growled with need. He could almost imagine how it would feel to have that shy little tongue move over his body. He couldn't remember a kiss being so…consuming. He had forgotten where they were. He had darned near forgotten who he was. He might be seriously hot for Violet but he wasn't going to act on it. She was his best mate's kid sister, the baby of the family he adored.

It was a boundary he was determined not to cross. Or at least not to cross any further than he just had.

Cam released her hands and gave a relaxed smile he hoped disguised the bedlam of base needs in his body baying for more. 'That was quite a kiss.'

Violet gave him a distracted little smile that seemed to set off a rippling tide of worry in her toffee-brown eyes. 'Y-you caught me by surprise…'

Right back at you, sweetheart. 'Yes, well, I figured your workmate wasn't going to go away until we got it over with. Is she usually that persistent?'

'You caught her on a good day.'

Cam wondered how much bullying went on in that office. Violet was a gentle soul who would find it hard to stand up for herself in a dog-eat-dog environment. Even within the loving and loud bosom of her family, she had the tendency to shrink away to a quiet corner rather than engage in the lively banter. Before he could stop himself, he brushed a fingertip down the pinked slope of her cheek. 'You're completely safe with me, Violet. You do know that, don't you? Kissing is all we'll do if the need should arise.' *I hope fate isn't listening, otherwise you are toast.*

Her small white teeth sank into the pillow of her lower lip and she lowered her gaze to a point at the base of his neck. 'Of course.' Her voice was not much more than a scratchy whisper.

He stepped back from her. 'I'd better let you get back to work.'

She turned without another word and climbed the steps, not even glancing back before disappearing into the building when she got to the top.

Cam let out a long breath and walked on. It was all well and good to kiss her but that was as far as it could go. He wasn't what Violet was looking for. He wasn't the settling down type. Maybe one day he would think about setting up a home with someone, but right now he had too much going on in his career. That was his focus, his priority. Not relationships.

Marriage might work for some people, but it didn't work for others—his parents and their collection of exes being a case in point. Too many people got hurt when relationships broke down. It was like a boulder dropped into a pond; the ripples of hurt went on for years. He was still sidestepping the pain his parents' divorce had caused. It wasn't that he'd wanted them to stay together. Far from it. They hadn't been happy from the get-go because his mother had been in love and his father hadn't and then his father had dumped his mother for someone younger and more attractive and had been outrageously difficult about the divorce.

His mother had responded by being equally difficult and, inevitably, Cam had got caught up in the middle until eventually he'd been dumped at boarding school and left to fend for himself. In the years since, his parents had changed partners so often Cam had trouble keeping track of names and addresses and birthdays. He'd had to set up a database on his phone to keep on top of them all.

But he needed to get Sophia Nicolaides off his case and taking Violet was the way to do it. Sophia was too crafty to spot a fake. He couldn't bring someone he'd only just met to the dinner. It had to be someone he already felt comfortable with and her with him. Violet was shy around him, but then, she was shy around most people. It was part of her charm, the fact that she didn't flaunt her assets or draw attention to herself. He'd been upfront about the fact it wasn't a date and he was sure she too wouldn't want to compromise the friendship that had built up over the years.

At least they'd got the first kiss out of the way.

And what a kiss. Who knew that sweet little mouth could wreak such havoc on his self-control? He would have to watch himself. Violet wasn't street smart like the women he normally dated. She wasn't the sleep-around type. He wondered if she was still a virgin. Not likely since she was close to thirty, but who knew for sure? It wasn't exactly a question he'd feel comfortable asking her. It was none of his business.

Cam ran his tongue over his lips and tasted her. Even

if he never kissed her again, it was going to take a long time to forget that kiss.

If he ever did.

Violet tried on seven different outfits until she finally settled on a navy-blue velvet dress that fell just above the knee. It reminded her of the colour of Cam's unusual eyes. *Maybe that was why you bought it?* No. Of course not. She'd bought it because she liked it. It suited her. She loved the feel of the fabric against her skin. She slipped her feet into heels and turned to view her reflection in the cheval mirror.

Her flatmate, Amy, popped her head around the door. 'Gosh, you look scrumptious. I love that colour on you. Are you going out?'

Violet smoothed the front of her dress over her stomach and thighs, turning this way and that to check if she had visible panty line. No. All good. 'You don't think it's too…plain?'

'It's simple but elegant,' Amy said, perching on the end of Violet's bed. 'So who's the guy? Have I met him? No, of course I haven't because you've never brought anyone here, that I know of.'

Violet slipped on some pearl drop earrings her parents had given her for her twenty-first birthday. 'He's a friend of my brother's. I've known him for ages.' *And he kisses like a sex god and my body is still humming with desire hours later.*

Amy's eyes danced. 'Ooh! A friends-to-lovers thing. How exciting.'

Violet sent her a quelling look. 'Don't get your hopes up. I'm not his type.' Cam couldn't have been more succinct. *'Kissing is all we'll do.'* She hadn't turned him on… Well, she had, but clearly not enough that he wanted to take things further.

The doorbell sounded and Amy jumped off the bed. 'I'll get it. I want to check out your date to see if he passes muster. Flat twenty-three B has certain standards, you know.'

Violet came out a few seconds later to see Amy giving an impression of a star-struck teen in front of a Hollywood idol. Violet had to admit Cam looked heart-stoppingly fabulous in a suit. He wasn't the designer-wear type, but the sharp tailoring of his charcoal-grey suit fitted his tall frame to perfection and the white dress shirt and blue and grey striped tie highlighted the tanned and healthy tone of his skin and the intense blue of his eyes.

Cam's gaze met Violet's and a tiny invisible fist punched her in the stomach.

'You look stunning.' The deep huskiness of his voice was like a caressing stroke down the entire length of her spine. The way his eyes dipped to her lipgloss-coated mouth made her relive every pulse-racing second of that kiss. Was he remembering it too? How it had felt to have their tongues intimately entwined? How it had felt to taste each other, to feel each other's response? How it had felt to end it without the satiation both their bodies craved?

Violet brushed an imaginary strand of hair off her

face. 'This is one of my flatmates, Amy Kennedy. Amy, this is Cameron McKinnon, a friend from way back.'

When Cam took Amy's hand, Violet thought her flatmate was going to fall into a swoon. 'Pleased to meet you,' he said.

Amy's cheeks were bright pink and her mouth seemed to be having trouble closing. 'Same.'

Violet picked up her coat and Cam stood behind her and helped her into it. His body was so close she could feel its warmth and smell that intriguing blend of his aftershave. He briefly rested his hands on the tops of her shoulders before stepping away. While he was facing the other way, Amy gave her the thumbs-up sign, eyes bright with excitement. Violet picked up her purse and followed Cam to the door.

'Have a good time!' Amy's voice had a sing-song quality to it that made Violet feel like a teen going out on her first date.

Cam led her to his car, parked a few metres down the rain-slicked street. 'How many flatmates do you have?'

'Two. Amy and Stefanie.'

Violet slipped into the plush leather seat of his showroom-perfect convertible. There was no way she could ever imagine a couple of kids' seats in the back. His car was like his lifestyle—free and fast. Not that he was a hardened playboy or anything. But he was hardly a monk. He was a healthy man of thirty-four, in the prime of his life. Why wouldn't he make the most of his freedom? How many women had experienced that divine mouth? That gorgeous body and all the sensual delights it promised?

Probably more than she wanted to think about.

'I'm sorry about Amy back there,' Violet said after they were on the move. 'She can be a bit over the top.'

Cam glanced her way. 'Did I pass the test?'

Violet could feel an annoying blush creeping over her cheeks. 'The girls have a checklist for potential dates. No smokers, no heavy drinkers, no drugs, no tattoos. Must be gainfully employed, must respect women, must wear a condom... I mean during...you know... not at the time of meeting... That would be ridiculous.'

Cam's deep laugh made the base of her spine quiver. 'Good to know I tick all the boxes.'

Violet swivelled in her seat to look at him. 'So what's on your checklist?'

He appeared to think about it for a moment or maybe it was because he was concentrating on the traffic snarl ahead. 'Nothing specific. Intelligence is always good, a sense of humour.'

'Looks?'

He gave a lip shrug. 'Not as important as other qualities.'

'But you've only ever dated incredibly beautiful women. I've seen photos of them. Fraser showed me.'

'Mere coincidence.'

Violet snorted. 'Well-to-do men are selective when choosing a lover. Women, in general, are much more accepting over looks. It's a well-known fact.'

'What are you looking for in a partner?'

Violet looked at her hands where they were clutching her purse. 'I guess I want what my parents have—a partner who loves me despite my faults and is there for me no matter what.'

'Your parents are a tough act to follow.'

She let out a long sigh. 'Tell me about it.'

The dinner was at a restaurant in Soho. Cam's client had booked a private room and he and his wife were already seated at the table when they arrived. The man rose and greeted Cam warmly. 'So good you could join us. Sophia has been excited about it all day, haven't you, *agapi mou*?'

Sophia was excited all right. Violet could see the sultry gleam in those dark eyes as they roved Cam's body like she was mentally undressing him.

Cam's arm was around Violet's waist. 'Nick and Sophia Nicolaides, this is my partner Violet. Darling, this is Nick and Sophia.'

Partner? What was wrong with girlfriend? Partner sounded a little more…permanent. But then he wanted to make sure Sophia got the message loud and clear. 'Darling' was a nice touch, however. Violet quite liked that. No one had ever called her that before. She got 'poppet' and 'wee one' from her parents and her grandad called her Vivi like her siblings did. 'I'm very pleased to meet you both,' she said. 'Cam's told me all about you. Are you in London long?'

'Until New Year,' Nick said. 'Sophia's never had an English Christmas before.'

Sophia looked like all her Christmases and New Year's Eves had come at once when she slid her hand through Cam's arm. 'You're a dark horse, aren't you?' she said. 'You never told us you had a partner. Are you engaged?'

Cam's smile looked a little tight around the edges as he disentangled himself from Sophia's tentacle-like arm. 'Not yet.'

Not yet? Didn't that imply he was actually considering it? Violet had trouble keeping her expression composed. Even though she knew he was only saying it for the sake of appearances, her heart still gave an excited little leap. Not that she was in love with him or anything. She was just imagining what it would be like if she was. How it would feel to have him look at her with that tender look he was sending her way and actually mean it. For real.

Sophia smiled but it didn't crease her eyes at the corners, although that could have been because of Botox. *Meow.* Violet wasn't normally the critical type but something about the predatory nature of Nick Nicolaides' wife irritated her beyond measure. Sophia looked like the type of woman for whom the word 'no' was a challenge rather than an obstacle. What Sophia wanted, Sophia got. No matter what. And Sophia wanted Cam. It was a wonder Nick couldn't see it. Or was Nick so enamoured with his young, stunningly beautiful wife he couldn't see what was right before his eyes?

Violet decided it was time to draw the line, not in

sand but in concrete. She gazed up at Cam with what she hoped passed for besotted devotion. 'I didn't know you were thinking along those lines this early in our relationship.'

He leaned down and dropped a kiss to her upturned mouth. 'It's never too early to say I love you.'

Violet smiled a blissfully happy smile. Who said she couldn't act? Or maybe she wasn't acting. Hearing him say those words, even though deep down she knew he didn't mean them, had a potent effect on her. No one, apart from her family, had told her they loved her. 'I love you, too, baby.' She turned her smile up a notch.

Nick slapped Cam on the shoulder. 'Let's have a drink to celebrate in advance of the announcement.'

Champagne was ordered and served and the glasses held up in a toast to an engagement that wasn't going to happen. It felt weird to be part of such a deception but Violet had no choice but to run with it. Sophia kept looking at her, sizing her up as if wondering what on earth Cam saw in her. Violet didn't let it intimidate her, which was surprising as, under normal circumstances, she would have retreated to the trenches by now.

Dinner was a long, drawn-out affair because Nick wanted to discuss business with Cam, which left Violet to make conversation with Sophia. Never good at small talk, Violet had exhausted her twenty question checklist before the entrées were cleared away.

Cam came to her rescue after what was left of their mains was removed. He excused them both from the table and escorted her out to the restroom. 'You're doing great, Violet. Hang in there.'

'If looks could kill, I'd be lying in a morgue with a tag on my big toe right about now,' Violet said through clenched teeth. 'She is *such* a cow. She's not even trying to hide how she's lusting after you. Why can't Nick see it? She's so brazen it's nauseating.'

Cam's mouth was set in a grim line. 'I think he does see it but he's in denial. I don't want to be the one to take the bullet for pointing it out to him. This project is too important to me. It's the biggest contract I've done and more could follow. Nick has a lot of contacts. Word of mouth is everything in my business.'

Violet studied his tense features for a moment. 'If she weren't married would she be the type of woman you'd be involved with?'

'God, no.' His tone was adamant. 'What sort of man do you think I am?'

'She's incredibly beautiful.'

'So are you.'

Violet moistened her lips. 'You're terrifyingly good at lying.'

His brows came together. 'You think I'm lying? Don't you have mirrors at your flat? You turned every head when you walked through the main restaurant just now.'

Keep it light. Violet smiled a teasing smile to cover her self-consciousness. Compliments had never been her strong point. She knew it was polite to accept them with thanks but she could never quite pull it off with sophisticated aplomb. And if people noticed her when she came into a room, she never saw it. She was always too busy keeping her head down trying *not* to be noticed. 'You *were* lying about the intended proposal.'

His dark blue eyes held hers in a lock that made the base of her spine tingle like sherbet. 'I can be ruthless when it comes to nailing a business deal, but not that ruthless.'

'Good to know.'

His phone pinged with an incoming message. His expression turned sour when he checked the screen.

'Sophia?' Violet's tone was incredulous. 'She texted you while her husband is sitting right next to her?'

Cam expelled a breath and pocketed his phone. 'Go and powder your nose, I'll wait for you here.'

Cam led Violet back to the private dining room. She had reapplied her lipgloss and it made her lips all the more tempting to kiss. *Get a grip.* This was an act, not the real deal. He wasn't interested in the real deal. Not with anyone just now and particularly not with a girl he had viewed as a surrogate sister for the last twelve years.

But then last Easter something had changed.

He had changed.

He had suddenly noticed her. As in *noticed* her. The way she smiled that shy smile that made the corners of her mouth tilt upwards and then quiver, as if uncertain whether to stay there or not. The way she bit her lower lip when she was nervous. The way she moved her body like a graceful dancer. Her beautiful brown eyes that reminded him of caramel. Her creamy skin with that tiny dusting of freckles over the bridge of her nose that he found adorable.

Adorable?

Okay, time to rein it in. He had no right to be thinking about her that way. If he crossed the boundary any further it had the potential to ruin his relationship with her whole family. Three generations of it. He had so many wonderful memories of spending time at Drummond Brae, the big old house set on a Highland estate just out of Inverness. He had met Fraser Drummond in his fourth year at university in London when they were both twenty-two. It felt like a lifetime ago now.

But he still remembered the first time he had visited the Drummond family. It was nothing like any of the families he had been a part of, his nuclear family in particular. He had been struck by their warmth, the way they loved and accepted each other; the easygoing bonhomie between them was something he had never witnessed outside of a television show. Sure, they argued, but no one shouted or swore obscenities or threw things or stormed out in a huff. No one went through an insanely bitter divorce and then refused to have the other person's name mentioned in their presence ever again. Violet's parents were as in love with each other as the first day they'd met. Their solid relationship was the backbone of the family, the scaffolding providing the safety net of stability that allowed each sibling to grow to their full potential. Even the way

Margie Drummond was taking care of her ill ninety-year-old father-in-law Archie was indicative of the unconditional love that flowed in the family.

Cam had become an ancillary part of that family in a way he wouldn't dream of compromising, even if it meant ignoring the persistent drumbeat of lust he had going on for Violet—the baby of the clan. Who was doing an excellent job of pretending to be in love with him at the moment.

But it was far more than the fear of compromising his relationship with her family that held him back. How could he even think about settling down when he was all over the place with work commitments? He was driven to succeed and the only way to succeed was to put everything else on hold. Work was his focus. His first priority. His only priority. If he got distracted now, he could jeopardise everything he'd worked so hard for since the day he'd been left at boarding school. He was used to being an island. Self-sufficient.

Violet resumed her seat next to Cam at the table and looped her slim arm through his, gazing up at him with those big brown eyes as if she thought the world began and ended and only made sense with him. This close he could smell her perfume, a bewitching combination of spring flowers that tantalised his senses until he felt slightly drunk. Or mad. Definitely mad. Mad with lust. He could feel it pounding in his pelvis when she leaned closer, her slim pale hand sliding down to his.

Her touch should not be having this effect on him. He was not a lust-crazed teenager. Normally he could control himself. But if she looked at his lap right now, he'd have some explaining to do. He still had some explaining to do after that kiss. He had been hard for her with one kiss. One kiss, for God's sake! What sort of tragic did that make him? Yes, he hadn't had sex in a while but he'd been busy since Easter… And no, it had nothing to do with seeing Violet that weekend. Nothing to do with noticing her in a way he had never done before.

Or had it?

Had he not pursued the many opportunities he'd had for a casual fling because something had gnawed at him since Easter? The sense that there had to be something more…something more than a few drinks or dinners, a few mostly satisfactory tumbles and a 'goodbye, thanks for the memories'?

For years he had been perfectly content with his lifestyle. He enjoyed the freedom to take on extra work without the pressure of being responsible for someone's emotional upkeep. He had seen both of his parents struggle and fail to meet the needs of each other and their subsequent partners whilst juggling the demands of a career and family. It had always looked like too much hard work.

But there was something to be said for feeling something more than basic lust for a sexual partner. Kissing Violet had felt…different somehow. The connection they had as long-term friends had brought a completely different dynamic to the kiss. He couldn't quite explain it. Maybe he would have to kiss her again... *There's a thought.*

'Smile for the camera,' Sophia said from the other side of the table, holding up her phone.

Cam smiled and leaned his head against Violet's fragrant one, her hair tickling his cheek, her closeness doing something dangerous to his hormones. The photo was taken and Sophia sat back with a Cheshire cat smile. He didn't trust that smile. He didn't trust that woman. He didn't trust his deal with Nick would be secure until the contract was signed, sealed and delivered. But Nick was dragging things out a bit. This trip to London was obviously part of the stalling campaign. Cam couldn't help feeling he was being subjected to some sort of test. Maybe Nick knew exactly what his flirty young wife was up to but wanted to see how Cam would deal with it.

He was dealing with it just fine. With Violet's help. But how long would he have to play pretend? This weekend was fine. But after that? There was only one more week before Christmas. If word got out... His gut seized at the thought. Why had he got himself into this? Seeing Violet in that café earlier had been purely coincidence.

Or had it?

He had felt drawn to that café as if a navigational device inside his body had taken him there. When he'd seen her sitting there all alone something had shifted inside him. Like a gear going up a notch. He had gone from *noticing her* to wanting her...as in *wanting* her. He had offered to take her to the party not because he felt sorry for her but because he couldn't bear the thought of some sleazy colleague trying it on with her.

Green-eyed monster?

You bet.

CHAPTER THREE

VIOLET WASN'T SURE she liked the idea of Sophia having photos of her and Cam but what could she do? She had to play along and pretend everything was fine. Thing was, it *felt* fine. Leaning against him, smiling up at him, looking into those amazingly blue eyes of his that crinkled up at the corners when he smiled—all of it felt so fine she had trouble remembering this was all an act. That it wasn't going to last beyond the weekend.

'Nick and I are going to dance at the nightclub down the road,' Sophia said. 'Come and join us.'

It wasn't an invitation—it was a command. One Violet would have ignored but for the forty million pounds that were hanging in the balance.

And because she didn't want Sophia to think she was one bit intimidated by her. It was how mean girls worked. They manipulated and caused trouble, striking mischief-making matches and standing back to watch the explosion like Lorna had done outside the office.

But there was another reason Violet walked into that nightclub on Cam's arm. She had never danced with anyone. Not since that party. She hated the crush of bodies. The threat of strangers touching her, even by accident as they jostled on the dance floor, had always been too threatening.

But if she danced with Cam it would prove she was moving on. Taking back the control she had lost. She had never danced with him, not even at one of her family's famous *ceilidhs*. He had always refrained from joining into the fun, citing the fact that he had no co-ordination or wasn't a true Scot and there was no way he was ever wearing a skirt. But this would be the perfect opportunity to get him on the dance floor. A legitimate excuse to be in his arms. Where she felt safe.

But Violet hadn't factored in the music. It wasn't the swaying-in-your-partner's arms sort. It was loud, an auditory assault that made conversation other than sign language virtually impossible. The nightclub dance floor was cramped with sweaty, gyrating bodies. It was exactly the sort of place she normally avoided. There wasn't room to swing a cat, let alone a dance partner.

But Sophia and Nick seemed to be enjoying every eardrum-splitting moment. They were jigging about, weaving their way through the knot of dancers as if they did it every day of the week. They waved to Cam and Violet on their way past, shouting over the music, 'Come and join us!'

Violet looked up at Cam, who looked like he was suffering from indigestion. She stepped up on tiptoe and cupped her hand around his ear. 'Are you going to ask me to dance? Because, if so, let me spare you the embarrassment of being rejected.'

'You call that dancing?'

A smile tugged at her mouth and she stepped up to his ear again. 'You ever get the feeling you were born into the wrong century? Give me a traditional Gay Gordon dance any day.'

He drew her closer in a quick squeeze hug that made her breath hitch. 'I feel about a hundred and fifty in here.'

'Age or temperature?'

He gave a crooked smile and took out his handkerchief—*why did classy men always have one?*—and gently blotted the beads of perspiration that had gathered on her forehead. Violet couldn't tear her eyes away from the deep steady focus of his. What was he thinking behind the screen of his gaze? His eyes dipped to her mouth, his lashes going to half-mast, giving him a sexily hooded look that made her belly quiver like someone bumping into an unset bowl of jelly. She moistened her mouth…not because it was dry but because she liked seeing him watch her do so. He moved closer, his thighs strong and muscular, so very male against her trembling legs. She felt the ridge of his arousal. It should have shocked her, would've shocked her, if it had been anyone else.

But it was Cam.

Who desired her even though he didn't want to. It was a force they were both fighting…for different reasons. Violet didn't want to waste time in a relationship going nowhere even if it was with the most desirable man she had ever met. Cam wasn't interested in finding a life partner. He didn't want to be tied down to family life. Understandable, given the atrocious example his parents had set. But Violet couldn't help wondering if deep down he was less concerned about his loss of freedom and more concerned about not being the sort of husband and father he most aspired to be. He was a perfectionist. Doing a good job wasn't enough for someone like Cam. If he put his mind and energy to something he did it brilliantly. That was why he was one of the most celebrated naval architects in the world.

'Let's go someplace else,' Cam said against her ear.

Had he suggested leaving because he knew she was uncomfortable in that environment? Violet couldn't help but be touched by his concern. 'But what about Nick and—?'

'They'll survive without us.' He took her hand and led her out of the nightclub. 'I'll send Nick a text to say we had to leave. He'll think I want to whip you away somewhere private.'

Please do! Violet followed him out of the nightclub to the wet and cold street outside. Within a few minutes they were in the warm cocoon of his car. But instead of driving her back to her flat he turned in the direction of his house in Belgravia. She hadn't been there before…although she'd walked past. Purely to satisfy her feminine interest, of course. During the drive he'd suggested a nightcap, which could have been code for something else but she took it at face value. Besides, going back to her flat, which would be empty now because both Amy and Stef had steady boyfriends and spent most weekends at their homes, was not the most exciting prospect.

Violet had to pretend to be surprised by the outside of the house when he pulled up in front of it. 'Is this your place? Wow! It's gorgeous. How long have you had it? It looks massive.'

'I bought it a year or so ago.' He led her up the black and white tiled pathway to the front door. 'I've done most of the renovations myself.'

Violet knew he was good with his hands; she had the humming body to prove it. But she hadn't realised he was a handyman of this sort of standard. The house was amazing. A showcase similar to those you would see in a home and lifestyle magazine. It was a three storey high Georgian mansion with beautiful features throughout. Crystal chandeliers tinkled above when Cam closed the door against the wintry breeze. The plush Persian carpet runner that led the way down the wide hallway threatened to swallow Violet's feet whole. The antique furniture made her mouth water. Some girls loved fashion and jewellery but anything old and precious did it for her. There were priceless works of art on the walls in gilt-edged frames. Sculptures on marble stands, a white orchid in full bloom on another softening the overall effect.

Cam led her through to a sitting room with a fireplace with a stunning black marble surround with brass trim. Twin cream sofas, deep as a cloud, sat opposite each other with a mahogany coffee table in between. A Louis XV chair was featured in one corner next to a small cedar writing desk next to a full bookcase. It looked like the perfect room for curling up with a book…or cuddling up with the one you loved.

Stop it. You're letting it go to your head.

Violet realised then with a little jolt that this was the first time they had been completely alone. At Drummond Brae there had always been members of her family about the place, if not in the same room. She had never truly been alone with Cam without the threat of interruption.

Violet turned from taking in all of the room to find him looking at her with an unreadable expression. The air seemed to tighten and then to crackle as if an invisible current was being transmitted through their gazes. She could feel her body responding to the magnetic presence of his. She was half a room away but it felt like a force was drawing her to him, a force she could not control even if she wanted to. 'Why are you looking at me like that?' she asked, barely recognising the breathy voice as coming from her.

'How am I looking at you?'

'As if you don't want me to know what you're thinking.'

His mouth lifted in a wry smile that tugged on something deep inside her. 'Believe me, you don't want to know what I'm thinking.'

'Try me.' *Did you just say that? Isn't that flirting? That thing you never do?*

He closed the distance in a couple of strides, standing close enough for her to feel the potent energy of his body calling out to hers. 'This is all sorts of crazy.' He didn't touch her. He just stood there looking down at her with that inscrutable expression on his face.

Violet disguised a tiny swallow. 'What is?'

She heard him draw in a breath, it sounded as if it caught on something on the way through. He lifted his hand, brushing the backs of his bent fingers down the slope of her cheek. 'Being alone with you. It's… ill-advised.'

Ill-advised? Violet wondered what other word he'd considered using. Dangerous? Tempting? Inevitable? All three seemed to apply. She looked at his mouth, knowing it was a signal for him to kiss her. Knowing it and doing it anyway. It was what she wanted. It was what he wanted. She might not be very experienced but she could tell when a man wanted to kiss a woman.

She lowered her lashes over her eyes, swaying towards him. *Kiss me. Kiss me. Kiss me.* She placed her hands on the wall of his chest. The feel of his firm male form beneath her palms sent a thrill through her body. It was like being plugged into a power source. She felt the sensual voltage from her palms to the balls of her feet…and other places. Places she mostly ignored, but not now. Her feminine core responded to his closeness with a tight, clenching ache. His head came down, his mouth hovering within a breath of hers as if some fraying thread of self-control was only just keeping him in check.

Violet took matters into her own hands...or mouth, so to speak. She closed the minuscule distance by placing her lips to his, her heart kicking in excitement when he made a low, deep groaning sound before he took charge of the kiss. His lips were firmer than the last time, not rough but with an undercurrent of desperation as if the self-control he had always relied on had finally let him down. She felt it in the way his tongue came in ruthless search of hers, tangling with it in an erotic dance that made her skin pop all over with goose bumps. The spread of his fingers through her hair made every nerve on her scalp tingle at the roots, his mouth continuing its sensual teasing until she was mindless with longing. His stubble grazed her cheek and then her chin but she didn't care. This was what she'd been hungering for all evening...or maybe for most of her adult life.

The insistent sound of her phone vibrating and chirruping from within her evening bag would have been easy to ignore under normal circumstances, but it was late at night. Late night phone calls usually meant something was wrong. And with her frail grandfather it was hard not to worry something terrible had happened. Violet eased back from Cam's embrace and gave him a wincing look. 'Sorry, better answer that. It might be urgent.'

'Sure.' He rubbed a hand over the back of his neck and stood back while she fished her phone out of her purse.

By the time Violet got her phone out it had stopped, but she frowned when she saw she'd missed six calls from her mother. There were three each from all of her siblings. Her stomach dropped like an elevator with sabotaged cables. She pressed speed dial and looked at Cam with a grimace as she braced herself for bad news.

'Mum? What's wrong? You called me—'

'Poppet, why didn't you tell me?' Her mother's clear voice carried as if Violet had put her on speaker. 'It's all over social media. I've had everyone calling to confirm it. We're so delighted for you and Cam. When did he ask you? Tell me everything. It's just so exciting! Grandad's taken on a new lease of life. He got out of bed and had a wee dram to celebrate. He says he's going to make it to your wedding and no one's going to stop him. Your father's beside himself with joy. Here, speak to him.'

Violet looked wide-eyed at Cam for help, mouthing, *What will I say?*

Cam gestured for her to hand him the phone. He took it and held it to his ear, his eyes on Violet's, his expression was calm on the surface, but she could see a tiny muscle in his jaw going on and off like a miniature hammer. 'Gavin? Yes, well, we were hoping to keep it quiet a little longer but—'

'Congratulations,' her father said. 'Couldn't have asked for a better son-in-law. You have my every blessing, Cam. You're already a big part of the family—this has just made it formal. You and our little Vivi. I'm so thrilled I can barely tell you. I know you'll look after our baby girl.'

After a few more effusive congratulations from both her parents, Cam handed back the phone to Violet and she was subjected to the same. This was the trouble with having parents who were enthusiastic and encouraging in anything and everything their children did. There was barely a space for her to put a word in. Finally her parents ended the call and Violet switched her phone off. Her siblings would be next. There would be another barrage of verbiage she wouldn't be able to contradict for fear of disappointing everyone.

But her brother and sisters would have to wait until she figured out what Cam was up to. Why hadn't he denied it? Why let it continue when so many people would be hurt when the truth came out?

'Okay, so apparently we're now engaged,' she said, shooting him a *please explain* look. 'Any idea how that happened?'

His mouth was set in a rigid line. 'Sophia Nicolaides must have made an announcement on social media with that photo she took of us at dinner. Do you know how many followers she has?' He turned away and let out a stiff curse. 'I should've known something like this would happen.'

'But we could've just denied it.'

He swung his gaze back to hers. 'You heard what your mother said. Your grandfather practically came out of a coma at the news. No, we'll have to run with it—at least until after Christmas.'

Violet's heart was doing a rather good impression

of having some sort of medical event. 'Why till after Christmas?'

'Because I don't want your family's Christmas to be spoilt,' he said. 'It's the time when everyone comes together. Your mother puts such a lot of effort into making it special for everyone. Can you imagine how awkward it would be if we were to tell them it's all a lie?'

Violet chewed her lip. He was right. Of course he was. Christmas was a big thing in her family and it would be ruined if she and Cam put them straight about the charade they were playing. And surely poor old Grandad deserved to have his last Christmas as happy as they could make it? It wasn't like Cam was going to keep this going for ever. He didn't want to settle down. The last thing he would want to do was tie himself down with a woman he wasn't in love with. He liked her, loved her even in a platonic sort of way, but he wasn't in love with her. She wasn't his type. She wasn't anyone's type.

'But we're going to have to tell them some time...'

Cam dragged a hand down his face, momentarily distorting his handsome features. 'I know, but there's too much at stake. And no, I'm not just referring to this deal with Nicolaides.'

'Apart from my family, what else is at stake?'

He let out a ragged-sounding breath. 'There's my family for one thing. I'm not sure I want to show up to my father's fifth wedding on Christmas Eve with a broken engagement under my belt. He'll never let me hear the end of it. I can hear everyone saying it now. *Like father, like son.*'

Violet could understand his point of view. From what she knew of his father, Ross McKinnon would make the most of any opportunity to rub in Cam's mistakes as a way to take the focus off his own behaviour. His mother, Candice, would also not let a chance like that go by, given Cam had been so critical of how both his parents had behaved over the years.

'Right, well, it looks like we run with it then.'

At least her office Christmas party would be less of an ordeal with him there as her fiancé. For once she would be spared the sleazy flirting from male colleagues, and at least there would be no more pitying looks from some of the women who thought it fine sport to make a mockery out of her being single. It was a win-win…she hoped.

Cam picked up his keys from the writing desk where he'd left them earlier. 'I'd better take you home. It's late.'

Violet's spirits slumped in disappointment. Didn't he want to finish the kiss they'd started? 'I don't have to be back by any set time,' she said. 'The girls are sleeping over at their boyfriends' so…'

His sober expression halted her speech. 'Violet.' The way he said her name with that deep note of gravity was a little disquieting to say the least. 'We're not going there, okay?'

There? Where was 'there'? All she wanted was a

little more kissing and…a little fooling around. Okay, *lots* of fooling around. Violet forced a smile.

He looked at her for a long moment, his eyes moving back and forth between each of hers in a searching manner that made her feel like someone was trickling sand down the column of her spine. 'I said we'd kiss and that's all.'

'Fine. No problem. Best to be sensible about this.' The words kept tumbling out. 'Way, way too awkward if we go there. I'm not your type in any case. Not enough experience for one thing.'

His brows formed a bridge over his dark-as-midnight blue eyes. 'How much experience have you had?'

Violet gave a self-deprecating grimace. 'Well…let's put it this way. I haven't been around the block, I got to the corner and then got kind of lost.'

His frown deepened. 'What do you mean?'

What are you doing? You haven't ever told anyone about…that.

Violet pressed her lips together, wondering if she should go any further. Would it make him see her differently? Make him judge her for being a naïve little fool to get into such a situation? But something about his concerned expression made her realise he would be the last person to pass judgement on her. 'I'd rather not talk about it…'

'You can tell me, Violet.' Cam's voice was so steady, so strong, so calm. But then he had always been a good listener. Violet remembered an occasion during her teens when she'd found herself telling him about the mean girls at school who had taunted her for not wearing the right label of clothes to a party. *What was it with her and parties?* Cam had listened to her frustrated rant and then assured her the girls were probably jealous because she didn't need designer wear to look gorgeous. Violet remembered blushing to the roots of her hair but feeling a strange sense of warmth every time she recalled that conversation since.

Telling him about what happened at that university party was not on the same level of having a moan about a bunch of vacuous schoolgirls at a teenage birthday bash. Telling him about the trauma of her first sexual experience would be laying herself bare. Opening old wounds that had never properly healed. But there was something about Cam that gave her new strength. Maybe it was time to get it off her chest so she could breathe without that lingering pinching feeling of shame.

'During my first year at university, I went to a party...' She took a short breath before continuing. 'I was trying to fit in instead of being on the outer all the time. I had a couple of drinks—too many drinks, really...'

Violet glanced up to see him frowning so intensely his eyebrows met over his eyes. But it wasn't a frown of disapproval or judgement, it was one of raw concern. It gave her the courage to continue. 'Things got a little hazy and I...well, I woke up and there were three...' She took a painful swallow. 'At first I wasn't sure if it was a dream—a nightmare or something. I was on a bed and there was a man, not someone I knew…'

'Did he…rape you?' Cam's voice came out sounding rusty as if he had trouble getting the words through his throat.

This time Violet couldn't quite meet his gaze but aimed it at a point just below his chin. 'I'm not sure… I don't remember that part. Can you call it rape if you don't remember anything? There wasn't just one man… I'm not sure if they were just…watching or…'

He took her by the hands and drew her close but not quite touching his body as if he was worried about making her feel uncomfortable after her confession. 'Did you report it?'

Violet shook her head. 'I couldn't bear anyone knowing about it. I didn't tell anyone, not even Mum or Rose or Lily. I felt so ashamed I'd got myself into that situation. I just locked it away and…and, well, I quit my studies. I couldn't help feeling people were looking at me differently around the campus…you know? I just thought it best to move on and pretend it never happened.'

He drew her against him in a gentle hug, resting his head on top of hers. 'I wish I'd been at that party because there's no way those lowlife creeps would have got away with that.' The deep resonance of his voice from his chest where it was pressed against hers was a strange sort of comfort. She felt safe in a way she hadn't felt in years. If only he had been there. If only she had been able to run to him and have him hold her, protect her. He was that type of man. Honourable. Chivalrous. There was no way he would spike anyone's drink and take advantage of a woman when she was too out of it to give proper consent. The world needed more men like Cam. Men who weren't afraid to stand up to bullies. Men who were brave and steadfast in their values. Men who treated women as equals and not as objects to service their needs.

Violet looked up at him. 'Thank you.'

He gently stroked her hair back from her face. 'It wasn't your fault, Violet. What those men did was wrong. You're not the one who should be feeling ashamed. They committed a crime and so did anyone else at that party who witnessed it and didn't report it.'

'I was so worried there might be…photos…'

He winced as if someone had stabbed him in the gut. 'Do you remember anyone taking any?'

Violet shook her head. 'No, but there was so much I didn't remember so I could never be sure one way or the other. It's made the humiliation of that night go on and on. For ten years I've worried someone out there has photos of me…like that, and I can't do anything about it.'

Cam's expression was tight with rage on her behalf. There were white tips around his mouth and his jaw was locked. 'Think of it this way. If photos were to surface they could be used as evidence in court. You could identify the perpetrators and lay charges.'

Violet hadn't thought of it that way and it was like a weight coming off her, like taking off a heavy backpack after a long, exhausting walk. She leaned her head against his chest, breathing in the clean male scent of him. He continued to stroke her head, gentle soothing strokes that made her feel as if she was the most precious person in the world instead of someone dirty, tainted, someone to be used for sport and cast aside.

Violet didn't know how long they stood there like that. It could have been seconds, minutes or even half an hour. All she knew was it felt as if she had come to a safe anchorage after years of tossing about in an unpredictable sea.

But finally he eased back from her, still holding her, his thumbs rhythmically stroking the backs of her hands. 'I want you to know something, Violet. You will always be safe with me. Always.'

Violet wasn't sure she wanted to be safe. The feelings she had for him were dangerous. Dangerous and exciting. 'Thanks…' *I think.* 'But please, I'd rather you didn't mention this to my family. I want to put it behind me. For good.'

'Am I the only person you've told?'

Violet nodded. 'Weird, huh? You of all people.'

His frown was still pleating his forehead. 'Why me of all people?'

She shifted her gaze. 'I don't know… I never thought I'd tell you. I guess I didn't want you to think of me… like that.'

He brought her chin up so her gaze came back to his. 'Hey.' His eyes were as dark as sapphires, his voice low and deep as a bass chord. 'I could never think of you like that and nor should you think of yourself that way. You're a beautiful person who had an ugly thing happen to her. Don't keep punishing yourself.'

Violet had spent years berating herself for being in the wrong place at the wrong time with the wrong personality. If she'd been less reserved, less trusting, more able to stand up for herself, then maybe it wouldn't have happened. For so long she had blamed herself for allowing herself to get into such a situation. But now that she had opened up to Cam, she could see how futile that blame game was. It was time to let it go and accept that it could have happened to anyone. She had been that *anyone* that fateful day.

Violet looked into his dark, caring eyes. Did this mean it was still hands-off? She still wanted him to kiss her. She wanted to be free from her past and experience being in a relationship with a man who respected her and treated her as an equal. Why couldn't Cam be that man? Cam who listened to her as if she were the only person in the world he wanted to hear talk. Cam, whom she'd trusted enough to tell her most shameful secret to, which, strangely enough, didn't feel so shameful now that she had shared it with him.

Cam's phone started ringing and he took it out of his pocket and grimaced when he saw the caller ID. 'Fraser.' He pressed the mute button. 'I'll call him later.'

Violet bit down on her lip. Fraser wouldn't give up in a hurry. She had yet to talk to him and her sisters. How soon before one of her family began to suspect things weren't quite as they seemed? What if it jeopardised Cam's contract? She didn't want to be responsible for ruining that for him, but nor did she want to be responsible for wrecking everyone's Christmas. 'This situation between us is getting awfully complicated… I'm not a very good liar. What if someone guesses this isn't for real?'

His hand cupped one side of her face, his touch gentle fire licking at her flesh. 'No one will guess. You're doing a great job so far.'

That's because I'm not sure I'm still pretending.

CHAPTER FOUR

CAM DROVE VIOLET back to her flat half an hour later. He was still getting his head around what she'd told him earlier. He'd had trouble containing his rage at what had happened to her. The frustrated anger at the way she had been treated gnawed at him. He had the deepest respect for women and felt sickened to his gut that there were men out there who would act so unconscionably. For all these years since, Violet had lived with the shame of being in the wrong place at the wrong time with the wrong people. It saddened him to think she blamed herself. *Still* blamed herself. No wonder she had no dating life to speak of. Why would she want to fraternise with men if she didn't know if she could trust them?

He didn't trust himself around her. Not that he would ever do anything she didn't want, but still. The attraction that had flared up between them was something he was doing his best to ignore. It was all very well pretending to be engaged for a couple of weeks. Kissing and holding hands and stuff was fine to add a little authenticity. More than fine. But taking it any further?

Not a good idea.

A dumb idea.

An idea that had unfortunately taken root in his brain and was winding its tentacles throughout his body like a rampant vine. He had only to look at Violet and those tentacles of lust coiled and tightened in his groin.

But how could he act on it? Even if it was what she wanted? It wouldn't be fair to her to get her hopes up that he could offer her anything more than a casual relationship. He hated hurting people. If he broke Violet's heart he would never forgive himself. Her family would never forgive him either.

Engaged via social media.

What a nightmare. How had he got himself into such a complicated mess?

Cam walked Violet to the door of her flat but when they got there it was slightly ajar. She stopped dead, cannoning back against his body standing just behind her. 'Oh, no…' Her voice came out as a shocked gasp.

Cam put his hands on her shoulders. 'What's wrong?' And then he saw what she had seen. The lock had been jemmied open, the woodwork around it splintered. 'Don't touch anything,' he said, moving her out of the way. 'I'll call the police.'

Within a few minutes the police arrived and investigated the scene. The police told Cam and Violet that several flats in the area had been targeted that night in the hunt for drugs and cash. Once they were allowed inside, Cam held Violet's hand as she inspected the mess.

And it was a mess. Clothes, shoes, books, kitchen items and even food thrown around and ground into the carpet as if the intruders were intent on causing as much mayhem as possible.

Cam could sense Violet's distress even though she was putting on a brave face. Her bottom lip was quivering and her brown eyes were moving from one scattered item to the next as if wondering how on earth she would ever restore order to the place. He was wondering that himself. 'I... I've got to call Amy and Stef,' she said in a distracted tone, fumbling for her phone in her purse and almost dropping it when she found it.

Cam would have led her to the sofa to sit down but it had been slashed with a sharp object, presumably one of the kitchen knives the police had since bagged and taken away for fingerprinting. He shuddered at the thought of what might have happened if Violet had been alone inside the flat when the intruders broke in. Who knew what this new class of criminals were capable of these days? It didn't bear thinking about. He picked up an overturned chair instead and set it down, making sure it was clean first. 'Here, sweetie. Come and sit down and I'll call the girls for you.'

Violet's expression was a mixture of residual fear and gratitude. 'Would you? I'm not sure I can think straight, let alone talk to anyone just now.'

Cam spoke to both of Violet's flatmates, telling them what had happened and that everything was under control now as he was organising an emergency locksmith to repair the lock. 'And don't worry about Violet,' he added. 'I'm taking her back to my place.'

Of course he would have to take her home with him. There was no question about it. He couldn't leave her in the trashed flat to lie awake all night in terror of being invaded again. Or worse. It was the right thing to do to take her home with him. What friend wouldn't offer a bed for a night or two? He wasn't one for sleepovers. He liked his space too much. But this was Violet. A friend from way back.

It was a pity his body wasn't so clear on the friend factor, but still. His hormones would have to get control of themselves.

While the locksmith was working on the lock, one of Violet's elderly neighbours shuffled along the corridor to speak to her. 'Are you all right, Violet?' the wizened old man said. 'I didn't hear a thing. The sleeping pills the doctor gave me knock me out for most of the night.'

Violet gave the old man a reassuring smile. 'I'm fine, Mr Yates. I'm glad you weren't disturbed. How's your chest feeling? Is your bronchitis better?'

Cam thought it typical of Violet to be more concerned about her elderly neighbour than herself. The old man gave her a sheepish look. 'The doc reckons I should give up smoking but at my age what other pleasures are there?' He turned his rheumy gaze to Cam. 'And who might you be, young man?'

'I'm Violet's—'

'Friend,' Violet said before Cam could finish his sentence.

Mr Yates's bushy brows waggled. 'Boyfriend?'

'Fiancé, actually,' Cam said with a ridiculous sense of pride he couldn't account for or explain. He knew it was beneath him to be beating his chest in front of an elderly man like some sort of Tarzan figure but he couldn't help it. *Boyfriend* sounded so…juvenile, and *lover*, well, that was even worse. Violet wasn't the sort of girl to take a lover.

Mr Yates smiled a nicotine-stained smile. 'Congratulations. You've got a keeper there in Violet. She's the nicest of the girls who live here. Never could understand why she hasn't been snapped up well before now. You're a lucky man.'

'I know.'

Once the locksmith had finished and Mr Yates had shuffled back to his flat, Cam led Violet back out to his car with a small collection of her belongings to see her through for a few days. Not that she could bring much as most of it had been thrown about the flat. The thought of putting on clothes that some stranger had touched would be horrifying for her. It was horrifying to him.

He glanced at her once they were on their way. She was sitting with a hunched posture, her fingers plucking at her evening bag, her face white and pinched. 'How are you doing?'

'I don't know how to thank you…' She gave a little hiccupping sound as if she was fighting back a sob. 'You've been so amazing tonight. I really don't know what I would've done without you.'

Cam reached for her hand and placed it on top of his thigh. 'That's what friends—or rather, fake fiancés—are for.' His attempt at humour didn't quite hit the mark. Her teeth sank into her lower lip so hard he was worried she would puncture the skin. She looked so tiny and vulnerable it made his chest sting. It made him think of how she must have been after that wretched party—alone, terrified, shocked, with no one she felt she could turn to. If only he had known. If only he had been there that night, he could have done something to protect her. Violet was the sort of girl who made him want to rush off for a white horse and a suit of armour. Her trust in him made him feel…conflicted, truth be told.

He wanted to protect her, sure, but he wanted her, period. Which was a whole lot of capital *T* trouble he could do without right now. Bringing her home with him was the right thing to do. Of course it was. Sure, he could have set her up in a hotel but he sensed she needed company. Her parents were too far away in Scotland to get to her in a hurry, so too were her brother and sisters, who lived in various parts of the country.

Cam was on knight duty so it was up to him to hold her hand.

As long as that's all you hold.

Violet had held off tears only because Cam had done everything that needed to be done. He'd taken charge in a way that made her feel supported and safe. The horror of finding all her possessions strewn around the flat had been such a shock. She felt so violated. Someone—

more than one someone, it seemed—had broken in and rifled through her and her roommates' things. They had seen her photo with the girls at Stef's last birthday celebration stuck on the kitchen door, which meant she might one day pass them in the street and they would know who she was but she would have no idea who they were. It was like being back on the university campus after that party. She didn't know who the enemy was. They had touched her clothing, her underwear. Invaded her private sanctuary and now it was defiled, just as her body had been defiled all those years ago.

Cam kept glancing at her and gently squeezing and stroking her hand. It was enormously comforting. Violet could see the concern, and the anger he was doing his best to suppress on her behalf. Was he thinking of what might have happened if she'd been in that flat alone? She was thinking about it and it was terrifying. How fortunate that he had walked her to the door. But then, of course he would do that. It was the type of man he was. Strong, capable, with old-fashioned values that resonated with hers.

His offer to have her stay with him at his house was perfectly reasonable given their friendship and yet… she wondered if he was entirely comfortable with it. Would it make it harder for him to keep things platonic between them?

Once they were back at his house, Cam carried her small bag of belongings—those she could stomach enough to bring with her—to one of the spare bedrooms. But at least her embroidery basket had been left intact. She was halfway through making a baby blanket for Lily's unborn baby and couldn't bear the thought of anyone destroying that.

'I'm only a door away over there.' Cam pointed to the master bedroom on the other side of the wide hallway. 'I'll leave my door open in case you need me during the night.'

I need you now.

'Thanks…for everything.'

He gave her one of those lopsided smiles of his that made her heart contract. 'You're welcome.'

Violet shifted her weight. 'Do you mind if I have a hot drink? I'm not sure I'm going to be able to sleep. Maybe a hot milk or something will help.'

'Of course.'

Violet followed him back down to the spacious kitchen and perched on one of the breakfast-bar stools while he went about preparing a hot chocolate for both of them. It was a strange feeling to be alone with him in his house, knowing she would be sleeping in one of his beds. Not *his* bed. He'd made that inordinately clear. But the possibility he could change his mind made her feel a thrill of excitement like someone had injected champagne bubbles into her bloodstream. She couldn't stop looking at his hands, couldn't stop imagining how they would feel touching her, stroking her. He had broad hands with long fingers with neat square nails. Capable hands. Careful hands. Hands that healed instead of hurt. Every time he touched her she felt her body glow with warmth. It was like she was coming out of cold storage. His touch awakened the sensuality that had been frozen by fear all those years ago.

He slid the hot chocolate towards her with a spoon and the sugar bowl. 'There you go.'

Violet took a restorative sip and observed him while he stirred his chocolate. He still had a two-fold crease between his eyes as if his mind was still back at her flat thinking up a whole lot of nasty scenarios, similar to the ones she was trying her best not to think about. 'I'll only stay tonight,' she said into the silence. 'Once the girls and I tidy up, I'll go back.'

His frown wasn't letting up any. 'Is that such a good idea? What if you get broken into again? The security there is crap. You don't even have a security chain on the door. Your landlord should be ashamed of himself.'

'It's actually a woman.'

'Same goes.'

Violet cradled her drink between her hands, looking at him over the rim of her cup when she took another sip. He had abandoned his drink as if his mind was too preoccupied. There were lines of tension running down either side of his mouth. 'I know this must be awkward for you…having me here…' she said. 'You know, after our conversation earlier about…only kissing.'

His gaze went to her mouth as if he couldn't help himself. 'It's not awkward.' His voice came out so husky it sounded like it had been dragged along a rough surface.

'I could go to a hotel or stay with a—'

'No.' The word was delivered with such implacability it made Violet blink. 'You'll stay here as long as you need to.'

How about for the rest of my life? Violet took another sip of her chocolate before setting the mug down. She had to stop this ridiculous habit of imagining a future with him. She was being a silly romantic fool, conjuring up a happy ending because she was almost thirty and Cam was the first man to treat her the way she'd always longed to be treated. It was her hormones...or something. 'I guess it kind of makes sense, me being here, since we're supposed to bc engaged.'

'Yes, well, there's that, of course.'

Violet slipped off the stool and took her mug over to the sink, rinsing it first before putting it in the dishwasher. She turned and found Cam looking at her with a frowning expression. 'I'm...erm...going to bed now,' she said. 'Thanks again for everything.'

He gave her a semblance of a smile that softened the frown a smidgen. 'No problem. Hope you can get some sleep.'

Violet was about to turn for the door when, on an impulse she couldn't explain let alone stop, she stepped up to where Cam was standing and, rising on tiptoe, pressed a soft kiss to his stubble-roughened cheek. His hands went to her hips as if he too couldn't stop himself, drawing her that little bit closer so her body was flush against his. His eyes searched hers for a long moment before dipping to her mouth. 'We really shouldn't be doing this, Violet. It only makes things more—'

'More what?' Violet said, pressing herself closer,

feeling the hardened ridge of him against her belly. 'Exciting?'

His hands tightened on her hips but, instead of drawing her closer, he put her from him, dropping his hold as if her body was scorching hot. His frown was severe but she got the feeling it was directed more at himself than at her.

'You're upset after the break-in,' he said. 'Your emotions are shot to pieces. It would be wrong of me to take advantage of you when you're feeling so vulnerable.'

Take advantage! Take advantage! Violet knew he was being the sensible and considerate man she knew him to be, but the fledging flirt in her felt hurt by his rejection. Why shouldn't they have a fling? It was the perfect chance for her to let go of her past and explore her sensuality without shame, without fear, with a man she not only trusted but admired and cared about. Why couldn't he see how much she needed him to help wipe away the past? 'I'm sorry for misreading the signals. Of course you wouldn't want to sleep with me. No one wants to sleep with me unless I'm coma-drunk. Why am I so hopeless at this?'

Cam took her by the shoulders this time, locking his gaze on hers. 'You're not hopeless at anything, sweetheart. You're a beautiful and talented young woman who deserves to be happy. I'm trying for damage control here. If we take this further, it will blur the boundaries. For both of us.'

Violet planted her hands on his chest, feeling the thud-pitty-thud-pitty-thud of his heart beneath her palm. The battle was played out on his features: the push of pulsating desire and the pull away of his sense of duty. Push. Pull. Push. Pull. It was mirrored in the rhythm of a muscle flicking in his jaw. 'But you want me…don't you?' she said.

He brought her up against his body, pelvis to pelvis, his eyes holding hers. 'I want you, but—'

'Let's leave the "but" out of it,' Violet said. 'If I were anyone else, you'd have a fling with me, wouldn't you?'

He let out a short breath. 'You're not a fling type of girl so—'

'But what if I was? What if I wanted to have a fling with you because I'm so darn tired of being the girl without a date, the girl who hasn't had proper consensual sex? I'm sick of being that girl, Cam. I'm turning thirty in January. I want to find the courage to embrace my sexuality and who better with than you? Someone I trust and feel safe with.'

It was clear she had created a dilemma for him. His expression was a picture of conflict. His hands tightened on the tops of her shoulders, as if torn between wanting to bring her closer and pushing her away. 'I don't want to hurt you,' he said. 'That's the last thing I want.'

'How will you hurt me?' Violet asked. 'I'm not asking you to commit to anything permanent. I know that's not what you want and I'm fine with that.' *Not exactly true, but still.* 'We can have a fling for as long as our pretend engagement lasts. It will make it appear more authentic.'

He cupped her face with the broad span of his hand while his thumb stroked back and forth on her cheek. 'Looks like you've thought all of this through.'

'I have and it's what I want. It's what you want too, isn't it?'

His frown hadn't gone away but was pulling his brow into deep vertical lines between his eyes. 'What about your family?'

'What about them?' Violet said. 'They already think we're…together. Why shouldn't we therefore actually be together?'

'There's something a little off with your logic but I'm not sure what it is.'

'What's logical about lust?'

His frown was back. 'Is that all this is?'

'Of course.' Violet suspected she might have answered a little too quickly. 'I love you but I'm not *in* love with you.'

His eyes did that back and forth thing that made her feel as if he was looking for the truth behind the screen of her gaze. 'The thing is…good sex can make people fall in love with each other.'

Violet cocked her head. 'So, I'm presuming you've had plenty of good sex. Have you ever fallen in love?'

'No, but that doesn't—'

'Then what makes you think you will this time?'

He blinked as if he was confused about her line of argument. 'I'm not worried about me falling in love, I'm worried about you.'

Violet raised her brows. 'What makes you think you'll be immune to falling in love?'

He opened and closed his mouth, seemingly lost for an answer. 'Sex for me is a physical thing. I never allow my emotions to become involved.'

'Sounds like heaps of fun, just getting it on with someone's body without connecting with them on any other level.'

His brows snapped together and he dropped his hands from her hips. 'Damn it. It's not like that. At least I know their names and make sure they've given full and proper consent and are conscious.'

Violet wasn't going to apologise for her straight talking. In her opinion he was short-changing himself if he stuck to relationships that were based on mutual lust and nothing else. What about sharing someone's life with them? What about growing old together? What about being fully present in a relationship that made you grow as a person?

All the things she wished for but hadn't so far been able to find.

'You remind me of Fraser before he met Zoe. He was always saying he'd never fall in love. Look what happened to him. A chance meeting with Zoe and now he's married with twins and he couldn't be happier.'

Cam blew out a frustrated-sounding breath. 'It's different for your brother. He's had the great example your parents have set. He's had that since he was a baby—all of you have. I had a completely different example, one I wouldn't wish on a partner and certainly not on any children.'

Violet studied his tense expression, his even more rigidly set body and the way his eyes glittered with bitterness. And the way he had put some distance between their bodies as if he didn't trust himself not to reach for her. 'What exactly happened between your parents that you're so against marriage?'

It was a moment or two before he spoke. 'They only got married because my mother got pregnant with me. They were pressured into it by both of their families, although to be fair my mother was in love with my father, but unfortunately he didn't feel the same. It was a disaster from the word go. The earliest memories I have are of my parents fighting. They're the only memories I have, really.'

'But that doesn't mean you'd conduct a relationship like that,' Violet said. 'You're not that type of person.'

He gave a short laugh that had a note of cynicism to it. 'Thanks for the character reference but it won't be needed. I'm fine with how my life is now. I don't have to check in with anyone. I'm free to do what I want, when I want, with whomever I want.'

'As long as they're not married to your richest client or are your best friend's kid sister,' Violet said with a pointed look.

He pressed his lips together as if checking a retort. 'Violet...'

'It's fine.' Violet turned away with an airy wave of one hand. 'I get the message. You don't want to complicate things by sleeping with me. I'm not going to beg. I'll find someone else. After our engagement is over, of course.'

It was a great exit line.

And it would have been even better if she hadn't stumbled over the rug on her way out.

CHAPTER FIVE

Cam swore and raked his hand through his hair until he thought he'd draw blood. Or make himself bald. What was he doing even *thinking* of taking her up on her offer of a fling? Violet was the last girl he should be thinking about. Tempted by. Lusting over. She was so innocent. So vulnerable. So adorable.

Yes, adorable, which was why he had to be sensible about this. She wasn't someone he could walk away from once the fling was over and never see or think of again. He would see her every time he was at a Drummond family gathering. He could avoid them, of course, but that would be punishing her family as well as himself.

Not that he didn't deserve to be punished for dragging her into this farce. If he hadn't asked her to that wretched dinner, none of this would have happened.

But if the dinner and the Christmas party tomorrow night weren't bad enough, now he had her under his roof in one of the spare bedrooms. Now he would spend the night, or however many nights she would be here, in a heightened state of arousal. Forget about cold showers, he would have to pump in water from the North Sea to deal with this level of attraction.

What was wrong with him?

Where was his self-control?

Why had he kissed her? That had been his first mistake. The second was to keep touching her. But he couldn't seem to keep his hands off her. As soon as she came within touching distance, he was at it again.

He had to stop thinking about making love to her. Stop picturing it. Stop aching for it. Just stop.

But truth was it was *all* Cam had been thinking about since running into Violet at that café. Which was damned annoying, as he'd never seen her that way before last Easter. For years she'd been one of the Drummond girls, just like Rose and Lily—a sister to him in every way other than blood. But it had all changed that last time he'd visited Drummond Brae. He could sense the exact moment when she turned her gaze on him. His body picked up her presence like a radar signal. His stomach rolled over and begged when she smiled at him. His skin tingled if she so much as brushed past him in a doorway. When his knees bumped hers under the table in the café he'd felt the shockwave travel all the way to his groin.

Even though she was safely in the spare room, he couldn't get her out of his mind. Her neat little ballerina-like figure, gorgeous brown eyes the colour of caramel, wavy chestnut hair that always smelled of flowers, a mouth that was shaped in a perfect Cupid's bow that drew his gaze more than he wanted it to. He had fantasies about that mouth. X-rated fantasies. Fantasies he shouldn't be having because she was like a sister to him.

Like hell she is.

Was that why he'd offered to bring her back here? Had some dark corner of his subconscious leapt at the opportunity to have her under his roof so he could take things to the next level? The level Violet wanted? The level that would change everything between them? Permanently. Irrevocably. How would he ever look at her in the future and not remember how her mouth felt under his? He was having enough trouble now getting it out of his mind. He could think of nothing else but how her mouth responded to his. How her lips had been as soft as down, her tongue both playful and shy. How her body felt when she'd brushed up against him. How her dainty little curves made him want to crush her to him so he could ease this relentless ache of need. How he wanted to explore every inch of her body and claim it, nurture it, release it from its prison of fear.

But how could he do that, knowing she had so much more invested in their relationship? She was after the fairytale he was avoiding because loving someone to that degree had the potential to ruin lives. If—and it was a big if—he ever settled down with a partner, he would go for a companionable relationship that was based on similar interests rather than the fickleness of love that could fade after its first flush of heat. His mother had paid the price—was still paying it—for loving without caution. It hadn't just ruined her life but that of several others along the way, as well. He didn't want that sort of emotional carnage. He already had feelings for Violet. Feelings that could slip into the danger zone if he wasn't careful. Having her here under his roof was only intensifying those feelings. The thought of her being only a few doors away was a form of torture. Making love with Violet would be exactly that: making love. Encouraging love, feeding love, nurturing it to grow and blossom. Sex was easy to deal with if he kept his feelings out of it. But having sex with Violet would be all about feelings. Emotions. Bonding. Commitment. All the things he shied away from because they had the potential to disrupt the neat and controlled order of his life.

He had to be strong. Determined. Resolute. Violet was looking for someone to give her heart to. She was vulnerable and it would be wrong of him to give her the impression an affair between them could go anywhere.

Why couldn't it?

Cam slapped the thought away like he was swatting away a fly. But it kept coming back, buzzing around the edges of his resolve, making him think of how it would be day after day, week after week, month after month, year after year with Violet in his life. Having her not just as a temporary houseguest but as a permanent partner. He wasn't so cynical that he couldn't see the benefits of a long-term marriage. He had only to look at Violet's parents to see how well a good marriage could work.

But how could he guarantee his would work? There were no guarantees, which was what scared him the most.

Violet didn't expect to sleep after the evening's disturbance. She thought she'd have nightmares about her flat being invaded but the only dreams she had were of Cam kissing her, touching her, making her feel things she'd never expected to feel. With time to reflect on it, she understood his caution about getting involved with her sexually. Of course it would be a risk. It would change everything about their relationship. Every single dynamic would be altered. You couldn't undo something like that. Every time she saw him at family gatherings in the future it would be there between them—their sensual history. He had only kissed her and held her and yet she was going to have a task ahead of her to forget about it. It was like his touch had seeped through every pore of her skin, tunnelling its way into her body so deep she instinctively knew she would never feel like that with anyone else. How could she? His touch was like a code breaker to her frozen sensuality. It unlocked the primal urges she had hidden away out of shame. He'd awoken those sleeping urges and now they were jumping up and down in her body like hyperactive kids on a trampoline.

Violet threw off the bedcovers and showered but when she looked at her overnight bag of belongings she'd hastily packed last night she knew she could never bring herself to touch them, let alone wear them. How could she know for sure if the intruders had touched them? What if she wore them and then out on the street the burglars recognised them as the ones they had rifled through last night? She had only the clothes she'd been wearing for the dinner last night. She didn't fancy putting them on again after her shower and, besides, the velvet cocktail dress was hardly Saturday morning wear. It was way too dressed up. If she went out in that get-up, she would look like she had been out all night. She rinsed out her knickers and dried them with the hairdryer she found in one of the drawers in the bathroom. There was a plush bathrobe hanging on the back of the bathroom door so she slipped it on over her underwear.

Cam was in the kitchen pouring cereal into a bowl when she came in. He looked up and Violet saw the way his eyes automatically scanned her body as if he was imagining what she looked like underneath the bathrobe. He cleared his throat and turned back to his cereal, making rather a business of sealing the inside packet and folding down the flaps on top of the box. 'Sleep okay?'

'Not bad...'

He took a spoon out of one of the drawers and then turned and opened the fridge for the milk. Violet drank in the image of him dressed in dark blue jeans and a black finely woven cashmere sweater with a white T-shirt underneath. There should be a law against a man looking so good in casual clothes. The denim hugged his trim and toned buttocks; the close-fitting sweater showcased the superb musculature of his upper body. His hair was still damp from a shower and it looked like his fingers had been its most recent combing tool, for she could see the finger-spaced grooves between the dark brown strands.

'What would you like for breakfast?' he said, turning from the fridge. 'I'm afraid I can't match your mother's famous breakfast spreads but I can do cereal, toast and fruit and yoghurt.'

'Sounds lovely.' Violet perched on the stool opposite him. 'Can I ask a favour?'

His gaze met hers. 'Look, we had this discussion last night and the answer is—'

'It's not about…that.' Violet captured her lip between her teeth. Did he have to rub it in? So he didn't want to sleep with her. Fine. She wasn't going to drag him kicking and screaming to the nearest bedroom. 'It's about my clothes. I need to get new ones. I can't bear wearing any of mine from the flat, not even the ones I brought with me, and I don't want to wear my cocktail dress because I'll look like I've been out all night.'

A frown pulled at his forehead. 'You want me to go…shopping for you?'

Did he have to make it sound like she'd asked him to dance naked in Trafalgar Square? 'I'll give you my credit card. I just need some basics and then I can do the rest myself once you bring those couple of things back.'

He blew out a breath and reached for a pen and a slip of paper, pushing it across the bench. 'Write me a list.'

* * *

Cam had never shopped for women's clothing before. Who knew there was so much to choose from? But choosing a pair of jeans and a warm sweater wasn't too much of a problem. The problem was he kept looking at the lingerie section and imagining Violet in the sexy little lacy numbers. He had to walk out before he was tempted to buy her the black lace teddy with the hot pink feathers. Or the red corset one with black silk lacing. Once he'd completed his mission, he was making his way back to his house when he walked past a jewellery store. He'd walked past that store hundreds, if not thousands, of times and never looked in the window, let alone gone in. But for some reason he found himself pushing the door open, going inside and standing next to the ring counter.

It's just a prop.

Violet's office party was tonight and what sort of cheap fiancé would he look if he hadn't bought her a decent ring? No need to mortgage the house on a diamond but that one at the back there looked perfect for Violet's hand. He didn't have too much trouble guessing her ring size; he had thought of her hands—holding them, feeling them on his skin—enough times to know the exact dimensions. Actually, he knew pretty much the exact dimensions of her whole body. They were imprinted on his brain and kept him awake at night.

Cam paid for the ring, placed it in his pocket and walked out of the store. Just as he was about to turn the corner for home, he got a call from Fraser. He couldn't avoid the conversation any longer, but something about lying to his best mate didn't sit too comfortably. 'Hey, sorry I haven't returned your calls,' he said. 'Things have been happening so fast I—'

Fraser gave a light laugh. 'You don't have to apologise to me, buddy. I saw the way you were looking at Vivi at Easter. Is that why you skived off to Greece? So you wouldn't be tempted to act on it?'

Maybe it had been, now that he thought about it. Cam often had to travel abroad at short notice in order to meet with a client, but the chance to go to Greece for a few months had been exactly the escape hatch he'd needed. He'd felt the need to clear his head, to get some perspective, to have a little talk to himself about stepping over boundaries that couldn't be undone. But the whole time he'd been away, Violet had been on his mind. 'Yeah, well, now that you mention it.'

'Great news, man,' Fraser said. 'Couldn't be more delighted. Zoe reckons this is going to be the best Christmas ever. Did you hear about Grandad? Talk about a turnaround. He's so excited for your wedding.'

The wedding that wasn't going to happen... Cam sidestepped the thought like someone avoiding a puddle. 'Yeah, your mum told me. It's great he's feeling better.'

'So when's the big day? Am I going to be best man? No pressure or anything.'

Cam affected a light laugh. 'I've got to get my father's fifth wedding out of the way first. We'll set a date after that.'

'What's your new stepmother like?'

'Don't ask.'

'Like that, huh?'

'Yep,' Cam said. 'Like that.'

Violet looked around Cam's house while he was out. It was a stunningly beautiful home with gorgeous touches everywhere but on closer inspection it didn't have a personal touch, nothing to hint at the private life of its only occupant. There were no family photos or childhood memorabilia. Unlike her family home in Scotland, where her mother had framed and documented and scrapbooked each of her children's milestones, Cam's house was bare of anything to do with his childhood. There were no photos of him with his parents. None of him as a child. It was as if he didn't want to be reminded of that part of his life.

Violet turned from looking at one of the paintings on the wall in the study when Cam came in carrying shopping bags. 'You've been ages,' she said. 'Was it frightfully busy? The shops can be a nightmare at this time of year. I shouldn't have asked you. I'm sorry but I—'

'It was fine.' He handed her the bags. 'You'd better check I've got the right size.'

Violet took the bags and set them on the cedar desk. She took out the tissue-wrapped sweater and held it against her body. It was the most gorgeous baby-blue cashmere and felt soft as a cloud. The other wrapped parcel was a pair of jeans. But there was another tiny parcel at the bottom of the second shopping bag. Her heart gave a stumble when she picked it up and saw the high-end jewellery store label on the ribbon that was tied in a neat bow on top. 'What's this?'

'An engagement ring.'

Violet's eyes rounded. Her heart pounded. Her hopes sounded. *Did this mean...? Was he...?* 'You bought a ring? For me?'

His expression was as blank as his house was of his past. 'It's just for show. I figured everyone would be asking to see it at your office party tonight.'

Violet carefully unpeeled the ribbon, her heart feeling like a hummingbird was trapped in one of its chambers. She opened the velvet box to find a beautiful diamond in a classic setting in a white gold ring. It was more than beautiful—it was perfect. How had he known she wasn't the big flashy diamond sort? She took it out of the box and pushed it onto her ring finger. It winked up at her as if in conspiracy. *I might be just a prop but don't I look fabulous on your hand?* She looked up at Cam's unreadable expression. 'It's gorgeous. But I'll give it back after Christmas, okay?'

'No.' There was a note of implacability to his tone. 'I want you to keep it. Think of it as a gift for your help with the Nicolaides contract.'

Violet held up her hand, looking at the light dancing off the diamond. She didn't like to think it might be the only engagement ring she ever got. She lowered her hand and looked at him again. 'It's very generous of you, Cam. It's beautiful. I couldn't have chosen better myself. Thank you.'

'No problem.'

Violet gathered up her new clothes and the packaging. 'I'm going to get dressed and head out to replenish my wardrobe. What are your plans?'

'Work.'

'On the weekend?'

He gave her a *that's how it is* look. 'I'll catch up with you later this evening. What time is your office party?'

'Eight.'

'I'll be back in time to take you. Make yourself at home.' He reached past her to open the drawer of the desk and took out a key on a security remote. He handed it to her. 'Here's the key to the house.'

Violet took the key and a rush of heat coursed from her fingers to her core when her hand came into contact with his. He must have felt it too for his gaze meshed with hers in a sizzling tether that made her wonder if he was only going to work to remove himself from the temptation of spending time with her. Doing…things. Wicked things. Things that made her blood heat and her stomach do cartwheels of excitement. 'Cam?' Her voice came out croaky and soft.

His eyes went to her mouth and she saw the way his throat moved up and down over a tight swallow. 'Don't make this any harder than it already is.' His tone was two parts gravel, one part honey, and one part man on the edge of control.

With courage she had no idea she possessed, Violet moved closer, planting her hands on his chest, bringing her hips in contact with his. 'Don't I get to kiss you for buying me such a gorgeous ring?'

His eyes darkened until it was impossible to tell where his pupils began and ended. His body stirred against hers, the swell of his erection calling out to her. Desire burned through every lonely corridor of her body, every network of nerves, every circuit of her blood. She became aware of her breasts pushed up against the fabric of her bathrobe, the nipples already tight, her flesh aching for human touch—Cam's touch. Her courage increased with every pound of his heart she could feel thundering under her palm.

His head came down at the same time she stepped up on tiptoe, their mouths meeting in the middle in an explosion of lust that sent a shockwave through Violet's body. It sent it through Cam's, too, for he grabbed her by the hips and pulled her hard against him, smothering a groan as his mouth plundered hers.

His tongue didn't ask for entry but demanded it, tangling with hers in a sexy combat that mimicked the intimacy both of them craved. This wasn't a chaste kiss between old friends. This was a kiss of urgency, of frustration, of long-built-up needs that could wait no longer for satiation.

Cam's mouth continued its thrilling exploration of hers while his hands slipped beneath the opening of her bathrobe, exposing her breasts. Violet shivered as the feel of his hand shaping her, cupping her, caressing her threatened to heat her blood to boiling. She'd had no idea her breasts were that sensitive. No idea how wonderful it felt to have a man's hand cradle her shape while his thumb moved back and forth across her nipple.

But it wasn't enough. Her body wanted more. More contact, more friction, more of the sensual heat his body promised. She pushed her lower body against his, relishing the delicious thrill it gave her to feel the potency of his arousal. She had done that to him. Her body stirred his as his stirred hers. It was a combustible energy neither of them could deny nor ignore any longer.

'This is madness,' Cam said just above her mouth.

Violet didn't give him a chance to pull away any further. She pressed closer, stroking her tongue over his lips, the top one and then the lower one, a shiver coursing through her when he gave another rough groan and covered her mouth in a fiery kiss. His hands gripped her by the hips, holding her to his rigid heat, the contact making Violet's inner core tingle and tighten with anticipation. How had she survived so long without this magical energy rushing through her body? Cam's touch made every nerve in her body cry out for more.

He pulled his mouth away, his breathing a little unsteady. 'Not here, not like this.'

Violet kept her arms around his waist, reluctant to give him the opportunity to break the intimate contact. 'Don't say you don't want me because I know you do.'

He gave her a rueful look. 'Not much chance of hiding it, is there? But I want you to be comfortable and making love on a desk or the floor is not my idea of comfortable.'

Before Violet could say anything, he scooped her up

in his arms. She gave a startled gasp and held on, secretly delighted he was taking charge like a romantic hero out of an old black and white movie.

They came to his bedroom door and he shouldered it open and carried her to the end of the bed, lowering her to the floor, but not before trailing her body down the length of his, leaving her in no doubt of his erotic intentions. He pressed another lingering kiss to her lips, exploring the depths of her mouth with a beguiling mix of gentleness and urgency. Sensations rippled through her body in tiny waves, making her skin sensitive to his touch like he had cast a sensual spell on her. But then he had. From the moment he had walked into that café, she had been under the heady spell of sexual attraction.

Violet pulled up his sweater and T-shirt so she could glide her hands over his naked skin. Warm, hard male flesh met the skin of her palms; a light smattering of masculine hair grazed her fingertips, the scent of his cologne teased her nostrils. She explored the tiny pebbles of his nipples, and then the flat plane of his stomach with its washboard ridges that marked him as man who enjoyed hard physical exercise.

Cam untied the waist strap of her bathrobe and sent his hands on their own sensual journey. Violet shuddered when his hands glided around her ribcage, not quite touching her breasts but close enough for her to feel she would die if he didn't. He brought his mouth to the upper curve of her right breast. He didn't seem in a hurry, but maybe he was giving her time to get used to this level of intimacy. He brushed his thumb over her nipple, a back and forth movement that made her body contract with want.

Rather than undress her any further, he set to work on his own clothes, taking each item off while his gaze was trained on hers.

Finally, he was in nothing but black underpants, and then and only then did he remove her bathrobe. Violet's belly did a somersault an Olympic gymnast would have been proud of when she saw the way his eyes feasted on her breasts. He cupped them in his hands with exquisite care, rolling his thumb over each nipple before lowering his mouth to subject her to an intimate torture that made her senses spin in dizzying delight.

He lifted his mouth off her breast and, kneeling in front of her, continued to kiss his way from her sternum to her belly button. Violet sucked in a breath, her hands on his shoulders, not sure she could handle what he was planning.

'Relax, sweetheart.'

Easy for you to say. Violet held her breath while he peeled away her knickers. The warmth of his breath on her intimate flesh made her spine weaken as if someone had unbolted her vertebrae. His mouth came to her softly, a light as air touch that made her knees tremble. He gently parted her, stroking her with his tongue, the sensation so powerful she pulled away. 'I—I can't...'

His hands were gentle but firm on her hips. 'Yes, you can. Don't be frightened of it. Trust me.'

Violet glanced down at him worshipping her body, his touch so tender, so respectful it made her see her body differently, not as something to be ashamed of and hidden away, but as something that was not only beautiful and capable of receiving pleasure, but also of giving it too. The rhythmic strokes of his tongue sent a torrent of tingles through her body, concentrating on that one point—the heart of her femininity. The tension grew to a crescendo until she was finally catapulted into a vortex that scattered her thoughts until all she could do was feel. Feel the power of an orgasm that swept through her like a hot wave, rolling through every inch of her flesh, trickling over every nerve ending, sending showers of goose bumps over her body, leaving no part of her immune. She was limbless, dazed, out of her mind as the aftershocks pulsed through her.

Cam brought his mouth back up over her stomach and ribcage, then her breasts, leaving a blistering trail of kisses on her tingling skin. He stood upright, drawing her closer, his mouth settling back on hers in a mind-altering kiss, the eroticism of it heightened by the fact she could taste her own essence on his lips and tongue.

Violet had thought herself too shy to draw his briefs from his body but somehow her hands reached for the elastic edge of the waistband and slid them away from his body. She took him into her hand—hot, hard, and quintessentially male. She stroked him with experimental caresses, her fingers drawing down from the base to the head and back again. It was so empowering to be an active part of a sexual encounter. The deep guttural noises he made added to her sense of agency.

She was doing this to him. She was the one he wanted. She was the one exciting him, pushing him to the limit of control.

Cam gently moved her hand away and guided her to the mattress behind her, coming down over her in a tangle of limbs, balancing his weight on his arms so as not to crush her. 'Comfortable?'

'Yes.' Violet was surprised she was capable of thought, let alone speech. The way he made her feel, so safe, so treasured, made the shame she had carried for so long slip further out of reach, like an old garment stuffed at the back of the wardrobe. It was still there but she could no longer see it.

Cam stroked her face with his fingertip, his eyes dark and lustrous. 'We don't have to go any further if you're not ready.'

I'm ready! I'm ready! Violet touched the flat of her palm to his stubbly jaw, looking into his eyes without reserve. 'I want you inside me.'

A flash of delight went through his gaze. 'I won't rush you and you can stop me at any point.'

He reached for a condom in the bedside drawer and deftly applied it before coming back to her. The choreography of their bodies aligning themselves for that ultimate physical connection was simple and yet complex. It was like learning the steps to a dance, one leg this way, the other that, her breasts pressing against the wall of his chest, her arms winding around his body to anchor herself. He gently probed her entrance, allowing her time to adjust to him just…being there. She felt the weight and heft of him waiting there but it wasn't threatening in any way.

He slowly entered her, waiting for her to relax before going any further. Violet welcomed him inside her body with soft little gasps as the sensation of him stretching her, filling her, tantalising her gained momentum. He began a slow rhythm that sent shivers of delight through her body, the friction of male against female making her aware of her body in a way she had never been before. Nerves she hadn't known existed were firing up. Muscles that had been inactive for most of her life were now being activated in a deeply pleasurable workout that had one sure goal. She could feel that goal dangling just out of reach, the thrill of her flesh building and building but unable to go any further. It was a frustrating ache, a restless urging for more. But, as if Cam could read her silent pleas for release, he brought his hand down between their bodies and sought the heart of her arousal. The stroking of his fingers against her tipped her into a free fall of spinning, whirling, dizzying sensations. They ricocheted through her in giant shudders, making her lose her grasp on conscious thought. She was in the middle of a vortex, vivid colours bursting like thousands of tiny fireworks behind her squeezed-shut eyelids.

Then the slow wash of a wave of lassitude… She was drifting, drifting, drifting…

But then she became aware of the increasing pace of Cam's thrusts as his own release powered down on him. She experienced every second of it through the sensitised walls of her body, his tension building to a final crucial point before he pitched forwards against her, his deep primal cry making something in her belly shiver like a light wind whispering over the surface of a lake.

Violet lay in his embrace, her fingertips moving up and down his spine while his breathing gradually slowed. She couldn't find the words to express what her body had just experienced. She felt reborn. As if the old her had been sloughed away like a tired skin. Her new skin felt alive, energised, and sensitive to every movement of Cam's breathing as his chest rose and fell against hers.

Should she say something? What? *How was it for you?* That seemed a little trite and clichéd somehow. How many times had he lain here like this with other women? How many other women? He might not be the fastest living playboy on the planet but he wasn't without a sex life. He just kept it a little more private than other men in his position. How many women had lain here in his arms and felt the same as her? Was what she had experienced with him run-of-the-mill sex? Or was it different? More special? More intense?

Violet knew she was being a fool for allowing her feelings to get involved. But this was Cam. Not just some hot guy she happened to fancy. Cam was a friend. Someone she had known for years and years and always admired.

They had stepped into new territory and it felt... weird, but not horribly weird. Nicely weird. Excitingly weird. Would he make love to her again? How soon? Would he get so hooked on having sex with her he would extend their 'engagement'? What if he fell in love with her? What if he decided marriage and kids wasn't such a bad idea? What if—?

Cam dealt with disposing of the condom and then looked down at her with a soft smile that made his eyes seem even darker. 'Hey.'

Violet hoped he wasn't as good at reading her mind as he was at reading her body. Her thoughts were running like ticker tape in her head. *Please fall in love with me. Please.*

'Hey...'

He brushed some stray strands of hair back from her face, his smile fading as a frowning concern took up residence instead. 'Did I hurt you?'

Violet had trouble speaking for the sudden lump in her throat. 'N-not at all.'

He picked up another strand of hair and gently anchored it behind her ear, holding her gaze with his. 'Sure?'

How was she supposed to keep her feelings out of this when he looked at her like that? When his hands touched her as if she were something so eminently precious to him he would rather die than hurt her? 'I'm sure.'

He leaned down to press a soft kiss to her mouth. 'You were wonderful.'

Violet traced the line of his mouth with her fingertip. 'This won't...change things between us, will it? I mean, no matter what happens, we'll always be friends, won't we?'

A flicker of something moved through his gaze like a passing thought leaving a shadow in its wake. 'Of course we will.' He took her hand and quickly kissed the ends of her fingertips before releasing it. 'Nothing will ever change that.'

Violet wasn't so sure. What if she couldn't cope with going back to normal? He might be able to go back to relating to her as he had always done, but she wasn't confident she would be able to do the same to him. How could she look at him and not think of how his mouth felt against her own? How could she not think of how his hands had stroked her most intimate flesh? How could she not think of how his body had awakened hers and made her feel things she hadn't thought were possible to feel?

Not just physical things, but emotional things.

Things that might not be so easily set aside once their fling was over.

CHAPTER SIX

CAM WAITED WHILE Violet had a shower and got changed. He would have joined her but he was conscious of allowing her time to recover. God, *he* needed time to recover. So much for keeping his distance. So much for his self-control. Where had that gone? He hadn't been able to resist the temptation of making love to her. So apparently they were having a fling. It didn't feel like any fling he'd ever had before. He had never known a partner the way he knew Violet. Her trust in him had heightened the experience. Every touch, every kiss, every stroke, every whimper or gasp of hers had made his pleasure intensify. It was like having sex for the first time but not in a clumsy, awkward way, but in a magical, mutually satisfying way that left his body humming like a plucked string.

Somehow the thought of spending the afternoon working didn't hold its usual appeal. Even a yuletide cynic like him had to agree there was no greater place to be before Christmas than in London. He wasn't much of a shopper but Violet needed a new wardrobe and he would rather spend the time with her than chained to his desk.

Violet came down the stairs wearing the jeans and baby-blue sweater he'd bought her. Cam had trouble keeping his hands to himself. He ached to slide his hands under the sweater and cradle the perfection of her breasts. To feel those pink nipples embed themselves into his palm. To feel her body quake with pleasure when he touched her.

She smiled at him shyly, her cheeks going a faint shade of pink as if she too were recalling their earlier intimacy. 'I thought you were going to work?'

Cam shrugged. 'It can wait.' He took her hand and brought it up to his mouth. 'I probably should warn you I'm not the world's best shopper but I'm pretty handy with carrying bags.'

Her eyes shone as if the thought of him accompanying her pleased her as much as it pleased him. 'Are you sure you're not too busy? I know how much men loathe shopping. Dad and Fraser are such pains when we try to get them through a department store door.'

Cam looped her arm through his. 'I have a vested interest in this expedition. I have to make sure Cinderella is dressed appropriately for the ball tonight.'

A flicker of worry passed through her gaze. 'I never know what to wear to the office party. There's a theme this year… *A Star-Struck Christmas*. Last year it was *White Christmas*. The year before it was *Christmas on the Titanic*.'

'You could turn up in a bin liner and still outshine everyone else.'

Her smile made something in his chest slip sideways. 'I really appreciate you coming with me. I can't tell you how much I hate going alone.'

Cam bent down to press a kiss to her forehead. 'You're not alone this year. You're with me.'

Cam wasn't much of a party animal but even he had to admit Violet's firm put on a Christmas extravaganza that was impossible not to enjoy. It occupied the ballroom of one of London's premier hotels and the decorations alone would have funded a developing nation for a year. Giant green and gold and red Christmas bells hung from silken threads just above head height. Great swathes of tinsel adorned the walls. A fresh Christmas tree was positioned to one side of the room, covered with baubles that looked like they had been dipped in gold. Maybe they had. There was an angel on the top whose white gown glittered with Swarovski crystals. The music was lively and fun. The food was fabulous. The champagne was top-shelf and free flowing.

Or maybe he was having a good time because he was with the most beautiful girl at the party. The shimmery dress he'd helped Violet choose skimmed her delicate curves so lovingly his hands twitched in jealousy. The heels she was wearing put his mind straight in the gutter. He couldn't stop imagining her wearing nothing but those glossy black spikes and a sexy come-and-get-me smile.

Cam had been ruminating all afternoon over whether he had done the right thing in making love to Violet. Who was he kidding? He was *still* ruminating. It was like a loop going round and round in his head. *What have I done?*

It was fine to put it down to hormones, but he wasn't some immature teenager who didn't know the meaning of the word self-control. He was a fully grown adult and yet he hadn't been able to walk away.

Had he done the wrong thing?

His body said *Yes*.

His mind said *Yes, but.*

The *buts* were always going to be the kicker. Violet wasn't like any other casual lover he'd met. She'd been in his life for what seemed like for ever. He'd seen her grow from a gangly and shy teenage girl to a beautiful young woman. She was still shy but some of that reserve had eased away when they'd made love. Sharing that experience with her, being the one to guide her through her first experience of pleasure with a partner had been special. More than special. A sacred privilege he would remember for the rest of his life. Her trust in him had touched him, honoured him, and made him feel more of a man than he had ever felt before.

But...

How could he give her what she wanted when it was the opposite of what he wanted right now? Violet came from a family where marriage was a tradition that was celebrated and treasured and believed in. She wanted the fairytale her parents and siblings had.

It wasn't that Cam was so cynical he didn't think marriage could work. It did work. It worked brilliantly, as Margie and Gavin Drummond demonstrated and their parents before them. But Cam's parents' example had made him see the other side of the order of service: the stonewalling, the bitter fights, the disharmony, the petty paybacks, the affairs and then the divorce lawyers, not to mention years of estrangement where the very mention of the other person's name would bring on an explosive fit of temper.

While Cam didn't think he was the type of person to walk out on a commitment as important as marriage, how could he be sure life wouldn't throw up something that would challenge the standards he upheld? The promises people made so earnestly in church didn't always ring with the same conviction when life tossed in a curve ball or two.

It was all well and good to be confident he would stand by his commitment, but it wasn't just about his commitment. The other person would have to be equally committed. How could he be sure Violet, as gorgeous and sweet as she was, would feel the same about him in ten weeks, let alone ten years or five times that? Watching his parents go through their acrimonious divorce when he was a young child had made him wary about rushing into the institution.

He had never had any reason to question his decision before now. It had always seemed the safest way to handle his relationships—being open and honest about what he could and couldn't give. Yes, some lovers might have been disappointed there was no promise of a future. But at least he hadn't misled them.

But sleeping with Violet had changed things. Changed *him*. Made him more aware of the things he would be missing out on rather than the things he was avoiding. Things like walking into a party hand in hand, knowing he was going to leave with that hand still in his. Knowing the smile she turned his way was for him and no one else. Recognising the secret look she gave him that told him she was remembering every second of his lovemaking and she couldn't wait to experience it again. Feeling the frisson of awareness when she brushed against him, how his body was so finely tuned to hers he could sense her presence even when she was metres away.

Had he ever felt like that with anyone else? No. Never. Which wasn't to say he wouldn't with someone else…someone other than Violet. His gut swerved at the thought of making love to someone else. He couldn't imagine it. Couldn't even picture it. Couldn't think of a single person who would excite him the way she excited him.

It will pass. It always does.

Lust for him was a candle not a coal ember. It would flare for a time and then snuff out. Sometimes gradually, sometimes overnight.

But when he looked at Violet, he couldn't imagine his desire for her ever fading. Because his desire for her wasn't just physical. There was another quality to it, a quality he had never felt with anyone else. When he'd made love to her it had felt like an act of worship rather than just sex. Her response to him had been a gift rather than a given. The fact she trusted him enough to feel able to express herself sexually was the biggest compliment—and turn on—he had ever experienced.

But...

How was he going to explain the end of their 'engagement' to her family? How was he going to go back to being just friends? How would he be able to look at her and not remember the way her mouth had felt when she'd opened it for him that first time? How her shy little tongue had tangled with his until his blood had pounded so hard he'd thought his veins would explode? How would he be able to be in the same room as her without wanting to draw her into his arms? To feel her slim body press against his need until he was crazy with it?

Maybe he was crazy. Maybe that was the problem. Making love to her was the craziest thing he'd done in a long time.

But...

He wanted to make love to her again. And again and again.

God help him.

Violet was coming back from a trip to the ladies' room when she was intercepted by three of her workmates, including Lorna.

'Congratulations, Violet,' Lorna said, eyeing her engagement ring. 'Gracious me, that man of yours was quick off the mark.' Her gaze flicked to Violet's abdomen. 'You're not pregnant, are you?'

If there was one time in her life Violet wished she didn't have the propensity to blush, this was it. Could Lorna tell the engagement wasn't real? After all, Violet hadn't mentioned anything about dating anyone, not that she talked about her private life that much at work. But women working together for a long time tended to pick up on those things. Besides, conversations around the water cooler tended to show how boring her life was compared to everyone else's. 'No, not yet but it's definitely on the to-do list.' *Why did you say that?*

Lorna's smile didn't involve her eyes. 'When's the big day?'

'Erm…we haven't decided on a date yet,' Violet said. 'But some time next year.' *I wish.*

'So how did he propose?'

Violet wished she'd talked this through a little more with Cam. They hadn't firmed up any details of their story apart from the fact—which was indeed a fact—they had met via her older brother. How would Cam propose if he were going to ask her to marry him? He wasn't the bells and whistles type. There wouldn't be any skywritten proposals or football-stadium audiences while he got down on bended knee. That was the sort of thing his father did, even on one memorable occasion making the evening news. Cam would choose somewhere quiet and romantic and tell her he loved her and wanted to spend the rest of his life with her. Her heart squeezed. *If only!* 'It was really romantic and—'

'Ah, here's Prince Charming himself,' Lorna said as Cam approached. 'Violet's been telling me how you proposed.'

Cam's smile never faltered but Violet knew him well enough to notice the flicker of tension he was trying to disguise near his mouth. He slipped an arm around Violet's waist and drew her close against him. 'Have you, darling?'

Violet's smile had a hint of *help me* about it. 'Yes, I was saying it was terribly romantic…with all the roses and…stuff.'

'What colour?' Lorna asked.

'White,' Violet said.

'Red,' Cam said at exactly the same time.

Lorna's artfully groomed brows rose ever so slightly. But then she smiled and winked at Cam. 'You have good taste. Violet's a lucky girl to land a man who knows his way around a diamond dealer.'

'She deserves the very best,' Cam said.

'Yes, well, she's waited long enough for it,' Lorna said and with a fingertip wave moved on to return to the party.

Violet released a long jagged breath. 'She suspects something. I know she does. We should've talked about the proposal.' She spun around so her back was to the party room. 'I feel such an idiot. And, for the record, I hate red roses.'

'I'll make a note of it.'

Violet searched his expression but he had his blank-wall mask on. 'So how would you propose if you were going to?'

His brows moved together over his eyes. 'Is that a trick question?'

'No, it's a serious one,' Violet said. 'If, and I know it's a very big "if", but if you were to ask someone to marry you how would you go about it?'

Cam glanced about him. 'Is this the right venue to talk about this?'

Violet wasn't going to risk being cornered by another workmate for details of their engagement. Nothing would out a charade faster than someone cottoning on to a clash of accounts of an event from witnesses. 'We're out of earshot out here. Come on, tell me. What would you do?'

He blew out a short breath. 'I'd make sure I knew what the girl would like.'

'Like what colour roses?'

He gave her a droll look. 'What have you got against red roses?'

Violet gave a lip shrug. 'I don't know… I guess because they're so obvious.'

'Right, then I'd make sure we were alone because I don't believe in putting a woman under pressure from an audience.'

'Like your father did with wife number three?'

'Number two and three.' Cam's eyes gave a half roll.

'So no TV cameras and news crews?'

'Absolutely not.'

Violet looked back at the party in the next room. 'We should probably go and mingle...'

'What's your dream proposal?' Cam asked.

She met his gaze but there was nothing to suggest he was asking the question for any other reason than mild interest. 'I know this sounds a bit silly and ridiculously sentimental, but I've always wanted to be proposed to at Drummond Brae. Ever since I was a little girl, I dreamed of standing by the loch near the forest with the house in the distance and my lover going down on bended knee, just as my father did with my mum and my grandfather did with my grandmother.'

'Your would-be fiancé would have to have a meteorological degree to predict the best time to do it.' Cam's tone was dry. 'Nothing too romantic about being proposed to in sleet or snow.'

Violet's smile was wistful. 'If I was in love I probably wouldn't even notice.'

Half an hour later, Violet turned back to Cam after listening to a boring anecdote from one of her co-workers who'd had one too many drinks. Cam was staring into space and had a frown etched on his brow. 'Are you okay?' she said, touching him on the arm.

He blinked as if she'd startled him but then he seemed to gather himself and smiled down at her. 'Sure.' He slipped an arm around her waist and drew her closer. 'Did I tell you you're the most beautiful woman in the room?'

Violet could feel a blush staining her cheeks. Did

he mean it or was he just saying it in case other people were listening? She felt beautiful when she was with him. What woman wouldn't when he looked at her like that? As if he was remembering every moment of making love to her. The glint in his dark eyes saying he couldn't wait to do it again. 'Don't you feel a little... compromised?'

'In what way?'

She glanced around at the partying crowd before returning her gaze to his, saying sotto voce, 'You know... pretending. Lying all the time.'

He picked up her left hand and pressed a kiss to the diamond while his eyes stayed focused on hers. 'I'm not pretending to want you. I do and badly. How long do we have to stay?'

Violet's inner core tingled in anticipation. 'Not much longer. Maybe five, ten minutes?'

He dropped a kiss to her forehead. 'I'm going to get a mineral water. Want one?'

'Yes, please.'

'Hey, Violet.' Kenneth from Corporate Finance came up behind her and placed a heavy hand on her shoulder. 'Come and dance with me.'

Violet rolled her eyes. She went through the same routine with Kenneth every year at the Christmas party. He always had too much to drink and always asked her to dance. But, while she didn't want to encourage him in any way, she knew Christmas for him was a difficult time. His wife had left him just before Christmas a few years ago and he hadn't coped well with the divorce.

Violet turned and gently extricated herself from his beefy paw. 'Not tonight, thanks. I'm with my...fiancé.'

Kenneth looked at her myopically, swaying on his feet like his body couldn't decide whether to stand or fall. 'Yeah, I heard about that. Congrats and all that. When's the big day?'

'We haven't got around to settling on that just yet.'

He grabbed her left hand and held it up to the light. 'Nice one. Must've cost a packet.'

Violet didn't care for the clammy heat of his hand against hers. But neither did she want to make a scene. The firm had strict guidelines on sexual harassment in the workplace but she felt sorry for Kenneth and knew he would be mortified by his behaviour if he were sober. 'Please let me go, Kenneth.'

He lurched forwards. 'How about a Christmas kiss?'

'How about you get your hands off my fiancée?' Cam said in a tone as cold as steel.

Kenneth turned around and almost toppled over and had to grab hold of the Christmas tree next to him. Violet watched in horror as the tree with all its tinsel and baubles came crashing down, the snow-white angel on the top landing with a thud at Violet's feet, her porcelain skull shattering.

The room was suddenly skin-crawlingly quiet.

But then Kenneth dropped to his knees and picked up the broken angel and held it against his heaving chest. His sobs were quiet sobs. The worst sort of sobs because what they lacked in volume they made up for in silent anguish.

Violet went down beside him and placed a comforting hand on his shoulder. 'It's all right, Kenneth. No one cares about the tree. Do you want us to give you a lift home?'

To her surprise Cam bent down on Kenneth's other side and place his hand on the man's other shoulder. 'Hey, buddy. Let's get you home, okay?'

Kenneth's eyes were streaming tears like someone had turned on a tap inside him. He was still clutching the angel, his hands shaking so much the tiny bits of glitter and crystals from her dress were falling like silver snow. 'She's having a baby... My ex, Jane, is having the baby we were supposed to h-have...'

Violet had trouble keeping her own tears in check. How gut-wrenchingly sad it must be for poor Kenneth to hear his ex-wife was moving on with her life when clearly he hadn't stopped loving her. She exchanged an agonised glance with Cam before leaning in to one-arm-hug Kenneth. She didn't bother trying to search for a platitude. What could she say to help him recover from a broken heart? It was obvious the poor man wasn't over his divorce. He was lonely and desperately sad, and being at a party where everyone was having fun with their partners was ripping that wound open all over again.

After a while, the music restarted and the crowd went on partying. Cam helped Kenneth to his feet while some other men helped put the tree back up.

Violet collected their coats and followed Cam and Kenneth out to the foyer of the hotel where the party was being held. She waited with Kenneth while Cam brought the car to the door and within a few minutes they were on their way to the address Kenneth gave her.

He lived in a nice house in Kensington, not unlike Cam's house, but Violet couldn't help thinking how terribly painful it must be for Kenneth to go home to that empty shell where love had once dwelled, where plans had been made and dreams dreamt.

Once they were sure Kenneth was settled inside, Cam led Violet back to his car. 'Sad.'

'I know...'

'Did you see all the photos of his ex everywhere?' Cam said. 'The place is like a shrine to her. He needs to find a way to move on.'

'I know, but it must be so hard for him at Christmas especially.'

He gave her hand a light squeeze. 'Sorry for being a jerk about him touching you.'

'That's okay, you weren't to know.' She let out a sigh. 'It must be terrible for him, seeing everyone else having a good time while he comes back here to what? An empty house.'

'Does he have any other family? Parents? Siblings?'

'I don't know...but even if he did, wouldn't being with them just remind him of what he's lost? It's hard when you're the only one without a partner.' Violet knew that better than anyone.

Cam nodded grimly. 'Yeah, well, divorce is harder on some people than others.'

Violet glanced at him. 'Your mother took it hard?'

The line around his mouth tightened. 'I was six years old when they finally split up. A week or two after my father moved out to live with his new partner, I came downstairs one morning to find her unconscious on the sofa with an empty bottle of pills and an empty wine bottle beside her. I rang Emergency and thankfully they arrived in time to save her.'

No wonder he was so nervous about commitment. Seeing the devastation of a breakup at close quarters and at such a tender age would have been nothing short of terrifying. 'That must have been so scary for you as a little kid.'

'Yeah, it was.' He waited a beat before continuing. 'Every time I went back to boarding school after the holidays I was worried sick about her. But she started seeing another guy, more to send a message to my father than out of genuine love. It was a payback relationship—one of many.'

'No wonder you break out in a rash every time someone mentions the word marriage,' Violet said.

'Divorce is the word I hate more. But you can never know if it's going to happen or not. No one can guarantee their relationship will last.'

Violet wanted to disagree but deep down she knew what he said was true. There were no guarantees. Life could change in a heartbeat and love could be taken away by disease or death or divorce. Just because you were in love didn't mean the other person would remain committed. She knew many women and men who'd been devastated by their partners straying. But she believed in love and commitment and knew she would do her best when she fell in love to nurture that love and keep it healthy and sustained.

What do you mean—when you fall in love? Haven't you already?

Violet waited until they'd gone a few blocks before speaking again. 'Cam? I have to do something about my flat tomorrow. I really should have done something about it today but I couldn't bring myself to face it. But I can't leave that mess for the girls to clean up on their own.'

'Do you have to go back there?'

Violet glanced at him again. 'What do you mean? It's where I live.'

'You could live somewhere else. Somewhere safer, more secure.'

'Yeah.' Violet sighed. 'Somewhere heaps more expensive too.'

There was a silence broken only by the swishing of the windscreen wipers going back and forth.

'You could stay with me for as long as you like,' Cam said. 'Until you find somewhere more suitable, I mean. There's no rush.'

Violet wondered what was behind the invitation. Was it solely out of consideration for her safety or was he thinking about extending their relationship until who knew when? 'That's a very generous offer but what if you want to start seeing someone else after we break up after Christmas? Could be awkward.'

'Everything about this situation is awkward.'

Violet looked at the tight set of his features. 'Are you regretting…what happened this morning?'

He relaxed his expression and reached across the gear console and captured her hand, bringing it over to rest on top of his thigh. 'No. Maybe I should, but I don't.'

'I don't regret it either.'

His eyes met hers when he parked the car. 'Your family is going to be hurt when we…end this.'

Why had he hesitated over the word 'end'? Who would end it? Would it be a mutual decision or would he suddenly announce it was over?

'Yes, I feel bad about that. But at least it's not for long,' Violet said. 'Once Christmas is over we'll say we made a mistake…or something and go back to normal.'

He studied her for a long moment. 'Will you be okay with that?'

Violet gave him a super-confident smile. 'Of course. Why wouldn't I be? It's what we agreed on. A short-term fling to get me back on my dating feet.'

His expression clouded. 'You have to be careful when you're dating guys these days. You can't go out with just anyone. It's not safe when there are so many creeps on the prowl. And don't do online dating. Some of those guys lie about their backgrounds. Anyone can use a false identity. You could end up with someone with a criminal past.'

Violet wondered if he was cautioning her out of concern or jealousy or both. 'You sound like you don't want me to date anyone else.'

He paused before responding. 'I care about you, Violet, that's all. I don't want you to become a crime statistic.'

'I'm sure I'll manage to meet and fall in love with some perfectly lovely guy, just like my sisters have done,' Violet said. 'I'm just taking a little longer than they did to get around to it.'

He opened his car door and came around to hers but, instead of tension, this time there was a self-deprecating tilt to his mouth. 'Sorry about the lecture.'

Violet smiled and patted his hand where it was resting on the top of the doorframe. 'You can lecture me but only if I can lecture you right on back. Deal?'

He bent down to press a kiss to the end of her nose. 'Deal.'

CHAPTER SEVEN

CAM WOKE FROM a fitful sleep to find the space next to him in the bed was empty. He sat bolt upright, his chest seizing with panic. Where was Violet? When he'd drifted asleep she had been lying in his arms.

Calm down, man. She's probably gone to the bathroom.

He threw off the bedcovers and, snatching up a towel, wrapped it around his hips and padded through his house, checking each room and bathroom upstairs but there was no sign of her.

'Violet?' His voice rang out hollowly. His blood chugged through his veins like chunks of ice. His skin shrank away from his skeleton. He was annoyed at his reaction. What did it say about him? That he was so hooked on her he couldn't let her out of his sight? Ridiculous. She had a right to move about the house without asking permission first. Maybe she'd had trouble sleeping with him in the bed beside her. After all, she'd never been in a proper relationship before. Sharing a bed with someone took some getting used to, which was why he generally avoided it.

'Violet?'

Where could she be? Had she gone outside? He tugged the curtains aside but the back garden was as quiet and deserted as a graveyard. It was three in the morning and it was bitterly cold. Had she gone back to her flat? No. She wouldn't go there without backup. He flung open the sitting room door, then the study.

All empty.

'Are you looking for me?' Violet appeared like a ghost in the doorway of the study.

Relief flooded through Cam like the shot of a potent drug. 'Where were you?'

Her eyes did a double blink at the edginess of his tone. 'I was reading in the breakfast room.'

Cam frowned so hard his forehead pinched. 'Reading?'

Her tongue snaked out and left a layer of moisture over her lips. 'I was…having trouble sleeping. I didn't want to disturb you. You seemed restless enough without me putting on the light and rustling pages.'

Cam forked a hand through his already tousled hair. 'You should've woken me if I was disturbing you. Was I snoring?'

'No, you were just…restless like you were having a bad dream or something.'

He had been having a bad dream. It was coming back to him now in vivid detail. He had been alone in a run-down castle. The drawbridge was up and there was no way in or out. Loneliness crept out from every dark corner, prodding him with tomb-cold fingers. The yawning emptiness he felt was what he had seen on Kenneth's face when they'd returned him to his home last night: the absence of hope, the presence of despair, the bitter sting of regret.

But it was a dream. It didn't mean anything. It was just his mind making up a narrative while his body rested. It didn't mean he was worried about ending up alone in a castle with nothing but cobwebs and shadows to keep him company. It didn't mean he was subconsciously regretting his stance on marriage and commitment. It meant he was dog-tired and working too hard. That was what it meant. That. Was. All. 'Sorry for wrecking your beauty sleep. Next time just give me a jab in the ribs, okay?'

Violet's shy smile tugged like strings stitched on to his heart. 'It was probably my fault more than yours. I've never spent the night with anyone before.'

Of course she hadn't. She might have felt all sorts of uncomfortable about sharing the night with him in his bed. Cam put his hands on her hips and brought her closer. 'I'm not much of a sleep-over person myself.'

A flicker of concern appeared in her gaze. 'Oh... well, then, I can sleep in one of the spare rooms if you'd—'

'No.' Cam brought his mouth down to within an inch of hers. 'I like having you in my bed.' *More than I want to admit.*

Her hint of vanilla danced over his mouth. 'I like it too.'

Cam covered her mouth with his, a shockwave of need rushing through him as her lips opened beneath his. He moved his lips against hers, a gentle massage to prove to himself he could control his response to her. But within seconds the heat got to him, the flicker of her tongue against his lower lip unravelling his self-control like a dropped ball of string. He splayed his fingers through her silky hair, holding her face so he could deepen the kiss. She gave a soft whimper of approval that made his body shudder in delight.

Her body pressed against his, her breasts free behind the bathrobe she was wearing. Knowing she was naked underneath that robe made him wild with need. He untied the waistband, still with his mouth on hers, letting it fall to her feet. He glided his hands over her breasts and then he brought his mouth to each one in turn, caressing the erect pink nipples with his tongue, gently taking them between his teeth in a soft nibble. She smelt of flowers and sleep and sex and he couldn't get enough of her.

He brought his mouth back to hers, his hands holding her by the hips so she could feel what she was doing to him. The ache of need pounded through his body, the primal need to mate driving every other thought out of his brain.

He should have taken her upstairs to the bed but he wanted her now. *Now.*

The hunger was in time with his racing pulse. He

wanted her on the floor. On the desk. On the sofa. Wherever he could have her. He dragged his mouth off hers. 'I want you here. Now.'

Violet's eyes shone with excitement. She didn't say anything but her actions spoke for her. She stroked her hands down his chest to his abdomen, deftly unhooking the towel from around his waist and taking him in her hands. Her touch wreaked havoc on his control. Red-hot pleasure shot through his body, luring him to the abyss where the dark magic of oblivion beckoned.

Cam had to stop her from taking him over the edge. He drew her hand away and guided her to the floor. He kissed his way down from her breasts to her belly, lingering over her mound, ramping up her anticipation for what was to come. She squirmed and whimpered when he claimed his prize, her body bucking within seconds of his tongue moving against her. Her cries of pleasure made him want her all the more. Her passion was so unfettered, so unrestrained it made him wonder if she would find the same freedom to express her sexuality with someone else.

Someone else...

Cam tried to push the thought aside but it was impossible. It was ugly, grotesque thinking of Violet with some other guy. Someone who might not appreciate her sensitivity and shyness. Someone who might pressure her into doing things she wasn't comfortable with doing. Someone who wouldn't protect her at all times and in all places.

That's rich coming from the guy who hasn't got a condom handy.

Violet must have sensed Cam's shift in mood for she propped herself up on her elbows to look at him. 'Is something wrong? Did I do something wrong?'

Cam took her by the hand and helped her to stand. 'It's not you, sweetheart. It's me.' He handed her the bathrobe before picking up his towel and hitching it around his waist. 'I didn't bring a condom with me.'

'Oh…'

'Unlike other men, I don't have them strategically planted in every room of the house.' *But maybe I should.*

Her lips flickered with a smile. 'That's kind of nice to know…'

'I'm selective when it comes to choosing partners.' He only ever chose women he knew he wouldn't fall in love with: safe, no-strings women who were out for a bit of fun and a tearless goodbye at the end of it. Women who didn't look at him with big soulful brown eyes and pretend they didn't feel things they clearly felt.

How was he going to end this?

Do you even want to?

Cam played with the idea of extending their affair. But how long was too long and how short was too short? Either way, it still left him with the task of facing her family and saying the happy ever after they were hanging out for wasn't going to happen.

And that wasn't even the half of it. What about what Violet felt? No matter how much she said she was only after a short fling, he knew her well enough to know she was only saying that to please him. Would it be fair to continue this, knowing she was probably falling in love with him? God knew he was having enough trouble keeping his own feelings in check. Feelings he couldn't explain. Feelings that crept up on him at odd moments, like when Violet looked at him a certain way, or when she smiled, or when she touched him and it sent a lightning zap of electricity through him. Feelings he couldn't dismiss because Violet wasn't a temporary fixture in his life.

The longer he continued their affair, the harder it would be to end it. He knew it and yet…and yet…he couldn't bring himself to do it. Not until after Christmas. Grandad Archie surely deserved to have his last Christmas wish?

Violet made a business of tying the bathrobe back around her waist. 'I suppose you're careful to choose partners you're not likely to fall in love with.'

'It's easier that way.' Maybe that was why he never felt fully satisfied after an encounter even when the sex was good. Something always felt a little off centre. Out of balance, like only wearing one shoe. He never let a relationship drag on for too long. A month or two maximum. It made him look like a bit of a player but that was the price he was prepared to pay for his freedom.

Violet gave him a smile that didn't quite make the grade. 'Lucky me.'

Cam frowned. 'Hey, I didn't mean I chose you for that reason. You're different, you know you are.'

'Not different enough that you'll fall in love with me.'

'Violet—'

She held up her hand. 'It's okay, I don't need the lecture.'

Cam took her by the shoulders again. 'Are you saying you're in love with me? Is that what you're saying?'

Her eyes did everything they could to avoid his. 'No, I'm not saying that.' Her voice was hardly more than a thread of sound.

Cam tipped up her chin, locking her gaze with his. 'This is all I can give you. You have to accept it, Violet. Even if we continued our relationship past Christmas, it would still come down to this. I'm not going to get married to you or to anyone just now.'

Her shoulders went down on a sigh. 'I know. I'm being silly. Sorry.'

He brought her head against his chest, stroking her silky hair with his hand. 'You're not being silly. You're being normal. I'm the one with the commitment issues, not you.'

Her arms snaked around his waist. 'Can we go back to bed now?'

Cam lifted her in his arms. 'What a great idea.'

Violet had arranged with Cam to take her back to her flat on Sunday afternoon to help Amy and Stef with the clean-up, but while she was getting breakfast ready while Cam checked some emails, Amy phoned.

'You're not going to believe this,' Amy said. 'But last night old Mr Yates in twenty-five was smoking in bed and started a fire—'

'Is he all right?' Violet asked.

'Just a bit of smoke inhalation but both our flats are uninhabitable from the water damage,' Amy said. 'The landlady is furious and poor Mr Yates won't want to face her in a hurry.'

'So what will we do?' Violet asked. 'Are we expected to clean it up or will a professional cleaning service do that?'

'Cleaning service,' Amy said. 'I'm not going in there until the building's secure. The ceiling might come down or something. Stef's going to move back in with her mum and I'm going to move in with Heath. We've talked about moving in together for ages so this nails it. What about you? Will you stay with Cam now that you're officially engaged?'

'I... Yes, that's what I'll do,' Violet said. What else could she say? *No, Cam doesn't want to live with anyone*?

Cam came in at that point and smiled. It never failed to make her shiver when he looked at her like that. He stroked a hand down her back while he reached past her to take a mug out of the cupboard next to her. It was the lightest touch but it sent a tremor of longing through her flesh until her legs threatened to buckle.

Violet said goodbye to Amy and put her phone on the bench. 'I have a slight problem…'

'What's wrong?'

She explained about the fire and the water damage. 'So, I have to find somewhere else to live.'

It was hard to read his expression beyond the concern it showed while she had related the events of last night's fire. He turned to one side to take out a tea bag from a box inside the pantry. 'You can stay here as long as you need to. I told you that the other day.'

'Yes, but—'

'It's fine, Violet, really.'

'No, it's not fine,' Violet said. 'A couple of weeks is okay, but any longer than that and things will get complicated.' *More complicated than they already were.*

'What if I help you find a place?'

'You don't have to do that.'

'I'd like to,' he said. 'It'll mean I can give the security a once-over.'

Violet gave him a grateful smile. 'That would be great, thanks.' She waited a beat before adding, 'What's happening with the contract with Nicolaides? Is it secure yet?'

'Not yet.' Cam pulled out one of the breakfast-bar stools. 'I have some drawings to finalise. Sophia keeps altering the design, I suspect because she wants to drag out the process.'

'Has she sent you any more texts?'

'A couple.'

Jealousy surged in Violet's gut. 'When's she going to get the message? What is wrong with her?'

He gave a loose shrug. 'Some women don't know the meaning of the word no.'

Violet would have to learn it herself and in a hurry. 'I think it's disgusting how she openly lusts over you while her husband is watching. Why does he put up with it?'

'He's too frightened to lose her,' Cam said. 'She's twenty years younger than him. And she brings a lot of money to the relationship. Her father left her his empire. It's worth a lot of money.'

'I wouldn't care how much money someone had. If I couldn't trust them, then that would be it. Goodbye. Have a good life.'

He stroked a fingertip down her cheek, his smile gently teasing. 'If you think Sophia's bad, wait till you meet my father's fiancée.'

Violet frowned. 'You want me to meet her?'

'My dad's organised drinks on Wednesday night,' Cam said. 'If you'd rather not go, then—'

'No, it's okay. Of course I'll go. You went to my boring old office party, the least I can do is come with you for drinks with your father.'

Cam's father, Ross, had arranged to meet them at a boutique hotel in the centre of London. Violet hadn't met Ross McKinnon before but she had seen photos of him in the press. He was not quite as tall as Cam and his figure showed signs of the overly indulgent life he led. His features had none of the sharply chiselled definition of Cam's, and while he still had a full head of thick hair, it was liberally sprinkled with grey. His eyes, however, were the same dark blue but without the healthy clarity of Cam's. And they had a tendency to wander to Violet's breasts with rather annoying frequency.

'So this is the girl who's stolen my son's hard heart,' Ross said. 'Congratulations and welcome to the family.'

'Thank you,' Violet said.

Ross pushed his fiancée forward. 'This is Tatiana, my wife as of next weekend. We should have made it a double wedding, eh, Cameron?'

Cam looked like he was in some sort of gastric pain. 'Wouldn't want to steal your thunder.'

Violet took the young woman's hand and smiled. 'Lovely to meet you.'

Tatiana's smile came with a don't-mess-with-me warning. 'Likewise.'

Cam was doing his best to be polite but Violet could tell he was uncomfortable being around his father and new partner. Ross dominated the conversation with occasional interjections from Tatiana, followed by numerous public displays of affection that made Violet feel she was on the set of a B-grade porn movie. Clearly she wasn't the only one as several heads kept turning at the bar, followed by snickers.

Ross showed no interest in Cam's life. It shocked Violet that his father could sit for an hour and a half in his son's company and not once ask a single question about his work or anything to do with his private life. It made her feel sad for Cam to have had such a selfish parent who acted like a narcissistic teenager instead of an adult.

Violet was relieved when Cam got to his feet and said they had to leave.

'But we haven't told you what we've got planned for the honeymoon,' Ross said.

'Isn't that supposed to be bad luck?' Cam said with a pointed look.

Ross's face darkened. 'You can't help yourself, can you? But Tatiana is the one. I know it as sure as I'm standing here.'

'Good for you.' Cam's tone had a hint of cynicism to it and Violet wondered how many times he had heard exactly the same thing from his father. Ross was the sort of man who treated women as trophies to be draped on his arm and summarily dismissed when they ceased to pander to his bloated ego.

Violet quickly offered her hand to Ross and Tatiana. 'It was lovely to meet you. I hope the wedding goes well.'

Ross frowned. 'But aren't you coming with Cameron?'

Violet realised her gaffe too late. 'Erm…yes, of course, if that's what you'd like.'

'You're part of the family now,' Ross said. 'We'd be delighted to have you share in our special day, wouldn't we, babe?'

Tatiana's smile was cool. 'But of course. I'll aim the bouquet in your direction, shall I?'

Violet's smile felt like it was stitched in place. 'That'd be great.'

Cam took her by the hand and led her out of the hotel. 'I did warn you.'

'How on earth do you stand him?' Violet said. 'He's impossibly self-centred. He didn't ask you a single thing about your work or anything to do with you. It was all about him. How amazing he is and how successful and rich. And Tatiana looks like she's young enough to be his daughter. What on earth does she see in him?'

'He paid for her boob job.'

Violet rolled her eyes. She walked a few more paces with him before adding, 'I'm sorry about the wedding gaffe. I didn't think. Do you think they suspected anything was amiss?'

'Probably not,' Cam said. 'They're too focused on themselves.'

'Poor you,' Violet said.

He gave a soft smile. 'You want to grab a bite to eat before we go home?'

Go home. How…permanent and cosy that sounded. 'Sure. Where did you have in mind?'

'Somewhere on the other side of the city so there's no chance my father and Tatiana will chance upon us.'

Violet gave him a sympathetic look. 'I swear I am never going to complain about my family ever again.'

'There's no such thing as a perfect family,' he said. 'But I have to admit yours comes pretty close.'

Violet adored her family. They were supportive and loving and always there for her. But the pressure to live up to the standards her parents had modelled for her always made her feel as if she wasn't quite good enough, that she would never be able to do as brilliant a job as they had of finding love and keeping it. It was one of the reasons she had never told her mother or her sisters about what had happened at that party. Although she knew they would be nothing but supportive and concerned, she'd always worried they would see her differently...as damaged in some way.

'I know, but it's hard to live up to, you know? What if I don't find someone as perfect as my dad is for my mum? They're such a great team. I don't want to settle for less but I'm worried I might miss out. I want to have kids. That makes me feel under even more pressure. It's all right for guys; you can have kids when you're ninety. It's different for women.'

'If it's going to happen it'll happen,' he said. 'You can't force these things.'

'Easy for you to say. You have a queue of women waiting to hook up with you.'

He gave her hand a tiny squeeze. 'I'm only interested in one woman at the moment.'

At the moment.

How could she forget the clock ticking on their relationship? It was front and centre in her mind. Each day that passed was another day closer to when they would go back to being friends. Friends *without* benefits. It would be torture to be around Cam without being able to touch him, to kiss him, to wrap her arms around him and feel his body stir against her. It would be torture to see him date other women, knowing they were experiencing the explosive passion and pleasure of being in his arms.

What if she never found someone as perfect for her as Cam? What if she ended up alone and had to be satisfied with being an aunty or godmother instead of the mother she longed to be? She had been embroidering baby clothes since she was a teenager. She'd made them for her sisters and brother's wife Zoe each time they were expecting but she had her own private stash of clothes. It was her version of a hope chest. Every time she looked at those little vests and booties and bibs she felt an ache of longing. But it wasn't just about having a baby, she realised with a jolt. She wanted to have *Cam's* baby. She couldn't think of anything she wanted more than to be with him, not just for Christmas but for ever.

After dinner they walked hand in hand through the Christmas wonderland of London's streets. Violet had always loved Christmas in her adopted city but being with Cam made the lights seem all the brighter, the colours all the more vivid, the hype of the festive season all the more exciting. When they walked past the Somerset House ice-skating rink, Cam stopped and looked down at her with a twinkling look. 'Fancy a quick twirl to work off dinner?'

Violet looked at the gloriously lit rink with the beautifully decorated Christmas tree at one end. She had skated there a couple of times with Stef and Amy but she'd felt awkward because they had brought their boyfriends. The boys had offered to partner her but she'd felt so uncomfortable she'd pretended to have a sore ankle rather than take them up on their offer. 'I'm not very good at it…' she said. 'And I'm not wearing the right clothes.'

'Excuses, excuses,' Cam said. 'It won't take long to go home and change.'

Within a little while they were back at the rink dressed in jeans and jackets and hats and gloves. Violet felt like a foal on stilts until Cam took her by the hand and led her around until she felt more secure. He looked like he'd been skating all his life, his balance and agility making her attempts look rather paltry in comparison.

'You're doing great,' he said, wrapping one arm around her waist. 'Let's do a complete circuit. Ready?'

Violet leaned into his body and went with him in graceful sweeps and swishes that made the cold air rush past her face. It was exhilarating to be moving so quickly and with his steady support she gained more and more confidence, even letting go of his hand at one point to do a twirl in front of him.

Cam took her hand again, smiling broadly. 'What did I tell you? You're a natural.'

'Only with you.' *And not just with skating.* How would she ever make love with someone else and feel the same level of pleasure? It didn't seem possible. It wasn't possible because there was no way she could ever feel the same about someone else.

Once they had given back their skates, they walked to the London Eye, where Cam paid for them to go on to look at the Christmas lights all over London. Violet had been on the giant Ferris wheel a couple of times but it was so much more special doing it with Cam. The city was a massive grid of twinkling lights, a wonderland of festive cheer that made all the children and most of the adults on board exclaim with wonder.

Violet turned in the circle of Cam's arms to smile at him. 'It's amazing, isn't it? It makes me get all excited about Christmas when usually I'm dreading it.'

A slight frown appeared on his brow. 'Why do you dread it? I thought you loved spending Christmas with your family.'

Violet shifted her gaze to look at the fairyland below. 'I do love it…mostly, it's just I'm always the odd one out. The one without a partner. Apart from Grandad, of course.'

His hand stroked the small of her back. 'You won't be without a partner this year.'

But what about next year? Violet had to press her lips together to stop from saying it out loud. Once Christmas was over so too would their relationship come to an end. All the colour and sparkle and excitement and joy would be snuffed out, just like someone turning off the Christmas lights.

'No one knows what the next year will bring,' Cam

said as if he had read her thoughts. 'You could be married and pregnant by then.'

I wish...but only if it were to you. 'I can't see that happening.' Violet waited a moment before adding, 'Would you come to my wedding if I were to get married?'

Something flashed across his face as if pain had gripped him somewhere deep inside his body. 'Would I be invited?' His tone was light, almost teasing, but she could sense an undercurrent of something else. Something darker. Brooding.

'Of course,' Violet said. 'You're part of the family. It wouldn't be a Drummond wedding if you weren't there.'

'As long as you don't ask me to be the best man,' he said with a grim look. 'My father's asked me to be his and that'll be four times in a row.'

'Wow, you must be an expert at best man speeches by now.'

'Yeah, well, I hope this is the last time but I seriously doubt it.'

Violet thought of her parents and how loving and committed they were to each other and had been from the moment they'd met. They renewed their wedding vows every ten years and went back to the same cottage on the Isle of Skye where they'd spent their honeymoon on each and every anniversary. How had Cam dealt with his father's casual approach to marriage? Ross McKinnon changed wives faster than a sports car changed gears. How embarrassing it must be for Cam to have to go through yet another wedding ceremony knowing it would probably end in divorce. 'Maybe this time will be different,' she said. 'Maybe your dad is really in love this time.'

Cam's expression was a picture of cynicism. 'He doesn't know the meaning of the word.'

CHAPTER EIGHT

THE NEXT DAY Cam came home from work with the news that his contract with Nick Nicolaides had been signed that afternoon.

'Let's go out to celebrate.' He bent down to kiss Violet on the mouth. 'How was your day?'

Violet looped her arms around his neck. 'My day was fine. You must be feeling enormously relieved. Was Sophia there at the meeting?'

'Yes, but she was surprisingly subdued,' he said. 'I think she might've been feeling unwell or something. She got up to leave a couple of times and came back in looking a bit green about the gills. Too much to drink the night before, probably.'

Violet's brow furrowed. 'Could she be pregnant?'

He gave a light shrug. 'I wouldn't know, although, now that I think of it, Nick was looking pretty pleased with himself. But I thought that was because we finally finalised the contract.'

'Maybe being pregnant will help her settle down with Nick instead of eyeing up other men all the time,' Violet said.

Cam stepped away to shrug off his coat, laying it over the back of a chair. His expression had a cloaked look about it, shadowed and closed off. 'A Band-Aid baby is never a good idea.'

Violet knew he was bitter about his parents and the way they had handled his arrival in the world. Did he blame himself for how things had turned out? How could he think it was his fault? His parents were both selfish individuals who ran away from problems when things got the slightest bit difficult They moved from relationship to relationship, collecting collateral damage along the way. How many lives had each of them ruined so far? And it was likely to continue with Ross McKinnon's next marriage. No wonder Cam wanted no part of the type of marriage modelled by his parents. It was nothing short of farcical. 'True,' she said. 'But a baby doesn't ask to be born and once it arrives it deserves to be treasured and loved unconditionally.'

A frown pulled at Cam's forehead. 'We haven't discussed this before but are you taking any form of oral contraception?'

Violet felt her cheeks heat up. It was something she had thought about doing but she hadn't got around to making an appointment with her doctor to get a prescription. There hadn't seemed much point when she wasn't dating regularly. But now…now it was imperative she kept from getting pregnant. The last thing Cam would want was a baby to complicate things further, even though she could think of nothing more wonderful than falling pregnant with his child. 'I'm not but I'm sure it won't be a problem—'

'Condoms are not one hundred per cent reliable,' he said, still frowning.

Violet felt intimidated by his steely glare. Why did he have to make her feel as if she was deliberately trying to get pregnant? There were worse things in the world than falling pregnant by the man you loved. Much worse things. Like not getting pregnant at all. Ever. 'I'm not pregnant, Cam, so you can relax, okay?'

A muscle tapped in his cheek. 'I'm sorry but this is a big issue for me. I don't want any mishaps we can't walk away from.'

Violet cast him a speaking look. 'You'd be the one walking away, not me.'

His frown deepened. 'Is that what you think? Really? Then you're wrong. I would do whatever I could to support you and the baby.'

'But you wouldn't marry me.' It was a statement, not a question.

For once his eyes had trouble meeting hers. 'Not under those circumstances. It wouldn't be fair to the child.'

Violet moved away to fold the tea towels she had taken out of the clothes dryer earlier. 'This is a pointless discussion because I'm not pregnant.' *And I wouldn't marry you if I were because you don't love me the way I long to be loved.*

'When will you know for sure?'

'Christmas Day or thereabouts.'

A silence ticked past.

Cam picked up his jacket and slung it over his arm. 'I'm going to have a shower.' He paused for a beat to rub at his temple as if he was fighting a tension head-ache. 'By the way, thanks for doing the washing. You didn't need to do that. My housekeeper will be back after Christmas.'

'I had to do some of my own so it was no bother.'

He gave her a tired-looking smile. 'Thanks. You're a darling.'

Violet disguised a despondent sigh. *But not* your *darling.*

Cam couldn't take his eyes off Violet all evening. They had gone to one of his favourite haunts, a piano bar where the music was reflective and calming. She was wearing a new emerald-green dress that made her creamy skin glow and her brown eyes pop. Her hair was loose about her shoulders, falling in soft fragrant waves he couldn't wait to go home and bury his head in.

But there was something about her expression that made him realise he had touched on a sensitive subject earlier. Babies. Of course he'd had to mention contra-ception. He had the conversation with every partner. It was the responsible thing to do. A baby—*he*—had ruined his mother's life. It had changed the direction of her life, her career plans, her happiness—everything. A thing she unfortunately reminded him of when she was feeling particularly down about yet another bro-ken relationship.

But Violet wanted a baby. And why wouldn't she? Her siblings were growing their young families and she was the only one left single.

Not quite single...

Cam picked up his glass and took a measured sip. Weird how he felt...so committed and yet this was supposed to be temporary.

Violet raised her glass, a smile curving her lips. 'Congratulations, Cam. I'm so happy for you about the contract.'

'Thanks.' He couldn't think of a single person he would rather celebrate his contract with. It wasn't as if either of his parents were interested, and while Fraser was always thrilled for him when he won an award or landed a big contract, it wasn't the same as having someone who wanted your success more than their own.

'About our conversation earlier...' Cam said.

'It's fine, Cam,' Violet said. 'I understand completely.'

'It's tough on women when they get pregnant. I realise that,' Cam said. 'Even today when there is so much more support around. It's a life-changing decision to keep a baby.'

'Did your mother ever consider...?' Violet seemed unable to complete the sentence.

'Yes and no.' Cam leaned forward to put his glass down. 'She kept me because by doing so she thought she'd be able to keep my father. But when that turned sour, she decided she wished she'd got rid of me so she could have continued her studies.'

Violet frowned. 'She told you that?'

He gave an I'm-over-it shrug. 'Once or twice.'

'But that's awful! No child, no matter how young or old, should hear something like that from a parent.'

'Yes, well, I was an eight-pound spanner in the works for my mother's aspirations. But I blame my father for not supporting her. He got on with his career without a thought about hers.' Cam passed Violet the bowl of nuts before he was tempted to scoff the lot. 'Have you ever thought of going back and finishing your degree?'

Her mouth froze over her bite into a Brazil nut. She took it away from her mouth and placed it on the tiny, square Christmas-themed napkin on the table between them. 'No… I'm not interested in studying now.'

'But you were doing English Literature and History, weren't you?' Cam said. 'Didn't you always want to be a teacher?'

Her eyes fell away from his and she dusted the salt off her fingers with another napkin. 'I'm not cut out for teaching. I'd get too flustered with having to handle difficult kids, not to mention their parents. I'm happy where I'm working.'

'Are you?'

Her eyes slowly met his. 'No, not really, but I'm good at it.'

'Just because you're good at something doesn't mean you should spend your life doing it if it bores you,' Cam said. 'Why don't you study online? Even if you don't teach, it will give you some closure.'

Violet pushed her glass away even though she had

only taken a couple of sips. Her cheeks were a bright shade of pink and her mouth was pinched around the edges. 'Can we talk about something else?'

Cam leaned forwards, resting his forearms on his thighs. 'Hey, don't go all prickly on me. I'm just trying to help you sort out your life.'

Her eyes flashed with uncharacteristic heat. 'I don't need my life sorting out. My life is just fine, thank you very much. Anyway, you need to sort out your own life.'

He sat back and picked up his glass. 'There's nothing wrong with my life.'

Her chin came up. 'So says the man who only dates women who won't connect with him emotionally. What's that about, Cam? What's so terrifying about feeling something for someone?'

Losing them.

Like his mother had lost his father and gone on to lose every other partner since in a pattern she couldn't break because the one person she had loved the most hadn't wanted her any more.

Cam didn't want to be that person. The person left behind. The person who gave everything to the relationship only to have it thrown away like trash when someone else more exciting came along.

He was the one in control in his relationships.

He started one when he wanted one.

He left when it was time to go.

'We're not talking about me,' Cam said. 'We're talking about you. About how you're letting a bad thing that happened to you rob you of reaching your full potential.'

'But isn't that what you're doing? You're letting your parents' horrible divorce rob you of the chance of long-term happiness because you're worried you might not be able to hang on to the one you love.'

So what if he was? He was fine with that. It wasn't as if he was in love with anyone anyway. *You sure about that?* Cam blinked the thought away. Of course he loved Violet. He had always loved her. But it didn't mean he was *in* love with her.

Yes, you are.

No, I'm not.

The battle went back and forth in his head like two boxing opponents trying to get the upper hand. He was confusing lust with love. The sex was great—better than great—the best he'd ever had. But it didn't mean he wanted to tie himself down to domesticity. He was a free agent. Marriage and kids were not on his radar. Violet was born to be a mother. Any fool could see that. She went dewy-eyed at the sight of a baby. She embroidered baby clothes for a hobby, for goodness' sake. Even puppies and kittens turned her to mush. She had planned her wedding day since she was a kid. He had seen photos and home videos of her and her sisters playing weddings. Violet had looked adorable wearing her mother's veil and high heels when she was barely four years old.

How could he ask her to sacrifice that dream for him?

Violet began chewing at her lip. 'Are you angry at me?'

Cam reached across and took her hand. 'No, of course not.' He gave her hand a gentle squeeze. 'Would you like to dance?'

Her eyes lit up. 'You want to dance?'

'Sure, why not?' He drew her to her feet. 'I might not be too flash with a Highland fling but I can do a mean waltz or samba.'

Her arms linked around his neck, bringing her lower body close to the need already stirring there. 'I didn't mean to lecture you, Cam. I hate it when people do that to me.'

Cam pressed a soft kiss to her mouth. 'I'm sorry too.'

Violet had always been a bit of a wallflower at her home town's country dances. She stood at the back of the room and silently envied her parents, who twirled about the dance floor as if they were one person, not two. But somehow in Cam's arms she found her dancing feet and moved about the floor while the piano played a heartstring-pulling ballad as if she was born to it. His arms supported her, his body guided her and his smile delighted her. 'If you tell your brother about this I'll have to kill you,' Cam said.

Violet laughed. 'Someone should be videoing this because no one's going to believe I've got through three songs without doing you an injur— Oops! Spoke too soon.' She glanced down at his feet. 'Did I hurt you?'

'Not a bit.' He guided her around the other way, drawing her even closer to his body.

Violet loved the feel of his arms around her, but

the slow rhythm of the haunting melody of lost love reminded her of the time in the not too distant future when those words would apply to her. How long had she been in love with him? It wasn't something she could pin an exact time or date to. She had always thought falling in love would be a light bulb moment, a flash of realisation that this was *The One*. But with Cam it had been more of a slow build, a gradual awareness the feelings she had towards him were no longer the platonic ones she had felt before. It was an awakening of her mind and body. Every moment she spent with him she loved him more. Which would make the end of their affair all the more difficult to deal with. Had she made a mistake in letting it go this far? But then she would never have known this magic. She would never have known the depth of pleasure her body was capable of giving and receiving.

The song ended and Cam led her back to their table in the corner to collect their coats. Violet suppressed a shiver when his hands pulled her hair out from the back of her collar when he helped her into her coat. She turned back around to face him and her belly did a flip at the smouldering look in his eyes. 'Time to go home?' she asked.

His mouth tilted in a sexy smile. 'If I make it that far.'

They barely made it through the door. Violet slipped out of her coat and walked into Cam's arms, his head coming down to connect his mouth with hers in a hungry kiss that made her whole body tingle. His tongue entered her mouth with a determined thrust that mimicked the intention of his body. She sent her tongue into combat with his, stroking and darting away in turn, ramping up the heat firing between them.

His hands went to the zipper at the back of her dress, sending it down her back, his hand sliding beneath the sagging fabric to bring her closer to the hardened length of him. His mouth continued its passionate assault on her senses, his teeth taking playful nips of her lower lip, pulling it out and releasing it, salving it with his tongue and then doing it all over again.

Desire roared through Violet's body with a force that was almost frightening in its intensity. She clawed at his clothing like a woman possessed, popping buttons off his shirt but beyond caring. She had to feel his hot male skin under her hands. *Now.* She unzipped him and dragged down his underwear, taking him in one hand, massaging, stroking up and down until he was fighting for the control they'd lost as soon as they'd stepped through the door. She sank to her knees in front of him, ignoring his token protest and put her mouth to him.

He allowed her a few moments of torturing him but finally hauled her upright, pushing her back against the wall, ruthlessly stripping her dress from her, leaving her in nothing but her tights and knickers and heels. He cupped her mound, grinding the heel of his hand against her ache of longing, his mouth back on hers, hard, insistent, desperate.

Violet fed off his mouth, her hands grasping him by the buttocks, holding him to the throb of her female flesh. 'Please…*please…*' She didn't care that she was begging. She needed him like she had never needed him before.

Cam pulled off her tights, taking her knickers with them. He left her hanging there while he sourced a condom, swiftly applying it and then coming back to her, entering her in one deep thrust that made her senses go wild. He set a furious pace, unlike anything he had done before. It was like a force had taken over his body, a force he couldn't control. The same force that was thundering through her body, making her gasp and whimper and arch her spine and roll her hips to get the friction where she needed it most.

He hooked one of her legs over his hip and caressed her with his fingers, triggering an earthquake in her body. It threw her into a tailspin, into a wild maelstrom of sensations that powered through her from head to toe. Even the hairs on her head felt like they were spinning at the roots.

Cam followed with his own release in three hard thrusts that brought a harsh cry out from between his lips.

Violet's legs were threatening to send her to a puddle of limbs on the floor at his feet. She grasped at the edges of his opened shirt, which she hadn't managed to get off his body in time. 'Wow, we should go dancing more often.'

He gave a soft laugh, his breathing not quite back to normal. 'We should.'

Violet pulled her clothes back on while he dealt with

the condom and his own clothes. If anyone had told her she would have acted with such wanton abandon even a week ago, she would have been shocked. But with Cam everything felt…right. She had the confidence to express herself sexually with him because she knew he would never ask her to do something she wasn't comfortable with. He always put her pleasure ahead of his own. He worshipped her body instead of using it to satisfy himself.

'We'll have an opportunity to dance at my father's wedding on Saturday,' Cam said once they had gone upstairs to prepare for bed.

Violet stalled in the process of unzipping her dress. 'You're not really expecting me to go with you, are you?'

He was sitting on the end of the bed, reaching down to untie his shoelaces, but looked up with a partial frown. 'Of course I want you there. We can fly up to Drummond Brae that evening. The wedding's in the morning so we should make it plenty of time for Christmas.'

Violet sank her teeth into her lip. 'I don't know…'

'What's wrong?'

'Your father won't mind if I don't show up. He won't even notice.'

'Maybe not, but I want you there. I'm the best man. Dad's arranged to have you with me at the top table.'

Violet thought about the wedding photos that would be taken. How she would be in all the family shots that for years later everyone would look at and say, *'There's the girl who was engaged to Cam for two weeks.'* It was bad enough with it being all over social media. But at least everyone would forget about it after a while. But a wedding album wasn't the same as cyberspace. It would be a concrete reminder of a charade she should never have agreed to in the first place.

However, it wasn't just the fallout from social media that had her feeling so conflicted about his father's wedding. It was the wedding ceremony itself, the sanctity of it. How she felt she would be compromising someone else's special day by pretending to be something she was not. How could she cheapen a ceremony she held in such high esteem? It would be nothing short of sacrilege. 'I don't think I belong at your father's wedding.'

He got up from the bed and tossed his loosened tie to the chest of drawers. 'You do belong there. You belong by my side as my fiancée.'

Violet pointedly raised her brow. 'Don't you mean your *fake* fiancée?'

A flicker of annoyance passed over his features. 'You didn't have any problem with lying to your workmates and your family. Why not stretch it to my family as well?'

'I'm not going, Cam. You can't make me.'

Cam came up to her and placed his hands on her shoulders. 'We're in this together, Violet. It's only till after Christmas. Surely it's not too much to ask you to come with me.'

Violet held his gaze. 'Why do you want me there? It's your father's fifth marriage, for pity's sake. It'll be a farcical version of what marriage is supposed to represent. I can't bear to be part of it. It would make me feel as if I'm poking fun at the institution I hold in the highest possible regard. Why is it so important to you that I be there?'

He dropped his hands and stepped away, his expression getting that boxed up look about it. 'Fine. Don't go. I don't blame you. I wish I didn't have to go either.'

Violet realised then how much he was dreading his father's wedding. Just like he had dreaded meeting his father for drinks. If she didn't go to the wedding then he would have to face it alone. Surely it was the least she could do to go with him and support him? He'd supported her at her office Christmas party. He'd supported her through the ordeal of her flat being broken in to. He'd been there for her every step of the way. It was a big compromise for her but wasn't that what all good relationships were about? She came up behind him and linked her arms around his waist. 'All right, I'll go with you but only because I care about you and hate the thought of you going through it alone.'

He turned and touched her gently on the cheek with his fingertip. 'I hate putting you through it. If it's anything like his last one it will be excruciating. But it'll be over by mid-afternoon and then we can fly up to Scotland to be with your family.'

Violet stepped up on tiptoe to plant a kiss to his lips. 'I can't wait.'

* * *

The church was full of flowers; every pew had a posy
of blooms with a satin ribbon holding it in place. On
each side of the altar was an enormous arrangement
of red roses and another two at the back of the church.
Violet sat in the pew and looked at Cam standing up at
the altar with his father. Ross was joking and banter-
ing with the other two groomsmen and, even though
Violet was sitting a few rows back, she wondered if he
was already a little drunk. His cheeks were ruddy and
his movements were a little uncoordinated. Or perhaps
it was wedding nerves? No. Ross McKinnon wasn't the
type of man to get nervous about anything. He was enjoying being the centre of attention. He was relishing
it. It was jarring for Violet, being such a romantic. She
loved weddings where the groom looked nervous but
excited waiting for his bride to arrive. Like her brother
Fraser, who had kept checking his watch and swallowing deeply as the minutes ticked on. It had been such
a beautiful wedding and Cam had been a brilliant best
man.

Violet looked at Cam again. He looked composed.
Too composed. Cardboard cut-out composed. He met
her gaze and smiled. How she loved that smile. He only
did it for her. It was *her* smile. The way his eyes lit up
as if seeing her made him happy. She was glad she'd
come to the wedding. It was the right thing to do even
if the wedding was every type of wrong.

The organ started playing the 'Wedding March' and
every head turned to the back of the church. There

were three bridesmaids who were dressed in skimpy gowns that didn't suit their rather generous figures. Had Tatiana deliberately chosen friends who wouldn't upstage her? Not that anyone could upstage Tatiana. Violet heard the collective indrawn breath of the congregation when the bride appeared. Tatiana's white satin gown was slashed almost to the waist, with her cleavage on show as well as the slight bulge of her pregnancy. Violet looked on in horror as Tatiana's right breast threatened to pop out as she walked—strutted would be a more accurate description—up the aisle. The back of Tatiana's dress was similarly slashed, this time to the top of her buttocks, which her veil was not doing a particularly good job of hiding.

Ross looked like he couldn't wait to get his hands on his bride and made some joking aside to Cam that made Cam's jaw visibly tighten. Violet felt angry on his behalf. What a disgusting display of inappropriateness and poor Cam had to witness every second of it.

It got worse.

Ross and Tatiana had written the vows but they weren't romantic and heartfelt declarations but rather a travesty of what a marriage ceremony should be. Finally they were declared man and wife and Ross and Tatiana kissed for so long, with Ross's hand wandering all over his new bride's body, that several members of the congregation snickered.

The reception was little more than a drunken party. How Cam managed to get through his speech while his father cracked inappropriate jokes and drank copious amounts of champagne was anybody's guess.

When Cam sat back down beside her, she took his hand under the table and gave it a squeeze. 'This must be killing you,' she said.

'It'll be over soon.' He gave her a soft smile. 'How are you holding up?'

Violet curled her fingers around his. 'I'm fine, although I feel a bit silly up here at the top table. Tatiana doesn't like it. She keeps giving me the evil eye.'

'That's because you outshine her,' Cam said.

Violet could feel herself glowing at his compliment. His look warmed her blood. The look that said *I want you.* 'I'm going to powder my nose. Can we leave after that, do you think, or will we have to wait until your father and Tatiana leave?'

He glanced at his watch. 'Let's give it another hour and then we'll go.'

On her way back from the ladies' room, Violet saw Cam's father leading one of the bridesmaids by the hand to a corner behind a large arrangement of flowers. The bridesmaid was giggling and Ross was leering at her and groping her. Violet was so shocked she stood there with her mouth hanging open. Did Ross have no shame? He'd only been married a matter of hours and he was already straying. Did the commitment of marriage mean nothing to him?

Violet swung away and went back to where Cam was waiting for her. She couldn't stay another minute at this wretched farce of a wedding. Not. One. Minute.

She felt tainted by it. Sullied. Defiled by listening to people mouthing words they didn't mean and watching them behaving like out of control teenagers. No wonder Cam was so against marriage. Apart from her brother and sisters' weddings, all he had seen was the repeated drunken mockery of what was supposed to be the most important day in a couple's life. No wonder he was cynical. No wonder he couldn't picture himself getting married in the near future.

'What's wrong?' Cam said when she snatched up her wrap from the back of the chair.

'I can't stay here another minute,' Violet said. 'Your father is feeling up one of the bridesmaids out in the foyer.'

Cam's expression showed little surprise about his father's behaviour. 'Yes, well, that's my father for you. A class act at all times and in all places.'

Violet tugged his arm. 'Come on. Let's get out of here. My flesh is crawling. Oh, God, look at Tatiana. She's got her tongue in the groomsman's ear. She's practically doing a lap dance on him.'

Cam took Violet's hand and led her out of the reception room. 'Sorry you had to witness all that craziness. But I'm glad you came. It would've been unbearable without you there.'

Violet was still seething about his father's and Tatiana's behaviour when they got home to change and collect their bags for their evening flight to Scotland. 'I can't believe you share any of your father's DNA. You're nothing like him. You're decent and caring and principled. I'm sure if you were to get married one day in the future you won't be off canoodling with one of the bridesmaids within an hour or two of the ceremony. What is wrong with him?'

Cam paused in the action of slipping off his coat. But then he resumed the process of shrugging it off and hanging it on the hallstand with what seemed to Violet somewhat exaggerated precision. 'We've had this conversation a number of times before,' he said. 'I don't want to get married.'

Violet felt his words like a rusty stake to her heart. Not married? *Ever?* She had heard him say it before but hadn't things been changing between them? Hadn't *she* changed things for him? He cared about her. He talked to her. *Really* talked. About things he'd not spoken of to anyone else. He had invited her into his home. Was his heart really still so off-limits? How could he make love to her the way he had and not have felt anything? He'd bought her an engagement ring, for goodness' sake. He could have bought something cheap but he'd chosen something so special, so perfect, it surely meant he cared more than he wanted to admit.

Violet understood now why he was so wary of marriage. But deep down she had harboured hope that he would see how a marriage between them would be just like the marriage between her parents: respectful and loving and lasting. 'You don't really mean that, Cam. Deep down you want what I want. What my parents and siblings have. You've seen how a good marriage is conducted. You can't let your father's atrocious behaviour influence you like this. You're not living his life, you're living yours.'

Cam's expression went into lockdown. Violet knew him well enough to know he felt cornered. A frown formed between his eyes, his mouth tightened and a muscle ticked in his lean cheek. 'Violet.'

'Don't *do* that,' Violet said, frustrated beyond measure. 'Don't use that schoolmaster tone with me as if I'm too stupid to know what I'm talking about. You're not facing what's right in front of you. I know you care about me. You care about me much more than you want to admit. I can't go on pretending to be engaged to you when all I want is for it to be for real.'

The tenseness around his mouth travelled all the way up to his eyes. They were hard as flint. 'Then you'll be waiting a long time because I'm not going to change my mind.'

Violet knew it was time for a line to be drawn. How long could she go on hoping he would come to see things her way? What if she stayed in a relationship with him for months and months, maybe even years, and he still wouldn't budge? All her dreams of a beautiful wedding day with her whole family there would be destroyed. All her hopes for a family of her own would be shattered. She couldn't give that up. She loved him. She loved him desperately but she wouldn't be true to herself if she drifted along in a going nowhere relationship with him. She had to make a stand. She couldn't go on living in this excruciating limbo of will-he-or-won't-he? She had to make him see there was no future without a proper commitment.

No fling.

No temporary arrangement.

No pretend engagement.

Violet drew in a carefully measured breath, garnering her resolve. 'Then I don't want you to come home to Drummond Brae with me. I'd rather go alone.'

It was hard to tell if her statement affected him for hardly a muscle moved on his face. 'Fine.'

Fine? Violet's heart gave a painful spasm. How could he be so calm and clinical about this? Didn't he feel anything for her? Maybe he didn't love her after all. Maybe all this had been a convenient affair that had a use-by date. *Be strong. Be strong. Be strong.* She knew he was expecting her to cave in. It was what she did all the time. She over-adapted. She compromised. She hated hurting people's feelings so she ended up saying yes when she meant no. It had to stop. It had to stop now. It was time to grow a backbone. 'Is that your final decision?' she said.

'Violet, you're being unreasonable about—'

'*I'm* being unreasonable?' Violet said. 'What's unreasonable about wanting to be happy? I can't be happy with you if you're not one hundred per cent committed to me. I can't live like that. I don't want to miss out on all the things I've dreamt about since I was a little girl. If you don't want the same things then it's time to call it quits before we end up hurting each other too much.'

'It was never my intention to hurt you,' Cam said.

You just did. 'I have to go now or I'll miss the flight.' Violet moved past him to collect her bag from his room upstairs. Would he follow her and try and talk her out of it? Would he tell her how much he loved her? She listened for the sound of his tread on the stairs but there was nothing but silence.

When she came back downstairs with her overnight bag he was still standing in the hall with that blank expression. 'I'll drive you to the airport,' he said, barely moving his lips as he spoke.

'That won't be necessary,' Violet said. 'I've already called a cab.' She took off her engagement ring and handed it to him. 'I won't be needing this any more.'

He ignored her outstretched hand. 'Keep it.'

'I don't want to keep it.'

'Sell it and give the money to charity.'

Violet placed the ring on the table next to his keys. Did it have to end like this? With them acting like stiff strangers at the end of the affair? She'd taken a gamble and it hadn't paid off. It was supposed to pay off! Why wasn't he putting his hands on her shoulders and turning her around and smiling at her with that tender smile he reserved only for her? She turned back to face him but if he were feeling even half of the heartache she was, he showed no sign of it. 'Goodbye, Cam. I guess I'll see you when I see you.'

'I guess you will.'

Violet put on her gloves and rewound her scarf around her neck. *Do* not *cry*.

'Right, that's it then. I'll have to collect the rest of

my things when I get back. I hope it's okay to leave them here until then?'

'Of course it is.'

Another silence passed.

Violet heard the telltale beep of the taxi outside. Cam took her bag for her and opened the front door and helped her into the taxi. He couldn't have given her a clearer message that he was 'fine' with her decision to leave without him.

Violet slipped into the back of the taxi without kissing him goodbye. There was only so much heartbreak she could cope with. Touching him one last time would be her undoing. She didn't want to turn into a mess to add insult to injury. If it was over then it was over. Better to be quick and clean about it. Apparently he felt the same way because he simply closed the door of the taxi and stood back from the kerb as if he couldn't wait for it to take her away.

'Going home for Christmas?' the cabbie asked.

Violet swallowed as Cam's statue-like figure gradually disappeared from view. 'Yes,' she said on a sigh. 'I'm going home.'

CHAPTER NINE

CAM STOOD WATCHING the taxi until it disappeared around the corner. *What are you doing?* Being sensible, that was what he was doing. If he chased after her and begged her to stay then what would it achieve? A few weeks, a few months of a relationship that was the best he'd ever had but could go no further. That was what he would have.

He walked back into his house and picked up the engagement ring off the table. It was still warm from being on Violet's finger. Why was he feeling so... numb? Like the world had dropped out from under him.

Violet had blindsided him with her ultimatum. He was already feeling raw from his father's ridiculous sham of a wedding. She couldn't have picked a worse time to discuss the future of their relationship. Seeing his father act like a horny teenager all through that farce of a service, and then to hear via Violet he had been feeling up one of the bridesmaids at the reception had made Cam deeply ashamed. So ashamed he'd wanted to distance himself from anything to do with weddings. The word was enough to make him want to be ill. Why had she done that? Why push him when they'd already discussed it? He had been honest and upfront about it. He hadn't told her any lies, made any false commitments, allowed her to believe there was a pot of gold at the end of the rainbow. They hadn't been together long enough to be talking of marriage even if he was the marrying type. If he were going to propose for real—*if*—then he would do it in his own good time, not because it was demanded of him.

Go after her.

Cam took one step towards the door but then stopped. Of course he had to let her go. What was the point in dragging this out till after Christmas? It wasn't fair to her and it wasn't fair to her family. She wanted more than he was prepared to give. She wanted the fairytale. Damn it, she *deserved* the fairytale. All her life she had been waiting for Mr Right and Cam was only getting in the way of her finding him.

He paced the floor, torn between wanting to chase after her and staying put where his life was under his control. He blew out a long breath and went through to the sitting room. He sat on one of the sofas and cradled his head in his hands. His chest felt like someone had dragged his heart from his body, leaving a gaping hole.

If this was the right thing to do then why did it feel so goddamn painful?

Violet hadn't worked up the courage to tell her parents she and Cam were finished when her mother texted to ask what time they would be arriving. She told her mother they would be arriving separately due to his father's wedding commitments. She knew it was cowardly but she couldn't cope with their disappointment when hers was still so raw and painful. Checking into that flight at Heathrow had been one of the loneliest moments of her life. Even as she'd boarded the plane, she had hoped Cam would come rushing up behind her and spin her around to face him, saying he had made the biggest mistake of his life to let her leave.

But he hadn't turned up. He hadn't even texted or phoned. Didn't that prove how relieved he was that their relationship was over? By delivering an ultimatum she had given him a get-out-of-jail-free card. No wonder he hadn't argued the point or asked for more time on their relationship. He had grabbed the opportunity to end it.

Violet's mother met her at the airport and swept her into a bone-crushing hug. 'Poppet! I'm so happy to see you. Your father's at home making mince pies. Yes, mince pies! Isn't he a sweetheart trying to help? But you should see the mess he's making in the kitchen. We'll be cleaning up flour for weeks. Now, what time is Cam coming? There are only two more flights this evening. I've already checked. I hope he doesn't miss whichever one he's on. I've made up the suite in the east wing for you both. It's like a honeymoon suite.'

Violet let her mother's cheerful chatter wash over her. It reminded her of the time when she'd come home after quitting university. She had kept her pain and shame hidden rather than burst her mother's bubble of happiness at having her youngest child back home. It wasn't that her mother wasn't sensitive, but rather Violet was adept at concealing her emotions.

Her father was at the front door of Drummond Brae wearing a flour-covered apron when Violet and her mother arrived. He came rushing down the steps and gathered her in a hug that made her feet come off the ground. 'Welcome home, wee one,' he said. 'Come away inside out of the cold. It's going to snow for Christmas. We've already had a flurry or two.'

Violet stepped over the threshold and came face to face with a colourful banner hanging across the foyer that said: *Congratulations Cam and Violet.* Helium balloons with her and Cam's names on them danced in the draught of cold air from the open door, their tinsel strings hanging like silver tails.

Her grandfather came shuffling in on his walking frame, his wrinkled face beaming from ear to ear. 'Let's see that ring of yours, little Vivi,' he said.

Violet swallowed a knot that felt as big as a pine cone off the Christmas tree towering in the hall in all its festive glory. She kept her gloves on, too embarrassed to show her empty ring finger. How on earth was she going to tell them? The rest of the family came bursting in, Fraser and Zoe with their twins Ben and Mia and then Rose and Alex with their boys Jack and Jonathon. And, of course, Gertie the elderly golden retriever who looked like the canine version of Grandad with her creaky gait and whitened snout.

'Aunty Violet! Did you bring me a present?' Ben

asked with a cheeky grin, so like her brother Fraser it made Violet's heart contract.

'Can I be your flower girl?' Mia asked, hugging Violet around the waist.

Rose and Lily greeted her with big smiles and even bigger hugs. 'We've already started on the champagne,' Rose said. 'Well, not Lily, of course, but I'm drinking her share.'

'When's Cam arriving?' Lily asked.

'Erm…' Violet felt tears burning like acid behind her eyes. 'He's…hoping to make it in time for Christmas dinner.' *Coward.*

Her brother Fraser came forward and gave her a big hug. 'So pleased for you guys. Always knew Cam had a thing for you.'

'I thought so too,' Rose said, grinning. 'He wasn't himself at Easter, do you remember, Lil? Remember when I asked him to take in a hot cross bun to Vivi and he got all flustered and said he had to make a call? Classic. Absolutely classic.'

Lily's smile made her eyes dance. 'I'm so thrilled for you, Vivi. All three of us will be married. How soon will you start a family? It'd be so cool to have our kids close in age.'

Gertie came up to Violet and slowly wagged her tail and gave a soft whine as if to say, *What's wrong?*

Violet could stand it no longer. 'I—I have something to tell you…'

Rose's eyes lit up as bright as the lights on the Christmas tree she was standing near. 'You're pregnant?'

Violet bit her lip so hard she thought she would break the skin. 'Cam and I are…not engaged.'

The stunned silence was so profound no one moved. Not even the children. Even the tinsel and baubles on the Christmas tree seemed to be holding themselves stock-still. Everyone was looking at her as if she had just told them she had a disease and it was contagious.

'Oh, poppet.' Her mother came to her and gathered her in her arms, rocking her from side to side as if she were still a baby. 'I'm so sorry.'

Her father joined in the hug, gently patting her on the back with soothing 'there, there's' that made Violet sob all the harder.

Rose and Lily ushered the children away and Fraser helped Grandad back into the sitting room near the fire. Lily's husband Cooper and Rose's husband Alex came in late and, taking one look at the scene, promptly walked back out.

'What happened?' Violet's mother asked. 'Did he break it off?'

'No, I did. But we weren't even engaged. We were pretending.'

Her mother frowned. 'Pretending?'

Violet explained the situation through a series of hiccupping sobs. 'It's my fault for being so pathetic about going to the office Christmas party on my own. I should've just gone alone and not been such a stupid baby. Now I've hurt everyone and ruined my friendship with Cam and spoilt Christmas for everyone too.'

'You haven't spoilt anything, poppet,' her mother

said. 'Take the banner down, Gavin. And get the kids to pop the balloons. I'll take Violet upstairs.'

Violet followed her mother upstairs, not to the suite prepared for her and Cam but to her old bedroom. All her childhood toys were neatly arranged on top of the dresser and some on her bed. Violet's books were in the bookshelves, waiting for her like old friends. It was like stepping back in time but feeling out of place. She wasn't a child any more. She was an adult with adult needs. Needs Cam had awakened and then walked away from as if they meant nothing to him.

As if *she* meant nothing to him.

Her mother sat on the edge of the bed beside Violet. 'Are you in love with him?'

'Yes, but he doesn't love me. Well, he does but not like that.'

'Did you tell him you loved him?'

Violet gave a despondent sigh. 'What would be the point? He never wants to get married. He doesn't want kids either.'

'I expect that's because of his parents,' her mother said. 'But he might change his mind.'

'He won't.'

Her mother hugged her again. 'My poor baby. I wish there was something I could do or say to help you feel better.'

Violet wiped at her eyes with her sleeve. 'I love him so much but he's so cynical about getting married. Deep down, I don't really blame him after attending his father's fifth wedding today. It was awful. So awful you wouldn't believe.' She described some of what went on and her mother made tut-tutting noises and shook her head in disgust.

'Did you press him for a commitment after you came back from the wedding?' her mother asked.

Violet looked at her mum's frowning expression. 'You think I should've waited?'

Her mother squeezed her hand. 'What's done is done. At least you were honest with him. No point pretending you're happy when you're not.'

Violet's bottom lip quivered. 'He's the only one for me, Mum. I know I won't be happy with anyone else. I just know it.'

Her mother gave her a sad smile. 'For your sake, poppet, I hope that's not true.'

Cam packed up Violet's things for when she was ready to collect them. He could have done it any time between Christmas and New Year because she wouldn't be back till the second of January as they had planned to spend the week with her family. But he was feeling restless and on edge. He kept telling himself it was better this way. That it was wrong to drag things out when he couldn't give her what she wanted.

But when he came to her embroidery basket, his heart gave a painful spasm. He opened the lid and took out the creamy baby blanket Violet was in the process of embroidering with tiny flowers. He held it to his face, its softness reminding him of her skin. He could even smell her on the blanket—that sweet flowery scent that made him think of spring. He put the blanket back inside the basket and took out a pair of booties. They were so tiny he couldn't imagine a baby's foot small enough to fit them. He started to picture a baby…one he and Violet might make together: a little squirming body with dimpled hands and feet, a downy dark head with eyes bright and clear and a little rosebud mouth.

What if Violet were pregnant? They had been careful but accidents could happen. Should he call her? No. Too soon. He needed more time. Time to get his head together. He wasn't used to feeling this level of emotion. This sense of…loss. The sense of loss was so acute it felt like a giant hole, leaving him empty and raw.

Cam picked up a tiny jacket that had sailing boats embroidered around the collar. He rubbed his thumb over the meticulous stitches, wondering what it would be like to have a son. His father hadn't been an active father in any sense of the word, but Cam couldn't imagine not wanting to be involved in your child's life. How could you not be interested in your own flesh and blood? Being there for every milestone, watching them grow and develop, reading to them at bedtime—all the things Violet's parents had done and were now doing for each of their grandchildren when they came to stay.

He put the sailing boat jacket down and picked up a pink cardigan that was so small it would have looked at home on a doll. There were tiny rosebuds around the collar and the cuffs of the sleeves. What would it be like to have a daughter? To watch her grow from babyhood to womanhood. To be there for her first smile, her first tooth, her first steps. *Gulp.* Her first date. Walking her down the aisle. One day becoming a grandfather...

Cam had never thought about having his own children. Well, he had thought about it but just as quickly dismissed it. Like when he had walked into the sitting room at Drummond Brae at Easter and seen Violet curled up on the sofa with a baby's bonnet in her hands. It had been a jarring reminder of the responsibility he'd spent his adult life actively avoiding.

But now he wondered why he was working so hard when he had no one to share it with. What was the point? Would he end up some lonely old man living out his end days alone? Not surrounded by a loving family like Grandad Archie in the winter of his life. No one to tell him they loved him, no one to be there in sickness and in health and everything in between. No laughter-filled Christmases with all the family gathered around the tree exchanging gifts and smiles and love.

Cam put the pink cardigan back inside the basket and closed the lid. What was he doing? It was best this way. Violet was better off without him and his crazy family who would do nothing but stir up trouble between them if given half a chance. He wasn't cut out for marriage and commitment. He was too driven by his career, by achieving, by the next task waiting on his desk. He didn't have the time to invest in a long-term relationship.

Cam had been to three of his father's previous weddings and never once taken much notice of the vows. But when he'd heard his father make all those promises earlier that day it had made Cam's gut churn to realise his father didn't mean a word of them. They were just words, empty, meaningless words because his father had no intention of committing to his new wife other than in an outward way by standing up in church in front of family and friends. His father didn't mean them on the inside, in his heart where it counted. Anyone could say they would love someone for the rest of their life but how many people actually meant it? Violet's parents obviously had. So had her grandad Archie and Maisie Drummond when they had married sixty-five years ago.

Cam knew if it were him up there saying those words with Violet by his side, he would make sure he meant them. His heart gave a kick as the realisation dawned. This was why he had avoided marriage and commitment all this time—because he had never been able to picture himself saying those words with any sincerity. But with Violet they meant everything. He loved her with all his heart and mind and soul. He worshipped her with his body, he wanted to protect her and stand by her in sickness and in health, in pregnancy and childbirth.

What a damn fool he had been. Letting her walk away when he loved her so much. Loved her more than anything, more than his freedom, which wasn't such a great thing anyway. True freedom was in your ability to love someone without fear, without conditions, loving without restraint.

The love he felt for Violet was bigger than his fear of abandonment. It was bigger than the need to protect himself from hurt. He couldn't control life and all its vagaries. Life happened, no matter how carefully you laid plans. He thought of Violet's poor workmate Kenneth, so hung up on his ex-wife he was unable to move on with his life. Cam didn't want to be like that. Too afraid to love in case he lost it.

He loved Violet and he would make sure nothing and no one destroyed that love. They would face the future together, a dedicated team who had each other's backs no matter what.

Cam glanced at his watch. He would have to hotfoot it but he could make the last flight if he was lucky.

Violet was determined her family's Christmas would not suffer any more disturbance after her tearful confession. She joined in with the family board games—a Drummond tradition late at night on Christmas Eve while everyone drank eggnog—and laughed at her father's corny jokes and patiently repeated everything for Grandad, who was hard of hearing. Her mother kept a watchful eye on her, but Violet did her best to assure her mum she was doing just fine, even though on the inside she felt a cavern of emptiness.

She couldn't stop wondering what Cam was doing. Was he spending Christmas with his mother or alone? Or had he hooked up with someone new? It wasn't like him to do something like that but what if he wanted to press home a point? He wanted his freedom, otherwise wouldn't he have come after her by now? Called her? Texted her? Given her a fragment of hope? No. He hadn't. It didn't seem fair that she was up here in the Highlands of Scotland nursing a broken heart while he was in London living the life of a playboy. Did he miss her? Was he thinking about her?

'Well, we're off to bed,' Fraser announced, taking Zoe's hand. 'The kids will be up at four, looking for their presents.'

Zoe gave Violet a sad look. 'Are you okay, Vivi?'

Violet put on a brave smile. 'Rose and I are going to work on that bottle of champagne over there, aren't we, Rose?'

Rose gave her an apologetic look and reached for her husband Alex's hand. 'Sorry, Vivi, but I've had too much already.'

'Don't look at me,' Lily said, placing a protective hand over her belly. 'I'm knackered in any case.'

'Will you take Gertie out for a wee walk, poppet?' her mother asked. 'Your father and I have to stuff the turkey.'

Violet shrugged on her coat and put on her gloves and took the dog outside into the crisp night air. There were light flurries of snow but it wasn't settling. So much for a magical white Christmas. Maybe it was going to be one of those miserable grey and gloomy ones, which would be rather fitting for her current state of mind.

Gertie wasn't content with waddling about the garden and instead put her nose down to follow a scent leading down to the loch. Violet grabbed a torch from the hall table drawer and followed the dog. The loch was a silver shape in the moonlight, the forest behind it a dense dark fringe.

Violet stood at the water's edge, feeling the biting cold coming off the sheet of water while Gertie bustled about in the shadows. An owl hooted, a vixen called out for a mate.

A twig snapped under someone's foot.

Violet spun around, shining the torch in the direction of the sound. 'Who's there?'

Cam stepped into the beam of light. 'It's me.'

Violet's heart gave an almighty lurch. 'Cam?'

He shielded his eyes with his arm. 'Will you stop shining that thing in my face?'

'Sorry.' She lowered the torch. 'You scared the heck out of me.'

He came up closer, the moonlight casting his features into ghostly relief. Gertie padded over and gave him an enthusiastic greeting as if she had suddenly turned into a puppy instead of the fifteen-year-old dog she was. Cam leaned down to scratch at the dog's ears before straightening. 'I'm sorry about earlier today. I was wrong to let you leave like that. I got flooded with feelings I didn't want to acknowledge. But I'm acknowledging them now. I love you, Violet. I love you and want to spend the rest of my life with you. Will you marry me?'

Violet stared at him, wondering if she was hearing things. 'Did you just ask me to marry you?'

He smiled so tenderly it made her heart skip a beat. Her smile. The one he only used for her. 'I did and I want to have babies with you. We can be a family like your family. We can do it because we're a team who are batting for each other, not against each other.'

Violet stepped into his waiting arms, nestling her head against his chest. 'I love you so much. It tore my heart out to leave you but I had to. I wasn't being true to myself or to you. Your father's wedding brought it home to me. I couldn't go on pretending.'

'After you left I started thinking about my father and that ridiculous sham of a wedding,' Cam said. 'He doesn't love Tatiana enough to die for her. He's using her as a trophy to prove his diminishing potency. He uses every woman he's ever been with like that. I know I won't do that to you. I couldn't. You mean the world to me. I couldn't possibly love anyone more than I love you.'

Violet gazed up at him. Was this really happening? Cam was here. In person. Asking her to marry him. Telling her he loved her more than anyone else in the world. 'It was a bit mean of me to push you on commitment so close to your father's wedding,' she said. 'No wonder you backed away. The mere mention of the word *wedding* after that debacle of a ceremony would've been enough to make you run for cover.'

He gave her a rueful smile. 'Your timing was a little off but I got there eventually. I'm sorry you had to go through an awful few hours thinking we were over. After you left I sat in numb shock. Normally when a relationship of mine comes to an end I feel relieved.

Not this time. Can you forgive me for being so block-headed?'

Violet linked her arms around his neck. 'I'm never leaving again. Not ever. You've made all my dreams come true. You've even proposed to me by the loch.'

He grinned and drew her closer. 'I reckon we've got about sixty seconds before your family come down here to check if there's a reason to celebrate Christmas with a bang or we both freeze to death. Will you marry me, my darling?'

Violet smiled so widely her face ached. 'Yes. A million times yes.'

'Once will be more than enough,' Cam said. 'From here on I'm a one-woman man.'

She stroked his lean jaw, now dark and rough with stubble. 'I've been a one-man woman for a lot longer. I think that's probably why I never dated with any enthusiasm. I was subconsciously waiting for you.'

His eyes became shadowed for a moment as if he was recalling how close to losing her he had come. 'How could I have been so stupid not to see how perfect you are for me all this time?'

Violet smiled. 'Mum saw it. She's going to be beside herself when she hears you're here. Did anyone see you coming up the driveway?'

'I'm not sure. When I pulled up I caught a glimpse of you heading towards the lake with Gertie so I came straight down here.'

'They made a banner for us,' Violet said. 'It was a

bad moment when I saw it hanging in the hall. I hadn't told them we were over at that point.'

He winced. 'Poor you. Well, we'd better tell them the good news. Ready?'

Violet drew his head down to hers. 'Not yet. Let's treasure this moment for our kids. I want to tell them how you kissed me in the moonlight, just like Grandad did to my grandmother in exactly this spot.'

'Hang on, I'm forgetting something.' He took out the ring from his pocket and slipped it on her finger. 'I don't want to see that come off again.'

Violet smiled as she twirled the ring on her finger. Her hand had felt so strange without it there. Like someone else's hand. The diamond winked at her as if to say, *I'm back!* 'I can't believe this is happening. I felt so lonely and lost without you.'

'Me too,' he said. 'I was so afraid of losing you that I ended up losing you. I will regret to the day I die not following you out of my house and bringing you back. I wanted to but I kept thinking you were better off without me.'

There was the sound of twigs snapping and a few hushed whispers. Cam's eyes twinkled. 'Looks like the family has arrived. Shall we make an announcement?'

Violet drew his head down to hers. 'Let's show them instead.'

EPILOGUE

Christmas Eve the following year...

CAM LOOKED AROUND the sitting room at Drummond Brae where all Violet's family were gathered. Correction. *His* and Violet's family. The last few months since his and Violet's wedding in June had shown him more than ever how important family was and how much he had missed out on having a proper one growing up. But he was more than making up for it now. He glanced at Violet where she was sitting almost bursting to tell the family her good news. *Their* good news. He still couldn't believe they were having a baby. Violet was just past the twelve-week mark and there could be no better Christmas present for her parents than to tell them they were about to have another grandchild.

He smiled when Violet's gaze met his. He never tired of looking at her; she was glowing but not just because of being pregnant. She had completed her first semester of an English Literature degree. He couldn't have been prouder of her. Of course she topped her class.

Grandad Archie was sitting with a blanket over his legs and a glass of whisky in his hand and looking at Violet with a smile on his face. That was another miracle Cam felt grateful for. Grandad Archie, while certainly not robust in health, was at least enjoying life surrounded by his beloved family. Even Kenneth, Violet's workmate, had started dating again. Cam had introduced him to a young widow who worked part-time in his office and they'd hit it off and had been seeing each other ever since.

Poor old Gertie, the golden retriever, hadn't been so lucky; her ashes were spread out by the loch not far from where Cam had proposed to Violet. But there was a new addition to the family, a ten-week-old puppy called Nessie who was currently chewing on one of Cam's shoelaces.

'Vivi, why aren't you drinking your eggnog?' Grandad Archie asked with a twinkle in his eyes. 'Is there something you have to tell us?'

Cam took Violet's hand just as she reached for his. He squeezed it gently, his heart so full of love he could feel his chest swelling like bread dough. 'We have an announcement to make,' he said. 'We're having a baby.'

'Ach, now I'll have to live another year so I can wet the wee one's head,' Grandad said, grinning from ear to ear.

Violet's mother grasped her husband's hand and blinked back happy tears. 'We're so thrilled for you both. It's just the most wonderful news.'

Violet placed Cam's hand on the tiny swell of her

belly and smiled up at him with her beautiful brown eyes brimming with happiness. 'I love you.'

Cam bent down and kissed her tenderly. 'I love you too. Happy Christmas, my darling.'

'Okay, knock it off you two,' Fraser said with a cheeky grin. 'The honeymoon's been over for six months.'

Cam grinned back. 'Not this honeymoon.' He gathered Violet closer. 'This one's going to last for ever.'

* * * * *

If you enjoyed this story, check out these other great reads from Melanie Milburne:
HIS MISTRESS FOR A WEEK
THE MOST SCANDALOUS RAVENSDALE
ENGAGED TO HER RAVENSDALE ENEMY
AWAKENING THE RAVENSDALE HEIRESS
RAVENSDALE'S DEFIANT CAPTIVE
Available now!

MILLS & BOON®

MODERN™

POWER, PASSION AND IRRESISTIBLE TEMPTATION

A sneak peek at next month's titles...

In stores from 17th November 2016:

- **A Di Sione for the Greek's Pleasure** – Kate Hewitt *and* **Married for the Sheikh's Duty** – Tara Pammi
- **The Greek's Christmas Bride** – Lynne Graham *and* **The Desert King's Secret Heir** – Annie West

In stores from 1st December 2016:

- **A Royal Vow of Convenience** – Sharon Kendrick *and* **The Guardian's Virgin Ward** – Caitlin Crews
- **The Prince's Pregnant Mistress** – Maisey Yates *and* **Surrendering to the Vengeful Italian** – Angela Bisse

---

Just can't wait?
Buy our books online a month before they hit the shops!
www.millsandboon.co.uk

Also available as eBooks.

MILLS & BOON®

EXCLUSIVE EXTRACT

Natalia Di Sione hasn't left the family estate in years,
but she must retrieve her grandfather's lost book of
poems from Angelos Menas! The lives of the brooding
Greek and his daughter were changed irrevocably by a
fire, and Talia finds herself drawn to the formidable
tycoon. She knows the untold pleasure Angelos offers is
limited, but when she leaves with the book, will her
heart remain behind on the island?

Read on for a sneak preview of
A DI SIONE FOR THE GREEK'S PLEASURE
by Kate Hewitt

"Talia…" Angelos's voice broke on her name, and then,
before she could even process what was happening, he pulled
her towards him, his hands hard on her shoulders as his
mouth crashed down on hers and plundered its soft depths.

It had been ten years since she'd been kissed, and then
only a schoolboy's brush. She'd never been kissed like this,
never felt every sense blaze to life, every nerve ending tingle
with awareness, nearly painful in its intensity, as Angelos's
mouth moved on hers and he pulled her tightly to him.

His hard contours collided against her softness, each
point of contact creating an unbearably exquisite ache of
longing as she tangled her hands in his hair and fit her
mouth against his.

She was a clumsy, inexpert kisser, not sure what to do
with her lips or tongue, only knowing that she wanted more
of this. Of him.

She felt his hand slide down to cup her breast, his palm

hot and hard through the thin material of her dress, and a gasp of surprise and delight escaped her.

That small sound of pleasure was enough to jolt Angelos out of his passion-fogged daze, for he dropped his hand and in one awful, abrupt movement tore his mouth from hers and stepped back.

"I'm sorry," he said, his voice coming out in a ragged gasp.

"No…" Talia pressed one shaky hand to her buzzing lips as she tried to blink the world back into focus. "Don't be sorry," she whispered. "It was wonderful."

"I shouldn't have—"

"Why not?" she challenged. She felt frantic with the desperate need to feel and taste him again, and more importantly, not to have him withdraw from her, not just physically, but emotionally. Angelos didn't answer and she forced herself to ask the question again. "Why not, Angelos?"

"Because you are my employee, and I was taking advantage of you," he gritted out. "It was not appropriate…"

"I don't care about appropriate," she cried. She knew she sounded desperate and even pathetic but she didn't care. She wanted him. She *needed* him. "I care about you," she confessed, her voice dropping to a choked whisper, and surprise and something worse flashed across Angelos's face. He shook his head, the movement almost violent and terribly final.

"No, Talia," he told her flatly. "You don't."

Don't miss
A DI SIONE FOR THE GREEK'S PLEASURE
by Kate Hewitt

Available December 2016

www.millsandboon.co.uk

MILLS & BOON®

Why shop at millsandboon.co.uk?

Each year, thousands of romance readers find their perfect read at millsandboon.co.uk. That's because we're passionate about bringing you the very best romantic fiction. Here are some of the advantages of shopping at www.millsandboon.co.uk:

* **Get new books first**—you'll be able to buy your favourite books one month before they hit the shops

* **Get exclusive discounts**—you'll also be able to buy our specially created monthly collections, with up to 50% off the RRP

* **Find your favourite authors**—latest news, interviews and new releases for all your favourite authors and series on our website, plus ideas for what to try next

* **Join in**—once you've bought your favourite books, don't forget to register with us to rate, review and join in the discussions

Visit **www.millsandboon.co.uk**
for all this and more today!